2016

The Warp in the Weave

Crime by Design, Book 2

A novel by

Jane Lynn Thornley

RiverFlow Press

D1520961

The Warp in the Weave *by Jane Thornley*

ISBN-13:978-1514187920

ISBN-10: 1514187922

The Warp in the Weave by Jane Thornley

To Nancy Tarr Hart, with whom my travels to Turkey and beyond have illuminated my path.

The Warp in the Weave *by Jane Thornley*

The Warp in the Weave by Jane Thornley

The Warp in the Weave *by Jane Thornley*

ACKNOWLEDGMENTS

My thanks to Fran Mues for her astute editorial eye and enthusiastic support and to Heidi Hugli for always being in my corner.

1

Max and I huddled together under the awning as a sudden October downpour sluiced the Knightsbridge streets. Upstart rivulets streamed the curbs, causing pedestrians to pop their umbrellas and dive for cover.

Despite the English deluge, getting wet didn't worry me as much as getting burned.

I stared at the gallery across the road, a little broad-windowed shop with gilt lettering scripting *Carpe Diem Fine Antiques* above a sentry of ornamental greenery. "It all looks very posh."

"Don't let that fool you. Foxy thinks because his wife was related to an earl or something, that makes him king of the hill. He's as crooked as the rest of them, just does it in better tailoring."

I stepped back against the wall as a bus whooshed around the corner in a blur of double-decker red. "Maybe I should go in alone."

"It's me he wants to see."

"Is that why it's taken him four months to answer your call?"

"My old friends don't talk to me these days, Phoebe. I'm a has-been in this business. I just rang and rang until he agreed to see me. Probably wants me off his back."

"All the more reason why I should go in by myself."

"You don't know these criminal types."

"I know you, don't I?"

"Ouch."

Being in the company of my godfather did not bring out my higher self. "Okay, so we'll go in together. Just promise me you won't lose your temper. I know you've been drinking."

"Just a nip." He sighed. "Do you have the goods?"

I fingered the pouch in my pocket. "Sure."

"That'll make old Foxy twitch. Well, my dear, it's 4:30 and the appointment time. Take my arm and let's go."

I linked my arm through his as we splashed across the zebra crossing that carved safe passage between three converging streets. A black cab hooted at us seconds before we reached the opposite sidewalk.

"Look left," Max said.

"I've been crossing streets for over three decades. I know how to do it."

"I just don't want anything happening to you."

"It's a little late for that."

He wiped his mouth with his sleeve and looked away.

"You look so dapper today, almost like your old self," I said as a peace offering.

"You look a right corker, too."

My godfather had applied the sartorial splendor at my insistence. Rather than slumping around in his usual dressed-to-depress blue jeans and tattered sweaters, today he sported gray flannel trousers, a heather-hued cashmere turtleneck, and his black leather jacket, the sum of which added up to more money than most citizens earned in a month. Only the crocodile boots suggested that the tall man with the silver mane was not minted in some rich British enclave but the product of a far wilder frontier. I, on the other hand, had styled my curly red hair into some semblance of sleek in an effort to pass as an urban sophisticate, which I clearly was not. Perhaps I'd become too comfortable with fraud in general.

"Expect to be escorted into one of his little client salons and plied with tea and cakes. I'd prefer a good shot of Scotch myself but don't worry, I won't ask." He patted my hand.

"Good. Beer is already competing with your aftershave."

"Stop worrying."

"Worrying is all I do. I'm good at it."

"Here we are."

Carpe Diem Rare Antiques' strategically placed topiary all but obscured the interior view. It was the kind of place one visits by appointment only or, at the very least, rings the bell and waits for admittance based on assessment of one's net worth.

"Here the book is judged by its cover, I see."

"And the book better have wads of cash for pages, or no one's getting past the title." Max stabbed the bell with his index finger. "Bloody nuisance," he muttered. "Does he want business or not?"

"So he caters to a wealthy clientele?"

"The kind with silver spoons up their butts."

A man opened the door, a security guard. His blue serge uniform bore the badge of an elite company. "Mr. Baker, madam." The man greeted Max and nodded at me. "You have an appointment, I understand."

"Good day, Rutgers. How's the wife and new pup? Still chewing up the furniture? That would be the dog I'm referring to, not your wife, unless she's long in the tooth, too." Max bellowed out a laugh.

But Rutgers didn't share the joke. He stepped back to let us enter, his face expressionless. "Follow me, please."

We entered a narrow gallery stretching ahead of us in a hush of subdued lighting. At regular intervals, display pedestals rose from the floor, haloed in light pools illuminating rare objects encased in glass. In passing, I glimpsed a Russian icon triptych, what looked to be an ancient Greek gold necklace in remarkable condition, and even a collection of emerald snuffboxes that might be Persian. Closer investigation was not allowed. Rutgers ushered us along like a border collie herding sheep, yapping at us with a battery of "this way, this way" every few seconds.

At one point, Max veered towards a door to the left but the guard hailed him back.

"This way, Mr. Baker." Rutgers pointed towards the back of the gallery.

"But that's not the way to the salon."

"Mr. Fox prefers to meet you back here. Follow me, please."

"In the bloody storeroom? What are we, delivery boys?"

But the storeroom it was. We stepped through a steel door into a large but meticulously tidy utility room stacked in cartons and hanging shelves.

"Have a seat, please." The guard indicated a long steel packing table where three chairs had been arranged. The only decoration appeared to be a stack of brown envelopes beside a spool of tape on one end. No tea and cakes.

"I'll stand," Max said.

"Me, too."

"Suit yourselves." Rutgers turned his back to buzz an intercom announcing our arrival while I stared around at the crates, safes, and shelves. I'd have given anything for x-ray vision just then. What secret treasures were kept in reserve in the back recesses of Carpe Diem?

"One step up from the back door," Max muttered.

"Literally," I remarked, pointing to the steel version set into the back wall.

"Just shows how far I've fallen in the arts and antiquities business."

"In the black market, you mean," I whispered. "Which, given the circumstances, means you've actually come up in the world."

"Ssh. Don't say that too loudly around here. Foxy's probably listening in." He pointed to a camera following our every move from its ceiling recess.

Before I could say anything further, the door opened and in walked a short middle-aged man with a burly build encased in a fine grey suit sporting a bright yellow silk tie. The bizarre impression of a bulldog-schnauzer mix swathed in silk gabardine struck me hard. Even the tufts of gray hair sticking out above his ears added to the effect.

The man extended a hand first to Max. "Maxwell. It's been a long time."

"Through no bloody fault of mine."

And then to me. "This must be your lovely partner, Miss McCabe, I presume?" He took my hand firmly in his, squeezing it as if testing an orange for ripeness. "I am Rupert Fox, Sir Rupert Fox."

4

"Pleased to meet you, Sir Rupert," I said, smiling. I gripped his hand firmly and met his eyes. "You may call me Phoebe minus the miss. You have a gorgeous shop and a brilliant editorial eye. I couldn't help but appreciate the range and exquisite nature of the objects while race-walking down your gallery. Most look museum-worthy."

"Indeed they are, Phoebe. As you know, museums oft pass on many exquisite works due to the lack of funds, at which point, the private collector steps in." He smiled, pulling away his hand after administering one last squeeze. "I do try to gather the most unique and valuable of specimens to bring pleasure to my clients worldwide. Perhaps I could provide a personal tour of my exhibits sometime?"

"Not bloody likely," Max said, glowering. "We didn't come here for a tour, did we, Phoebe?"

I still held Mr. Fox's small blue eyes with mine. "Nevertheless, I'd love to see your collection. Perhaps we can arrange another time?"

"Certainly, and I'm most sorry Rutgers rushed you along."

"Which brings us to why we're here," Max interjected. "Phoebe, show him the goods."

Max ignored my pointed glance. Turning towards the table, I pulled the fold of velvet from my pocket and spread it across the surface with a subdued flourish. I next positioned a pectoral cross mid-center of the deep blue background while coiling the length of its pearl necklace around the gilded centerpiece like a lustrous serpent. "The original belonged to Queen Isabella of Spain, circa 1561. The pivotal emerald is estimated to be approximately 22.5 carats and the rope is compiled of 325 pearls mixed with sapphires."

Max slipped a color photograph of a painting beside the necklace. A striking woman, swathed in elaborate velvet robes the color of bleeding rubies, her long neck framed in a high ruffed collar, stared out with the kind of regal bearing that commanded time itself. "A portrait of the queen painted in 1561 shows her wearing the exact piece, proving its provenance."

Mr. Fox's eyes widened. He cleared his throat and reached trembling fingers towards the piece, lifting it carefully from the velvet. He weighed it in his hand briefly before letting the

5

necklace flop to the table in a clatter of ceramic on oak. "This is a fake."

"It's a copy, of course. Do you think we'd carry about a priceless object like that around town if we had it?" Max countered.

"But we don't have it. That's why we're here," I added smoothly. "It's a replica, albeit a clever one, don't you think?" My brother knew his stuff.

"Where is the original?" Mr. Fox asked.

"That, Foxy, is what we hope you'll tell us," Max said. "Phoebe and I have visited all my old dealer friends to see if anyone has heard if the original-or maybe one of the companion pieces—is circulating. You're the biggest fish by far, if you know what I mean. You cater to clients with a taste for such rare and priceless objects with pockets deep enough to land them. I hoped that you might have—"

Mr. Fox flexed the fingers of his right hand, his eyes hooded. "You hoped I'd implicate myself in an illegal sale? That sounds more your style than mine, Baker. I have no interest in black market dealings."

"Since when? You sure as hell looked interested enough a second ago."

"Mr. Fox," I interjected, "We only want information. We'd hoped you might have heard something which might help us locate my brother and his friends. Of course we're not implying you'd deal in black market goods."

"I bloody am. You and every damn dealer in the city have probably heard of what happened in Bermuda last January," Max added. "You know about the Oak Island heist, don't deny it. We're just trying to track them down, our family members, I mean. I don't care a damn about the treasure, but there were copies made of all the missing pieces and this is the only one we have in hand. Have you heard of anything like this—Spanish, possibly Aztec— being fleeced in London or on the international black market? Spit it out, Foxy. I know you have eyes and ears everywhere."

"Of course I know about your fumbled heist. You were double-crossed by your own son, as I understand, not to mention your former girlfriend, both of whom took off with the hoard, leaving you empty-handed. Such a sorry tale of greed and the pitifully double-crossed. Indeed, you have my deepest sympathy on both counts. To be both duped and cuckolded is enough to send any man to drink. Is it true that that devilish handsome half-breed son of yours took up with your mistress, the delectable Miss Maggie? Well, well, a very sorry tale indeed. Yet, I assure you, I have no pertinent knowledge to aid your search."

I could feel Max go still beside me, absorbing the verbal blows.

"Look, Mr. Fox," I began. "Coming here was a mistake, but there's no need for verbal sucker punches. Sorry you wasted our time. We'll just leave. Come on, Max."

But Max stood frozen to the spot, fixing Foxy with fierce blue eyes. "You know something, Foxhole. Spit it out or Interpol just might learn something you'd rather keep hidden."

I placed a warning hand on Max's arm.

Rupert Fox withdrew his hands to his sides, his shoulders stiffening. "Leave my premises immediately so as not to further waste my time or yours." He shot a quick glance to Rutgers, who jerked upright from his leaning post.

Max caught his glance. "After all these years that we've done business together and you can't even throw me a scrap of information? Do you think so little of me?"

My fingers dug deeper. "Max, let's get out of here."

"What I think of you has always been and remains irrelevant, Baker, but let us be clear on one thing: We were never 'in business together.'"

"I'm only looking for my son, can't you understand that? I don't care about the treasure." Max splayed his hands on the desk and leaned towards Mr. Fox. "We don't know where the hell it is, get that? But if you know something and are keeping it from me, I—"

"You'll what?" Fox snapped his fingers and Rutgers was at his side in seconds. "You'll growl and threaten to bite me with your toothless jaws? Don't be so pitiful. Rutgers, escort Mr. Baker out. We are finished here."

"I'm not finished with you, Foxy, not until I say we are. I know things about you that you wouldn't want New Scotland Yard hearing about. I—"

I pulled Max away from the table, grabbing the necklace in passing, and headed in the direction the guard pointed, straight towards the back door. I called over my shoulder. "Too bad you couldn't deign to help us."

Fox nodded towards Rutgers, a gesture I caught but didn't understand. The guard responded with a flick of his hand while Mr. Fox stood motionless, watching the eviction.

What happened next occurred so quickly, I had no time to react. Suddenly, Rutgers shoved Max into the back alley while simultaneously pulling me backward into the room.

2

I swung around to face Rupert Fox. "What do you think you're doing?"

"Please don't be alarmed, but we truly must speak privately, away from your combustible godfather. I assure you, I mean no harm, Phoebe. I'll just ask a few questions and answer a few of yours in reciprocation. We both have information the other needs. I believe we can help each other."

"Why couldn't you be more collaborative a few minutes ago?"

"In truth, Maxwell quite rankles me. My apologies for being rude."

"So you do know something?"

"I believe I can help, yes."

I took a deep breath, expelling it slowly. "Rutgers can't harm Max."

"No harm will befall Maxwell, at least none for which I am responsible. Rutgers will merely escort him to the end of the street, where he will no doubt lumber off the nearest pub in which to drown his sorrows. You may phone him to ease your mind. In fact, it's best you do in case he takes it upon himself to call the police."

Pulling my cell phone from my pocket, I pressed the speed dial. Max picked up in seconds. "Phoebe, are you all right? What's that bludger doing to you?"

"Nothing. Calm down. He says he wants to talk privately and I'm all right with that. Is Rutgers still with you?"

"The mongrel left, presumably scurrying back to his master. I don't like you alone with that slippery bastard. Tell him to let you go immediately or I'll just call the coppers sooner than later."

"No, I said. Wait for me somewhere I can find you when I'm finished here. No police unless I give the word, got that?"

"I'll wait for you at the pub at the end of the street. Call the moment you're out."

I pressed END and deposited the phone back in my pocket. Turning to Mr. Fox, I said, "So, talk."

"First, let's retire to my salon where we'll be more comfortable. Allow me to dispel your unfortunate first impressions of me."

Down the length of the hushed gallery we went until he ushered me into a dark green-walled room furnished in tobacco-brown leather chairs and hung with illuminated hunting pictures. The effect reminded me of some swanky gentlemen's club fragranced with lingering cigars, only the no smoking signs proved the ambiance served as staging only.

A tea tray sat on a marble table beside a fireplace where a low-burning fire glowed. I wondered idly whether Rutgers had dashed back in time to play serving maid. I amused myself picturing the guard trussed up in a frilly apron setting out a paper-thin Nippon tea set, yet I'd seen no sign of him or anyone else in the gallery minutes ago.

"Ah, the salon," I remarked, taking a seat beside the cushion, a richly colored knitted piece of fruits and flowers. I proceeded to stroke the pillow as if comforting a lap dog.

"My late wife's piece. Lovely, isn't it?"

"Yes, but you need more color in here, maybe a few richly colored rugs. I have the perfect solution in my shop."

Sir Rupert beamed. "Oh, my. You are in the trade, aren't you? I shall take your advice. Perhaps I may drop by?"

"If you're interested in purchasing something, certainly. Is this where Max thought you'd be meeting us today?"

"Indeed. Forgive my bad manners, but I did not want Maxwell to have chummy notions."

"But you want me to have chummy notions?"

"You and I have a better chance for a mutually beneficial relationship and, besides, I find Maxwell rather tiresome these days. Tea, Phoebe?"

"Yes, please, Rupert." I watched him pour the steaming liquid into the delicate Japanese cups. "I hope you aren't suggesting more than just an exchange of information?"

"No, my dear, I assure you I am no aging Don Juan hoping to snare a lovely young woman. Even though my dear wife has passed, that would be most inappropriate. My interest is respectfully professional."

"In other words, you're hoping I can lead you to the pot of gold at the end of the proverbial rainbow." I poured milk into my cup, stirring the liquid into a cloudy caramel with a tiny spoon, the very same kind of silver suppository Max believed Foxy attracted. "Sorry to disappoint you but I know nothing."

"I understand that both your brother and your boyfriend were involved in the Bermuda heist."

"First of all—and I'm just going to say this once, so please pay attention—Noel Halloran is not and has never been my boyfriend. How did that rumor start? Never mind. The important thing is it's not true. If you think befriending me will somehow lead you closer to the Treacherous Trio, you're wrong."

He arched his eyebrows, two caterpillar growths that perfectly complemented the ear tufts. "And yet, a few pieces of the hoard have been trickling into the market of late, meaning your Treacherous Trio is on the move." I paused, lips on the rim of my cup. He read my surprise. "Yes, I have word from my network that a small collection of Aztec gold has been acquired by a Mexican museum."

"But museums don't buy illicit pieces without legal provenance."

"Some are unscrupulous enough to do exactly that, especially if it means acquiring something of great cultural value for considerably less than it's worth and, may I remind you, provenance can be faked just like everything else. Public coffers are not always deep. My contacts say they have attempted to purchase the pieces at a much higher price, but the seller seemed determined to have the gold returned to the country of its origin and to a museum, at that. A rather altruistic touch, don't you think?"

"Seller, not sellers? There was there only one?"

"Only one initiating the transaction, yes."

"Male or female?"

"Male, I believe."

"Red hair or dark?"

"My understanding is that the transaction was performed by an intermediary, which is often the case, so no direct contact transpired. The museum's buyer met the agent in an undisclosed European city, and the seller offered an impressive, though completely bogus, provenance trail with enough details to satisfy all but the most expert scrutiny."

"Forgeries."

"Yes. I understand your brother is a master forger. His skill, I presume, extends to sketches and maps?"

"Sketches, maps, artifacts, you name it." I lowered the tea cup to my lap untouched. "Is that why you think these pieces were part of the Bermuda heist?"

"No, there is more compelling evidence. The pieces match the description Alistair Wyndridge published two months ago in his autobiography, and because the style of the transaction—accepting a below-market price without the benefit of an auction—smacks of Dr. Noel Halloran."

"Why?" The tea was growing cold. I couldn't bring that cup to my lips without risking spillage.

"I believe Miss Maggie is far cleverer than Max ever gave her credit and I confess to knowing little about your elusive brother, but I have had dealings with Dr. Halloran in the past. He is an archaeologist first, criminal second. Many are the times he's chastised me with passionate diatribes regarding obtaining pieces for private collectors when he believed they should be in the hands of the public domain, preferably museums and art galleries. He's what I consider a crusader. Tedious though he can be, I rather admire him for that. The world is a better place with convictions, don't you think?"

"A crusader?" I said, nearly snorting. "Well, why not? Crusaders stormed off to foreign lands to raze temples to the ground in the name of conviction."

"Do I detect a note of sarcasm? Oh, indeed I do. My point is that sale has Halloran's mark all over it," Rupert continued. "Dr. Noel Halloran is on the move."

Noel's face flashed across my mind: the honey-skinned, exotic beauty of mixed racial parentage-Australian Aborigine combined with Max's Celtic bog of a gene pool. "Why, because he may have chosen to fleece the stolen goods at a lower price? Couldn't he have done that for expediency sake just to get quick cash?"

"There was nothing expedient about this. In all ways, it was carefully planned and executed."

I took a deep breath. "Okay, but why are you telling me this?"

"For your safety and information: Halloran's having you followed."

"What?"

"My dear, you have become the target of increased scrutiny over the past few weeks. Several competing interests are keeping you in their sights, but one in particular has been identified as a friend of Noel Halloran's."

My hand jerked. I caught the cup just as it tipped tea and milk over my lap. "Sorry."

"Please, do take this napkin to mop that up. There now. Much better. There is a lavatory just around the corner if you'd like to use cold water."

I waved away the offer. The last thing I cared about was a pair of soggy thighs. "Why would Noel have me followed? I can understand the black market types but why him? He knows I don't have the loot. That doesn't make sense."

"Think, my dear. Noel Halloran is an impassioned archaeologist fixated on securing artifacts no matter what the cost. Just because he has successfully wrested away a fortune from your hapless godfather and that Bermudian author chap doesn't mean he's finished. My no, for there is a world filled with undiscovered treasures and artifacts waiting for the talented extractor, and you can believe Noel Halloran is keeping his eye on them all."

"You mean, he's already onto something new?"

"Of course. The Bermuda venture only served to finance future operations. Whatever and whenever he finds something of interest, he will be looking to unearth them, and those objects will require storage, and, eventually a market. Naturally, I am most interested in helping him with the latter but you, my dear, can certainly be of assistance in the storage department. What better place to secure stolen artifacts than the gallery he already knows intimately, having worked there himself for several years? My dear, he used you once and plans to do so again."

"Over my dead body." My Irish roots always prevented me from uttering those words but that didn't stop me now. "He wouldn't dare come back to London. It's too risky."

"Maybe he doesn't have to."

"Which means?"

"All he need do is send a package or shipment, something which looks legitimate and which you might hide without even knowing."

"I get the feeling you know more about this than you're saying."

"Should you accept my help, my knowledge will be at your disposal. Naturally, until such time as we are in a cooperative partnership, I must keep some key matters to myself. What I have told you thus far should serve as a taster."

"And I should trust you because?"

"Because you must trust somebody. Your godfather is totally unreliable at the moment; your family is either dead or crossed over to the dark side, shall we say, and; black market cutthroats are closing in on you by the minute. Who better to help you navigate than one with my vast experience, not only as a fellow gallery owner, but as one who has many contacts, many ears and eyes, plus considerable protective muscle? I will place my expertise and resources at your disposal. Let me help. You want to find the trio as do I, but for different reasons. No, I am not interested in having them arrested but I am interested in their past and future operations. Doesn't that make ours the perfect collaborative relationship?"

"An illegal relationship, as you well know. We've been cooperating with the police all along. Why should that change?"

"Do you really believe the international police protect stolen artifacts, let alone those threatened by their absconding? Their goal is to return such items to the registered owners but supposing that individual or institution came by the item illegally or, at the very least, through devious means? Priceless antiquities have long complicated histories."

"I've heard that line before. I didn't buy it then and I don't now."

"The short story is the police needn't know. I will merely enter the scene as your consultant assisting you with gallery management while Maxwell is indisposed. More importantly, I'm offering you protection, Phoebe, something the police won't. I have the resources to keep you safe against the multiple interests trailing you, protection of which you have every need."

"Nobody's made a move. Why would they?"

"The London underworld finds you most interesting—sister and probable lover of the thieves, how enticing, perhaps useful as a hostage? You make the perfect mark. Do you realize that Max has been babbling into his cups all over London, blubbering on about how he was hoodwinked out of a fortune, until every two-bit crook in the boroughs knows about it, including your affiliation with the thieves? One will make a move someday soon, Phoebe. You are the most vulnerable. Make sure you're not also the most defenseless. I'll provide you with a bodyguard. All you need do in return is to keep me informed should anything suspicious happen on your gallery premises or beyond. We are not at cross-purposes with one another. Most importantly, I mean no harm to anyone you care about. My interests lay only in objets d'art"

I carefully replaced the cup on the table and got to my feet. "I'm not interested. Thank you for the offer but I have to go now. Max will be worried." I stepped towards the salon door.

"Wait. Please."

I paused.

"My offer stands. You may need my help some day or, at the very least, my advice. Take my card. Don't hesitate to call if you need anything."

Pocketing the card, I strode from the salon and down the length of the darkened gallery. Only when Rutgers appeared from the shadows to unlock the door, did the dealer speak again. "Do give thought to my offer but don't wait until it's too late. Matters will only grow more treacherous in the coming weeks."

Rutgers held the door as I stepped out onto the early evening. "Mr. Baker's at the Cock and Bull at the end of the road. Shall I walk you there, miss?"

"No, thanks." I shrugged my carpet bag more comfortably over my shoulder and headed off down the rain-slicked street.

3

Pubs in London merge from the cacophony of lights and traffic like beacons of comfort, only these days Max couldn't seem to find comfort anywhere else. When he didn't answer his phone, I proceeded directly to the Cock and Bull. I slipped through the throng of natty suits and stylish work attire to find him hunched over a beer at the bar. I touched his arm.

"Phoebe! I was getting bloody worried about you." By his bleary eyes, I knew he was also getting bloody drunk. "What did he say?"

"Nothing. He thinks I know more than I do. What else is new?"

"He's the last one. We've come up empty. No place left to turn."

"What kind of talk is that? We have the gallery, don't we? Let's go home."

"No, I'm just going to have a little drink."

"Max, you've had enough. Come with me. We promised Rena we'd close the gallery for her today, remember? She's got a date with Marco. Come on, I'll buy you supper after we lock up. How about Asian fusion at the Paper Tiger?"

He dropped his gaze. "You go, sweetheart. I'll catch up with you later."

"Max, don't do this, please."

"Don't do what? Be the adult I am and do what I damn well please? Don't nag. I'll be home when I get there, maybe in an hour."

"Fine." But I knew I wouldn't see him in an hour, maybe even not that evening. For some reason, I always tried to keep up the fantasy, as if that helped. I plowed my way to the exit, elbowed along the way by the socializing business folk lubricating their evening by a pint or two. Alcohol, companionship, and merriment—was I really missing something? All of it just made me lonelier.

Flipping up my collar, I darted down the road, intent on taking a shortcut to our shop. The streets were packed by harried workers dashing for home, the traffic lights slicking the wet streets with color. As much as I loved London's energy, that rhythm and punchy creativity mixed with tradition, that night all I craved was a return to a smaller world where layers of memory gilded every street and home lay just around the corner.

Only home would never be that close for me again.

The faces passing me only intensified my alienation. *The apparition of these faces in the crowd; petals on a wet, black bough,* lines from Ezra Pound, came to mind. Poetry helped. Color helped. Knitting sustained me. When lost at sea, cling to whatever moves you. The gallery and my little top floor flat had become my sanctuary.

The underground to Kensington Church Street was a relatively short hop on the Piccadilly Line, but I'd rather cross the Antarctic in bedroom slippers than pack myself in with all the evening commuters so I strode right past the Knightsbridge Station. Catching a cab was next to impossible this time of night so I chose to walk. At least it had stopped raining.

I swerved out of the pedestrian stream and into a fast-food restaurant to pick up supper. Tonight I'd feast on an avocado and shrimp salad, a lemonade, and just because I could, a gooey chocolate brownie. Chocolate offered comfort more reliably than humans. Chocolate betrayed nobody, hurt nothing, except maybe a waistline or two. On impulse, I added a carton of stew for Max in case he returned to the office in time, though I knew he wouldn't. Fooling myself again.

Taking my bounty to the register line, I mused over my meeting with Foxy, niggled by his offer for protection. Nothing about Sir Rupert inspired confidence, especially his trumped-up story of Noel having me followed. More likely I'd follow him; that is, if I could ever find enough information to begin tracking him down.

Foxy would have done a better job at convincing me with a city or a contact name, something, anything concrete I could use to find the bastard. As it was, he had nothing to offer but thinly veiled intimidation and an offer which was no offer at all. I'd stay the course, go home and spend an evening the way I always did: Eat while studying tomes on antique carpets and then retire upstairs to my flat for an hour of knitting before bed. Though lonely in many ways, I'd nested out a little niche of my own in the big city, a way of shrinking the unwieldy urban world down to size.

The familiar tingle began spidering down my spine just before I reached the cashier. Turning quickly, I scanned the faces around me. Everyone stood with British patience awaiting their turn. If someone found me particularly interesting, they kept it well-shielded. All the tables lining the walls were filled with heads-down diners grabbing a quick bite. No one even looked at me, yet I knew I was being watched. Why didn't they leave me alone? Turning back to the queue, I paid the cashier, stuffed my dinner packages into my carpet bag, and bolted.

With the October darkness falling heavily down across the streets, all illusions of safety scuttled into the shadows. Harrods loomed ahead on the opposite side, beckoning me in with the golden glow of a luxury cruise ship afloat on an ink-black sea.

I dashed across the road and dove into the department store. Glass cases of shiny objects, a display of Hermes scarves, and a kiosk of Paddington-like bears blurred past. I accidentally bumped into a willowy sales associate, apologized, and ran on. I wasn't so much panicked as annoyed, but I wasn't going to make stalking me easy for anyone.

I took the escalator to the second floor and then dashed straight for the elevators at the rear wall. Moments later, I was back on the escalators heading down to the first floor, rushing towards the nearest exit. I never looked over my shoulder or paused for so much as a nanosecond, but by now I'd attracted the attention of the security troop patrolling the floors like stealthy operatives. I only smiled at the polite "May I be of assistance?" and slipped out the Basil Street exit just as a woman disembarked from a cab. Nabbing the ride in her wake, I gave the driver the address, and sank back into the seat.

Foxy only confirmed what I already knew. I'd been followed almost the moment I arrived in London. It began as a prickle between my shoulder blades while strolling through Covent Garden just weeks after I arrived and intensified the day I spent in the Victorian and Albert Museum roaming the textile gallery. Someone had entered one of the exhibit rooms behind me and, since I had been alone just seconds before, I sensed his presence. The moment I turned towards him, he scurried away as if caught pilfering the crown jewels. All I grasped was an impression of an elderly man in a tweed suit.

That marked one of those connective seconds when I realized this wasn't the first time. After that, I'd often catch a figure staring at me from a street corner only to dart down a side road as I approached. By height and build, I knew it wasn't always the same person, sometimes not even the same sex. Sometimes, my stalker was young and sometimes much older, sometimes dressed in a suit, and sometimes in jeans, but always intensely interested in me.

As if I knew anything. Did they really think that following me would reveal the Tricky Trio's hideout? Those three had to be holed down somewhere far away from London. Not one of them had ever been in contact with either of us. My own brother and Max's own son had amputated us from their lives like gangrenous limbs.

All I had to go on was the sense of being watched in a city where a million strangers accompanied my every step. Who would listen? I gazed out the window. Traffic hemmed in the cab on either side as we wove through London's congested tributaries. I'd have been back at the shop had I walked. Fishing in my bag for my phone, I dialed Serena, our gallery assistant, who picked up in one ring. "Rena, I'm running late. Sorry. I wanted to get back early so you could leave. I don't suppose Max called to let you know?"

"No Max, Phoebe, but relax. Everything is all right, yes? Marco canceled."

"Again?"

"Again. When his love life cooks, mama gets shoved to the back of the stove. Jennifer forgives again."

"All the women forgive him." Marco Fogarty, Serena's son and an aspiring actor, ground girls' hearts under his booted heels like candy wafers, but Mom stuck to his sole like gum.

"Marco is being Marco and mothers are made to be all-suffering, yes? But girlfriends, what is their excuse?"

I laughed. "Hormones! We're just approaching Kensington Church Street now. I should be there in a few minutes. See you soon."

Only it took 15 minutes before the cab finally slid in front of Baker & Mermaid Art and Fine Antiques. I paid the driver, jumped out, and paused, temporarily transfixed by the site of our shop. Though not as prestigious as Carpe Diem, Baker & Mermaid had much more curb appeal. I had worked hard to eradicate all vestiges of Maggie, Max's former girlfriend and assistant, who had composed the gallery to look somewhere between a high-end dress shop and a Sears decorating store. Now it presented itself for what it was: a purveyor of fine textiles and antiques, many of which fell into the (legal) artifact category.

A gilded mermaid, suspended on scrolled wrought iron hinges curved her magnificent tail around the shop sign as if hugging it close. My symbol since childhood, she was my soul's pilot light, my reminder to keep swimming no matter how rough the seas. Both the sign and the partnership were an extravagantly generous gift from Max in honor of my arrival in London. Part apology, part heart-felt offering, and possibly also an act of consolation for our mutual losses, it still touched me in all my deepest places.

"I know she is magnifico, Phoebe, but will you crick your neck staring like that?"

My gaze shot down to Serena framed in the doorway, her head cocked to one side. Crud, how long had I been standing exposed on the street? "She gets me every time."

Serena grinned. A striking presence with hair colored a deep pink and shaped into a smooth bob, today she wore a long black tunic over leggings, her attire accessorized with clusters of vintage necklaces looped one over the other. I knew she'd be wearing attar of roses in honor of all things rose but tomorrow might choose another color theme and be scented accordingly. I only hoped I looked and smelled that good in my sixties.

"My only complaint is the bra, oh, the bra!" Serena continued, mock-cupping her bosom. "Ouch. Can she not find a more comfortable bra than that? Marks and Spencer has a sale this week."

I stepped towards the door. "I think in mermaid terms, clam shells are the ultimate in shape-wear, kind of like Spanx on the half shell."

Rena laughed and clapped her hands. "I'm sure you are right."

She'd already closed the shop for the day. The back gallery space hung in darkness with just the two Ushak carpets in the window illuminated in a glory of golds and reds. It would break my heart the day one or both went home with someone else, though we desperately needed a big sale.

"I'm sorry I didn't get here sooner. I took a cab."

"I see." Rena stepped aside as I entered, locking the door behind me. "Would not the tube be faster?"

"Probably." I breathed deeply her rose fragrance and lowered my carpet bag to the floor. "Only I can't quite adjust to traveling in a cylinder."

I resisted the urge to double-check the deadbolt and scan the street through the glass for possible pursuers. What difference would that make? Everybody knew where I lived by now.

"In another year or two, you will be proper Londoner. I am almost glad that Marco stood me up tonight so that we can speak alone. I must say something."

Surely she wasn't going to hand in her notice? Serena Fogarty had been my right hand since I assumed part ownership of the gallery. She had once owned a gallery herself with her husband in Bath but, after his sudden death a decade ago, she came to London with a teenage son and a bag-load of debt. She'd been working the booths at Portobello Road and other shop jobs until the day six months ago when she arrived at Baker & Mermaid. Her application felt like a stroke of divine intervention.

"Is everything all right?" I asked.

"So I hope." She studied my face, her hands clasped before her like a supplicant. "Phoebe, maybe this is not my business and so I overstep my place, but I think you must know, yes? Your name is on the door, too." Her English, though excellent, couldn't quite eradicate her Italian imprint.

"I should know," I nodded. "Know what?"

"It is about Max."

I stared at her for a moment. My loyalty to my godfather remained unshaken no matter what. Discussing him with an employee didn't feel right, and yet, Serena verged on a friend and would never broach something unless it was important. "Right, so how about sharing supper with me first? I picked up some fodder on the way home."

"I couldn't possibly carve into what surely must be a banquet in a bag."

"Stew, salad, and a brownie the size of a truck, are you kidding me? I'm surprised I haven't gained half a pound just saying brownie out loud. You can't leave me to tackle it alone. That thing is huge."

"Chocolate?"

"Completely."

"Then I will be there for you tonight, but you must promise to let me cook for you soon, something truly magnificent like squash ravioli, my specialty, yes?"

"From one of your family recipes? Absolutely." I picked up my bag and strode halfway down the gallery towards the glass staircase. That staircase was one of the few things of Maggie's renovation that remained after Max tried abolishing her memory from his existence. Extravagantly engineered in Plexiglas, it slipped upward to a kind of observatory-cum-workspace landing that seemed to float over the center of the gallery like my own stairway to heaven. I claimed it as my office and arranged for the assistant's desk to be located near the back. The idea of sailing over art and textiles in my own dream come true was too perfect to resist.

One more level up and hidden from view lay Max's third-story office with my flat tucked around the corner and down the hall. When Max had first acquired the building decades ago, he gutted the first and second floors to make a lofty display area suitable for hanging impressive objects like antique rugs. In those days, Maggie strove to hone the area with a modernistic edge. Just thinking of her now made my teeth ache. Physical responses to

Noel and my missing brother, though similar, were far more painful and hovered about my heart and gut. My response to Maggie's duplicity was simpler, a seething anger that provided an easier target. Devious, conniving, and superficial pretty much summed up my adjectives for her.

In my suspended office above, I cleared a corner of my desk, spread a pashmina for a tablecloth, and set out the knives and forks we kept in the tea alcove. Rena and I ate in companionable silence interspersed with Marco tales and anecdotes. Some unspoken agreement passed between us that we'd avoid unpleasant topics until suitably fed and watered. As it turned out, my takeout dinner accommodated us both. Though a bit of stew remained, the brownie didn't stand a chance.

"Well, I guess it's time to get to the crux of it," I said, shaking crumbs into the wastebasket.

Rena sighed. "Maybe we could have a cup of tea first?"

"You know, for an Italian-born, you certainly have adopted British mores. I mean, you ask for tea like you mean it."

She brightened. "You have wine?"

I laughed. "No, sadly. I downed the last of my Chablis last night."

Rena shrugged. "Wine is always best but, after twenty-five years, I adapt."

"Right, so I'll plug in the kettle."

Rena followed me downstairs to the back room where a tea-making stand and water cooler sat just inside the door. Boxes, crates, and mailing tubes cluttered the rest of the space surrounding a long oak table. Max had collected rare objects for years, storing them in every available corner until such time as they either took their turn on the gallery floor or faded into oblivion. Most of the really valuable objects were gone now but in a space the size of a single garage, it looked more like the Old Curiosity Shop than a business storeroom. Still, I'd know if something else were hidden there, wouldn't I?

"Someday I want the luxury of organizing this properly," I remarked.

"But why not now?"

I flicked on the electric kettle. "First I have to scale the mountainous learning curve that comes with being a gallery owner.

I'd like to have been a textile expert by last month. There's so much to learn."

"You work too hard. You study all the time—study, study, study. What about love?"

"Love?" I made a face. "Please. I've given up on men." I almost gave up on people, too. "Okay," I said turning around. "About Max."

Rena sighed. "Right. The check you signed for me last week?"

"Your salary? Of course."

"My bank called to say it had not cleared."

I stared at her. "As in bounced?"

"Like a rubber ball-boing-de-boing," she made bouncing motions with her hand. "The one two weeks ago, same."

"That's impossible. Maybe I messed up the date or forgot to sign it?"

"You never mess up dates, Phoebe, and am I not careful to get either one or both of your signatures? There is more. Please wait here."

She slipped from the room and returned moments later to lay a stack of envelopes snapped together with an elastic band on the table. "I don't know what to do with them. I place them on Max's desk every morning, and every day I see them in the same place. The pile mounts."

My icy fingers pulled the stack from the rubber band, quickly flicking through the unopened letters, requests, invitations, and two envelopes stamped FINAL NOTICE. I opened one, staring at a collection notice referencing one of our suppliers.

"Oh, crud." I tossed them on the desk. Collection agencies? Bounced checks? Had our bank account bottomed out? "It can't be." Max was rich. Evidence of his wealth greeted me every morning in this very building, followed me around in strings of gifts, had, in fact, enveloped me since my father died and I left Nova Scotia to join him in London. What was happening?

"Phoebe, I am so sorry. I had hoped this would all just go away." Rena flapped her arms like an escaping bird.

I pressed my index finger between my temples to reset my brain, then dropped my hand, straightened my shoulders, and faced her. "You did right to tell me. Let's just handle this one step at a time. First, you need your salary. I'll transfer money from my personal account into the company and provide you with another check that you can cash tomorrow. Next, please leave me all the information you have regarding the accounts—ledgers, books, passwords, whatever. Does Max keep everything upstairs?"

Serena nodded. "There is an automated bookkeeping program which I try to keep up to date but Max doesn't provide me current information. He jots things down in a ledger in his desk, I think, but," she shrugged, "I am unsure."

"I haven't paid any attention to the accounts. I've just assumed too much."

The kettle began to boil. I moved to pour water into the nearby pot but Rena laid her hand on mine. "Forget the tea, yes? You have much on your mind. I will gather what I have and leave you now. I am certain you will get everything sorted out. Anything you need from me, anything at all, you ask."

4

Hours later, I still sat in Max's upstairs office poring over the ledgers. It didn't take an accountant to see how more money had been siphoned out of Baker & Mermaid than had been going in. The list of sales over the prior months had been small, something Max attributed to a poor economy as well as his sudden jettison into the legal trade, which he claimed cost him many high-ticket customers. Meanwhile, I'd spent far too long caught in the illusion that we were rich while he went far too long letting me believe it. Why hadn't I paid attention? Why didn't I ask questions, insist he go over the books with me?

I logged onto my bank account, still based in Halifax where my father's estate had yet to close, and checked my balances. The bottom line of my checking account delivered another shock: Almost twenty thousand dollars had been mysteriously deposited two days ago. I stared in disbelief. What was happening? With my brother and co-heir of my father's diminutive estate missing, I had yet to receive anything from Dad's will or even put the cottage up for sale. I lived on the ample salary Max paid, which I deposited into a British bank, but this? I now had over fifty thousand dollars that wasn't mine.

I checked the time: eleven o'clock in London meant seven o'clock back in Nova Scotia. My friend, Nancy, a lawyer, would still be at her office closing things down for the day. I sat staring unfocused at Max's collection of antique inkwells lining the wall before pushing back the chair, padding downstairs to my glass landing, and dialing my home province. She picked up on the first ring. "Nancy?"

"Phoebe, is everything okay?"

"I just discovered Baker & Mermaid is broke."

"How serious is it?"

"Serious enough, but that's not my only worry. I told you that someone deposited money in my account two weeks ago? So far, the bank hasn't been able to determine the source, but another deposit came through yesterday, a big one. It shows up online as 'Undisclosed Transfer'."

Nancy paused for a moment. "Toby."

"Of course it's Toby, who else? The bank said it was a wire transfer and gave the name of a bank in Switzerland but couldn't identify the owner."

"They wouldn't or couldn't. It's not illegal to give someone money, and bank transfers and money wires happen all the time, often anonymously. Switzerland specializes in anonymous wealth."

"Yes, but surely I have the right to accept or refuse the gift?" I stared into the empty air over the balcony. Saying that aloud sounded plain foolish.

"The right to refuse large infusions of money? I doubt banks have that request often enough to require stipulations."

"If he's trying to appease his conscience or otherwise make up for what he's done to me and Dad, he can forget it. But, look, what if he's using me to launder money?"

"Do you really believe Toby would do that?"

"Ask me if I thought any of the things he's done were possible a year ago."

"Point taken. Here's another thing: Someone's been infusing your dad's account with money, too. Remember when I told you how the bank statements showed an aberration from one month to the next? Typically in probate cases, the bank account pays outstanding bills, fees, and such, which means the assets should be going down until we finally close it out, except for the premium savings accounts, of course. But, and this is a big but, your dad's checking account has been increasing incrementally, first by hundreds, now by thousands, and what's more, it's been going on since long before your dad died. We were impressed by how much we thought he saved in his lifetime, but after studying his accounts, I've reached the conclusion that someone, presumably Toby, has been augmenting your father's account all along."

I pressed a finger against my forehead. "Okay, so Toby took care of Dad's expenses—good for him. That's what we kids are supposed to do for our ailing parents if we can—but to continue after he's gone means he has no compunction about using me to further his own ends. How little I knew my brother."

"He's still your brother and loves you, regardless of what compulsions feed him. Maybe he sees padding your father's assets as one way of taking care of you down the road? In six more years, he'll be declared legally dead and all of that inheritance goes to you."

"Unless I expose him first, which I will. And how do we know he isn't just hiding it from the government? It's tainted money. I don't want his apologies or his belated brotherly love, and certainly not his money, except-"

"Except you've decided to use it."

Sometimes she just knew me too damn well. "Except I need it to pay Serena's salary and keep Baker & Mermaid afloat. If I don't, we'll go under. I can't let that happen. This gallery means more to me than I ever expected. It's like all I have left."

"You have far more left than the gallery, but I understand how you're clinging to it right now. Still, technically what you're doing is illegal, which you know already."

"Sure, I know that but I'm not stealing anything, just borrowing something already stolen. Anyway, I've sent the request to the bank to transfer the funds into the company until I can repay it. That will give me time to get the gallery where it needs to be while I go after the Treacherous Trio."

Nancy laughed a melodious rumble. "That's why you left the law. You just can't do black and white. You always get snarled in the gray zone."

"I like blended colors."

"Which can get pretty muddy."

"At the time I quit law school, I they called it a 'rebellious refusal to accept rules unconditionally'."

29

"Sounds right. You know I'll have to share my suspicions to investigators, should they start poking around your father's estate?"

"Of course, but you wouldn't volunteer the information, would you?"

"I should."

I squeezed my eyes shut. Of course she should. What was I thinking? "Don't hold anything back, please. I don't want you mired in any of this or your firm associated with obstructing justice just because I am. Once I track down the three of them, I'll pass their heads over to them on a plate and will look mighty fine in the eyes of the law."

"Just try to stay alive while you're doing it, will you? This is the black market we're talking about."

"Don't I know it. We visited one of Max's old comrades in crime today, a Sir Rupert Fox, and he's definitely dealing in stolen goods, though he wouldn't admit that. He says he has information that Noel has already begun fencing the goods to a Mexican museum while making on that he was more interested in returning the plunder to their rightful countries than money. He called Noel 'altruistic'. How's that for a joke? He claimed the duplicitous criminal treasure hunter might try using the gallery to hide stolen artifacts."

"Do you think that's a possibility?"

"Nothing that bastard does would surprise me but I don't see how he could have hidden anything here since the heist. Anyway, for months I've just been keeping my head down trying to build a life for myself but all that poison keeps seeping back and tainting everything. I'll never be free unless those three are in jail."

"But you don't need to be the one to put them there. This is dangerous stuff. Maybe you do need a bodyguard."

"Another person dodging my heels, you mean? Somehow that doesn't sound comforting. Besides, he's probably already having me followed."

"Tell the police."

"No. I need flexibility. If the trio have begun fencing the loot, somewhere, somehow, they'll trip up, leave a trail, and I'll be on it. I don't need the police following me on that adventure."

"Phoebe, what are you saying? Leave it to the authorities. It's their job to find the thieves, not yours."

"But this is personal and I'm taking it very personally. It's my brother and my—hell, I don't know what Noel was—anyway, he made it personal, too."

"Could you just think with your head instead of your heart for once? Don't act impulsively."

"Sure."

"Wish your 'sure' meant something."

"I'll try."

"Try really hard."

Speaking with Nancy left me feeling amazingly fortified, like taking a tonic for my resolve. Only, such boosts lasted only until the next stray thought sent me off on a tangent. We hung up promising to talk soon.

Shoving myself away from the desk, I padded down the glass steps to the gallery. It was almost twelve and night had sunk the space in a kind of subterranean glow. The street lamps cast long bars of illumination across the floor, brushing against the cases and artifacts that centered the space.

The family of Asian celadon incense burners on the long oak table now swam in a ghostly gloom and all the carpets and textiles lining the walls had withdrawn their brilliance. And yet, if I closed my eyes, I could imagine every detail of every piece—the wild Shekarlu Persian rug with its mellowed ocher and rusted reds, the trio of folk kilims dancing in pattern and color, the Greek 18th century bridal embroidery with its precise stitchery, and even the circular motifs that centered the deep green background of the Zoroastrian shawl.

We had forty-five pieces of textile art displayed here with another ten upstairs in my apartment to be brought down as pieces sold. These expressions of humanity sat hushed in the dark yet I swear could hear them speaking a thousand languages in my heart.

These were my favorite moments, alone in the gallery surrounded by these textiles and glorious objects. Rarely a night passed when I didn't descend from my aerie to stroll the gallery like some spirit on the prowl. Mostly, I counted my blessings, marveling over being here, alone amid all this majesty.

I thought of my mother from whom I learned my love of textiles; I thought of my dad, gone now these seven months, who had once regarded his womenfolk's love for color and fiber an honor that had enlightened his life; thought of my brilliant, twisted, missing brother, and then quickly swerved away.

Why did it feel as if every step I took to mend my life, only unraveled it farther?

5

My apartment had originally been Max's storeroom attic tucked under the dormers of this building and, before that, probably servants' quarters to some elegant Georgian family. With the cramped spaces and odd-angled walls, it needed plenty of refurbishment to make habitable.

Down came walls to open up the rooms, wooden floors were buffed and polished, bright new windows installed, plus Max added a bathroom and mini kitchen. Into this lovely new world that had become my land of new beginnings, I marched a collection of Art Nouveau tiles along the mantle, hung framed stained glass windows, graced the available hanging areas with antique rugs, and focused shots of color and pattern everywhere. My mother's loom occupied the center of the sitting area, leaving the rest of the furniture—a chair, two side tables, and a carved bookcase—hugging the walls like second-rate citizens. Stuffed with yarn as well as books, my well-padded bookcase made a particularly dazzling accent along with the pieces of knitting I draped everywhere.

Over the mantle hung *Tide Weaver*, the tapestry I'd created with Mom and Toby years ago. Sometimes it still hurt to look at it but mostly I'd come to take comfort in its presence. The energy from my mother's creative spirit lay embedded in those threads along with some aspect of all I once believed my family represented.

Admiring my apartment that morning, I wondered why I hadn't asked how much that renovation cost. Actually, I had, only Max had refused to answer.

Gulping down a kale smoothie, I grabbed my jacket. Our shop hours ran from ten am to seven pm on Wednesdays and, because I lived upstairs, I always opened the gallery in the mornings and ran it solo until Serena arrived at eleven o'clock. Today I wished I'd arranged for her early arrival so I could dash around the corner to Max's townhouse. I knew he wouldn't arrive until much later and what I had to say needed saying immediately and preferably in private. Since he wasn't answering the phone, either, I'd just have to wait.

I deactivated the security system and strolled around the gallery flicking on the lights, including the brace of halogens focused on the magnificent carpets lining the walls. Each textile deserved a personal greeting. Beginning nearest the door, I walked around the perimeter of the gallery, saying each textile by name like a benediction. Nearest the front on the left-hand side, the red and blue silk Gansu carpet I called Cloud-head for its distinctive border, was my first, after which I made my way around and back to the right-hand side to finish with the nineteenth century Northwest Persian rug I'd dubbed Magic Garden. Name something and you grant it dignity. Greet it by that name and you give it life.

Each carpet was special, rare and inspiring. My loomed divas required acknowledgment of their incredible beauty and will to survive. Some had been smuggled out of conquered castles as war trophies; others had made their way across steppes and plains as part of a family's most treasured possessions; and all represented the human need to enrich our world in color and pattern. I was honored to be in their presence every single day and vowed never to forget it. I had been known to refuse a sale based on my assumed unworthiness of the buyer. Did they really plan to let their puppy pee on it?

Down the center aisle ran our series of oak tables placed end to end over which we hung green Tiffany turtle-back glass lamps. Captured in each light pool lay clusters of tribal jewelry, carved celadon incense burners, and collections of small, rare objects grouped amid pots of African violets and miniature palms—Serena's and my idea, which we thought brilliant. The violets and greenery added an air of living grace over the inanimate objects like finding artifacts in a jungle garden.

I had just finished switching on the Tiffanies and testing the plants for water when the doorbell rang. I looked up, startled, watering can in hand. Rarely did customers arrive this early and yet the outline of a man stood back-lit against the sun. I checked the time on my phone: one minute after ten o'clock. Okay, so I was a minute late. Then I had a thought: Supposing this was one of my stalkers come to check me out? Oh, hell. They would have done the checking out long before. Besides, I couldn't very well refuse to answer the door. I had a business to run.

I strode forward in my best store manager mode, thinking that, if I had to, I could trip the emergency alarm located under the long table. As an added precaution, I kept one hand on the phone in case I had to speed-dial the cops.

Unlocking the door, I smiled up at the tall man in a greatcoat, with dark hair curling out from under a broad-brimmed hat and a long mustache that could have come straight out of Dr. Zhivago. His eyes were deep-set and silky brown like a stallion's glossy flank and for a moment I fell into their light.

"Hello, Phoebe."

My throat constricted. "Noel?"

"Back up," he said in a low voice. "Make on like I'm a customer. Say you have something put aside for me and walk towards the back to the camera's blind spot where we can talk."

I stepped back. "You're crazy coming here."

"I have to talk to you and this is the only way. Give me a minute."

I desperately wanted to talk or hit him with my fists, kick him in the shins or considerably higher, anything but continue the cold silence I'd been plunged into for months. Yet, to have him show up now? I wasn't prepared. I could hardly breathe. Still, I turned half in shock and began walking toward the back, gripping my phone in one hand but sliding the watering can onto the table in passing.

"Sorry to arrive so early," he said in a loud voice, the Australian jaunt replaced by a clipped British affectation. "I would have phoned but my blasted cell isn't on the ball today. Bloody nuisance! I had to come into the city anyway, so I thought I'd just swing around."

"I'm so glad you did, mister, ah, Drummond? I have the item you requested put aside for you right back here," I said, my voice a little too chirpy.

"Oh, jolly good."

Jolly good? I led him right into the far corner behind Lena's desk. The moment we were out of camera range, I dropped my phone on the desk, swung around and delivered such a closed-fist blow to his face that it left my hand throbbing. I stood for stunned seconds staring at my hand before bursting into tears. "Look what you've done! I've never hit another human being in my life!"

"You shot me a few months ago."

"That was different. I wasn't aiming for you."

He reached out to bring me to him but I pushed him away.

"Don't touch me. Don't you ever touch me."

He dropped his hands, those fine long-fingered, pilfering, criminal hands. "Okay, so I deserved that. Much worse, probably, but I—"

"Probably? Definitely, you sleazy, criminal, low-life, art-thieving bastard!"

"Will you cut the inspired adjectives and just listen for a moment?"

I wiped my eyes on the back of my sleeve and stepped towards him, so wired by pain and fury, I couldn't think straight. "How dare you come back here after all you've done to your father, to me. You don't care about anybody but yourself, you bastard!" I'd rehearsed this first meeting again and again, but my cache of spring-loaded barbs failed to launch.

"I do care. Why do you think I'm here?"

"To steal something else, how the hell do I know? Are the Elgin Marbles taken yet?"

He suppressed a laugh but the eyes fixed on mine brewed something darker. "At least once by the British, but I suppose we could steal them back for Greece. How's Father?"

"What do you care?" God, why couldn't I say something intelligent?

He spread his gloved hands. "I've always cared."

"Bullshit!"

"Phoebe, look, you're angry, I get that. You should be. How could I expect anything else? But I never stop thinking you. I can't bear that I put you in danger. Since Bermuda, I've had someone looking out for you and Father on a constant basis. Now my man tells me you've got a batch of thugs, detectives, and even Interpol types tailing you. He says they're so thick, they practically form queues on your heels. I had to come see for myself, find out what the hell's going on, and screw the risk. What is going on?"

"Are you serious? Look around, Noel. I'm trying to rebuild my life while shaking everyone's conviction that I must be in some way involved with your heist, your mess-up. You and my own damn brother have sunk Max and me so deep, we have to claw our way out, and you ask me what's going on?"

"Interpol's watching."

I tried to steady my breath, rein in my thunder, think. "And I assured them that the moment one of you appears, I'll tell them. I want nothing more than to see you all rot in jail."

He took a deep breath, his expression shooting glib one minute and silk-softened the next. "I'm not even going to try to apologize, because nothing I say will ever be enough, at least not now, not like this. It would take a hell of a lot longer than the time I've got today to fill you in with what really happened in Bermuda, let alone what's going on now."

"I have it on good authority that you've begun fencing the goods."

"Foxy told you, I suppose-yes, I know you and Father went to see him—but it's a hell of a lot more complicated. I just can't explain the details here and now. I'm leaving the country today, but I had to see you. God, you look so good, like I imagined only better. I love your hair." He looked as if he wanted to touch my face but thought better of it.

"It's the full story I want and I want it now. If you can't stick around long enough to tell it, maybe I'll just ring the alarm so you'll have to. You'll have plenty of time to talk in prison."

"It's about Toby."

"Toby? Do you mean my missing brother Toby? The one who hasn't bothered to contact me for a year Toby?"

He nodded solemnly. "He wants to see you, Phoebe, desperately, but can't. I've come to give you a message from us both, really. We're not the monsters you think." He took a deep breath, and in that instant I realized how sunken his cheeks were under the disguise, how his usual buoyancy had flat-lined into a tightrope of anxiety and pain. I should have felt deliriously happy over his suffering but I didn't. "Toby wants you to know that—" He paused.

"That what?"

"That he loves you."

"He doesn't know the meaning of love. Love would have kept him near while Dad was dying; love wouldn't have left me to die inside for all these months and plunge me into such danger. And where is he, anyway?"

Noel's dark eyes fixed on my face, his mouth twisted down. "Hell pretty much describes it."

"No details, eh? I'm supposed to just wait for answers forever?" I pushed past and sprang for the display table. In an instant, I had flicked the switch, turning to face him triumphantly as the siren ripped through the air.

"Oh, bloody hell, Phoebe! I haven't even told you about the Goddess with Vultures kilim yet, and now you're just going to have to figure it out by yourself." He lurched for the door, hat pulled low over his face. "Leave it alone for godsakes!" He paused by the door. "And I meant what I said, all of it."

"What Goddess with Vultures kilim?" I called out after him but he slipped into the street and was gone.

6

Giving my statement to the metro police was a waste of time. Try explaining why you rang the alarm on someone who made no attempts to threaten or harm you physically, let alone steal anything. He didn't even break in. Technically, no crime had been committed.

"He's a known criminal. Contact Interpol," I told them. "They know the background and, in the meantime, an international art thief may be already escaping the country. Why are you just standing there?" I mentioned nothing about Noel's personal comments or the remark about a goddess-with-vultures kilim. I mean, one was personal and the other simply inscrutable—a goddess with vultures? After an hour of senseless questioning, they finally left. I turned to find Serena watching me.

"Your lover really returned?" she asked, her face alight with expectancy.

"He's not and never was my lover. He kissed me once, that was it. Maybe twice. Big deal," I said. "Besides, he's a snake, the linchpin in the crime mechanism that ran the whole heist operation, an archaeologist shit-head." Admittedly, I needed work on my descriptors.

"But the archaeologist shit-head is very handsome, yes?"

"What does that have to do with anything?" I rubbed a hand over my eyes thus smearing my mascara. I hated makeup. Why should a woman in tears be further humiliated? "He actually had the nerve to come back here and talk to me, said he wanted to tell me he wasn't the monster I thought he was. Can you believe it? Like he'd risk capture for that? He came for another purpose, the bastard." I didn't mention the kilim to Serena, either.

"He must care about you very much."

"Care about me?" I stared at her in disbelief. "You call that caring? Did he really think I wouldn't pull the alarm on him, that I wouldn't alert the police after everything he's done?"

"He told you about your brother?"

"He said Toby couldn't come to me in person—must have been too busy planning the next heist or something—but wanted me to know he wasn't a monster." I laughed. "I mean, give me a break. I know a monster when I see one."

"Did he try to kiss you?" Serena asked.

"Serena, stop thinking life is like an Audrey Hepburn movie. It's not. It's more like a horror flick spliced together with a bad sitcom where everybody flubs the punch lines. No, he didn't try to kiss me. He tried to touch my face and I whacked him across the cheek so hard I thought I broke a finger. God, I hate that man." I held up my right hand. "To think I risked my knitting hand for the likes of him. And the most galling thing is that I burst into tears. Where is Max, anyway? He should have been here an hour ago. God, I hope Noel didn't visit him, too. That would really mess him up. He's not answering his damn phone!"

"Phoebe, Max does not come in early any more. Some days, never, and you know how he hates phones. He probably turned it off, yes?" Serena answered gently. "Try to calm yourself. I will make tea, yes?"

"No tea." I couldn't bear to see her watching me with those large eyes luminous with sympathy or some hope that my life story would somehow end with happily ever after. I took a deep breath. "I have to see Max. Cover for me, please."

"Of course, Phoebe, always."

I grabbed my carpet bag and left, relieved to be on the move, my fury lessening once my boots hit the sidewalk. I needed strength, not adrenalin. The police might catch Noel yet. After all, how long could a tall man dressed like an escapee from the Russian front go without attracting notice?

Halfway down the street, my phone rang. I answered it without even checking the caller's identity.

"Phoebe? Rupert Fox here. I understand you rang the alarm on a visitor this morning."

I veered out of the pedestrian traffic to stand against a brick wall. "How the hell do you know that? Are you having my gallery watched?"

"Part of the time, yes. What did he say, if you don't mind me asking?"

"I do mind you asking, so leave me alone." I pressed END and pocketed the phone. Damn him and everyone else to hell.

Continuing to Max's townhouse, I dropped into Costa for takeaway coffee and pastries, his eye-openers of choice. Holding the bag, I continued along the busy street. Noel claimed he would be leaving that night, but for where? Why hadn't I asked him any real questions, and what did he mean about a goddess kilim? More damn mysteries and innuendos. Maybe Foxy knew something. Maybe I shouldn't have been so quick to hang up on him?

Horns honked, cars and motorcycles whizzed by, leaving me breathing the fumy air sharpened by the late autumn chill. Turning the corner, I arrived on Bedford Gardens, a residential street of mostly brick and stucco townhouses with manicured lawns and tiny gardens abloom with fall roses. Approaching Max's white corner property with its three stories and five bedrooms, I was struck anew by the signs of neglect.

Maggie, once his mistress of external appearances, had kept the window boxes filled with seasonal delights arranged through a pricey subscription florist. Now, the greenery stuffing the lacquered black boxes so obviously hailed from Christmas past that they could be harboring ghosts. The building cried out for a fresh brightening of white paint, and the small patch of grass out front had already lost the war to weeds.

I mounted the stairs and rang the bell, checking behind me for possible stalkers. I half expected to see Noel but knew in my heart that he was long gone, damn him. He only came just long enough to mess up my head but hopefully left his father alone. In any case, no one looked suspicious, not that that meant anything.

After several moments of no response, I unlocked the door with my key, dropped my carpet bag onto the foyer chair, and stepped into the hall. I stopped dead staring ahead at the empty wall opposite. That spot had once held Max's prized Ersari-Bashir carpet from central Asia, an intricately patterned masterpiece, a design improvised by the weaver in a rare illustration of creative independence. Gone. I felt a cry build at the back of my throat.

"Max?" I called out.

"Phoebe? Back here."

Back here meant the kitchen, a light-washed room overlooking the narrow topiary garden. Those topiaries, once shaped like chess pieces, now resembled a gathering of mangy gnomes stumbling towards the back door.

My godfather, disheveled and unshaven in his bathrobe, sat at the kitchen table, a piece of gnawed toast minus a plate in front of him.

"Morning, Phoebe, dear. Come to drag me to work, have you?" He didn't meet my eyes.

I placed the coffee and croissant on the table. "Not exactly. Anything new?"

"Nothing," he said in a flat voice. No Noel then, thank god. He'd tell me that much.

"I came to talk. When were you planning to tell me?"

He half turned to look at me without meeting my eyes. "Tell you what?"

"That Baker & Mermaid is broke."

His anguished expression nearly cracked my heart. He studied his toast while I flipped the lid on my coffee cup, willing myself to stay strong. I couldn't tell him everything would be fine; I couldn't operate on denial one moment longer.

"How'd you find out?"

"Serena's payroll check bounced like Indian rubber. Twice."

He rubbed his bloodshot eyes. "I meant to have enough ackers in there to cover the checks but I fell short. I thought I could fix this, Phoebe. I tried."

"So you sold the Bashir? That must have fetched a bundle."

"Not as much as you'd think but I needed to turn it quick to get the cash."

"Why didn't you say something? I could have saved you from selling the Bashir. You loved that carpet."

He shook his head, his hair looking particularly leonine that morning. "It's just an object, Phoebe, not a person. I thought I could get the money right into the gallery account, but the taxes needed paying first, plus a pile of other bills." He rubbed his eyes again. "Phoebe, love, I can't shore things up any longer. I can't do it. There's so much I didn't tell you. She drained my accounts. She siphoned all the money in my checking account, dinged my savings, and piled so much debt on my credit cards, I've had to pay it off in installments."

I lowered myself into the chair opposite him, my gaze skimming the stacks of dirty dishes lining the marble counter top. "Maggie," I said, while taking a sip of my latte. Just saying her name left a bitter taste on my tongue no Italian roast could wash away.

"Maggie."

"Didn't you cancel the cards months ago?" I sounded so calm.

"I should have, but I put a dick on her and he said he could track her more easily if I left them open."

"Dick?"

"Dick Tracy, private eye."

"You hired a private eye and didn't tell me that, either?"

"Sorry, love, but you had a lot on your hands settling into the gallery so I thought I'd just do this on my own. The cops aren't doing anything."

I swallowed a mouthful of brew and took a deep breath. "So, you hired this dick and he told you to keep your credit cards open even though they were in the hands of a woman who had just stolen millions worth of treasure and kicked you in the nuts? Good advice."

"She's being tailed by Interpol. What was she thinking?"

"How about that she needs money? I know that's a bit obvious but, what the hell, some fool's bound to fall for it. Boy, has she got your number. Where did your private investigator say she'd been last?" These were all questions I should have had the presence of mind to ask Noel, not that he'd tell me the truth.

"Paris. She racked up over 5,000 pounds at Chanel last month."

"Wouldn't want to miss out on the new fall line even on the run. Hell, Max. Did you finally cancel the cards?"

"A couple of weeks ago, but I can't even afford to keep the dick going any longer now. I'm broke, Phoebe. I'm done."

"You're not done; we're not done. Has Noel been involved in stealing your personal assets, too?" Even saying his name aloud hurt. Seeing his damn sexy face this morning hurt worse, but I needed to exorcise all my devils any way I could.

He shook his head. "I don't know. Don't think so. Maggie handled our personal accounts. Noel was more keen on getting the artifacts and sourcing the art." He let out a groan. "We can't make it, Phoeb. We don't have the cash flow or the clients. The moment I went legal, all my connections dried up."

"So we'll build the gallery back up, this time with clients not willing to stash ancient stolen ethnography. We'll establish a new reputation and rise to the top of the antique carpet and textile world. We will not, I repeat, will not, go simpering into the twilight because a bunch of thieving bastards we thought loved us picked our pockets and smashed our hearts."

He gazed at me startled. "But—"

"No buts! I'm siphoning a little of my own savings into Baker & Mermaid. I'll cover Serena's salary, pay our creditors, and begin establishing a new reputation. We're not the same company, so of course we need different clientele." I took a few more gulps of coffee.

"Whatever cash you have in your savings isn't going to get us out of this mess."

"Maybe not right away but it will help in the short term. At least it's a plan, a way to keep moving forward. What else can we do?"

"Sell the gallery."

He could have slapped me in the face. For a moment I couldn't speak, and when I did, it came out in an explosion. "Like hell! Never, ever, ever, will we sell Baker & Mermaid!"

"I know it hurts, sweetheart, but we have to do what we have to do. I gave you half the gallery so we could run it together but we're about to go tits up. I may have a buyer. Bloke kind of just showed up when I needed him most, though he's a crafty bludger, ruthless, maybe, but he offered cash. Bought the carpets, too. Cuts a hard deal. Says he's interested in our stock and will take over the gallery, too, as either an investor or a buyer. Jason Young."

I placed my hands palms down on the table. "Ever think this buyer could be working for Sir Foxy? He'd buy us out in a nanosecond. Ever wonder why? Wonder what they're all after? Tell this Jason Young to take a frosty leap. Better yet, give me his number and let me tell him."

He shot me a quick, startled glance. "Phoebe, he's offering us a way out."

"Into what? No job, no future? A life of half-assed jobs doing something you hate?" I flipped the lid to his coffee and passed it over. "Drink up and listen carefully, Max: We are not selling the gallery, not as in ever. You'd need my signature to authorize a sale and you're not getting it, understand?"

"If we sell, we can start fresh, get out from under this debt."

"Max, this gallery is my fresh start and I'm not letting it go. Thank you from the bottom of my heart for giving it to me, but don't kick me in the gut by trying to rip it away. I'll buy you out first."

"With what?"

"I'll find a way and my Max would never go down without a fight or let a few bills, a bastard son, and a tricky ex keep him down."

"Don't call Noel a bastard. I would have married his mom if I knew."

"I'm not referring to his parentage but to his behavior. And don't change the subject. The point is, we're going to get back on top, find them, and get our lives back."

His stricken eyes said it all. "I'm stonkered. I have nothing left."

"You've got me and I've got you. All you need is to get off the booze so we can get our business back on its feet so you don't go off doing fool things with your broken heart instead of your head."

"Sweetheart—"

"Don't sweetheart me! Look at yourself. You're so consumed by self-pity, you can't find your way out of a paper bag. You're vulnerable in heart and mind and circumstance, and drinking is making it worse. You need help. Face it, you're alcoholic."

"I am not!" he slapped his fist against the table hard enough to send the knife skittering off the table edge. "I just like a drink once in a while."

I caught the knife in my hand and returned it to his plate before jumping up and flinging open the cupboards. "Like morning, noon, and night? What's this?" I pulled out a bottle of scotch wedged in among the tomato and Worcester sauces. "Good for eggs, maybe? And what's this?" I opened up the cabinets over the sink to find a jumble of half-opened liquor bottles. "I suppose this is a food group, now?"

"Everybody's got liquor in their cupboards in case of company, Phoeb."

"In your case, liquor is the company." I began opening the bottles one by one and pouring the contents down the drain.

Max heaved himself out of his chair and stood by, watching as if I'd slit his wrist to let him bleed to death. I didn't look at him, couldn't look at him. What had he become? They did this to him.

"Where's the rest?" I asked when I finished the last mickey of gin.

"Don't have any more," came the muffled reply.

"Don't lie to me! It's bad enough you're hiding things, which you swore you'd never do again, but lying is more than I can take."

I heard a snorting noise and looked up to find him collapsed over the table, crying into his arms, my big, strong, brave, flamboyant, deteriorating godfather crying like a child. I wanted to join him, bawl my eyes out and rage against the cruelty of the human heart but, right then, fury drove me on.

I'd get Maggie for this. I didn't care whether I had to tear the universe apart molecule by molecule, she'd pay for the damage done to him. Bad enough to make a fool out of a man but to keep twisting the knife? Noel might have been his son but he never promised him what Maggie did. My brother's masterful forgeries and strategic planning, Noel's duplicitous thievery and underhanded charm, they'd pay, too, each individually in different ways, but Maggie infuriated me the most just then. She wanted Max destroyed even after the main blow had been delivered.

Why hadn't I drilled Noel for information while I had the chance? He might have let something slip. Maybe, at that very moment, an Interpol team was intercepting him at Heathrow, shackling him with handcuffs, and dragging him into custody. Maybe I'd get to spit in his face instead of just whacking it.

It took me almost an hour to comb the house, nabbing bottles from hiding places under beds, in drawers, in wastebaskets. I emptied them all while wincing at every dust-limned vacancy I encountered on the walls. Each one had once held a personal treasure. Max must have been selling off his possessions for months while I blithely traipsed along thinking the world ran on magically lubricated hinges.

In his study, I found so many bottles, I needed a laundry basket to carry them to the bathroom sink. Once I finished draining the alcohol, I took the card for a cleaning service I found on his desk and made an appointment for a full house-cleaning. Just as I hung up from the cleaners, my glance caught a second business card slipped under a dirty coffee mug. I picked it up: Jason Young. Rare Ethnographic Art. New York, New York. Pocketing the card, I began gathering up the dirty clothes strewn over the upstairs floor and stuffing them into pillowcases, dragging them down to the foyer to be picked up by the linen service.

When I entered the kitchen over an hour later, I found Max still sitting at the table staring into space. "You know I can buy more juice, Phoebe," he said without meeting my eyes.

"I know that, Max, but I'm desperately hoping you won't. I'm praying you care enough about me to start pulling yourself together because I need you and miss you. You promised me you'd be my family, that you'd never let me down, and just once I want someone I care about to keep their damn promises. You can start by booking yourself into a detox facility until you regain your equilibrium. Do it for me. I need you back. I just don't want to do this alone."

Max said nothing, just sat there staring at his clasped hands. Suddenly weary, I made for the door. Stopping just on the kitchen threshold, I turned. "Max, do you know anything about a goddess-with-vultures kilim?"

"A goddess what?"

"That's what I thought."

7

"Mr. Young, this is Phoebe McCabe." I sat in Max's office glued to the phone after spending most of the afternoon going through more piles of unattended paperwork. How many major auctions had we missed, how many prime opportunities to network with potential clients? We could never rebuild our reputation unless we got to these events, but attending international exhibitions and conferences took capital we didn't have.

I set all the invitations to art and textile auctions aside, topping the pile with a postcard invitation to the major exhibition of the year in Istanbul taking place that same week. I couldn't make voice contact with Jason Young no matter how many times I tried. Finally, I left a message on his answering machine.

"Whatever agreement you think you have with my partner, Max Baker, is null and void considering that a) you do not have my signature on whatever he signed-it was probably a napkin he signed, anyway—and b) my godfather was probably inebriated at the time, making any quasi-contract void. Cease and desist from pursuing either me, Max Baker, or this gallery, or I will take legal measures." I hung up the phone and stared at the wall. Well, that sounded officious. It was frightening how quickly my old legalese kicked in. And here I thought I was beyond all that.

I pulled Sir Rupert's card from my pocket and stared at it. He had jotted his private cell number in fountain pen onto the gallery's thick creamy bond. Well, damn. I keyed in the number and waited.

"Sir Rupert Fox speaking."

"Phoebe McCabe here. Do you know of a Jason Young?"

He cleared his throat. "Possibly. Why do you ask?"

"You know why I'm asking, Rupert. If you want us to cooperate, start by telling me who he is and what he wants."

"In the spirit of reciprocation, isn't it time that you also shared information?"

I sighed. "Fine. My visitor assured me that he is not a monster and that he's worried about me. Touching, don't you think? He didn't get to say much else before I pulled the alarm."

"Are you certain?"

"Of course."

"And I am certain you are not being forthcoming with me, my dear. Nevertheless, in the spirit of cooperation, I will say that Jason Young is an alias. He goes by other names and identities but is most definitely connected to antiquities business. Use extreme caution when engaging with him. He will have ulterior motives."

"Who doesn't?"

He chuckled. I'd never heard a sound so aptly named. "Very true. What are your dealings with him?"

"Not my dealings but Max's. I've never met the man but recently he purchased many of Max's prized carpets at bargain basement prices and even made an offer on the gallery."

"Which pieces?"

"Why does that matter?"

"I'm a collector. Naturally, I'm interested."

"You don't deal in textiles so I don't see why you would. Or," I paused, "are you now changing specialties?"

"No, I am still primarily interested in smaller items. In any case, I suggest you prevent Maxwell from engaging in any further dealings with Jason Young. If money is the issue, I will double any offer he makes, both on carpets and on the gallery itself. If you need a buyer or money, I am he. Has this Jason Young pretender been into the gallery?"

"Not to my knowledge, but since I don't know what he looks like, I really can't be certain."

"I know what he looks like. I will put a watch out for him."

"No, I didn't ask for that kind of help, just information."

I hung up shortly after, fearing I had just cracked the lid on Pandora's box. I couldn't squander time fretting over it, in any case. There were just too many other anxiety inducers.

After a few minutes passed with me searching online for prime London detox facilities and jotting down numbers, I moved into researching goddesses with vultures, unearthing obscure references to Neolithic pagan beliefs. In the middle of skimming one of these entries, I looked up to see Serena at the door.

"Phoebe, there's a man in the gallery to see you, a Mr. Walker."

"I don't know a Mr. Walker. Is he interested in anything specific?"

"I don't think so. He just says he must speak with you. He looks a bit, let's say, shady. It's closing time but I wait until he leaves, yes?"

I turned to check the monitors but it seemed that my mysterious customer remained in the blind spot. He was either close to Rena's desk or on the opposite side by the storage room door.

I mustered a smile. "I'm sure it will be fine, Mama Serena. No need to babysit. Isn't Marco keeping his date with you tonight?"

"Yes. I meet him and girlfriend numero uno for an early supper and then see the dress rehearsal for his big play. This is all good. I will study what's between them, yes? See how long they'll stay together this time."

"Better not be late for that and you do look gorgeous."

"Because I'm wearing your gift, see?" She spun a little pirouette, flaunting the multihued, predominantly pink wrap I'd knit for her.

"Just tell this Mr. Walker I'll be down in a minute."

I checked the security monitor again but the man stayed out of view. Perhaps he understood exactly how these systems worked. Not a comforting thought. Still, the emergency switch was never far away.

Downstairs, moments later, I finally spied him turning one of the carved jade incense burners in his hands. First impression: medium height, muscular, fortyish, dressed in a navy pea jacket and jeans, with a bullet-bald head.

Serena hovered around the desk feigning random acts of tidying.

"It doesn't say Made in China, if that's what you're looking for," I said as I approached, keeping my tone light. "But since it's Ming dynasty, it could."

"Made in China for the collector types, then? I thought I saw one a lot like this in Camden market last week. Probably a knock-off. Fakes are getting increasingly clever."

"So are crooks. The real thing can be identified by certain features like the sculptor's initials inscribed on the bottom."

"Oh. Yes, I see that now. Still, I suppose even those can be fabricated, can't they?"

"They can, but that's the real deal. Are you looking for something in particular?"

The man carefully replaced the piece amid the violets and turned to face me. "I'm Agent Walker, Sam Walker, from the International Criminal Police Organization, commonly known as Interpol." He held up his badge—his photo plus the symbol of the globe over a gold sword and pair of scales.

"Interpol? Okay, I expected to hear from you today. Heard about my visitor, right?"

The man's face was arresting. A massive scar zipped across his shaven head from the right side of his forehead to his cheek, bisecting one eyebrow and hitching the eye into a perpetually half-shocked expression. Yet the sum total of the man wasn't unattractive as much as startling.

His mouth twisted into a wry right-side smile. "Old soccer injury," he remarked, pointing to the scar before holding out his hand. "You must be Ms. McCabe."

The East London accent enhanced the impression of a back-alley scrapper or retired rugby player rather than an international law agent. Soccer player, I reminded myself. I detected distinct musculature beneath the jacket. This was Interpol? He looked more like a bouncer from an East End club.

"Yes, that's me. All the Interpol agents I've met to date have worn dark suits, or at least the Canadian versions."

"What, as in Men in Black?"

"More like the Matrix."

He whistled between his teeth and smiled a twisted grin. "My boss wears a suit but I like your uniform idea better. Must put the request in at head office for full leather trench coats to enhance our sartorial reputation."

"That's the least you could do. You came to ask me about Noel Halloran, right?"

"I did, Ms. McCabe. I'm sure you are aware that both you and Max Baker have been persons of interest for some time regarding the disappearance of millions of pounds worth of stolen antiquities. We understand your relationship with the suspects so we weren't surprised when this one turned up, a former boyfriend, I understand?"

"You understand wrong. Halloran and I were never in a relationship. And you must also be aware that Max Baker and I are cooperating fully with the authorities and I did, after all, sound the alarm."

"That you did."

"I am hiding nothing."

"So I understand."

I plunged my hands into my pocket. "Good, because I witnessed the event under investigation but wasn't involved in it, as I've said to various authorities many times over. I believe that Max Baker met with the Canadian branch of your organization, too. We've been fully cooperative every step of the way. No one wants to bring those bastards to justice more than we do."

"I'm just wondering why Halloran paid you a visit today. What did he say to you?"

"A lot of personal nonsense like that he and my brother care about us and they're not the monsters I think they are, blah blah. Said he could explain everything but didn't have the time. Said my brother couldn't come to see me himself but they wanted to make sure I was all right."

"And what did you say?"

"I whacked him across the jaw and called him a bunch of names." For reasons I couldn't understand, I was loath to say anything about the enigmatic Goddess kilim. "I also ranted at him for putting me in this mess that results in having all kinds of criminal types dodging my heels. Then I rang the alarm."

"I understand the impetus for that, certainly, but we really could have used more information."

"So, you'd rather I hadn't called the police but tried to sit him down and grill him for incriminatory details he'd never reveal? Maybe offer him a coffee? He's not stupid, Agent Walker. He wouldn't tell me anything."

"And yet, had you kept him talking while alerting us covertly, we may have apprehended him."

"Sorry. That didn't occur to me. I admit I was rather worked up. I take it you didn't apprehend him, then?"

"A tall man in a fake mustache and a broad hat? No. I'm sure he dispatched that disguise quickly and travels under an assumed name and false passport. He'd have to or he'd never get as far as he has."

"But he's very tall, at least six feet four."

"That's not unusual."

"He also has a multiethnic genetic blend—part Australian Aboriginal, part European kaleidoscopic mix, which means he could adapt to nearly any nationality. Halloran is his paternal grandmother's maiden name, by the way. He refused to take Max's. Oh, I get your point." I shrugged. "I don't see what else I can tell you."

"Why didn't Halloran attempt to see his father, too?"

"My godfather's been drinking too much. Noel hinted that he didn't think reaching out to him was such a good idea under the circumstances, and I'd say he was right."

"And your brother?"

"What do you mean?"

"Halloran didn't say anything more about him?"

"Only that he couldn't come see me himself but he didn't specify why."

"But you haven't heard from your brother since the incident?"

"No."

He turned and began strolling around the gallery, studying each of our carpets and artifacts like a casual browser rather than an investigator on the prowl.

I caught Serena's eye and nodded for her to leave. She made a face, picked up her bag, and headed for the door.

"I want the three of them captured, too—no exceptions. Do you think I'm hiding one of them behind a carpet?" I followed after him.

"Not necessarily. If Halloran contacted you, maybe your brother will next."

"If he does, you'll be the first to know."

He peered down at the Kenyan beaded loin cloth we kept in a glass inset embedded in one of the tables. "I don't understand why Halloran would come for the sole reason of proclaiming his innocence to you. It seems more likely he had other intentions."

"I thought that, too, but he was only here for a few minutes and never left my sight except when I rang the alarm."

I heard a click-click-click on the glass at the front door and turned to see Serena waving on the other side. Dusk had already fallen behind her and she was making little throat-slitting motions. I'm fine. Go away. I mouthed. Reluctantly, she turned and left. When I turned back to Walker, he was watching me.

"You were present when they escaped with the treasure, I understand."

"Yes. They left us in the cave half-dead. Toby was in the background somewhere playing mastermind but I hadn't had contact with him or seen him in over a year. He had been missing just before the heist. I had no idea he was behind this at first."

"And even though he's your brother, you want to see him in jail?"

Oh, I got it: This was a loyalty test. "Absolutely. My brilliant missing brother infiltrated his lover's estate long enough to fabricate reproductions of a fortune's worth of jewels and artifacts and stage it so that Alistair Wyndridge wouldn't be the wiser. He plotted with Maggie and Noel to escape with the real treasure the night Max and I almost died—Tobias McCabe, my brother, thief, mastermind, and monster, has to pay for what he's done, too."

Walker whistled between his teeth. "And you're pissed."

"He left my poor sick dad never knowing whether his son lived or died, which may have contributed to his death. His disappearance certainly caused his stroke so, yeah, I'm pissed."

"And you feel the same way about Halloran?"

"Yes, minus the sibling love."

He smirked. "So, it's revenge you're after?"

"It's justice I'm after, Agent Walker. I want the three of them brought to their knees. I want them to go to jail, pay the price of deception, betrayal, and greed."

He held up his hands. "Okay, you're very convincing, Ms. McCabe. Just checking to see if you're still on the right team."

"I am, I assure you. Will you keep me informed about the investigation? Oh, and by the way, I've heard word that Halloran has fenced some of the gold to a Mexican museum."

"Did he tell you that or Sir Rupert Fox?"

I stared at him. "Are you following me, too?"

"Of course and Sir Rupert has always been on our radar."

"What is Interpol doing, anyway, besides waiting and watching and tailing innocent people? We've heard nothing from you guys in months. Max hired a private investigator who pegged Maggie's last known location somewhere in Paris, probably near a Chanel atelier. What have you done?"

"We're on the case, Ms. McCabe and, up until now, the trail has gone cold. Now the thieves are on the move and much more likely to leave a trail. Are you certain Halloran didn't say anything else or have time in the gallery alone?"

"Positive."

"And nothing else irregular has occurred to your knowledge?"

I thought of my magically refilling bank account. "No, nothing. But listen, I want to be there when you bring them in. This is personal for me. I need to be part of the operation in some way."

His mouth crooked into that diagonal grin, maybe just the tiniest bit patronizing. "Not possible, I'm afraid. Standard procedure. Best to stay out of that part of the operation, Ms. McCabe. It's dangerous on multiple fronts, the least of which is tracking a fortune of jewels and artifacts across Europe with a bunch of ruthless thugs on its heels. Besides, emotions as high as yours can throw a spanner in the works of any investigation. A cool head must prevail in these matters or somebody's going to end up dead."

"Are you trying to frighten me?"

"Hope so. You already know you're being followed, yet you're not anxious?"

His eyes were an unsettling bleached blue, like denim parched under the desert sun. "I'm uneasy, sure."

"Besides us, who are certainly no risk to you, do you have any idea who else might be keeping an eye on you?"

"Maybe every two-bit scumbag who thinks we can lead him to the missing treasure. I've seen four, maybe five, different people stalk me. How do I make them stop? I don't have the loot, have never had it."

"You've been showing a replica of a necklace around. That's a bit like waving a red flag, don't you think?"

Now the patronization was unmistakable. "That wasn't my idea. Max started making the rounds without me knowing, and when I found out how he'd been threatening every dealer along the way, I tried to intervene." I fingered stitch markers in my pockets. For some reason, I also found a pair of thread snippers.

"Let's just say that wasn't wise. You're already on the radar."

Breathing out slowly, I nodded. "It seemed the only way I could alleviate a bad situation."

"By making it worse? I'll take that necklace replica, if you don't mind. It will help our investigation."

I shrugged. "Sure. It's in my desk drawer. I'll get it for you."

Moments later, I poured the phony jewels into Walker's hand, amazed at how much it hurt to relinquish that little memento. Walker pocketed it without comment. "Thank you. Here's my cell number." He passed me a card. "Put it on speed-dial in case Halloran reappears. Don't sound the alarm, send me a message on the sly and we'll take it from there, if you can, but don't do anything that will jeopardize your safety. You don't know what these bastards are capable of."

"Yes, I do."

"We'll be in touch."

I followed him to the door, pocketing the card. "Wait, how can I help this investigation besides alerting Interpol?"

"Stay vigilant. Stay in close contact with me at all times. Don't go out after dark alone—that sort of thing. Common sense, really. If anything suspicious happens, contact me ASAP. Both you and your godfather are key to this investigation. Your presence is already drawing them out, making them careless."

"In the meantime, I'm supposed to stand around and look bait-like?"

He smiled. "That shouldn't be too hard. You seem good at attracting all the wrong kind of attention."

I secured the door behind him and watched as he strode out of sight. Don't take chances? Everything I did these days was one big roll of the dice. Exhausted, I shut off the gallery lights and retired upstairs for the night.

8

I sat knitting late into the evening, grappling with multiple loose ends, most of which threatened to hang me. Even my knitting seemed infected. So many false starts since I began my carpet-inspired intarsia piece, I seemed to be forever ripping out stitches. I couldn't turn my mind off long enough to set the pattern on the needles. I continually miscounted, knitting blue into a motif meant to be red.

Too tired to think, I headed for bed but, before turning in, I opened the door to the hall and padded down to Max's office in my bare feet. Every night I checked the security panel before bed. Max had expanded the system when I moved in so that motion sensors had been installed in key areas of my flat. By checking the panel, I could visually scan the monitors to ensure that the perimeter sensors were activated and that the alarms set to alert the police station in case of a breach. This more or less electronically tucked me in for the night. Living alone on top of thousands of pounds of ethnographic inventory had its perils, as if I didn't bring enough of my own into the mix.

Tonight the system lights all glowed green, happily activated against possible threats. The monitors revealed the gallery hanging dark and still. Even the sidewalk outside lay empty. I yawned.

On the way down the hall towards my flat, I paused by the stairs, staring down into the deep shadows pooling around my suspended office. A bit of street and display light limned the edges of the landing glass like a halo. Still, I'd forgo my usual solitary communion with the textiles that night. The darkness didn't seem quite so friendly.

I fell into bed wired, afraid I'd never still my mind. Noel. Max. Interpol. Sir Foxy. Damn, damn, damn. Just when I thought I'd never get to sleep, something woke me. I blinked into the darkness, befuddled. A red light pulsed from the other side of the room. Not my digital clock. That was green, so what was that blinking?

The motion detector! I jolted upright. That didn't make sense. Why wasn't the alarm ringing? Nobody could move around the premises without setting off a god-awful ruckus. It would arouse the neighborhood until manually switched off. So, whoever was moving around had to be familiar enough with the system to deactivate the alarm. Max, maybe Noel.

But why would Max enter the gallery in the middle of the night? I could think of two possibilities, neither of them likely: He decided to pilfer the inventory to pay bills or he was too drunk to make it home and decided to camp out in the office. Noel, on the other hand, was capable of anything, and if Foxy was right about his agenda, it made perfect sense. He knew how to enter the gallery after hours, but surely Max had changed the codes? But maybe he knew how to override them. Maybe he was stashing jewels on the premises that very minute.

Not this time. I plunged my feet onto the floor and stood up, keening my senses into the darkness. It was deathly silent. No sound, no footsteps, no creak of doors opening around my tiny flat. He had to be downstairs. I retrieved my iPhone from the bureau and crept out of my bedroom, crossing the sitting room to the hall door. I needed to see what he was up to before confronting him, maybe even catch him in the act. In any case, I needed to stick my nose outside the safety of my apartment and head for the office.

For once, I wished I had a gun. I'd shot him once by accident, but did I really think I could pull the trigger deliberately? No way and he knew it. A gun in my hand would be a useless deterrent against Noel Halloran. I entertained myself with nonsense thoughts while zipping down the hall, dashing past the stairs and risking a quick glance down to the depths below. Reaching the office, I lowered myself into Max's chair without eliciting so much as a squeak and stared at the monitors. Something moved in the storeroom. I held my breath as the camera followed a dark figure raking a flashlight across the shelves. What was he up to down there? Either hiding something or seeking something and damn him all to hell either way.

I picked up Walker's card, which I'd left on the desk earlier and tapped in the number. After an excruciating number of rings, he picked up, his voice muffled. "Yes?"

"Phoebe McCabe here. I have an intruder in my storeroom. No alarm went off. I think it's Noel."

"Where are you?"

"In the office upstairs."

"Stay put. I'm on my way." He hung up.

As if I'd just sit there while Noel Halloran messed with my gallery the way he did with my life. Pocketing my cell, I crept silently down the stairs. Once on the gallery floor, I could see the flashlight beam sweeping the storeroom shelves. I'd surprise him, make him talk, explain whatever he had intended to say earlier, and catch it all on security camera. I wouldn't allow my emotions to rule my head this time.

I reached the storeroom door ready to call out his name and froze. The light had flicked off. Stilling my breathing, I listened into the darkness and sensed it listening back. "Noel?" I ventured. No answer, just that full, tense silence. I knew then that it wasn't him. I turned, thinking I'd spring for the safety of my apartment, but something hit me from behind and knocked me to the floor.

9

I stood with my kimono thrown over my nightshirt answering questions as the police and Walker combed the premises.

"We could call an ambulance," Officer Howell said again.

"I don't need one. I was just winded," I repeated, rubbing my chin where it hit the floor. "He knocked me down and exited the building, I said."

"And you didn't get a good look at him?" the officer asked. Her tone remained courteous and professional with just the right touch of sternness.

"No."

"And yet you decided to confront him by yourself?"

"I thought I knew him."

"Accosting a burglar while a crime is in progress is not advised," she told me, "even if you think you recognize the perpetrator." Something about her manner made me think she was a rookie on one of her first assignments.

"The alarm wasn't tripped," I explained again. "And I called Agent Walker immediately."

"And you are certain nothing was taken?"

"As certain as I can be. My business partner, Max Baker, is on his way over and he knows the storeroom inventory better than I."

No sooner had I uttered those words when in dashed Max, sleep-tousled and still in his bedroom slippers, dark circles smudging his eyes. I could just see his old Bentley illegally parked outside. The stink of stale alcohol followed him around.

"Phoebe! Are you okay?" He hugged me against him before I could reply. "Officer, have you caught the suspect yet? What was taken?" he said over my head. "Phoebe?"

I pushed myself away. "I'm fine, Max, and we don't know if anything was taken. I can't tell—certainly nothing from the main floor. The intruder spent time in the storeroom. I thought it might be somebody we knew."

He looked at me, shocked. "Maggie? Noel?"

"But it wasn't."

"You sure it wasn't a faulty alarm like what went off yesterday?"

"That wasn't a faulty alarm, Max. That was me getting nervous because a suspicious-looking guy dropped by. A little trigger-happy, that's all. This is different."

Max turned to look towards the back of the gallery where two other officers and Agent Walker still inspected the space. He gave my shoulder a quick squeeze before dashing towards them.

"Mr. Baker," Officer Howell called. "I'd like to ask you a few questions first."

As she briskly took after him, I sagged against the center table. It had been a damn long night. Rest ended seconds later when Agent Walker strode up to me, his scarred face so tense, it was as if leather had been stretched across bone. "I told you to stay put, Ms. McCabe."

I tested my chin again with my index finger. Probably bruised. "I thought it was Noel back again and that I could get him to talk."

"I didn't suggest that you risk your safety."

"But I wasn't hurt, okay?

"No, it is not okay. Had you done as I requested, I could have spread a net around the gallery and caught the intruder on the premises."

I nodded. "Mea culpa and all that."

"I'll be back to continue this later. Excuse me a moment." With that, he turned towards the storeroom.

"Wait."

He paused.

"Whatever you do, please don't let Max know that Noel came here yesterday."

Walker cleared his throat. "Ms. McCabe, as a co-owner of this gallery, Mr. Baker is a key component in this investigation and—"

"I don't care. He's not well. Leave him alone."

Without a word, he turned and sauntered towards the storeroom, leaving me hanging around like a third shoe. I took that opportunity to dash upstairs to dress. Throwing on an art-knit sweater and jeans, I was back down in the gallery just as Howell finished tapping notes into her tablet. Her team was already exiting the gallery carrying bags of equipment.

"I believe we're done here for the moment, Ms. McCabe. I suggest you change the codes immediately. Officer Singh has received a list of staff from Mr. Baker and will be questioning them in due time, as well as reviewing a copy of your security footage. In the event that you discover something missing, by all means give us a call citing that incident number in the left-hand corner." She passed me a sheet of paper. "Illegal entries and thefts are still within our jurisdiction, Ms. McCabe. Please remember that." She left, her team traipsing after, one nodding his head as he passed.

Clearly she wasn't thrilled that Interpol infringed on her turf. Metro handled local crime and Interpol networked with all agencies for the international felonies. Art theft was almost always international, while break and entry would inevitably be local.

After locking the door behind Metro, I joined Max and Walker out back. Thankfully, Sunday morning meant the gallery would stay closed that day. "Well?"

Max looked up from counting boxes and shook his head. "Nothing missing." He pointed to the safe gaping open. "I even checked in there—not that I keep anything of value there since Maggie fleeced me."

Walker poked his shiny head up from under the table. "Who operates your security system?"

"Diamond and Dew, a major firm, as you know," Max said, rubbing his eyes. He almost sounded like his old self, though definitely a short-tempered version.

"I know they're legitimate and bond their staff, but they also encrypt codes through their phone system. Every time the alarm trips, a message is sent to their server pinning the exact time of the break-in as well as who the code was attributed to. Do you each use unique codes?"

I looked at Max.

"I gave you Maggie's old code," he told me.

"Great." Codes were the last thing I thought about when I arrived at the gallery months ago.

"Was it the same system you had operating while your son worked here?" Walker asked.

"What kind of a fool question is that?" Max barked. "Of course it was. What are you getting at?"

"I'm covering all the bases, Mr. Baker. Some crackerjack who knows what he's doing might be able to break the system, but let's assume for now that someone used one of your codes. That usually means somebody who knows it."

"Maybe it was Serena," Max said. "She's as honest as they come but maybe she let hers slip to that twit of a son."

"No way," I said. "But why would anyone enter the gallery and take nothing? It doesn't make sense."

"Maybe they were staking the place out, planning on making a return visit," said Max.

Walker shook his head. "That wouldn't be clever, would it? May as well post their intentions on Twitter. You'll need to change the system. I can recommend a company that uses state-of-the-art technology. Even if the audible alarm isn't tripped, a silent warning gets posted to the depot. I'd like to look around further, if you don't mind."

"We do mind," Max growled. "And who the hell are you to sniff around our place, anyway? This isn't your jurisdiction! Metro is handling this. Get a warrant."

"Max!" I shot him a warning. "We're cooperating with Interpol, remember?" And to Walker I added. "Of course you may look around. Where do you want to start?"

"Your security system. Metro took a copy of your footage but I'd like to take a look myself."

"It's upstairs. I'll show you."

"Thanks for not telling him about Noel's visit. You see what I mean by Max's mood," I said on the way upstairs to the office. "He's finding everything a bit of a struggle lately and I don't want him getting hurt."

"Right. Interviewing him has been like dancing with a combine harvester. Sure he's not hiding something?"

"He's not, at least not in the way you mean," I assured him. "He's getting pangs of paternal remorse, that's all. Don't worry. I'll make sure he cooperates."

As if I could.

I left Walker in the office and rejoined Max in the storeroom.

"Max, why are you blocking Interpol's investigation? So what if he checks the premises or reviews our security records? We have nothing to hide."

Max leaned over the table. "Look Phoebe, the fewer people we've got mucking around, the better."

"Why?"

"Just because."

"That's not an answer."

He straightened. "Supposing Noel or Toby do get in touch with one of us?"

I waited. "And?"

"And, do you really think we're going to turn in our own flesh and blood?"

"Damn right. Don't go turning to mush on me. They're criminals."

Max shrugged. "So was I a year ago, remember? Events changed me. Maybe they've changed, too."

"How does that matter? They stole from Alistair, stole from you."

"Look, Phoebe, Noel can take what he wants—he's my son. I owe him, and who says Toby's even involved in this? That's just conjecture on your part. Nobody's seen him—but Maggie needs her pretty little neck throttled. Her, I can turn in, no problem."

"Okay," I threw up my hands. "Let's continue this discussion upstairs. I need coffee. I'm obviously suffering from auditory hallucinations."

I managed to steer him upstairs and into my kitchen, nodding at Walker perched in the office in passing. As I plugged in the kettle and filled the coffee basket, it occurred to me that Walker probably witnessed our discussion in the storeroom from the security cam. Well, so what?

"Max," I said carefully, keeping my voice calm. "You've got to get a grip. If they think you're hiding something, or might aid Noel in any way, you'll be culpable, could even go to jail as an accessory to a crime. You're damn lucky Alistair didn't press charges as it was."

He rubbed his eyes. "I don't care."

"Well, I do, damn it!" I banged the coffee tin on the counter. I leaned there, my fists clenched so tightly my knuckles whitened. "Since when did you cross Noel off our most wanted list?"

"Noel's my son," he muttered, not meeting my eyes. "Hell knows I've been a rotten father to him. I owe him."

"He's an adult responsible for his own actions. Your parenting has nothing to do with it."

"So, we're family, that's what I'm saying. We don't go after family."

I slapped one hand against my forehead. "How could you forget what happened less than a year ago when your son got away with a fortune's worth of treasure and left us flopping around that cave like a couple of dying mackerel? And he can't 'take what he wants' if it isn't his."

"He's my boy," Max mumbled, choking up.

"Has he been to see you, is that it?"

"Hell, no, but I wish he would."

Turning back to the counter, I exhaled my relief while pouring water over the coffee press. "I'm going after the three of them and I don't care whose DNA is involved."

"Can't you forgive them?"

"No. Who else has a code to our security system?"

He didn't respond.

I placed the brew things onto the table, grabbed the sugar and milk, and sat down across from him, my eyes never leaving his face. "Max?"

He kept his gaze on the mug. "Me and you and Rena. That's it."

"Not Noel?"

Max's eyes met mine. "Noel and I shared a code. You don't think he broke in last night?"

"Of course not." I'd already told him that. Besides, tonight's intruder had been focused on finding something, shoving me to the ground the way you'd kick aside a rabid dog. Noel would never do that. "Noel would have said something or tried to seduce me or some nonsense."

"Yes, he would. He cares about you," Max said, staring down at his mug. "Anyway, if it's my code he used to get in last night, I'll just say it was me that came in and I was plastered or something."

"Max, think: The camera recorded last night's activities. They may not be able to identify the intruder from those tapes but they can tell height and body shape. Who knows the security system better than Noel? He's not going to get caught on camera. The police already have a copy of the security tape and Walker's reviewing it now. Did you hear me say it couldn't be Noel?"

"Well, then. That's a good thing," he said, brightening.

I shook my head. My godfather was so confused. How could I confess to him that his son had paid me a visit yesterday or about the magic refilling bank account? I'd never felt so damn alone in all my life.

I poured coffee into two mugs, slid one over to him, and attacked mine with a couple of scalding sips. "It's not a good thing," I said wearily. "Nothing's a good thing anymore."

"Don't help the cops, Phoebe," Max said. "Please."

"I know what side I'm on, Max. I thought you did, too."

A knock on the door down the hall interrupted us. "Come in," I called. When Walker entered moments later, I held my mug up. "Can I offer you a coffee, officer? Oh, wait. You're an agent, not an officer. Sorry. I forgot my law enforcement nomenclature."

"Sam is fine. 'Agent Walker' makes me sound a bit like one of those computer viruses making the rounds."

"Fits," Max said under his breath.

Walker ignored him. "Thanks for the offer but I'll catch one later. Just wanted to ask if you would call in to Diamond and

Dew to request the entry and exit stats. I could get it from Metro only after a bit of paperwork. This would be faster."

"Sure."

Max refused to look at him.

I pulled my phone from my pocket and pressed the speed dial for the security depot number and waited. In a moment I had given my password and was speaking with a dispatcher. When I finished, I laid the phone on the table and announced. "No alarms, silent or otherwise, went to Diamond and Dew last night, but they have a report of activation and deactivation times being faxed over now. The report will show which employee number touched the system last night, but apparently only we have the names associated with the employee number." I turned to Agent Walker. "Make sense?"

"It does. Do you have a list of the code assignations?"

Max nodded. "I gave them to Metro. Why should you get one?"

"I saw a copy on top of the desk. The fax from the depot should come in momentarily, too," I told him.

He nodded. "Thanks. I'll return to the office, then." In a second he was gone.

"What's with that face of his," Max remarked after he'd left.

"He said it was a soccer injury."

"Soccer? Looks like someone tried to split his melon open with a hatchet."

"Does it matter?"

Suddenly Max reached across the table and clutched my hand. "Don't do this, Phoebe. Let the cops do what they do. Don't help them."

I wrenched away my hand. "When I came to London, it was with the understanding that we would track down the trio together. You actually said that. Now, you're softening up but I'm not. I don't care how badly you think you treated Noel or his mother long ago. He needs to be held accountable for his actions."

He left his hand stretching towards me. "You told me he said he loved you."

"I said nothing of the sort. I told you it looked like he was on the verge of making such a declaration just seconds before leaving me in the cave. Wow, such passion: 'I wish it could be different, Phoebe, but I'm outta here and, by the way, that priceless object you've got slung around your neck is a fake,' or something like that. Do you seriously think I bought that?" I waved my hand in dismissal. "Max, you're letting your emotions get bogged down in self-recrimination. Stay the course with me."

"I can't. I want no part of this. Look, I've been dry for nearly 24 hours. I'm trying, okay? Give me a chance to make all this up to you. I know I'm letting you down, but is it too much to ask that I might salvage two relationships at the end of this?"

Tears stung my eyes. The man just wanted his family, wanted to be loved, wanted to do something for someone he loved. Who didn't? For a minute I thought I'd start sniveling and say anything he wanted to hear. But no. I plucked a paper napkin off the table and blew my nose. "Yes, it's too much to ask. If you think turning a blind eye on your wayward progeny is going to repair that relationship, you're wrong. Noel's got his own demons."

"Yeah, and I got mine."

"Max, glad that you're trying to get off the bottle. It can't be easy. Why are you trying to do it alone? You could book yourself into detox for a month to get back on your feet. Do it for me. I'll pay."

He looked like I'd slapped him. "You still think I need to be shrink-wrapped? I'm not going to one of those places where you sit around in a group and spill your guts."

"You spill your guts in pubs, why not do it while sober?"

"That's not fair. Maybe I'm looking for comfort in all the wrong places but that doesn't make me an alcoholic. And where are you getting all this money from?"

The shouting attracted an audience. I looked up to find Walker standing in the doorway. "Give us some privacy, okay?"

"My apologies. The fax came in and I knew you'd find it interesting."

He entered and passed me the page, which I spent a few seconds scanning. "Who is employee 33?" I asked Max.

"You, Maggie," Max replied.

"Okay, so it was me who activated the alarm at the regular time last night, but employee number 45 deactivated the system at 2:45. Employee 45 is?"

Max dug his fingers into his wild gray hair. I couldn't hear his mumbled response.

"Pardon?"

"Me and Noel."

"But neither you nor Noel were in here tonight, so now we have to figure out who used that code. Maybe you let it slip to someone?"

"I'd never do that." Yet, by the way he buried his head in his arms, I knew even he didn't believe that.

"What are the next steps, Walker?" I said, sounding more together than I felt. My externals may as well have been glued together with adhesive and fairy dust because inside I was coming undone.

"I'll continue reviewing the security backups. I see you keep them for two weeks before they get overwritten—bad move—but at least that's a place to start. And I think I'll take you up on the coffee offer, if you don't mind."

"She does mind," Max grumbled through his hands. "Why don't you just bugger off and leave us in peace?"

"Right," I countered brightly. "I'll make a new batch and bring it to you."

"Much appreciated." The agent got the message and quickly exited again.

Meanwhile, Max remained sagged into his forearms, as if all the air had escaped him. I sprang from my chair and threw my arms around his shoulders. "Max, I love you, no matter how cantankerous and snarly you get. You're all I've got left. I'm asking you, begging you, to book into a facility and let me do what you can't manage right now. Serena can help. She used to run a gallery, remember? You've been making bad decisions, doing things under the influence, not thinking straight. Hell, you tried to sell the gallery to that Jason Young creep and practically gave away your favorite carpets. It has to stop. There's no shame in needing help. You've been stonkered. Give yourself time to heal. Do it for me."

Soon he was crying and I joined in this time, slobbering all over his jacket. When he left 20 minutes later, he still hadn't promised me a thing but he seemed shaken enough to give it some thought.

By the time I returned to the office down the hall, fresh coffee in hand, I found Sam Walker still glued to the monitor. "Look at this," he said, not looking up.

I joined him on the edge of the desk. "What are you doing?"

"Replaying the security footage back to where the drive overwrote itself a couple of weeks ago. You should keep fresh drives on hand and store the old, at least until you review them all. I gather you haven't checked these in a while."

"I didn't think I had to," I said miserably. Since the alarm hadn't gone off, why would I? "What have you found?"

"Take a look."

I peered at the monitor as he rewound to a date marked two weeks earlier. A dark figure could be seen crossing the gallery to the storeroom. He spun the rewind further until that same figure was now inside the storeroom on the same night. I swallowed and straightened, unconsciously gripping my stomach. "Somebody's been in here before?"

"Same somebody, is my guess. At least once, maybe more, but I can't tell because the disk gets recorded over every two weeks. I'll review all the old reports from Diamond and Dew to see how many times this blighter's been entering the gallery."

While I slept upstairs, somebody had been prowling around downstairs. My gut felt like I'd swallowed an electric fan. "Yes, please."

"You request them and I'll get right on it. Otherwise, I'll need to go through New Scotland Yard to get clearance, which takes too much time."

I nodded.

"This guy look familiar to you?"

"No," I said in a small voice.

"Medium height—maybe five ten—dressed in a black track suit with a ski mask. Gloved. Yeah, he's probably not wearing his usual threads. Again, he doesn't take anything, just studies the place. A bit freakish, that, but since the cameras don't reach the far corners on either side of the door, you can't see everything he does. Otherwise, it's like he's casing the place. You should get on to changing those codes, ASAP, and get a locksmith over here to change anything with a keyed entry, too. Otherwise, I'd have said leave everything as is and we'll stake it out to catch the perp, but it's too late now."

"Right."

"How are you holding up?"

"Fine," I lied. Some stranger had been crawling all over my gallery while I slept. How good does it get?

And then Agent Walker's cell rang. He held it pressed to his ear, listening intently, before turning to me. "It's New Scotland Yard. A body matching our intruder's description has just been found in a dumpster behind Sheffield Terrace."

10

Imagining Noel dead on a slab hit me as brutally as a sucker punch. It didn't need to make sense to leave me reeling. I knew it wasn't him but it could have been.

Later, I endured Scotland Yard's excruciatingly polite questions as Walker sat in. At times, it almost seemed as though they considered me a suspect. Maybe they sensed I was hiding something, and who could blame them? So far, I'd failed to mention the Anatolian Vulture Goddess let alone my magic bank account. Then, in the midst of the interrogation, in came the identification of the dead man as Fred Haze, aka Jason Young. I stared dumbfounded when Walker told me the news.

"Do you know him?" he asked.

"A Jason Young tried to buy the gallery from Max a couple of days ago, and I tried to phone him since to tell him to bugger off but he never got back to me," I said. "I never met him."

"Looks like he was looking for something, since the same bloke's been sniffing around in the gallery more than once." Walker fixed his chill blue eyes on my face.

"I have no idea what he was looking for, I swear," I said, my voice quivering with exhaustion. It's like the last bit of news had ripped away all the scaffolding that had been propping me up for days. "Look, I'm exhausted. Can I just go home now? I have nothing left to say."

Walker gave me a lift home, and though he wanted to come in and probably grill me further, I practically shut the door in his face. After setting the security system, I trudged towards the stairs. My cell rang before I reached the landing.

"Hello, Phoebe. Rupert Fox here. Is this a secure line?"

I gripped the railing. "It's my cell number, Rupert. You know how secure those aren't."

"As I feared. May I drop by for a moment?"

I was so weary, I wanted to melt into the stairs. "Yes, but make it short."

"I'll be there directly."

A black car dropped him off moments later, as if he had been circling the gallery waiting to pounce. After locking the gallery door behind him, I led him upstairs to my flat. Yes, it felt like I was opening the cookie jar to a ravenous rat but I saw no other way to ensure privacy.

He studied my decor in open curiosity. "I do approve. Very colorful and eclectic. Ah, and you are a knitter, I see."

He picked a ball of yarn from a basket on the floor and studied the label. "Hand-dyed silk in a perfect shade of orchid. How exquisite. My late wife would have loved this. As for me, I find yellow to be the most heavenly hue with which to knit."

I couldn't process that just then. "Please sit." I indicated one of my two tapestry upholstered chairs. *And take your hand off my balls.*

He carefully returned the yarn to its nest. "It may surprise you to learn that I knit also," he said, lowering himself among the green vining motifs. "Mostly jumpers, though I have been known to do the occasional pair of argyle socks. In fact," he lifted his gray gabardine pant leg a few inches to reveal a flash of sock knit in fine-gauge gray, blue, and yellow. "Quite a feat, even if I do say so myself. These are remarkably comfy. I prefer Fair Isle in a multitude of colors so diverse I am tempted to use crewel floss."

"Did you really come here to discuss the textile arts?" The topic might be a favorite of mine, but I preferred the discourse some other time with some other person.

"I'm merely establishing a bond."

"I'm not in the mood."

I'm sure his ear tufts wiggled when he sighed. "Very well, onto business. I understand you had a visitor last night and the chap wound up murdered."

"And you must know the identity of that visitor so don't play games." I sat down across from him and picked up my mindless knitting project, an unborn wrap I kept on hand as both a pacifier and to while away the hours during television shows. Intarsia was out of the question at the moment. "So, did you kill Jason Young?"

"My dear, I am many things, but a murderer isn't one of them. What would be my motive? Oh, my, but watching you knit causes my fingers to itch so. I don't suppose you have a spare project I might work on for a few rows? Maybe a nice sock? I can follow any pattern, even work lace."

"I don't follow patterns and I don't do socks." I stabbed my needle into a seed stitch and glowered across at him. "How do I know you didn't kill him?"

"Why would I? I did have him followed, it's true, and knew the chap paid an unauthorized visit to your gallery in the wee hours more than once, but I am embarrassed to say that last night my hireling refused to wait outside the gallery until he emerged. Indomitable behavior, not in the least bit professional. Let us just say that I henceforth relieved him of his duties. As a result, I have only just heard—and by just, I mean 45 minutes ago—that this Jason ended up in the undignified position of being quite dead in a dumpster. Shot, I understand, which is vastly better than being strangled or garroted, though the end result is the same. May the final punctuation of my life's sentence never be so ignoble. Nevertheless, his demise is alarming. Matters are accelerating, my dear, as I feared they would. I do hope you are taking this very seriously and are reconsidering my offer."

I picked up a length of thick crimson cashmere. "Who killed him if not you?"

"Ah, there's the rub. My informant told me that our Mr. Young—what a tiresome name; surely he could have envisioned a more interesting alias—was himself being tailed by an undisclosed interest."

I paused, the red yarn looping around my hand as if my fingers were slashed and bleeding.

"I would choose a different hue for that row, maybe something in the magenta line? I fear a subtle clash."

"A subtle clash is an oxymoron. Why would this pseudo-Jason Young infiltrate my gallery repeatedly?"

"I would hasten to say he was either looking for something or planting something."

"But what?"

"I suspect you may have a clue to that, my dear. Why not tell me so I can assist you properly?"

I knit furiously for several stitches. "Isn't the missing Bermuda treasure what they're all after?"

"No, in fact, which is what I am attempting to say, albeit with perhaps too gentle a hand. I have reason to believe they may be seeking another cache and, if you don't yet possess the clues as to what it is and where it's been hidden, you had best hasten to educate yourself."

My project fell to my lap.

"I am convinced the clue lies in this building. Let us comb the premises together this very minute," he continued.

"Absolutely not."

He rose, smoothing his trousers down over his beefy legs. Eye to eye, he wasn't much taller than I. "Very well then, I see this meeting is at an end. Such a shame. Now, finish your row and I will show myself out."

I got to my feet and hastened after him. "You will not show yourself out. I'll escort you to the door."

"Very well," he sighed.

At the front door, he turned to face me. "Phoebe, I know you don't trust me and, naturally, I do understand why, but let me repeat that I mean you no harm, nor Maxwell, for that matter. I simply have little patience with drunkards in general, hence my abrasive and unforgiving nature around the man. My father was a drunkard and such behavior dredges up unfortunate memories."

"Max is going to get help."

"I do hope so." He glanced towards his shoes, old-fashioned brogues as black and shiny as a beetle's back. "If you do successfully convince him to enter a detox facility—detox is such an unfortunate word—may I recommend the Dayton Fields clinic. It has an excellent reputation on all counts and requires a full 28 days' residency commitment."

"Dayton Fields. I'll remember that."

"Good, good. Let me also offer a little advice: Avoid saying anything of note over the phone. Your lines are tapped and I'm guessing by three or four interests."

"Including you, I suppose?"

"Of course. May I recommend that all conversations of a sensitive nature be initiated using this." He passed me a phone. "Naturally, I took the liberty of keying in my own number should you ever wish to chat."

I turned the Android over in my hand. "You actually expect me to give you the sole opportunity to eavesdrop on my private conversations?"

He smiled. "I assure you the phone is encrypted and nearly impossible to trace, not to mention top drawer in all respects. You could use it as our secure line."

"If it's not secure from you, it's not secure. Besides, I have a smart phone of my own."

"They are never as smart as you think so it's best to be prepared. Good day to you." He nodded once and stepped out the door to stride across the sidewalk to a waiting black sedan.

***

Back in my flat later, I ripped out the crimson rows I had slashed across my wrap and wound a ball of magenta to add in at some point. I fell asleep on the couch with the knitting curled on my chest like a fibery cat, dreaming of death and destruction with all the men I loved/hated playing starring roles.

I awoke with a jolt hours later. Daylight had bled from the room, leaving the lounge stained in shadows. I quickly flicked on the lamp, breathing easier once the color seeped back to the carpets, the weavings, the yarn. Hell, was I going to be afraid of the dark now? The locks had been changed, the security codes renewed, with everybody and everything on high alert. Surely I was safe?

My personal cell phone was ringing. That must have been what woke me. I snatched it off the table after picking up Foxy's version by mistake. "Hello?"

"Phoebe, are you all right?"

"Max!" I hadn't been able to contact him all afternoon so his voice spread balm across my fraying nerves. "Look, could you phone me back on my flat's land line?"

"Yeah, sure."

The house phone rang seconds later. "You think you're being tapped?"

"Probably. So, did they grill you like a planked salmon, too? I saw you down the hall at Scotland Yard but couldn't catch your eye before they took you in."

"I got drilled by those wowsers, all right. Acted like I was some kind of suspect. How could I be when that two-bit sleaze was murdered while we were with the cops?"

"Was he?"

"Damn right."

"I guess so." I lowered myself back to sitting. "I was so busy saying over and over again that I wasn't hiding anything that I must have missed that part."

"The man they identified as Jason Young—though that was only one of his aliases, apparently—died at 3:35 a.m. while we had Metro police and Interpol mucking around our gallery. How rich is that?"

I took a deep breath and lowered myself back to sitting, letting my eyes fall on my Tide Weaver tapestry for moral support. "So, that means what? That someone knocked him off just after he left the gallery last night? But what was he looking for? Why was he even there?"

"Damned if I know, but if I hadn't been with the police at the time, I would have been a prime suspect. The dead guy broke into our gallery, the same dude who bought my prized carpets while I was in my cups, or so the story goes. That could be some kind of motive, I guess. I knew what the coppers were thinking—bloody stodgers. I wanted that snipe-faced Walker to ask me: 'Where were you between the hours of 3:30 a.m. and 4:45?' just so I could say 'with you, idiot.'"

I smiled. He sounded so normal, so Max-like, the same old irascible, pugnacious Max. He'd probably already had a few drinks pumping him up. "But what was he doing in the gallery if not stealing something?"

"That part's got me stumped."

"And someone's been following me, besides the usual Interpol watch, I mean."

"Yeah, honey, I know. I hired a bloke to keep an eye out for you—a good head, straight-up. Worked as a bouncer in a couple of big-name clubs. He's scampered off somewhere since but I couldn't afford to keep him on longer, anyway. Before he went AWOL, he told me a couple of guys were staking out us both."

"What?" The word escaped me like a croak. "You hired a bodyguard and a private eye without telling me? I've had so many people tailing me, I'm surprised they didn't form a line."

"I didn't want to spook you too soon. I thought I'd wait until I could find out who they were before saying anything. I still don't know and it's left me buggered. Now the gallery's been broken into and that guy murdered. Maybe Noel knows we're targets so he's hired his mate to protect us but then someone knocked him off?"

I closed my eyes. "You're not back on this Noel as good guy theme, are you?"

"Look, my boy could be protecting us. Maybe he's hired people to keep us safe and didn't just leave us swinging in the wind."

"What difference does it make? We're still on the gallows, aren't we? And we don't know who's following us. Agent Walker says it may be multiple interests."

"I want you to leave town for a couple of weeks, maybe go home to visit Nancy in Nova Scotia until things cool down."

"And what about you?"

"What about me?"

"Are you going into rehab or not?" Silence followed. "I'm not going anywhere unless you book into detox."

He gusted a sigh. "I'll go if you get out of town for a while."

We hung up agreeing to mutually consider our ultimatums. The last thing I wanted was to run away just as matters began heating up. Yet I desperately wanted Max in detox, too. Now what?

I logged onto my laptop to check my bank account again and stared at the bottom line. Another 10,000 pounds sterling had been deposited. I had the deep sense that Toby knew the gallery was in trouble and that I'd use the money to keep it afloat rather than declare it to the authorities. He knew me that well.

Why did love come with so much pain? I thought back to Dad in those last weeks of his life. He'd been so confused and kept insisting that his son had been to see him, something I knew to be impossible. Weeks after the heist and his long lost son suddenly appears after visiting hours to see his father? The hospital staff insisted no one had signed in and Dad's dementia had progressed to such an extent that whole swathes of memory had fallen off his map. No, my brother had a lot to answer for and the part that got me most went far beyond mere legalities.

But I needed that money and he knew it.

I shuffled into the kitchen to make myself a cup of chamomile tea, which I took downstairs. The gallery hung still with just the street light shifting through the plate glass up front.

Nobody would take this away from me. Ever. Clutching my mug, I strolled into the storeroom and switched on the light, shutting the door behind me in case someone peering too deeply into the gallery mistook us for open. This would be my first time alone there since the late Jason Young entered for no known reason and wound up dead.

So, I thought, gazing around the narrow space, what had been his real mission? He had entered this room multiple times while I slept upstairs. What was he looking for? To be surrounded by thousands of dollars of rare ethnographic objects and to walk out empty-handed didn't make sense. He had to be seeking something specific but what if not the stolen jewels? There was no place to hide something in these concrete walls except inside the boxes and crates that lined the shelves. Max had gone through everything.

We did have an inventory of sorts, one that Maggie had compiled over a year ago and that Max ignored the way he did everything his ex had touched. Though I'd plucked it from the files and handed it to him while the police were here, most of what I saw Max do earlier seemed run by memory. He claimed he knew every damn thing inside the storeroom so what was the big deal? I watched him open all the crates, check the boxes against the content lists taped on the front of each, and run a visual scan over, behind, and inside every object. Nothing was missing, he insisted.

I needed to check myself and use the inventory as a place to start. We had acquired only a few pieces since it had last been compiled, all of which I recognized intimately, so it would still be useful. Picking up the file, I began going over everything against the sales records for the last year. After an hour of tedium, I still was no further ahead. Everything had been accounted for, as far as I could see. I tossed the file on the table in disgust.

Staring unfocused at the shelves, I suddenly remembered the day Max first took me for a tour through the gallery. I had been so excited that I couldn't stop videoing the experience with my phone. Part enthusiastic record-keeping, part my quirky need to capture places and spaces of personal importance, I had acquired a visual record of the gallery as it was that first day nine months earlier, shelf by shelf. I'd even shot a selfie version of me mock-introducing one of the rugs.

I pulled my iPhone from my pocket and began scrolling through the photos and videos until I landed on the storeroom group. By holding the phone up, it was relatively easy to compare the before shots against the shelves. I recognized the same boxes with the same contents or slightly depleted, all duly recorded on the packing note and corresponding sales records. We'd sold two jade pieces and replaced the ones in the gallery with two more, leaving one remaining in storage. The crates containing the carved African masks hadn't moved because no one had yet bought the carvings still on the floor. We only had so much room and would often circulate our pieces in and out of storage.

The five rolled carpets still leaned against the wall, bundled in plastic and antihumectant paper, some brown, some still in their white shipping covers, waiting for the hanging beauties on the walls beyond to sell or to take a break. Only one major carpet had sold in the last nine months.

I paused. We had replaced the Kuba rug with the Cloud Head, meaning there should only be four carpets in waiting. Why did we have five?

Pulling the rolls away from the wall, I checked the stickers in the left-hand corner against the inventory records. Max always inspected each item when it arrived before rewrapping it, or at least he used to. Every carpet was accounted for except one.

My heart pounded as I hefted the roll up onto the table. I was about to slice the string and cut the wrapping when my gaze landed on the shipping label—not the usual computer print-out, not accompanied by the standard brokerage labels and custom stamps. The printing on the label affected me so violently, I dropped the knife.

I backed away like I'd been burned. I stood there, heart thundering, staring at the white, bubble-packed roll as if it contained a ticking bomb. It may as well have, since the moment I opened that thing, I knew the course of my life would explode in some crazy, uncontrollable way all over again.

After several moments, I approached, staring at the label warily. It was addressed to me. The writing matched my brother's art printing, the kind he used to label his artwork and iconic cartoons—almost runic, as if carved deep into ancient stone—unmistakably his.

The return address claimed it had been sent from an *Erdogan Sevgi Carpets and Kilims, Sultanahmet, Istanbul*. The customs label stated only CARPET and cited the worth at 2,000 pounds sterling, or about $3,700, not an unusual amount for a rug. Nothing about this package would attract attention unless someone recognize that printing, someone like me.

Call Walker, cried my more reasonable self, the part who had once studied law, tried to abide by the rules, attempted to remain steady and straight in a family of apparent criminals. This carpet or whatever it was didn't belong here, had been sent directly to me by a thief. But the thief was my brother and, for some reason, I called no one.

His printing delivered an unexpected blow filled with multiple levels of longing and pain that jettisoned me past anger into something else. He was my brother, my brother! What if I had misunderstood his actions and he really wasn't the monster I believed, as Noel insisted? What if he had been forced to steal the whole time, held by gunpoint while he forged a fortune's worth of jewels? What kind of sister was I not to at least hear him out? So, the other me, the one who couldn't abide rules, was susceptible to random acts of impulse, and reacted without reason, continued tampering with evidence.

I severed the strings and slit the white laminated paper, cut through the layer of bubble wrap down to a brown papered core. Inside, lay a roll measuring about three feet wide by six feet long, tied in regular intervals with more string. Once I cut those last cords, the brown paper curled away to reveal a very old textile—old by virtue of the back's discoloration, the thinning patches, which was all that I could see at first. Certainly it was a flat-weave, an old kilim in brown, rusty red, blue, and ivory wool.

An old kilim. Why would Toby send me this? Because he knew I'd love it? Because he was using it as a message, or both? I trembled on the precipice, shivering in the chill air of the lonely adult orphan craving something lost—a family, a home. Bringing the police into it would rip me from this one connection and transfer all the responsibility to an impersonal agency. How could I let that happen?

I blew on my fingers to warm them before spreading the carpet out on the table, tossing the brown wrapping to the floor, and staring fixedly at the old kilim.

I forgot to breathe. It was so old, how old I had no idea, but the faded wool motifs marching across the yellowed surface skipped over worn patches as if the carpet had honored many centuries, many floors and walls. Its vivid energy arrested the eye, seized the heart.

Vaguely female anthropomorphic shapes repeated across the rows, each wearing a skirt, arms held upward with something in the hands, and all bearing odd curled headdresses. Startling, dramatic and powerful, the figures called out from some ancient place. Every figure bore a symbol over the torsos—either more hooked motifs or wiggly flame things—or were those birds on branches? Vultures, maybe? Yes, vultures! Goddesses with vultures! Lining the edge of the yellowed ivory field and expertly balanced amid the figures, more strange shapes cavorted in a stylized, geometric frolic.

My heart flipped and danced. My blood beat deep within my veins. I felt powerful and centered and connected to that carpet and everything else. For one instant, I knew the universe on multiple levels and believed myself part of some great dynamic.

I kicked off my shoes and climbed on top of the table to sit before it cross-legged like a supplicant. How many thousands of people had sat on or before this rug? This textile was so beautiful, so rare, so old, and so powerful that I temporarily forgot who I was. Those symbols impacted me beyond words, touching me in my deepest recesses, and I realized that here was the goddess-with-vultures kilim Noel referred to, the one I was not to touch but about which he didn't have a chance to explain.

This carpet connected me to my brother and possibly to Jason Young and to who knew what else besides. And all of them connected to Istanbul.

Minutes later, as if shaking myself out of a spell, I climbed back down and began tidying up the mess. First, I sliced off the return address and stuck it in my pocket before gathering up the wrappings to burn in the upstairs fireplace. I'd need to erase the security footage that witnessed me finding the carpet and all evidence that it had ever arrived.

If someone had asked me what the hell I was doing, I wouldn't have been able to find the words to explain.

11

I had never been to Istanbul, never journeyed anywhere so far from my own culture map, but all necessary details fell together quickly. Serena agreed to manage the gallery after I waved the invitation to the International Rare Textile and Ethnographic Exposition under her nose, explaining how I must attend.

The reception, in particular, interested me, despite the hefty fee. Imagine the contacts I could establish?

"Yes, you must go," she agreed soberly. "Mermaid & Baker needs new clients and a good profile, yes? That cannot come by staying here."

Then Max booked himself into the Drayton Fields detox center because I assured him I was going home to Nova Scotia for a few weeks, a necessary lie. On that same day, I found a seat sale with a direct flight to Istanbul packaged with a room at a hotel in the old city, only a short walk away from both the exhibition site and the return address of the kilim. It was as if, as Nancy claimed, the Universe conspired to clear my path.

Only Agent Walker tried throwing up speed bumps.

"Am I under some kind of advisory not to leave the country, is that it?" I asked him over the phone. The last thing I wanted was those startling blue eyes and that hijacked eyebrow focused on me in person.

"As I stated before, you're not under suspicion but a person of interest, but why the sudden decision to leave town and to Istanbul, of all places? Is there something you're not telling us?"

"What, like someone just ended up dead around the corner and that I might be feeling the need to get out of Dodge?"

"I would think that experience would put you on high alert."

I cleared my throat. "Agent Walker-"

"Sam, please."

Serena was mimicking a Frankenstein-like man lumbering around in front of me. I turned my back on her.

"Agent Walker," I began again, "I am trying to run a business under volatile circumstances. And, yes, I am under high alert, believe me, which is why I'd like to get away for a few days. Somebody connected to my gallery in ways I don't understand has just been murdered. Am I supposed to be calm? I need a break. I'm hoping my sudden exit will throw my stalkers off my tail and give me a bit of vacation."

"Istanbul is a huge city. We can't protect you as easily as we can in London and it's challenging enough here. Your stalkers will note your sudden relocation and will be sure to track you down wherever you go."

"Are you trying to scare me again?"

"Is it working this time?"

"Hell, no. Do you really think I feel any safer in London after all that's happened? I'm going and that's that." I turned back to find Serena standing with her arms crossed, frowning.

"Fine," he said, his voice taut. "I'll alert my colleagues at our Istanbul office and set up an appointment. Which hotel are you staying at?"

"I haven't booked one yet. Look Walker, I'm assuming you'll still be keeping an eye on the gallery while I'm gone? I've told my assistant not to be alarmed should you show up suddenly and start poking around. We've also discontinued our evening hours for the time being and are hiring a student to assist Serena so she's not here alone. You already know that you can't interview Max while he's in rehab so don't even try."

"His booking himself in there in the midst of what has become a murder investigation is very inconvenient. We-"

"Oops—customer just arrived. Got to go. I'll be in touch. Bye." I pressed END and placed the phone in its stand.

Serena stood studying me, today a vision in purple, wafting the scent of crushed violets. "He is not happy that you are leaving?"

"No, but the show must go on and all that." I waved the expo invitation in the air again like a battle standard. "Have you ever been to one of these?"

"Not that one. My husband and I went to the Brussels event once long ago—very grand! Lots of champagne!—but never to Istanbul. It is very exotic, yes? I understand the show is very fabulous. All those beautiful carpets. You will make good connections and have a very good break. And be very careful?"

"I will be careful, of course," I said, hoping I appeared confident and upbeat instead of driven and percolating with tension. "Traveling in a strange city requires nothing but common sense—never go out alone after dark and that kind of thing."

"Yes, so true. And no worrying over things back here. Jennifer and I will take care of the gallery."

I'd agreed to hire Marco's current girlfriend to help Serena in my absence. "You must be careful, too. Are you nervous?"

"About dead bodies and big scar-faced men? Never. About spending all day with Jennifer who moons over Marco, oh so lovesick, maybe." Rena fluttered her hands like flapping lips, or maybe she was miming a flight of lovebird wings.

I knew she wanted to know where the money was coming from, since the gallery had apparently gone from broke to moving at full speed in record time. Her salary had been paid and I'd hired Marco's Gwyneth Paltrow lookalike girlfriend to keep her company. Another new security system was being installed that afternoon and obviously I was paying for Max's expensive detox facility.

She had to know something was up but would say nothing to no one. If she noticed that the wrapping over the fifth carpet in the storeroom had changed, she didn't comment on that, either. I had removed one of my upstairs wall-mounted rugs and rolled it into brown paper to add to the inventory. If anybody had chanced to count five carpets in storage, I made certain five remained. Oh, and the flash drive containing the recent security footage had been mysteriously replaced by a brand new version, several, in fact. It seemed I was taking Walker's advice and keeping multiple backups on hand.

That afternoon, I dropped in to see an old colleague of Max's, this one still on friendly terms. Ivan ran a small newsagent shop on Kensington High Street that sold cell cards along with extra services, available to only those who knew how to ask. I waited until the tiny space emptied of customers before introducing myself.

"Phoebe! Yes, Max told me you come to London. Where is he? Still good?" A little guy with a wily junkyard look, I knew he'd immigrated from Bosnia as a political refugee years ago.

"Well, thanks. He's just feeling a bit under the weather today. Hey, look, Ivan, can you help me with this phone?" I passed him my Foxy cell. "Someone gave it to me as a gift and I want to make sure I can use it to do business without eavesdroppers."

He studied it for a moment, flipping it over in his hands as if he'd never seen one before. "One moment. I come right back." He winked and disappeared into a back room, emerging minutes later. "Someone put on tracking device. See, under cover?" He pointed to a tiny metal disk inserted under the phone's gel cover. I removed it, so no one know where you go."

"Thank you." I pocketed the Foxy phone and pulled out my own iPhone 6 Plus. "This one I use all the time. How do I keep it from sending location signals on me?"

"You must keep the locator lock off and not use GPS but still possible to track through the number always. You want to stay private, best to use this." He pulled a phone from under the counter. "Not pretty. Number untraceable. Use SIM card I sell and no one finds you. Throw away after wards."

"A burner phone? Perfect!" I left the shop as the proud owner of three cell phones to which I assigned each a different purpose. The Foxy phone I would keep as my information channel, since I was convinced that Rupert could be as useful to me as I to him; my own smart phone would be my map and location device should I ever need to be found; and my new burner phone was appointed my secure line for phoning home or whatever. I felt ridiculously pleased with myself.

As I marched towards my bank, I passed the tattoo shop I'd crossed a hundred times or more since moving to London. The proprietor always caught my eye since her entire body had been inked in a complex vining design of thorns and leaves. Sometimes she'd stand outside smoking and either wave or roll her eyes at me, depending on her mood.

The black-on-black-stud-and-leather goth vibe never really stroked my friendly gene but today she actually smiled. Despite the onyx lipstick, that smile dazzled me. I actually smiled back, then paused, and finally retraced my steps until I was standing in front of her, trying not to stare at the noose of thorns strangling her neck.

"Hi. I'm not really into tattoos but I have one." Stupid opener but I was short on verbal brilliance.

"And you're telling me this because?"

"Because I want another. I want you to tattoo me."

She grinned. "You're having me on, right? You're gonna tell me you want a skull swallowing a dagger or maybe one of my ultra-popular poison apple tats?"

"Both sound stunning in a toxic way, but no thanks. I'll show you what I want." I was such an impulse shopper.

Inside her tiny shop papered by sample designs, I perched at a table strung with drill pens and ink pots and showed her my phone's photo of my Goddess with Vulture kilim. "I want one of those motifs. Is that possible?"

"I can draw anything. What is it?"

"A goddess with vultures."

She studied the image intensely before her eyes met mine. "A goddess with vultures? You're bloody kidding! How cool is that? But if you want a proper goddess, I could draw her in black spandex with an eye-popping set of boobs with maybe bulging biceps and toned abs."

"And maybe a broadsword? No, thanks. My goddess is more spirit leader than ball-breaker. I want the image just as it appears in the photo—about two inches high and as wide." I pointed to a laminated paper of intricate thorns criss-crossing a Frida Kahlo portrait. "If you can do that, you can do delicate and intricate. I want your best work in full color."

"You'll get it. Where do you want her?"

"Someplace where the sun don't shine. I have a mermaid tat just above my left butt cheek so maybe on the other side?"

"What's the point of art if no one sees it, not even you? Are you ashamed of your goddess?"

That made me think. "Of course not. I just don't feel the need to advertise my icons. Put her someplace I can see but not the general public."

And that's how I ended up with a goddess motif just below my breasts. Yes, it was awkward as hell lying in the backroom with that ink drill buzzing into my delicate flesh and, just so you know, it hurt, but the results were spectacular. It almost made me wish I wore bikinis or had a lover who I could show her off to, but just knowing I bore a goddess with vultures on my person was enough.

My last task of the day was to extract 1000 euros in cash, which I stuffed in my shoulder wallet under my clothes.

By early the next morning, while the world still slept, I took a cab to Heathrow and boarded a plane to Istanbul, the folded Anatolian Goddess with Vultures kilim occupying every inch of my carry-on bag. That, my phones, and my knitting featured as my only critical in-flight necessities.

During the four-hour flight, I actually managed to lay the foundation of my intarsia design, a feat of logistics which involved taping my sketch to the upright tray and keeping my yarn tucked in tiny butterfly balls dangling from my needles. I refused flight hospitality to keep my workspace clear, but the moment I needed to change yarn colors, I put the project aside and returned to researching everything I could about Istanbul and Turkish culture over the in-flight Wi-Fi.

12

Istanbul engulfed me in a blur of vignettes. The cab drove past ancient walls, Roman aqueducts, aborted marble columns, all standing juxtaposed alongside modern glass and steel structures with swathes of the Miramar running a cool blue along the highway.

Three civilizations had risen and fallen here—Byzantine, Roman, Ottoman—and I glimpsed relics of all three standing side by side in a single glance. While the car inched through the traffic towards the hotel, I strained to see the minarets soaring cloudward, the market stalls and vendors, the textiles that blazed in shop windows and spilled into the sidewalks of nearly every street. Ancient, modern, traditional, and edgy-new, the city jostled a thousand contractions, defying visitors to pigeonhole it in a single one. Fifteen million people lived in this crossroad between Europe and Asia Minor, and I swear they were all cramming the streets that afternoon.

I booked into my hotel, relieved to find the Crown Plaza Old Town offering exactly the kind of anonymity I sought. The marble foyer with its glass and mirrored hall and grand, soaring ceiling sketched an impressionistic Ottoman ambiance with velvet chairs, silk drapes, and uniformed men rushing about doing somebody's bidding.

My room was on the third floor accessible by either a glass bullet-shaped elevator or stairs. Both led to an open balcony-style hall overlooking a marble subfoyer with more red cushioned chairs beside a dress shop. After depositing my passport and most of the cash along with my kilim in the room safe, I popped a piece of complimentary Turkish delight into my mouth and hit the streets.

The impact nearly knocked me over. If I thought London a bustle, I underestimated the effect of stirring in a few million more humans and cramming vehicles into ancient streets against a panorama of contrasting cultures and competing wares. I could have been dropped into a human sea where all I could do was move with the stream or be bowled over. Should I go uphill or down, cross the broad road with the tramway running down the center, or jump into a shop to regroup? I chose downward, following the route I'd memorized on my map, the one that would take me directly to my kilim's return address.

Men in jeans and leather jackets, women in head scarves wearing long trench coats over gowns, strode beside clusters of tourists and many young Turks of both sexes in the latest fashion. Passing faces looked Slavic, Asian, Caucasian, Indian, Mongolian, and any combination in between. Though humanity swarmed around me, I soon relaxed into the company of the multitude, thrilled by the energy rather than overwhelmed by its diversity. I was in Istanbul, Istanbul!

Soon the broad-faced office buildings and modern shops shrank away to be replaced by rows of tiny coffee houses, pomegranate juice vendors, trinket shops, and jewelry boutiques, with every imaginable item to lure the eye. Every fifth shop appeared to be a carpet or scarf merchant, all of which caused me to pause as I scanned the color-saturated windows. I soon learned that pausing before a store in Istanbul was never without consequence.

"Lady, I have a beautiful carpet to show you. Come see, please."

I shook my head and moved on.

"Lady, lady! Come see my carpets! Best in town. Very good price."

I recognized the mass-produced, possibly Chinese or Indian knock-offs in many windows and soon learned to feign indifference. The constant calls didn't annoy me so much as slow me down and never once did I feel threatened. I knew Turkey as an open, relatively free-thinking Muslim country vying for entrance to the European Economic Union but I had yet to see one female shopkeeper. Unsure of how to interpret the absence of my sisters in merchandising, I kept my head fixed straight ahead and forged on.

Once I paused against a wall long enough to check my map and when I looked up, a man had arrived at my elbow to offer directions. The friendliness and eagerness to help seemed genuine.

"The address is at the Arasta Bazaar," he told me. "You follow the tram line until you see the Blue Mosque, and the street is just behind there."

The Blue Mosque—a monument named after a color—how exotic did that sound? I'd read its history and longed to visit, but I was here on business not pleasure. And when I followed the human stream along the narrow sidewalk until the street fell away to my right in a wide expanse of flowers, fountains, and gilded minarets, it was all I could do not to gasp. But I had no time to explore. All I wanted was to find the return address and come that much closer to Toby. Would Noel and Maggie be here, too? This city made a perfect hiding place, an invitation to any person of any stripe to blend with the multitude. I had to be getting closer.

I couldn't help but stare at the Blue Mosque and wonder at the magnificent structure, both delicate and imposing all at once. Here in the plaza, pedestrians strolled, enjoying the autumn sunshine in the open spaces so different from the congestion beyond. Slowing my pace, I ambled along, stopping only long enough to purchase a stick of roasted corn from a sidewalk vendor. The scent had been tantalizing me. Nibbling on my spicy corn, it suddenly occurred to me that I didn't stand a chance of detecting stalkers here. In London, I just knew. Here, plunged into a foreign world, I wasn't certain my twitchy sixth sense would still function.

I purchased a bottle of water and carried on, enjoying the sunshine and stunning skyscape of gilded minarets and blue domes. Uniformed men mounted on upright motorized scooters zipped around the plaza and I recognized them as tourist police guarding visitors against pickpockets. One of them cheerfully pointed me in the direction of the bazaar.

Down a set of concrete stairs, past a busy outdoor cafe, through a throng of tourists threaded by young men delivering trays of tea, I arrived at last at the Arasta Bazaar. An outdoor pedestrian arcade lined with modern shops tucked into old gray stone walls, it displayed all that had made Turkey a trade crossroads for centuries.

My steps faltered. I was seeking Erdogan Sevgi Carpets, which I had yet to find, but to walk past the Isnik tile shops, the store selling silken robes and vests, the jewelry shop glittering with lapis and high-karat gold, the shop specializing in embroidered pillows, and, of course, all the other carpet stores, was nearly impossible.

Everything I loved and honored resided here, and the merchants knew how to display their offerings, how to jumble patterns and colors together so that each excited the other in a harmonious symphony. My eyes couldn't bear to pass them by without proper acknowledgment.

"Miss, I have more inside."

I looked up from where I stood transfixed before a window displaying a magnificent Ottoman-style carpet, not old but expertly crafted in brilliant hues and intricate patterns, probably at least 25 knots per inch. A young man wearing the Turkish street uniform of jeans and leather stood in the doorway smiling.

"Um, I'm only looking, thank you, but this is a gorgeous piece."

Before I knew, I was sitting in the shop, sipping the small glass cup of tea Erkan offered, appreciating the show as he rolled out carpet after carpet until the floor at my feet was an overlay of wool and weaves. Most were new, the products of either small households or the many carpet cooperatives that operated across Turkey. Though handmade, they were still commercial productions and not what interested me as a collector or dealer, though beautiful nonetheless. A few emerged that were clearly older, less regular, with discolorations in the hand-dyed wool. They were pleasing but not spectacular. I insisted to Erkan that I was only looking, which he ignored and proceeded to show me even more.

Without acknowledging my business interest in textiles, without even letting on that I knew anything about carpets whatsoever, I let him explain the difference between flat-weave kilims and the soumak, where colored yarns are wrapped around the warps. I did this mostly to confirm my own understanding and to check my knowledge of techniques against the seller's. The minutes ticked away until I shook myself out of my stupor. I couldn't keep doing this. I came here for a reason. "As much as I love these carpets, I don't plan on buying anything quite so new." I made the mistake of adding: "I'm really more interested in antique carpets."

"Never a waste of time, Miss. I am honored that you enter my store and accept my hospitality, but my friend across the street specializes in antique carpets. I take you to him but finish your tea first. No rush."

By the time I'd drained the last of my apple tea, Mr. Kalecik had appeared from across the street, eager to escort me across the arcade to his shop. Did I miss a hand signal or maybe a discreet phone call while I was mooning over pattern and color?

I'd figured out how it worked: Erkan would receive a commission from Mr. Kalecik should I buy anything, commissions being the grease in the wheels of Turkish commerce. A customer's refusals would be politely and pleasantly left unacknowledged as these expert salesman maneuvered buyers into a state of relaxation and stimulation piqued by more gorgeous textiles and genuine hospitality. My slack-jaw expressions of wonder made me an easy mark.

"Thank you," I said, replacing my glass on the silver tray. "As much as I would enjoy visiting your shop, I must leave it for another day. I have business with Erdogan Sevgi's. Could you point me in the right direction?"

If Erkan was disappointed because I named another dealer, it didn't show. He smiled broadly. "I take you there. It is just down the street."

"That is not necessary," beamed Mr. Kalecik, an older man in a suit and tie. "I can show her on my way back to my store."

"That's all right, really. Thank you both," I assured them. "I'll find it." Darting from the shop, I headed further down the arcade.

Erkan jaunted at my heels anyway and, since he had to be twenty years younger than Mr. Kalecik, could easily win the race. I hung a left-hand turn into a silk shop as a diversionary tactic but, even so, I caught Erkan nodding knowingly at the shopkeeper at the door. The deal had been struck.

I wove deeper inside, tucking myself behind racks hung with gorgeous wearables. Lost for a moment in a forest of silken sleeves and Ottoman-style embroidered tunics, I suddenly stopped caring who got what. Let percentages rule. I had more important things to do like explore all that luminous fabric. Something as pearly as the inside of an oyster shell caught my eye. Ensorcelled, I lifted out an embroidered tunic with vining green and blue embroidered tulips curling across the glossy space. It looked as though it would fit perfectly.

"That is pure silk, miss. Very fine. Made in Bursa in honor of similar robes once worn by Ottoman sultans. May I offer you coffee or tea?" the shop owner asked.

I smiled, resigned to my fate. "Yes, thank you. Apple would be lovely."

He signaled to a tea boy and helped me out of my jacket and into the tunic, which slipped over my tee shirt and hugged my body in a fall of pattern and luster. Embroidered by hand, not machine, in colors so perfect for my skin and hair that I suddenly appeared younger, smarter, and more interesting than I had ever been before. Wouldn't it look splendid over leggings, worn to the exhibition gala, to all the cocktail parties I never went to? I had to have it, only it was more money than I had ever paid for a single item of clothing.

I shifted gears, shoved back my flaccid air of defenseless appreciation, and joined Mr. Caesar for tea. After chatting on about how much I loved Istanbul, I eventually informed him what I'd be willing to pay for my tunic plus another one in pink for my friend back home. After all, I pointed out, I sold fine textiles in London and displayed a genuine Ottoman robe in my shop. I passed him my card, which he scrutinized before proceeding to bring out a few genuine Ottoman textiles from his back room. A gold-embroidered black wool felt lady's jacket, circa 1900, caught my interest and we negotiated until I purchased two tunics and the jacket at a fair price.

Pleased with myself, I headed down the street. This time I made it as far as the carpet bag shop.

"You have very good taste, lady," said the man at the door, indicating my carpet bag. "But that one is very worn and I can show you many others in much better condition."

I smiled and patted my bag. "This one is an old friend. It even saved my life once."

"That is a special friend, then. Maybe you would like to find it a companion?"

These guys were good. Somehow I ended up inside once again, drinking yet more tea and chatting over antique carpets and the businesses that made bags and boots out of damaged textiles. The Turks certainly were a sociable people, I decided, and, after purchasing a pair of carpet slippers, I finally escaped.

What was I doing? I couldn't afford this. I was spending dirty money. Even for what I considered a justifiable cause, I couldn't go overboard. Finally, I walked with determined purpose down the rest of the street, looking neither left nor right, my stomach sloshing tea as I went.

A man emerged from a shop near the end of the street and stepped directly in front of me so suddenly that I jumped back. Startled, I looked at his face, took in the hazel eyes studying me calmly, yet intensely, and took another step away. "Sorry. I guess I wasn't looking where I was going." Yet I swear, he bumped into me, not me into him. He bowed slightly without uttering a word. I hastily excused myself and hurried on. Fatigue must be affecting me more than I knew.

At last, I spied Erdogan Sevgi's Carpets, the most unassuming shop on the street and almost the last one before the stairs. A tiny window was piled with rugs and tribal textiles, with the best spot for sunset viewing claimed by a fat gray tabby. I knew at once this merchant was of a different breed. A small mustached man with long graying hair and kind eyes met me at the door.

"Do you like my cat? His name is Harput and he thinks himself the most honored of guests." He took a quick puff from the cigarette he held before quickly extinguishing it in a bowl by the door.

I grinned. "I can see that. All he has to do all day is lie around on gorgeous rugs. How lucky can you get, Harput?" I asked the cat who barely opened an eye in greeting. "Are you Erdogan Sevgi?"

"I am. Will you enter my shop? Excuse my smoking. Bad habit. My wife and daughter say to quit." He shrugged. "I try at home, but here I am weak. Come in. May I offer coffee or tea?"

"Oh, yes, thank you. Tea, please. Apple." I was grateful that the cups were small enough that I might find room for maybe one more before bursting.

A young man nodded at me and then dashed off to fill the order at the cafe across the street while I sat down on a bench of a narrow room where rolled rugs, stacks of cushion covers, and layers of other small textiles padded every available inch. A visitor could sit on the bench by the door or maybe perch on a tower of cushion covers or even on one of the narrow steps heading upward but, otherwise, the shop couldn't entertain many at once, which added to its cozy charm. Thus I sat padded in color.

A call to prayer blared into the air with a force no Muslim could miss. Slightly buzzy and metallic-sounding, it had to be a recording emitting from the nearest mosque. In seconds, a string of them erupted all over the city, haunting, almost mesmerizing. It was 5:00 o'clock.

Mr. Sevgi did not unfold one of the multiple prayer rugs lining his shop and perform his devotions. Instead, he smiled and watched as my gaze landed on salt bags, ornamental horse trappings, and several long antique kilims hanging in the narrow spaces above the forest of rolled carpets. A few Turkmen pieces added to the mix, but mostly I recognized Anatolian. My pulse quickened.

"You like the older textiles?" he asked.

"I do," I said. "I collect tribal kilims and soumaks, but nothing commercially made."

"Good! I am so glad to hear this. Many visitors come to Turkey and go to the big carpet farms. I say, yes, those carpets are hand-made but they are not from the heart, do you know what I say? These rugs come to me from the villages where the women work their own designs, not the same for the carpet farms. The carpet farms tell them what to make but, in the villages, the women do their own. It is getting harder and harder to find these."

"It's happening everywhere in almost every artisan art. On one hand, I understand why the women want the financial guarantees from the cooperatives but, on the other, experimentation and creativity are being quashed."

"Yes, yes!" said Mr. Sevgi excitedly. "I could not say it so well in English. You understand."

I fished out my card and passed it over. "Already I see many pieces here I may be interested in purchasing, but could you tell me first if you've seen this kilim?" I showed him my phone photo of my Anatolian vulture goddess. "It was sent to me in London from your shop's address. I'm hoping you can tell me about the man who sent it."

He took my phone and stared down at the photo, his expression not registering surprise. "But this is very old, fine piece and very valuable. I have never had such a kilim in my shop. It is very special, like a museum would want. I would never forget it if I had seen it."

I stared at him in disbelief. "But the kilim arrived in London with your return address on it. Swipe over to the next photo and you'll see the label."

He flicked his finger over the screen and shook his head. "This is not mine, not my writing or my label. Who would send you this with my address? I do not understand."

"I don't either. The sender didn't identify himself, only gave your address. I need to find out why it was sent to me and your shop has to be a clue. Do you know anything about the kilim?"

"It is from East-Central Anatolia, that I can tell. It is much like the one my friend found on one of her travels around Cappadocia. She is very interested in these kinds of kilims and is a scholar but collects, also," Erdogan said. "She has written many books. Here, I show you."

While he rummaged in a stack of books sandwiched among multicolored cushion covers, I sat down to sip the tea cooling on the ottoman. The hot brew warmed my icy fingers, but nothing quite reached the chill of my disappointment. Did I really think it would be that easy, that I could just walk into the shop, show the photo, and be handed a clue to Toby's whereabouts? That he had sent it to me as a message, I knew absolutely. I just didn't know how to read it. Again, I kicked myself for not listening to Noel.

Mr. Sevgi, who had insisted I call him Erdogan, returned with a book opened to the colored photo of another striking kilim. This one, labeled *Kilim Fragment East-Central Anatolia, 18th Century*, featured a white background with two six-sided medallions populated by bird-like figures and hooked squiggles similar to my goddesses only more stylized and compressed. It appeared to be one end of a much longer piece.

"The Goddess with Vultures," I acknowledged.

"The Anatolian Goddess with Vultures. Very old, see," Erdogan said. "My friend found it in a mosque and a museum purchased it. I would be lucky to find such a piece. The collectors go all over looking, but I must wait here for carpets to come to me. Not so many fine ones come anymore."

"Do you see that goddess often?"

"Not this. The hooked symbol—what do you call it?"

"Motif."

"Motif, yes. The hooked motif has been a traditional image in Anatolian kilims but not like this goddess. Look." He pointed to several kilims and runners which contained simplified versions of the design, goddesses who had lost their skirts and headdresses, their energy compressed into punchy geometric shapes.

"Erdogan, I need to find everything I can about this kilim and that motif. I'm a little desperate. Who can I ask, what can I do?"

"My friend, she is from London, too, but is here for the big carpet expo. I saw her only this morning. I will give her your email and maybe she will know more. She is writing another book."

"Thank you," I said. "I'm just so curious."

"Of course, yes, and very lucky to have such a beautiful piece given to you."

Luck wasn't the word. I felt more like Toby and the kilim had forced me into yet another adventure not of my choosing. I gave Erdogan my email address and watched as he typed in a quick message to a Dr. Eva Friedrich.

That done, I proceeded to select the best of Erdogan's pieces-two soumak salt bags used to carry salt to grazing animals on the steppes, both richly colored and festooned with tassels; one saddle cloth of deep Turkish madder-reds brewed with indigo trims; and four tribal kilims obviously from a villager intent to make something beautiful for her home rather than sell at the markets.

I imagined all of them hanging in glory around the gallery rather than languishing in my shop's current economic reality. Maybe these would help change our fortunes. Maybe I could promote them somehow and find a way to catch collectors' attentions? Because, I reminded myself, I had to save Mermaid &

Baker, not just find my brother and the source of his mysterious gift.

Right then, the scope of my multiple quests seemed monumental. Just before our deal ended, Erdogan handed me a ceramic disk with a bright blue eye mid-center. "For you, a gift, to protect you from evil."

I'd seen talismans like these all over Istanbul and understood them to be a ward against the evil eye but hadn't otherwise given them much thought. I smiled down at the piece and thanked Erdogan. "Do you think I need protection?"

"We all do, yes? In my country, we carry one of these to help keep the evil spirits away, a very old tradition."

And I needed all the protection I could get. I placed the disk on top of my purchases for Erdogan to ship back to London. Though he took the textiles, he passed the paper-weight sized ceramic back to me. "You keep with you." Nodding, I tucked it into my bag. Its weight couldn't add more burden to the baggage I already carried.

But I had no time to ponder further since I badly needed to use the bathroom. Erdogan's assistant escorted me from the shop to the public washroom tucked against a wall two doors down. Dusk was already falling and I had a long walk back to the hotel. Anxiety pinged my spine. Relieved to find a Western-model stall rather than the famed hole in the ground, I exited moments later, planning to say goodbye to Erdogan, arrange for the shipment of my purchases, and then bolt back to the hotel.

As I was stepping into the shop, I chanced to look over my shoulder and down the street, now thinning of pedestrians and shoppers. The man I'd bumped into stood outside the shop, smoking a cigarette. Though I couldn't see his face, I knew he was watching me.

13

Masses of people and traffic heaved in all directions, focused and deliberate. A dense stream swarmed uphill towards the Crown Plaza. All I need do was stay with the flow until I reached my destination.

I clutched my bag to my hip and dove in. Other than swerving to avoid a man barreling downhill with a wagon of bundled goods, I thought I was making good progress, only somehow I slipped into the tram-bound current dominating the sidewalk's right-hand side. This human surge poured up the Darülŏnun road ready to leap onto the zooming vehicle the moment it paused for intake. I was staring straight ahead, gaze fixed on the woman in front of me, when I found myself boarding along with the tram crowd. I tried to bolt backward but the forward pressure refused to yield.

Now I was squeezed in with the crowd speeding along the darkened street. I couldn't tell which stop to take. Though the sidewalks were ablaze with lights, nothing looked familiar and, to make matters worse, I didn't have a ticket. That sent me scrambling in my bag looking for change in an unfamiliar denomination, jabbing people with my elbows while the tram attendant looked sternly on. Yes, I researched Turkish lira, but try fumbling for alien coins when your fingers have no idea what they're seeking. I was so obviously a tourist, that at last the attendant abruptly signaled me to stop and continued on his way.

I had to be way past the Crown Plaza by now. Unfamiliar buildings zipped by. There was nothing to do but wade my way to the door and disembark at the next stop. I kept saying "excuse me" in English while following a man ahead obviously exit-bound, too.

Together we stepped from the tram into the street, only when he took off in one direction, I was left standing dumbfounded. Lights flashed everywhere, ringing bells sounded along with honking horns and shouting. Four trams were bearing down on me from two directions, with me stuck dead center feeling like I'd been dropped into a psychedelic pinball machine. Someone yanked me to safety just as a tram peeled to a stop inches away.

He rattled away at me, managing the words "be careful" in English before taking off. I nodded, gazing over his shoulder at another man jumping from an incoming tram. I recognized the smoking man immediately.

I turned and fled, not down the street towards the hotel but deeper into the congestion pooling around the depot, thinking I could find a place to hide. Vendors formed a row of brightly lit shops ahead—juice stands, food stalls, a coffee shop. I had no idea where I was heading, but soon the shops funneled downhill away from the main road.

A quick check behind and there he was, hands in pockets, following a few yards away. The food stalls changed to shawl and carpet stores, with many shopkeepers closing down for the night. I veered into one, planning to ask the vendor for help but when I turned to point out my stalker, he had disappeared.

"Yes, lady? You see my scarves. Beautiful scarves, yes?" The shopkeeper's arms were swathed with textiles. "Pashminas, miss. Pure cashmere."

"What's down the street?" I asked pointing outside.

"Grand Bazaar, Miss, but pashminas there all overpriced from China. Mine real Turkish."

I glanced down at his wares, recognizing the distinctive warp of Indian silks and patterning. I bought one anyway, wrapping it around my head as if preparing for a windstorm in the Sahara and exited the shop.

The Grand Bazaar might be busy enough to be safe, I reasoned. No one could accost me there, surely? And so I entered the oldest shopping mall on earth, instantly plunging into an overwhelming kaleidoscope of color, pattern, and gloss.

The tile work overhead alone would be enough to prompt wonder, but to stir into that heaps upon heaps of textiles, gold, and colored glass banked outside shops selling more of the same was overwhelming in my present state. I didn't know where to look, which way to turn.

Without thinking, I barreled down the long corridor, casting periodic glances over my shoulder, taking abrupt turns into smaller tributaries, saying "no thanks" at every vendor. First left and then right followed by two rights and more lefts. Since the Bazaar formed a labyrinth of corridors and tiled boulevards, the smoking man had as many places to hide, as I only probably knew the landscape better.

I was still a damn good dodger. I ducked under hanging pashminas, wove my way through corridors of tiny antique shops, always hiding among clutches of tourists where possible. Once, I dove into a carpet shop and darted to the depths of the salon.

"Please, do you have a back door?" I asked the vendor. "A man's stalking me."

"What does he look like?"

I described every second man in Istanbul—a dark-haired man of approximate height and average height wearing a leather jacket and jeans.

"Quick, this way." The young guy called something to his colleague while hastening me out a back door so narrow that we had to duck to pass.

"You call tourist police?" he asked.

"No time."

"I told my friend to keep customers in front until I return," he assured me. We emerged in a passageway lined with clothing. "Here not so busy. Go straight to outside street."

Straight? Nothing here was straight. He left me in what I assumed to be somewhere deep in the rear of the Bazaar. The ornate tiles and sleek shop windows melded into stalls of household goods crammed into narrow concrete corridors under canvas awnings. I could smell fresh air but saw no way out. After ten minutes of ambling, I finally stumbled upon a narrow cobbled street where all the shops had been shuttered by steel slats for the night. Except for the occasional car, the street was empty.

I took off downward towards what I assumed must be the main road, navigating by instinct alone. Every time a car passed, I'd turn, hoping to see a cab, yet all were private vehicles going way too fast to pay notice to the lone woman waving in the dark. Finally, a car slowed down. I turned to see a sleek black limo inching along at the top of the hill, its lights raking the sidewalk. No roof light, nothing to distinguish it as friendly. As I picked up my pace, the car followed. Fear stabbed hard.

I fumbled in my bag for one of my three phones, thinking I'd call 911. Was that even the right help number for Istanbul? Then, abruptly, something dark dropped over my head and simultaneously dragged me backward. I screamed and dug my heels into the pavement.

My attacker threw me down face-first on the ground and wrenched my arms behind my back and began binding my hands. I kicked and squirmed and cried for help.

"Shut up or I hit you," he said, his knees digging into my back. As he pulled the ropes tighter, I heard pounding footsteps. Somebody shouted. For blind seconds I heard scuffling as I tried to flop myself over. Footsteps rapidly retreated amid more shouting. I felt someone standing over me.

"My dear, just lay still for a moment until I cut these bindings. It is I, Sir Rupert Fox, come to your rescue. Nothing to fear now, I assure you. You are quite safe."

I stilled in shock. The hood was pulled from my head and I was helped to a sitting position. I found myself in a dark alley with Sir Rupert crouching beside me. My attacker had disappeared. "Foxy?"

"I prefer Rupert. My man is giving chase. Come, come. Let us proceed to the car where we can talk in comfort. Are you all right? No injuries, I trust?" He helped me to standing and retrieved my carpet bag and phone. "How can you possibly carry this bag without causing bodily harm?"

He led me to a black limo parked curbside, the same one I had seen earlier. The driver's side was empty with the keys dangling in the ignition. I slid into the back seat with Sir Rupert beside me and leaned against the leather, closing my eyes. "How did you know where I was?"

"Quite easily, as it happens. If you were attempting discretion, I fear you failed miserably. I did say I was having you followed, did I not? No prevarication there. My man told me you had taken a flight to Istanbul and the rest was relatively easy. I have some tea on hand for just such emergencies as this. Do you take milk and sugar?"

I opened my eyes and watched him pour liquid from a thermos into a little glass mug which he passed to me.

"Actually, I ask from habit only since I'm afraid I take mine with liberal lashings of both sugar and milk and, as you can see, I am without the necessary hosting supplies to honor specific requests. Nevertheless, I believe my preferred blend should fortify you."

My hands trembled when I took the mug. "I meant how did you know where I was in Istanbul?" Though I'd planned to swear off tea for a decade, the brew tasted amazingly good.

"Oh, yes. I presume you ask because you unfortunately removed my tracking device from my gift—very short-sighted on your part, Phoebe. How can I adequately protect you without knowing exactly where you are? However, there are other means. Would you like a biscuit with that, perhaps a Hobnob or digestive?"

A little tin emerged, the lid pried off, and the contents offered, each cookie swathed in tissue wrapping.

"What you mean is how can you easily track me to Noel and the next presumable hoard?" I chose a Hobnob and savored its oaten crunch.

"Well, that too, of course, but I am truly concerned for your safety and trust that tonight's episode serves to strengthen my offer. I've been watching since you arrived in Istanbul and, no, there's no point in asking how I came to know which hotel you were staying at. Following you today was more challenging, I admit—the crowds in this city—but once you arrived at the Arasta Bazaar, logistics became more manageable. It was there that my man noticed your stalker. When he returns from giving chase, hopefully we will be further illuminated on who exactly attempted the kidnapping."

"Kidnapping?" I passed my empty mug back to Foxy, who deposited in a wooden chest at his feet.

"Yes, of course. He bagged you, my dear, much as one does an exotic bird bound for market or even a fish, an angel fish, perhaps, though one would hope such lovely creatures would require more expert care. If he planned to kill you outright, no doubt you'd be quite dead by now. Such brutal acts can be achieved very quickly, I believe, via firearms, knives, garroting, an impressive range of dastardly implements. No, I fear your attacker planned to take you off somewhere, perhaps to question you more forcefully. Another treasure-seeker, no doubt. One of your many admirers. Ah, here he comes."

A man was approaching up the street, brushing himself off as he trudged along with something draped over one arm. Not Rutgers, I realized, but taller, dressed in dark jeans and a long coat, though equally well-muscled. He opened the driver's side door and poked his head inside. Brown wavy hair, not bad looking. "He got away, Sir Rupert," he said in an English accent. "Tackled him but he escaped my bloomin' grip. Left behind his jacket, though."

"Pass it over, Evan. Are you harmed?"

"A bruised rib or two, nothing serious. He's in worse shape. Think I broke some of his. Is the lady all right?"

"I'm fine, thanks. Were you tailing me in London, too?"

He grinned an amazingly white set of teeth, climbing in behind the wheel. "Sometimes. You can be very good at escaping trackers, ma'am."

"Practice."

I watched Foxy pat down the captured jacket, his gloved hands smoothing along creases and over pockets. "Ah, here we are." Out came a cell phone. "Aren't we lucky that he chose to keep his communication device so conveniently close?"

"Let me see it. He's my attacker." I held out my hand.

"But my quarry, my dear. Finders keepers."

I relinquished my claim to watch Foxy scan the smart phone. While he scrolled through the numbers, I explored the jacket more thoroughly.

"Not much of interest in here, I'm afraid," Foxy said. "A few Turkish numbers I will have checked plus a photo of some houses that may prove interesting. This is not a personal phone, is my guess. He uses it for business only. The man was Turkish, I presume?" he asked Evan.

"Yes."

"Probably a hired chap, then. The question is, who employed him?"

My searching fingers landed on stiff paper slipped in an inside lining pocket. A business card. I eagerly held it to the ceiling light, blinking in disbelief.

"Well, what is it?" Sir Foxy asked.

"*Margaret E. Buckmaster. Dealer Ethnographic Goods* followed by a phone number with an unfamiliar zip code. Maggie tried to have me kidnapped? But why? She knows I don't have the hoard."

Rupert tsk-tsked as he gently pried the card from my fingers. "Indeed, why does she wish to have a private word with you in such a remarkably unfriendly fashion?"

"We're not exactly on the best of terms, considering that the last time she tried to shoot me but, still. Why not just ask to meet me somewhere or approach me the way Noel did? I can't imagine Noel or Toby agreeing to such methods."

"I will find out more about this number, if this helps. No doubt she has ensured it can't be traced but I will see what I can do."

"Where to now, Sir Rupert?" Evan asked as the car began easing away from the curb.

"The Crown Plaza, please," I said.

"Miss Maggie will most likely try to nab you again, which is where I may be of service."

"You've already been very helpful but I'm still not planning on making you my best friend just yet. I'll let you know if I need anything but for now, I just want rest."

"Yes, of course you do. I shall call once I learn more about this number. In the meantime, be very cautious."

Outside the hotel, tour buses and taxis congested every spare inch of curb. I had no choice but to leap into traffic and run to the door.

Foxy called out something like "See you tomorrow," which I chose to ignore.

14

The first adhan of the day awoke me at dawn the next morning. Ringing strong and clear from the old mosque directly across the street, it startled me from a brief, deep sleep. Allahu Akbar (God is Great), the prayer began. Staring up at the ceiling, I tried to recall what little I knew of the words. I'd crammed a lot of research into the hours before my flight. Somewhere in this day-breaking passage I knew a special phrase had been added: *As-salaatu khayrun min'n-nawm*, or "Prayer is better than sleep."

I struggled to sitting and sighed. Prayer probably was better than sleep, but right then I could use a little more of both. I got up and set the coffee machine working and gathered up my knitting for a spell of sleepy solitude.

Knitting was the closest I came to devotional practice. The rhythmic stitches helped ease me into a nearly meditative state, loosening the noose of stress while helping me believe I could survive anything, that I connected in some profound way to all things great and small. How could I ever explain knitting as a spiritual experience to the uninitiated? Yet, it was in some profound way. Each in our own manner, we pray, we commune with the Universe, sometimes with no more than peace, needles, and yarn.

By eight o'clock, I was in the hotel cafeteria, scrolling through my email while devouring samples of breakfast fare from multiple cultures. Rice and eggs with a side of sweet halvah wasn't half bad. I was just forking a bit of a Japanese noodle mix into my mouth when a message from frieddoc@gmail.com popped up in my in-box.

Hello, Dr. Eva Friedrich here. I understand you are interested in the Goddess with Vultures kilim. How fortuitous that we are both in Istanbul. Meet me for lunch to discuss. The e-signature declared her to be *PhD Archaeology, University of London; Assistant Director of the British Institute of Archaeology in Ankara* (retired), and listed several published books.

That she was a bit pushy didn't bother me. I tapped out a quick response. *Lunch would be perfect. Where and when?* No more than three gulps of tea later and she responded, giving me the address for a restaurant she said was near the Blue Mosque. Meet me at 1:00 sharp. I'll be waiting. I asked how I'd recognize her but received no response.

After I drank the last of my tea, I plowed through the throngs to the lobby, where I claimed one of the few available empty seats and used my own iPhone to check in with Serena. Everyone knew I was here. I had nothing to hide on this phone.

"Is everything good, Phoebe?"

"Everything's great," I effused while tucking my legs closer against my chair to avoid a rolling suitcase attached to some harried tourist. My descriptions of the shops and bazaar almost caused Serena to hyperventilate across the airwaves.

"What did you buy, anything? Tell me!"

"Just a few items for the gallery but I did nab a fabulous robe." I described the tunic in detail while she emitted excited sounds but didn't mention my gift. That would be a surprise. "I'll wear it tonight at the International Rare Textile and Ethnographic Exposition reception."

"You will look so beautiful. Take a selfie for me and post it on Facebook! When will you return?" Did I only imagine the anxiety in her voice?

"Maybe the day after tomorrow or maybe later. I have an open ticket but I won't be away too long. Are you sure everything is all right?"

"Everything is fine," she assured me. "But I miss you and Max, too. I would go visit him but I am not allowed, yes?"

"No visitors for two weeks. It's one of the conditions of his treatment."

"Oh, well. It must be good. Things are quiet, so quiet. Except for Jennifer. She talks on and on about Marco. You would think I'd be happy to listen, but no."

"And Agent Walker hasn't been around?"

"No. All is calm. You go and have a good time and forget about everything here."

If only I could.

"What will you do today?" Serena wanted to know before the call ended.

"More shopping, maybe some sight-seeing," I told her, though that wasn't strictly true. If I were really on vacation, I'd be settling in for a day at the Topkapi Palace, perhaps visit the Islamic Museum of Art, the Hagia Sophia, and any one of the other major attractions.

I tried checking in with Nancy next but could only talk to her answering machine. The message I left was a synopsis of all I told Serena only, in Nancy's case, what I didn't say would be more important than what I did.

As I dropped that phone into my bag, one of the others began ringing. After fumbling a bit, I retrieved my Foxy phone.

"Phoebe, what are you up to today and how may I help?"

"And where are you, Rupert?"

"Sitting across from your hotel illegally parked. I traced Maggie's number but, alas, as expected, it is now a dead end. I suspect she uses a number of revolving phones to shield her location."

"But she must be in Istanbul somewhere."

"No doubt. Oh, dear. I do believe an officer is about to issue us a ticket. May I offer you a lift somewhere before we are accosted?"

"No thanks."

"It would be so much easier if you'd just share your agenda so I could help."

"Bye for now, Foxy."

I clicked off and checked the time, seeing I had about two hours left before lunch, enough time for a little couture browsing. Stepping outside to Darülünun, the curb attendant hailed me a cab. Before climbing in, I waved at Foxy and Evan as they were ordered on their way and then passed the driver the address for Istanbul's foremost upscale designer shopping area, Nişantaşı. Foxy would be far ahead of me unable to turn around by the time we were under way.

Fifteen minutes later, the cab left me at a glass and concrete promenade, leaving old Istanbul so far behind it was as if it had never been. Gone were the bazaars and the mosques, the sense that the city had grown up around its heritage, proud of all it once was and planned to become. This nondescript arcade could be dropped anywhere in the world where the wealthy forage. Only the Turkish signs below the English on the restaurants and cafes betrayed the country.

Shoppers thronged the street, mostly western-dressed though a few stylish traditional Turkish women strolled by with chic shoes visible beneath their robes. I didn't belong to the chic category. Though there were enough women dressed down much like me, most carried a status bag far removed from my beloved battered satchel.

I found the Chanel store easily. As a minimalist glass and black-trimmed salon with glossy depths stretching back from the street, it claimed its real estate with typical panache. Fixing a smile on my face, I slipped inside, inhaled the rarefied air of wealth and couture, and headed directly to a lean young sales associate dressed in basic black. She flicked her eyes across my person before raising her gaze to my face.

"Hi," I said, giving her a little wave. "Can you help me with something? I want to surprise my aunt with a gift."

Her eyes narrowed. I estimated her to be around twenty and to have fully embraced the notion that working in a couture shop elevated her above mere mortals. She couldn't look further down on me had I dropped down a storm drain. "How can I help with that?" she asked, her accent I tagged as Balkan.

"Well," I said, warming up to my ruse. "My aunt's totally Chanel and I know she comes here all the time because she's told me. So, I want to surprise her with a present, you know?"

The woman thinned her lips into a smile. "You should try maybe flowers. Flowers make nice gift." Which you might be able to afford.

I grinned. "No, no. I'm looking for a bag. She loves bags, especially Chanel. I'm sure she shops here."

"What would be her name?"

Maggie had to be using an alias so I pretended I hadn't heard. "Wait, if you see her picture, perhaps you'll recognize her. Here, look."

I pulled out my phone, tapped the photo icon, and began scrolling through all my pictures until I reached those I'd scanned before leaving London. One in particular was my collateral: me dressed in head-to-toe white Chanel lace, standing in the gymnasium on my high school graduation, the outfit compliments of my pseudo-aunt Maggie, who stood at my side beaming away. My excruciating embarrassment of wearing something that cost more than most families in my community earned in a couple of months was alleviated only slightly by my excitement at having my whole tribe there: Max, Mom, and Dad. Toby took the photo.

I had looked damned good, I now decided with the retrospect of maturity, but at the time, that dress represented all I never wanted to become. Maggie, always playing beneficent aunt, which in reality she wasn't on either count, was totally oblivious to both the social awkwardness and my feelings.

I passed the woman my phone. She stared down at the picture in total disbelief. The ragged little nonlabel creature standing before her was really the same young couture-clad swan in the photo? She didn't seem to recognize Maggie who also wore complete Chanel.

Then another, older associate who had been hovering nearby slipped up and peered over the younger woman's shoulder. "Ah, oui! Let me see." She took the phone from the woman's hands and studied the photo closely. "Yes, I know her, Madame St. Remis, oui? But her hair is not blond now but black." French accent. I guessed this woman was the salon manager and a Parisian import.

"Oui!" I said excitedly. "Ma tante! She always changes her hair color like Linda Evangelista!" I pulled that model's name out of my head in a desperate attempt to seem in tune, realizing in a flash I had to be a good decade or two out of date. I began rattling away in my best school French, trying to impart more Parisian than Nova Scotian Acadian into my accent. "She goes from black to blond to red. I never know what color her hair will be on any day!"

The woman nodded and passed back my phone, continuing in French. "I know those pieces from the archive, yes? The first collection Monsieur Lagerfeld created for Chanel. Magnifique! Do you still have the dress?"

"Mais, non. I was much younger then, as you can see, but I am certain Auntie collects all her pieces forever and ever. She never changes dress sizes like her hair color. When did you see her last?"

"But two days ago. We are tailoring pieces from the new collection for her. Wait. I will check my book."

Leave it to ma tante to put visiting a Chanel store on top of her weekly to-do list even while being hunted by Interpol. My hunch paid off, big time. I couldn't help but bless my gut instincts. I watched the woman slip away to a back room, leaving the younger sales associate to attempt belated friendliness. "You are not from here?" she asked.

"Obviously not," I said, dropping words rattling with cubes of chill.

Luckily, a group of Japanese shoppers flocked into the salon in a flurry of excitement, so the saleswoman left my side.

When the senior associate returned moments later it was to inform me that Madame St. Remis was indeed planning to pick up her purchases, tomorrow actually. "We said that we can deliver them to her hotel but, non, she insists to come into the shop herself, for more choosing, perhaps?"

"Of course! Never miss an opportunity to shop, that's my auntie. I will surprise her when she comes and have her select her own present. You won't betray me, will you?"

The woman placed a lovely manicured hand over her silk bodice. "Mais, non! Your secret is safe in my heart. I shall call you when she arrives, yes?"

"Yes, please. I will wait outside and then surprise her." I gave the woman the number for the blind phone and left the salon in a delirium of self-congratulation. If Maggie was here, Toby and Noel couldn't be far away.

15

Soon I was back in old Istanbul and the Sultanahmet area, the oldest part of one of the oldest cities on earth. The taxi slid to a stop outside a row of tall wooden houses crammed together on a narrow, cobbled street where the soaring golden minarets and blue domes of the famed mosque could just be seen above a tall stone wall.

I disembarked on the curving street that dipped down towards the Bosporus. The noon call to prayer erupted all over the city in an eerie yet beautiful cadence. I paid the driver and gazed around, expecting an obvious restaurant sign but here, away from the jarring cacophony of traffic and neon, everything had toned down. A sign for a boutique hotel swung lazily in the breeze.

"Phoebe McCabe, over here!"

A sturdy little woman beckoned to me from a doorstep of a narrow brown-shingled house.

"Dr. Friedrich?" I asked, approaching.

Wearing an army-green safari jacket with buttons straining across her ample chest and a pair of tan cargo pants with red socks tucked into sneakers, she appeared at odds with the old world surroundings. A brilliant red silk scarf wrapped around her neck multiple times added to the impression of an army officer gone tribal.

"I am she and you are Phoebe McCabe. Erdogan describes you to perfection: 'Lots of red hair,' he said." Her accent was posh British with a slight Germanic bite. She pumped my outstretched hand energetically.

"That's all he could say about me was my hair color?" I asked, trying to retrieve my hand. Her hair, by contrast, consisted of no more than a skim of iron gray strands plastering her scalp—efficient, practical, and to the point.

"To Turks, red hair is significant, though as to what it signifies depends entirely upon the beholder. Erdogan is a good chap and I consider him my friend. Doubtless, he pegged you accurately." The kyanite blue eyes twinkled with amusement.

"Pegged me how?"

"Follow me. We'll talk inside. I have a table reserved upstairs."

She mustered me up a narrow flight of stairs that led past two dimly lit floors. I glimpsed empty dining rooms set with white table cloths and silverware. Gas light sconces on the stairwell flickered over silk brocade walls hung with sepia photos among paintings depicting Ottoman life. A waiter dashed downstairs balancing a tray, greeting Dr. Friedrich in Turkish, smiling, and nodding while exchanging pleasantries.

At last we reached the top floor, where another gentleman threaded us through the busy dining area to a balcony overlooking the Blue Mosque. We maneuvered directly to a table tucked into a far corner flush against the railing.

Eva grinned. "Yes, yes, quite the tourist vista, I'd say, but I'd rather pay for a touch of privacy than be tossed into the milling throng of most Istanbul restaurants. This is a favorite. Be seated. Yes, right there. You are the guest and so claim the benefit of this most magnificent view."

I lowered myself down, watching as she unraveled the long patterned scarf from her neck and dropped her green canvas utility sack to the floor. I slipped my own carpet bag between my feet.

"There," she said, grinning over at me as she sat down with a thud. "Lovely piece you have there," she nodded towards my bag. "A fine old Ottoman textile—an early depiction of the traditional tulip design. The enterprising Turks are forever squeezing dollars out of their textile treasures, but who blames them but we motley scholars?" Her smile dimpled her cheeks with a deceptively cherubic sweetness. "So, Phoebe, let's dispense with both preliminaries and formalities. I understand you have acquired an Anatolian kilim of some note. Show me."

I opened my mouth but she silenced me with her hand as a waiter slipped up to our table. She gave him a battery of instructions in Turkish, only consulting me once. "Are you vegan?"

"Still a carnivore with vegan leanings," I assured her.

"Good show," and she finished giving our orders, leaving me perplexed. The last time someone ordered for me in a restaurant, I was five years old.

After the waiter disappeared, Eva turned back to me. "Well?"

"Well what?"

"The kilim, Phoebe. Let me see it."

I passed her my phone opened to the photo, which she took without giving it a glance. "I mean the original. I need to see the original."

"I didn't bring it," I said.

"Not here, perhaps, but I am quite certain you brought it to Istanbul. Don't be disingenuous with me, Phoebe. Be honest. Ex veritas scientia."

"Which means?"

"In truth knowledge. Be truthful and I can assist you."

"I only want to ask your opinion on the kilim. I wouldn't call that help."

"Don't quibble."

I said nothing further as I watched her focus in on the photo. Her eyes flickered as she pinch-widened the shot and peered down at the screen in quarter segments. When she lifted her gaze, her cheeks were flushed. "How did you come by such a specimen?"

"It showed up unbidden in my London gallery with Erdogan's return address."

"How extraordinary. Do you know who sent it?"

"Yes and no. It's complicated."

"Of course it's complicated. Luckily we have all lunch for you to untangle the specifics. Begin."

"Presuming I want to explain, which I don't. I mean, I don't know you, Eva. I'd hoped you'd share some knowledge with me, that's all. If I presume too much, my apologies for wasting your time. I'll just be on my way." I grabbed my carpet bag and raised my butt inches off the chair.

"Touchy, touchy. Do sit back down, Phoebe. Please." She waved me back, her tone softening. "I've become far too excited about these matters and tend to run a little roughshod over everything and everyone. Bad habit. Let me make amends. A woman on a mission must be forgiven. I'll disclose first, as a show of good faith, then it's your turn. Sound fair?"

"I've been getting that offer a lot lately. Go ahead."

"To begin with, I presume you comprehend the preliminary importance of this kilim?"

I still clutched my carpet bag in my lap ready to bolt. "You mean that it's definitely rare and a possible museum piece? Yes, I got that. I sell kilims and old textiles in London but admit to being still very much in learning mode. Anything else about this kilim's provenance, other than it's Anatolian and probably at least three hundred years old, is pretty thin on the ground with me."

"But you do know about the Anatolian Goddess, since you called the kilim by name?"

"I know she predates the current world religions, going back, in one form or another, to the earliest fertility goddesses in Neolithic cultures."

Eva grinned. "You said 'She'—I like that—She being the Queen of Heaven and Earth, the Divine Feminine, the manifestation of the connecting force between feminine and masculine, mother and child, life and death, and the essence of transformative spirit that enlivens all things."

I nodded, startled to hear a spiritual stream pour from Dr. Friedrich. "I guess," I said, relaxing my grip on my bag.

"The Anatolian Goddess forms the crux of my research and also lies at the center of a significant academic and theological controversy."

"What kind of controversy?"

"One that cost me my career and forced me into early retirement, as if that would stop me."

The waiter reappeared at that point, smiling pleasantly as he began pouring white wine into glass goblets. I tried protesting but Eva shooed away my refusal. "Certain Turkish wines are actually quite palatable, contrary to popular opinion. This is one of the better vintages and hails from a little vineyard outside of

Izmir—and, yes, Turkey is a Muslim country but one espousing moderate views, at least so far as wine is concerned."

Several small plates began appearing next: dishes of hummus, dolmades, small bowls of rice topped with various purees and olive oils, along with a basket of hot flat bread. Everything enticed me at once and I accepted Eva's insistence that I try a bit of everything. "Please, continue disclosing. I'll just eat and listen. What kind of controversy costs a scholar her career?" I asked before taking a bite of delicious bread.

"One that is connected to a theory not adequately substantiated by a significant archaeological find, in the view of her peers, and that also has the misfortune of being wildly unpopular with any number of competing interests, including several major religions. In other words, one that may threaten the world order."

I stopped chewing. "Go on."

"I once held the esteemed position of Assistant Director of the British Institute of Archeology in Ankara."

"I saw that on your email signature."

"Which they'd rather I stop using but, whatever our disagreements, they can't erase history. My book will redeem me in the eyes of my colleagues and tip the world on its end."

"Wow. But how does the kilim fit in with world-tipping?"

"Allow me to give a little background first. Feel free to stop me if I'm repeating things you already know. It's a bad habit left over from my lecturing days. Anyway, as you no doubt realize, traditional kilims serve as an expression of group identity, a way for a family within a clan to express how they are both unique and part of a larger community. Designs and motifs are passed down the centuries to modern times by generations of Anatolian women."

"Yes, got that. So far, you haven't disclosed anything enlightening. These dolmades are incredible."

"Try the wine."

I never could do boozy lunches with dignity, but I was in Istanbul looking out over the Blue Mosque. I took a sip, startled by a flash of sensory images of sun-ripened vines on my tongue, smiled, and swallowed more. Eva drank deeply, well into her second glass.

"As I was saying, these kilims are an ancient symbolic language as well as the unique creative manifestation of woman's art, since the men do not weave in Turkish culture."

"I know."

"At the heart of my research is the role of this visual language as it emerges across the centuries in Anatolia. When occasionally one finds motifs that predate even Mohammed in this ancient land, they denote a thread leading deep into the human heart, back before recorded history."

I paused. "Aren't all Anatolian motifs ancient?"

"Most are, but over time some have become diluted, corrupted, if you will, and may look little like their originals. The first images were more anthropomorphic."

"Like my vulture goddess."

"Exactly. Where once women honored their goddess by working her representation into their art for home and community, gradually this became more difficult as society changed around them."

"Religious beliefs, you mean?"

"Religion has altered every society the world over, for better and for worse, in unequal measure. As the churches, synagogues, and mosques arose vying for spiritual dominance, all headed by men, of course, the Divine Feminine was forced underground—suppressed, transmuted, and annihilated. Women, presumably the weaker sex, were diminished in kind. We were forced to adapt, to hide, to be subjugated, both societally and spiritually. To work an image of a recognizable primitive female deity into their art in some communities is very dangerous and could be seen as heretical even today. Eventually, they forgot the original meaning of the motifs."

I nodded. "A woman's role in 2400 BC must have been significantly different from now."

"Research has landed soundly on the prospects of a matrilineal culture at work in early humanity. We were not so quick to weigh down on the relative worth of one sex over the other back in the beginning. Some scholars remain convinced that early humanity revered the giver of life as being at least equal in worth to her protector, the warrior male, if not more so." Eva shook her head and refilled her glass. "Women might have come a long way, but in the wrong direction when you consider that God was once a she or, at least, not exclusively male."

"Imagine how the world would have evolved had our species not spent the last few thousand years in full warrior mode? What if motherhood and nurturing were heralded as the most desirable traits?" I said, sipping my wine. "How would it have looked? Where would we be today?"

"Perhaps we might not be teetering on the brink of annihilation at this very moment." Eva lifted her glass. "I propose a toast: to the Vulture Goddess. May She find her wings again for the sake of all humanity."

I clinked my glass to hers. "To the Vulture Goddess!" I took a deep drink of the crisp wine and sat back. "But where does the vulture come in?"

"Vultures were not always seen as the dirty, opportunistic scavengers we see them as today but rather as a revered and significant part of the cycle of life and death. They were the cleansers, the ultimate recyclers. The Goddess gave life knowing that death is inevitable, and one of her totems, the vulture—she was rather fond of big cats, too—helped in the transformation."

"Vultures and goddesses seem so incongruous somehow."

"To our modern way of thinking, perhaps. The Anatolian Goddess speaks in a visual language predating mankind's development of the written word."

"Initially, men transcribed while women described."

"You could say that. Our ancestors communicated visually and read the natural world around them to impart meaning to the universe. They saw how life came into being and then died, how certain creatures like the vultures participated in the great recycling." Eva sipped her wine and gazed away, past the Blue Mosque, past all the mosques, all the churches, all the synagogues.

"And?"

"And when I find a kilim like yours with that ancient motif almost intact, that close to the original goddess image, so unusually anthropomorphic, I know it can lead me closer to the truth. Somewhere in Anatolia several hundred years ago, a handful of women kept that motif alive, despite whatever secular pressures might attempt to influence their art. Somewhere I believe they still do."

"Still, as in today?"

"Quite possibly. I have seen enough of these images in similar kilim fragments of varying dates to lead me to believe that a family somewhere is still holding true to the ancient goddess across multiple centuries."

I swallowed, blinking back visions of circling vultures as the main dishes began arriving—lamb and beef kebabs and salad.

"Speaking of vultures, do eat!" my hostess exclaimed.

The next twenty minutes were a continuation of our feast, minus conversation. There was too much to enjoy and maneuver with the speared meat and various sauces. When finally, I sat back in my seat my stomach had expanded so much I could hardly breathe. "Oh, that was wonderful," I sighed.

Eva smiled. "I do so love to share a good meal with a friend, old or new."

"So, am I your new friend?"

"We share a certain passion."

"For kilims, you mean?"

"At the very least but it's much deeper than that. We are on the Goddess's business and we are meant to help one another."

"Pardon me?" The wine blurred my thoughts. "Me, on the Goddess's business? I don't think so. Really, the Goddess and I have only recently become acquainted." I closed my eyes.

"So you think."

"My days have become so fraught. Nothing is easy."

"Think how boring easy really is and be grateful you don't live that life. You said the circumstances around the kilim's arrival was complicated. Explain what you think you know."

I opened my eyes. "No, I mean, not so fast," I said, leaning forward. "Other than to give me a retrospective of Turkish tribal kilims and discuss the Goddess culture, what have you really disclosed?"

"You need to listen better, Phoebe. I said: supposing that family of women still protects the ancient goddess for reasons yet to be determined?"

"So?"

"Look around you, really look. How easy do you think it is for a traditional Turkish woman in a Central Anatolian village to protect the image of a prehistoric fertility goddess? In some households, women are not even permitted to pray in the mosques with the men. To some Muslim men, woman are restricted to house and home with no soul and little worth except as breeder, cook, and housekeeper. She often lives an internal life while her menfolk go forth into the world for stimulation. Is keeping the goddess alive a question of faith, resistance, or something else?"

Though my thoughts were jumbled, excitement still stirred as if I'd glimpsed something grand from far away and longed for a closer look. Or maybe I was just drunk. Probably the latter. Either way, I didn't see how the kilim linked with my brother.

"Help me find the answer, Phoebe. Let me see your kilim. It was sent to you for a reason. You're part of this somehow."

Yes, I knew Toby had sent that kilim to me for a reason; the man calling himself Jason Young had died for a reason. Noel dropped in to see me for a reason. Maggie tried to kidnap me for a reason. Foxy was tailing me for a reason. Where was I in all this and what did thieves have to do with goddesses? Was I the only one who didn't understand?

"She is calling to you. Heed Her call. Work with me here. Let me see your kilim in person. By assessing the dyes and wools, I may be able to hone in on the exact village, which to date has eluded me. Most of the kilims I've inspected so far have not been so complete. I must see it."

"Coffee," I said, waving my hand like a downing woman. I knew I was in no condition to make decisions.

Eva lifted a finger and a waiter darted to her side. "Coffee for my friend, please, Anin."

As the man dashed away, I sat studying my companion.

"I'm your strongest ally. We are both in service to the Goddess, whether you know it or not. Together, we'll vanquish our enemies."

For an instant I imagined Eva dressed in armor brandishing a sword. "But you don't even know who my enemies are," I pointed out. "I'm not even sure I do. Besides, it's overwhelming how many people suddenly want to be my friend."

"Ah," she nodded. "Which means you must have enemies."

I sat in silence for a few moments, my thoughts skittering around like fish in a bucket while Anin poured thick black coffee into tiny cups. Me, in service to the Goddess? Who was I but a lowly carpet monger struggling to extricate herself from her brother's criminal entanglements? And this former esteemed archaeologist was beginning to seem a little unhinged.

"That's Turkish coffee. Try it," Eva urged.

I took a sip. The brew burned sweet and strong down my throat. If only it would jump-start my brain, I might stand a chance of extricating myself from this lunch intact.

"We will attend together the International Textile gala tonight," Eva said with a nod. She leaned forward with elbows on the table, holding her tiny cup in both hands.

I blinked at her. "We will?"

"Of course. I'm sure you don't want to attend alone."

"How do you know I'm even attending?"

"I have seen the attendance list."

"You have?"

"I will introduce you to the key players in the ethnographic art world here in Istanbul, or at least those who think they are."

I could use a few key introductions. And maybe a nap. I nodded, trying to rouse myself. "What time is it now?"

"Two minutes to three and don't concern yourself with the tab. Lunch is my treat."

I stifled a yawn. "Oh, thank you. That's very kind. I'm so tired. I need to get back to the hotel or I'll be in no condition for tonight."

"What, no baklava? You haven't tasted baklava until you try it here."

"I really have to go. It's the wine." I rubbed my eyes and suppressed another yawn.

"If you must, go on then. Meet me in the lobby of your hotel at 6:30 sharp."

16

Once in my room, I was so relieved to find the kilim still tucked inside the safe that I hugged it to my chest like some long-lost lover. I spread it across the bedspread and hovered my hands reverently above the weave. So old, so incredible, so powerful. Did it really represent an underground spiritual movement running counter to social and religious norms for hundreds, maybe thousands, of years, or was Eva just a slightly unhinged though fervent scholar? Did I have the right to cloister it away as if it were truly mine? Toby had entangled me in this enigma. At least he could have sent proper instructions.

I didn't want to attend the gala with the hyper-insistent Dr. Friedrich any more than I wanted to go alone. Carefully, I returned the kilim to the safe and flopped onto the bed. Before my head hit the pillow, I struggled to recall if I had even told Dr. Friedrich where I was staying. I didn't remember one way or the other and in seconds I was past caring.

My phone rang me awake in what seemed like minutes but was nearly an hour later. "Phoebe, Sir Rupert here. I understand you are going to the reception tonight. May I offer you a lift?"

I bolted upright. "No, thanks. Did you wheedle an invitation?"

"My dear, I do not wheedle. Unfortunately, not being a textile aficionado means I am not on the mailing list and I have not been successful in acquiring an invitation. Most disappointing. I had thought to go as a pasha."

"I can picture you in a nice blue."

"I was thinking jonquil but, really, beggars can't be choosers. You do realize that your admirers may be present at this event?"

"If you're referring to Maggie, I doubt she'll ambush me in such a public place. As for the other two, I can only hope they'll be there."

"Do try not to be naive, Phoebe. I understand the event is in full Turkish costume so a potential threat could come in a multitude of disguises."

"I'll be vigilant. I'd better hang up and get dressed."

"Did you enjoy your lunch with Dr. Friedrich?"

I paused, half annoyed, half amused. He read my iPhone emails or he successfully tailed me after all? "It was delicious, thanks for asking."

"Do beware of the noted doctor, as certain events in her history may place her firmly the side of the enemy."

"Ah, you mean of the duplicitous, treasure-seeking kind?"

"Exactly."

"I have so many to choose from."

"Indeed. It is best not to align yourself with such individuals as they cannot be trusted."

"Good night, Sir Foxy." And I pressed END before turning the phone off.

Clutching my toiletries, I climbed into the shower, emerging twenty minutes later ready to force my coarse hair in line with miracle tonics and gels. Tackling my face next, I smoothed on a little foundation to de-emphasize my freckles and tried applying powder to contour my face, tricks I'd learned from Maggie eons ago but seldom applied. Chic never stuck with me so lately I mostly aimed for interesting.

Next, I dressed. The silk tunic fell across my body in a flow of pattern, dousing me with just enough confidence to believe I could make it through the night. When I finally emerged from the bathroom, my room message light was flashing. An automated voice informed me that an envelope awaited me at the desk. I grabbed my satchel, took one more glance at myself in the mirror, and exited the room.

Downstairs, the lobby was swarming from more incoming bus tours, the lineups at the reception desk straggling six to seven weary people deep. I waited in the queue impatiently, scanning the lobby for Dr. Friedrich. When I finally reached the desk, the agent passed me an envelope but couldn't tell me who delivered it and when. I scuttled through the throng and into one of the little antefoyers that branched from the main reception area. They were almost always empty. Perching on a velvet ottoman, I ripped open the envelope and there, scribbled on the back of a postcard, I read the following handwritten message:

MEET ME AT THE GALA AND HEAR ME OUT. N

Flipping over the card, I stared down at a picture of the Bosporus taken from the Topkapi Palace gardens. Noel at last. Finally, I'd get some answers.

"There you are!"

I blinked up at a red gold-embroidered robe belted over white harem pants and nearly dropped the card. The person inside the costume was nearly invisible. "Dr. Friedrich?" I peered under a coin-spangled fez with an attached veil. "Is that you in there?"

She laughed, apparently delighted by my consternation. "Had you fooled, did I not? Good show! I was obliged to have it shortened and widened, of course, but, at one time, it actually belted properly across my middle. Behold the perils of too many baklavas! There's nothing a carefully placed safety pin can't rectify."

"Or packing tape for extreme measures." I stood up, admiring every detail. "It's an Anatolian wedding dress, right?"

"Correct."

"It's gorgeous. I love that red," I said, all the time remaining distracted by Noel's note. Before the night was out, I'd have another chance to ask the right questions and perhaps even hear the answers.

"Thank you and you look quite the vision in that silk tunic, Phoebe. From that shop at the Arasta Bazaar, right? Splendid!"

I turned her around to study the veil's lace crochet edging and to admire the embroidered slippers. The ensemble appeared lovingly cared-for despite the scent of camphor.

"You'll see many people in traditional costumes tonight. The textile experts like to strut their proverbial stuff and nobody's prouder of their textile art than the Turks. Those who associate their dignity with standard suits and high fashion will just saunter about trying to look officious. We'll ignore those unless they have something interesting to say, which most don't. What's that in your hand?"

"Just a postcard." I shoved the card into my satchel and forced a smile. "Shall we walk, take a cab, what?"

"We'll take a cab. If not, we'll be stopping every six feet for photo ops. Tourists adore folk costume. I've been accosted five times just passing through the lobby. Come along."

Eva posed twice with visitors before we even made it to the door. Tourists believed her to be Turkish, a misconception she made no attempt to correct as she regaled the photographers with detailed accounts of Anatolian wedding costumes. I declined the urges from the Texan couple to include me in their selfie and hung back against the wall. The last thing I needed was to end up on Facebook or be Instagrammed across the world.

I slid next to one of the lobby shops that sold textile-covered boots and bags, thinking my patterned tunic might blend with the display. There, with my back to the glass, I stared out at the throng, searching for Toby or Noel. Would they be at the gala, too? Would I even recognize any of them before they spied me? Wouldn't it be thrilling to have the upper hand just once?

By the time Eva retrieved me, it had just turned 6:45. "You look rattled, Phoebe. What's wrong?"

"Nothing," I smiled. "I'm just not one for crowds."

"And yet you live in London and came to Istanbul." She stood peering into my face, her expression masked under the veil.

"You're not the veil type," I remarked.

She laughed. "They do very well when women use them for their own purposes, as I will be tonight."

"Are you trying to stay under wraps?"

"Rather. We'd better go."

"Oh, yes," I checked my phone. "Aren't we late?"

"They will lock the doors in 25 minutes so, yes, we must make haste. I'd rather not arrive too early and thus be conspicuous. Nevertheless, we don't want to miss the hors d'oeuvres, do we? The Museum of Islamic Art is sponsoring the event this year and they always present an impressive spread."

"You can't possibly be thinking of food after that enormous lunch."

"Nonsense. I can always accommodate food. Move along, Phoebe. Don't dawdle. We must push ahead of that clutch in front to nab the next cab." She tugged me through the revolving doors towards the curb, rattling off something in Turkish to the bellman, which resulted in us butting ahead to snatch the next taxi.

"What did you say?" I asked, sliding into the seat.

"That we were meeting government officials and couldn't be late."

"And are we meeting government officials?"

"Of course! These events are infested with them." She leaned forward and barked instructions to the driver before sitting back in the seat and patting my hand. "Calm down, Phoebe. You'll be fine. I won't let anyone eat you up. You do look a bit out of sorts. Just stick with me and smile."

The International Rare Textile and Ethnographic Exposition gala was being held in a building on the Topkapi Palace grounds. The invitations cost a hefty $500 in equivalent US dollars and were issued only to two hundred people per year. How Max made it to such an esteemed list, I'd never know.

My thrill mounted as we climbed from the cab to join a gathering milling about in front of armed guards. The sight of so many glorious costumes, both women and men swathed in silks and embroidery, thrilled me until the sight of gun-bearing men shot down my glee. And Noel planned to meet me in this armed fortress? It seemed crazy. On the other hand, here was an event where disguise and costume were nearly synonymous, making it a brilliant plan.

"Semi-automatic weapon seem a bit of overkill, no pun intended," I whispered to my companion.

"We're about to enter a venerable palace housing a fortune worth of priceless historical and religious artifacts. Feather dusters and slingshots would hardly have the desired effect. Just don't try stealing anything."

The Topkapi palace, home of the Ottomans for 400 years, naturally had armed guards. I just wasn't expecting so many, all looking as though infractions would be dealt with swiftly and probably at the end of a gun.

"Above all else, we are not to leave the prescribed area allocated to the event," Eva informed me, reading from a brochure we'd been handed as we waited in line outside the gates. "Which happens to be the royal harem this year, with some exhibits situated in the Imperial Hall. Oh, very good. One year, they piled us all in the Grand Kiosk, lovely with its view of the Bosporus and Marmara Sea, but a bit cramped. Here we go. Have your invitation in hand."

I did, watching as a guard inspected the card, checked me off on his computer, and passed me a name tag embellished like an Isnik tile strung at the end of a silken cord. Dropping it over my head, I noted with satisfaction the play of pattern and color against my tunic. I fervently hoped I'd glimpse those famed tiles that very night.

When it came to Eva, the guard hesitated. "Dr. Yilmaz?"

"That's correct."

I looked at her in amazement as the guard studied his computer. "It says here that Dr. Yilmaz is deceased."

"Also correct. There were once two and now only one. I am the Dr. Eva Yilmaz component. As you can see, I am still among the living. You can check your database going back two decades or more and find that I have attended many such events with my late husband. We were both doctors of archaeology. Obviously your current information requires an update."

"I apologize, Dr. Yilmaz. Please proceed." He passed her a name tag, which she pocketed quickly. In a moment she had waded ahead of me in the line.

I caught up to her standing in the next queue. "Dr. Yilmaz?" I whispered.

"My married name. I use either one or the other as it suits me."

"I didn't realize you had been married."

"Why would you? He was a renown Turkish archaeologist and a great man but that point didn't arise in our conversation. I, however, have fallen out of favor in Turkey so prefer to flash his name wherever possible, lest they block my entrance. Borek had a standing invitation; I do not. More later. Look ahead. We're entering the gates."

Questions took second place to my mounting excitement. Here I was about to visit the Topkapi Palace, or at least part of it, and not with thousands of visitors but as part of a small group of special guests. Feeling honored, I followed the other attendees through a double-turreted gatehouse that could have been the model for Disney's fairy castle, only authentic struck me as far more enchanting. Spotlights illuminated the venerable stone overhead as we passed through.

"The Gate of Salutation. Be prepared for a pat-down," Eva told me. "Security here will make Heathrow seem like a walk in the mall."

I spread my arms as a woman guard ran a metal detector up and down my limbs, remaining comfortable and relaxed right up until a guard at the next checkpoint demanded I pass over my carpet bag for the evening.

"What, why? Can't you just x-ray it and pass it back?"

"No bags permitted inside the grounds," the man explained. "We keep here."

Eva sidled up to me. "It's all right, Phoebe. They stand over them all evening like pit bulls with guns for teeth. It will be perfectly secure. What do you have in there that you can't part with? Nothing too valuable, I hope."

"My knitting."

The guard, who was performing a manual inspection of the contents, paused to lift out my project, which I'd carefully bundled and secured with my bamboo needles. He held it aloft like a fibrous octopus, the little balls of colored yarn dangling around his hands in woolly tentacles. "Please be careful."

He handled my project with the respect afforded to small furry animals and carefully tucked it back into my satchel. After placing the bag on a shelf behind him, he handed me a check tag.

"Impressive piece, from what I could see," Eva remarked. "I'm a hooker myself. Never could make good with those sticks."

"I keep forgetting that knitting needles second as dangerous implements to security folks. I might try stealing a jewel-encrusted sword by wielding a bamboo stick. Anyway, what did you do that keeps you from using Dr. Friedrich tonight?"

"Long story, Phoebe. I'll explain all another time. We must stay with these last stragglers."

Along with about eighteen others, we formed the last group admitted into the grounds before the gates closed. After that, I guessed guests would be turned away whether they were ticket-holders or not. Nobody I saw could be either my brother or Noel, regardless of attire, both men being over six feet tall. As for Maggie, the three women in our group were definitely shorter and wider than she.

We proceeded into a courtyard where lights and lanterns glowed among the gardens as if the stars themselves had entangled in the foliage. Music and the scent of roses and night jasmine infused the air. I fell under the spell, thinking how this moment, this symphony of the senses, must have been similar to what an Ottoman courtier experienced hundreds of years ago. All I wanted was to still myself in the moment and capture the swish of perfumed silks.

"You can almost imagine the sultan taking his pick-of-the-night concubine for a stroll around the gardens, can't you?" Eva asked.

I catapulted back to earth. "Oh, I forgot about that—the harem. Yes, I can picture it perfectly: the sultan strolling arm-in-arm with one of his many beautiful concubines, selected from his harem like the choicest chocolate from a box of delectables, all splendor amid roses and lamplight." I sighed loudly. "Only women as sexual slaves is a real mood spoiler for me. Being a member of the ruling gender in the Ottoman Empire must have seemed like a male fairy tale."

"Pardon me but I must interrupt. I see you completely misconstrue the sultan's responsibilities," a male voice interjected. Eva and I turned to find a man in a dark tuxedo walking beside us. Of middle height and age with closely cropped gray-streaked hair and matching mustache brushing his upper lip, he gazed across at me with a slight supercilious smile.

Though he had stood out as we entered the palace in the way of a black-clad crow amid a flock of extravagant tropical birds, I hadn't noticed him in the last 15 minutes. "Excuse my interruption but I couldn't help overhearing. I am Mr. Attar Demir, Director of Ottoman Studies and adviser to the Topkapi Palace historical review."

I extended my hand. "Please to meet your acquaintance." Before I could introduce myself, he continued. "Ottoman sultans actually lived quite a tedious life sequestered in their luxury. Sitting day after day, hour after hour, hearing the tedium of plaintiffs in his audience chamber, without the freedom afforded the simpler man."

"Poor guy," I said with little conviction.

"Yes, and where is the glory in such?" Mr. Demir said. "As for the harem—a little-understood but necessary feature of a culture that must assure the sanctity of the royal lineage at all costs—many sultans rotated among the harem to ensure that each woman be afforded the same opportunity to carry his seed, a great honor at the time. Therefore, not selected like 'choicest chocolate' at all."

Eva snorted behind her veil and positioned herself between me and Mr. Demir. "You mean it was more like a salmon fertilizing spawn."

"No so at all!" humphed Mr. Demir.

"No, of course not—my apologies. Salmon mass fertilize, whereas the sultan had to do it sequentially, night after night, that is, if he chose. How tedious, indeed."

Mr. Demir's face had assumed the hue of a ripening pomegranate. "My point is that women of the harem lived a far richer life than the poorer classes. Most considered it a step up in circumstances to be pressed into the Sultan's service."

"Slavery was considered better than being under the control of a poorer man?" I asked, leaning towards Mr. Demir.

"Women were not totally powerless in the Ottoman world. The mother of the sultan, for instance, exercised considerable influence in politics whether she came from slavery or not. Concubines of the sultan rose in rank according to ability."

"Influence is not true power, Demir. It is pleading and whispering and wheedling and persuasion, manipulation being often the only power women have been afforded historically," Eva stated.

Mr. Demir leaned towards my companion. "Eva Yilmaz, is that you under there? How could I mistake the tone?"

"It's still Doctor Eva Yilmaz, Demir."

"I am surprised to find you here, Eva. I thought you had retired and returned to London in a fitting resolution to the unfortunate incidents of the past."

Eva brushed aside her veil, revealing a reddened face with eyes sparking fiercely. "As much as I would enjoy revisiting old arguments on the interpretation of social and cultural mores in a historic context, my friend and I have come to have a jolly good time. Good night to you. Come along, Phoebe." She linked arms with me and steered me ahead of the group towards a long building ablaze with lights.

"An old sparring partner?"

"Indeed, but not one of the more pleasant ones. Never liked him but I wish I had kept my mouth shut instead of announcing my presence like that. Soon every officious little personage at this event will know I've returned."

"Returned to Istanbul, you mean?"

"To Turkey, the land of my passion."

"You prefer to go incognito?"

"As much as possible, indeed."

"Why's that?"

"Later, Phoebe. I promise to explain everything soon."

"I see you have a lot of water running under your bridge."

"In truth, a veritable storm drain. Come, let's join the melee."

We proceeded across the broad grounds surrounded by elegant buildings and tall trees, the uniformed guards replaced now by men dressed in the imperial uniform of former times—baggy white pants gathered into boots, long gold tunics, and tall, conical hats.

The men were positioned along a paved boulevard that led to a set of porticoes gracing a richly tiled exterior. My eyes flickered across tiles patterned in blue, white, and gold leaf as we stepped between the guards wearing yet another century's uniforms and on into a long room dazzling with more pattern and color. This country made my senses drunk.

Past the glittering wonder, I sought Noel but saw no one with his height and bearing. Where would he expect to rendezvous?

"Here is the gilded cage wherein those lucky women lived out their lives," Eva remarked. "The building houses 400 rooms and apartments surrounding a central courtyard where women could dally away their days waiting to catch one man's eye."

"How delightful," I remarked, feasting on the colors. "And they'd be warded by eunuchs, I suppose?"

"Absolutely. All male slaves lucky enough to hold this trusted position were relieved of their genitalia."

"Seems like a fair trade." I gazed around, seeking tall men in costume. I would enjoy nothing better than the sight of Noel Halloran dressed as a eunuch but doubted even his sense of irony would prevail there. Since a sultan probably selected the tallest and the strongest male slaves from many lands, Noel could easily pass as a guard.

The guests had donned a stunning array of costumes from various centuries, all resplendent as they milled about the long hall, sipping drinks and chatting while a quartet played in one of the side niches. Only a handful wore suits and modern attire, while most appeared to have plunged into the spirit of the evening, a celebration of Turkish historical dress across the ages.

My eyes glossed over the glory, resting on several sultans and pashas dressed in big pillowy hats festooned with jewels and feathers. Many women wore long gowns, some with short jackets typical of the last days of the Ottoman Empire, while others donned veils or displayed their faces below tall, fez-like headgear.

Everything sparkled, shone, and glowed against the background of intricate tiles and fabulous fabrics. Color scrolled in patterns, entwined in images, and gleamed across tiles along with silk, wool, and velvet. Forget minimalist. Here, no white space prevailed, or so I thought.

At first, all I could do was stand and stare, trying to bear up under the sensual assault until I glimpsed a few men in long white robes sailing through the gathering. Some wore tall camel-colored hats, while others wore skull caps, but all appeared like snowy pages weaving through an illuminated manuscript.

"Eva, who are those men in white?"

"They are traditional Muslims who more closely follow the path of Mohammed while those in the shorter white robes with the tall felt hats are from the Mevlevi order, more commonly known as the Whirling Dervishes or Sufis."

"The Sufis as in Rumi? I have heard of them."

"I do wonder if they are here as costume or if the order will be giving us one of their mystic dances? Oh, I do hope so. The Mevlevi are quite wonderful. They embrace love in the way of Rumi, and their dancing closely aligns with the sacred feminine practices of ancient Greece and beyond where dancing awakens the sacred communion. Of all Islamic sects, Sufism above all focuses on love, tolerance, and the elimination of personal ego."

"Are there women Sufis?"

"Not in the true sense but many women practice in secret. Islam, like all the major religions, doesn't permit women access to the higher spiritual orders, since we apparently have inferior souls or no souls at all, much the same in other religious practices. I have had many engaging conversations with Sufis, and there is much agreement among them that women have been excluded, not by the word of God but by the dictates of man."

I found myself staring at one of the men in the tall tan hats as he wove through the gathering, his back to me still, nodding at the guests along the way. He towered over everyone in stature, but the addition of the foot-high hat only made him seem like a moving turret. Something about his slow ambling stride seemed familiar.

"Phoebe." Eva touched my sleeve, "Come, I'd like you to meet an old friend."

I was reluctant to tear my gaze away, but Eva urged me forward towards a woman standing by the wall fountain dressed in a dark blue velvet robe trimmed in what looked like real fur. She turned to Eva quizzically as if not recognizing her at first, her wide almond-shaped eyes searching and intelligent.

"Talya, it's so good to see you again. It's me, Eva."

"Eva, Eva Yilmaz? Is that really you?"

"It is," Eva exclaimed, throwing back her veil. "I'd like you to meet my friend, Phoebe McCabe, here for the exhibition. Phoebe, this is Dr. Talya Beren, Director of the Turkish Costume division of the Museum of Islamic Art."

We shook hands, Talya's smile genuine and warm. "So happy you could join us, Phoebe. But dear Eva, I thought we might never see you again. You have been so quiet and I have missed you."

"My work keeps me busy, Talya, but I have been coming to Turkey off and on across the years, just not on official business. I've been keeping low to the ground. You know I would never be kept away so easily."

She nodded. "I know it well and would have been very disappointed had it been otherwise. We need more scholars of your ilk. Did you know that we have an Anatolian Goddess kilim on display tonight?"

Eva grinned. "Of course. This is why I am here and to accompany Phoebe, of course. Where is she?"

"I will show you. Follow me."

We left the crowded hall, bypassing the servants bearing trays of food and drinks, making our way through several rooms and down a hall guarded by men in more period uniforms until we reached a long corridor where the walls appeared paved by textiles under glass. Only a few guests stood admiring the exhibition.

"Oh," I gasped, drinking in the sight of antique rugs encased on either side. I yearned to soak up the detail of every textile, read every description, not rush a single moment, but Eva and Talya strode purposefully down the length of the corridor. I followed them to stop before a single kilim suspended as if in midair behind the glass.

"Behold, the best preserved of the Anatolian Goddess kilims to my knowledge," Talya announced. "I knew you'd want to see this one. If you hadn't come, I would have sent you a photograph."

Upon an indigo background, intersecting triangles with hooked extensions worked in rust, white, and cream wool, occupied the center field with banding flanks of hands-on-hips motifs in black and rust. Each motif mirrored the one below in double symmetry. Not as anthropomorphic as my kilim, the motifs only echoed my goddess without equaling her power, but it was still a stunning specimen.

I turned to Eva, finding her staring fixed at the kilim, hands pressed to her lips. "Eva?"

"There She is, Phoebe, my goddess, caught within the weave. Isn't She amazing?"

"She is," I agreed.

"I simply must inspect the back. Talya, please inform whomever is in charge that I must inspect the reverse of the kilim immediately."

My gaze caught Talya's, who turned away as if embarrassed or anxious or both. "That's not possible Eva, not tonight or probably at any other time, though I'd certainly be pleased to submit a request on your behalf."

"Why must I endure the tedium of a long wait when it would be easy to grant me this simple request in a timely manner? I am a scholar and deserving of such courtesy."

"Of course you are. It's just that it's a very rare piece—"

"Of course it's a very rare piece," Eva said, her voice rising. "Am I not partially responsible for assisting Turkey in recognizing the value of such kilims? Has my research been totally undermined; is that what you're implying?"

"I'm implying nothing of the sort. I'm only explaining that we have certain rules and regulations in place to protect our art and that immediately dismantling an exhibition on the spot at the request of one person, no matter how esteemed, is not practical. We keep it in a sealed environment for conservation reasons, you must understand that."

"But you must understand that somewhere in Anatolia at this very moment, unscrupulous thieves may be robbing a site connected to this kilim. All proof of the significance of this motif may be destroyed along with precious artifacts. It is imperative that I see the reverse now so that I can best assist the authorities to find this sacred site."

"Eva, you are not permitted to engage in archaeological activities in this country. You know this."

"You don't understand, Talya." Eva pressed her palm against the glass.

"Eva, don't! The sensors—"

A guard stepped forward, shouting: "Madam, stop!"

An alarm ripped the air just as I glanced down the hall and caught sight of the tall Sufi standing no more than 50 yards away—unmistakable face, arresting eyes, bone structure, and expression, watching me. I cried out and lunged down the hall, guards streaming past me in the opposite direction. Once at the door, he had disappeared.

The alarm blared relentlessly. Behind me, chaos erupted as Eva called out something in Turkish and both Talya's and the guards' voices joined the fracas.

I caught a glimpse of a white robe heading rapidly towards the harem main hall and bolted after him, eyes fixed on the tall hat bobbing above the heads of the guests.

He was exiting a side door to the grounds. Pushing my way through, I burst out into an unfamiliar lantern-lit courtyard and circled the fountain calling his name.

Turning in all directions looking for some sight of him, I finally caught a flash of white out of the corner of my eye. In seconds I was bounding across the garden towards the ghostly swirl of white skirts, oblivious of the guard calling out behind me.

I didn't tackle him so much as reach out to slow him down. In so doing, I grabbed his arm, which caused him to stop so suddenly that I whammed into him. He lost his balance, the force pitching us both into the rose bushes, me on top. Everything blurred. I only recall the guards lifting me off the holy man, who lay on his back in a probable state of shock. As he unfolded himself and climbed to his feet, I found myself staring at a much shorter man, a man who was definitely not Noel.

Two guards pointed rifles at me.

"Don't shoot! It's only mistaken identity!"

17

Eva and I sat together in my hotel room, she in the only chair and me perching on the bed opposite. We had hardly spoken since being escorted off the Topkapi Palace premises and forbidden to return, our passes revoked, both unceremoniously bundled into a cab and banished from the gala.

"If it weren't for Talya, we'd be in jail right now. Or, in my case, probably shot," I said, breaking the silence. "I don't know what she told those guards in the end but I swear she took our necks out of the noose."

"Yes," Eva said in a flat voice. "She insisted we were both mentally unstable and petitioned our release accordingly. Why would anyone take a pair of crazy women seriously?"

"Well, really, what did we do that was such an act of insanity? You touched a glass case while demanding an exhibited item be inspected by you on the spot, while I accidentally accosted a holy man. In an unauthorized part of the grounds," I added before stifling a laugh. Eva's appearance soon sobered me.

She sat, hands between her knees, staring at the floor. Somehow her red dress had been ripped, leaving the headdress dangling down her back by its shredded veil. Though her knitted Turkish slippers remained intact, for the first time I noticed they had been pulled over sneakers. If mentally unstable were a look, I thought guiltily, she'd nailed it.

"Your dress is ripped. Maybe I can try to repair it? I have scissors and thread somewhere."

"It was once my wedding dress long ago, so long ago. Thank you for the offer but I will just retire it as it is."

I got up and untied the veil, unwinding it gently from her neck and laying the ruined hat in her lap. "It's too special to leave ruined. It's symbolic and laden with memories."

"Perhaps."

"Everybody believed we were crazy readily enough, didn't they? The wacky Canadian attacking a Sufi accompanied by the retired archaeologist demanding to inspect a museum display," I said, gazing down at the top of the gray hair.

"I'm not retired, whatever they may think. Passion and commitment do not get old. It is because I spoke in an authoritative manner that they assume I must be unhinged. How dare I? If I still bore my previous title, they might grant me some measure of respect but, once stripped of that, I became nothing more than a mere self-important old woman. Why must becoming older relegate women to irrelevance?" Her gaze remained fixed on the carpet, but her tone now bristled with its usual energy. "Why must passion be suspect?"

"Woman should be seen as a sum of everything we were and are rather than as diminishing according to our biology."

"Sexual attraction is the measure by which society weighs us. Once, long ago, the old were revered, not marginalized. Perhaps, if enough of us refuse to be devalued, you just might inhabit a different world thirty years from now, Phoebe."

"In the meantime, I'd rather be a free crazy female than an imprisoned sane one any day. Would you like tea or something else to drink?"

"Thank you, no."

"How about something from the mini bar? We have to re-establish our dignity somehow. Chocolate helps." I opened the refrigerator door to assess the contents. "No chocolate here. Not a Turkish thing, I guess. Ugh, potato chips just won't do—too flaky. We need something rich and nuanced with flavor, much like ourselves. Wait, how about Turkish delight?" When Eva didn't answer, I shook the tiny ornate tin appreciatively, flipped the lid, and offered her contents.

"They all think I'm crazy," she said finally, plucking a piece of paper-wrapped jelly from the tin. "Mad, totally mad. How dare I enter that event and stomp and puff and make demands?" She looked across at me. "They don't listen, refuse to understand, and yet it was me, not Borek, who revealed the significance of the goddess motifs all those years ago. He found the site but I provided the overlay of significance."

"Why don't they know that?"

Eva sighed deeply, gazing out to space. "We had an agreement, Borek and I, the details of which are too complicated to explain tonight. Even then, I was too vehement in my convictions. A scholar must be stripped of passion and speak only from the intellect while remaining well-buttressed by concrete facts and citations. My facts are rather thin on the ground and I could not reveal the location, details the government demanded for other reasons. As a result, I fell into disgrace."

"Well," I said, returning to my perch and selecting a candy for myself. "We're safe now."

"Why did you jump the Sufi?"

"I didn't jump the Sufi. Eva, that sounds so judgmental."

"My apologies. Judgment is not my intention, I assure you."

"I kind of fell into him, really, because I thought he was someone else."

"You thought you recognized him?" Eva's eyes fixed on me, suddenly alert.

"I saw a man dressed as a Sufi earlier and I recognized him at once as somebody I needed to speak with. Even in the disguise, he was unmistakable. I might have finally got the answers I needed, but the alarm went off. Again." I studied the Turkish delight moments before taking the first bite. Pistachio and cherry. After chewing reflectively for a few seconds, I added: "Only, how did he get in? What's he up to in Istanbul, anyway, besides hiding, I mean?"

"Perhaps he also came to see the kilim at the exhibition?"

I turned, studying her as she studied me. "What is it about the kilim that is so interesting? Sure, I get the link to some anthropological marvel but there's something you're not telling me."

"The kilim will help us find something lost that must be regained at all costs."

"A tribe of women clinging to an ancient fertility sect?"

"That in itself would be enough."

"To an archaeologist, perhaps. The company this archaeologist keeps will be interested in something more marketable." I replaced the half-eaten piece of Turkish delight into its paper wrapper.

"Perhaps."

"When are you going to fill me in on all the details?"

"All will unfold as it should, regardless, for you are about the Goddess's business."

I shook my head vigorously. "I am not about the Goddess's business. Please stop saying that. I am here to purchase kilims for my shop and, yes, to find the person who sent me that kilim and his … friends."

"The Goddess sent it to you."

Maybe she was crazy. "The Goddess did not send me that kilim. I'm sure it had more to do with low-life vices like greed and avarice than any higher power."

"We are all part of a greater plan, Phoebe, our lives intersecting and entangling far beyond our understanding or awareness. We think we act independently when, in fact, our lives are but threads in the Goddess's loom. If I said God instead of Goddess would my words make more sense to you?"

"I would better understand your religious fervor, yes."

"Then substitute 'God' for 'Goddess', if you must. Continue to live in the patriarchal view of the world. When you can take a broader view, ask yourself how a Universal Spirit can be relegated to a gender?"

I looked away, confused. These spiritual proclamations left me reeling. No wonder her colleagues had lost confidence in her capabilities—an archaeologist muttering about goddesses? At the same time, everything she said had a ring of truth like a clear bell chiming in the wilderness so far away I could barely hear.

"That candy was just way too sweet for me this late at night." I tossed the half-eaten piece into the wastebasket and yawned. "Anyways, it's late and I need to get to bed. Are you okay to get home by yourself? Where are you staying, by the way?"

"I'm staying with my brother-in-law and his family not far away. I'll take a cab but, Phoebe," she reached across the distance between us and grasped my arm, "first let me see the kilim. I know you brought it with you. She would not let you leave it behind."

"She? Oh, you mean the Goddess." I hesitated, worried that the kilim might ignite another rant but wanting to comfort her any way I could. What harm would it be to show her the kilim? "Wait here," I said.

I left her standing by the bed as I strode around the corner to the short hall leading up to the door. Opening the closet, I crouched, tapping in the numbers for the digital safe. Relieved to find everything just as I left it, I pulled out my kilim like a sleeping baby.

Eva stood directly behind me, gaze fixed on my bundle.

"I asked you to wait," I said.

"I have waited far too long." She held out both hands as if in readiness to receive a holy child.

I brushed past her, returning to the bed to carefully unfold the kilim across the cover, Eva following me like a puppy. "I have to say, this specimen is much more impressive than the one we saw tonight." I said as I spread the textile open. "Look at it. So beautiful!" It never failed to impress me.

"Oh," Eva fell to her knees, in prayer, I thought momentarily, but, no, instead she gently turned the piece over and bent her head to study the back. A monocle-style magnifying glass appeared from somewhere—she carried one in her pocket?—and now traveled the kilim's reverse pressed to one eye. "Yes!" she muttered amid strings of Turkish.

"Is it what you expected?"

"No, yes! More, much more." The monocle dropped from her eye as she turned her sharp blue eyes to me. "Phoebe, I think I know where this originated."

"Really?"

"I can identify the exact area in Anatolia where the kilim was woven. See this," she pointed to a tuft of rusty wool that sprouted around the frayed parts. "Turkish red was developed by using madder root mixed with sheep's blood. Typically, the yarn was steeped, mixed with dung and olive oil, and steeped again, usually finished off with gall nut solution, which has a high level of tannic acid. However, sometimes whole forests were wiped out in wildfires, resulting in dyers needing to source alternative mordants through experimentation."

Despite the sudden switch to lecture mode, she fingered the tuft lovingly. "One such fire whipped across the steppes of a certain region in Anatolia three hundred years ago, destroying grasslands, forests, and nearly the entire village. The weavers thereafter needed to source alternate mordants in a region devastated by fire, resulting in an inferior dye that turned rusty brown rather than remaining red in the ensuing years. Hence, this kilim's striking discoloration."

She could flick from fevered to scholarly in seconds. "Fascinating," I remarked and meant it, but weariness had taken hold and I just wanted to go to bed. "Do you want to take pictures of it or something before you go?"

Eva turned back to study the kilim for a long moment. Sighing, she climbed to her feet and retrieved the monocle from the floor. "I suppose it would be useless to implore you to let me take the kilim for safekeeping?"

"Totally."

"And yet you must recognize that its value far exceeds even its museum worth and should be under better protection than a hotel safe? Any employee could access that safe with a little finagling."

"I'm not letting it go. It was given to me for a reason."

"And so it was. The Goddess has entrusted you with its care. If you won't, in turn, entrust it to me, then I beseech you to come with me to Anatolia to find the village of its origin. Help me find what's lost."

"Explain exactly what you mean by what's lost?"

"It's a very long story, best told when we have much time, which is currently not the case. Come with me, Phoebe."

"No." I didn't mean to sound so abrupt but I was tired of her mystic references and just wanted answers, preferably served in block print. "I mean, thank you for the offer but I simply can't. I'm here to find what's lost, too, but I'm looking for something of the human variety, and when I find them, I plan to serve up some very ungoddess-like retribution. Besides, I have a few more errands to run here in Istanbul and then I must return to London. I have a gallery to manage and just too many loose ends to go on a road trip."

Eva sighed. "Very well, but don't be surprised if the Goddess sends you in unexpected directions. My cell number is at the bottom of the card I left on the bed. Call me when you change your mind."

"What do you mean by when? I won't change my mind," I said while holding the door.

She gathered up her ruined fez, stuffed the veil into her bag, and strode towards me. "The Goddess may change it for you."

18

"Serena?" I pressed my iPhone against my ear as I backed up against a low wall. Behind me lay a strange octagonal building the guide book didn't identify, while ahead, a lovely park. I'd already seen Sir Foxy's limo coasting along the streets. Luckily there'd been no place for him to pull over. Though I kept his phone off, I did wave a couple of times.

"Phoebe! I have been so worried—no call, no emails! Say you are too busy to phone me every hour but that everything is so fantastic."

"I'm too busy to call you every hour, maybe even every day, Serena. I just haven't had a moment to call. I have a few errands to run and then I'll be home soon. Everything is so fantastic as in impossible to believe. More on that when I get home. I'm supposed to leave the day after tomorrow, which isn't too far away. Is everything good at the shop?"

"Everything is fine. You must not worry about a thing."

"Oh, good." I kneaded my neck muscles with my spare hand. "And Agent Walker?"

"Nothing—no shocked eyebrow, no shiny head."

"I expected him to be haunting you, pressing for details. I just don't get that guy."

"Be glad he is elsewhere chasing real criminals, yes? But the exhibition, tell me, was it is as magnificent as you hoped?"

"Oh, yes, the exhibition certainly exceeded every expectation." Thoughts of that fiasco hit me like a taser. "I'll tell you all about it once I'm home."

Then my burner phone began ringing. "Rena, I've got to go. I'm standing on a street and it's crazy here. I'll talk soon." I clicked off and tossed one phone into the bag while scrambling around for the other. Precious seconds were squandered finding the right one, and I ended up pressing TALK mere seconds before the call disconnected.

"Hello?"

"Mademoiselle? Il est Madame a la Chanel."

"Oui!" I turned my back on the street traffic to better hear.

She told me in hurried French that Madame St.Remis had just called to confirm that she would be picking up her order within the hour. Could I come over immediately?

"I'll be there waiting outside. Please don't give me away," I said in French. The prospects of finally cornering Maggie excited me so much, I could barely contain myself—the hunter closing in on prey, so often stalked; finally I was the hunter.

Scrambling to the curb to hail a taxi, it suddenly occurred to me that I couldn't track Maggie with my red hair blazing or risk Foxy tagging along. Subterfuge was critical. Luckily, the perfect disguise was an easy find.

I slipped into a small shopping arcade wedged between two large buildings. After scouting a few shops, I located one catering to traditional Turkish working women and hastily purchased a headscarf, or hijab, and a long navy trench coat.

The shop attendant smiled but asked no questions when a western woman burst into her shop requesting traditional attire to wear over jeans. Her graciousness extended to assisting me with the proper application of the headscarf. She explained in excellent English how the wearing of the hijab had once been banned but now reinstated by the present government. I gathered that this arrangement satisfied her, but I did nothing to encourage details. Precious minutes were ticking by. Supposing Maggie picked up her loot in minutes and went on her way?

Upon exiting the shop, I realized my biggest signature was slung over my shoulder. That bag offended Maggie in every category of mandatory chicness. In desperation, I bought a large cheapo backpack from a street vendor and shoved my carpet bag inside. That done, I was ready for stalking.

I hailed a cab and explained to the driver that I needed him to wait outside a shopping arcade while I went into a store. His English was good but my explanation complex. He needed to wait but be ready to drive really fast once I came out. "Why you not call another cab when finished?" he asked. I assured him that wasn't possible but I'd pay him well. We struck a deal and I climbed into the car.

"Bad traffic always," he said as we pulled into the stream of cars and began weaving across town. No sign of Foxy's black limo followed.

"Yes, I can see that." I sank against the seat. What would I do when I finally tracked her down? I always did best thinking on my feet even if it meant breaking a limb along the way. I meant that literally since I still bore the scars on my leg from my last burst of impulse.

"You married Turkish?" the driver asked.

"Pardon?" Oh, I realized, he referred to the hijab. "Yes. Engaged," I told him. "My soon-to-be husband is from Istanbul." I scrambled to embellish further. "I must keep the mother-in-law happy." I nodded and smiled.

He gazed at me in his rear view mirror, his expression puzzled. "You will be Muslim?"

"Ah, no. I don't know," I said, flustered. Why would a western woman wear a hijab if she wasn't converting to Islam?

"My wife wears hijab. I not force but her father, he say she must."

"But does she want to?" I asked, avoiding asking why either a husband or a father had the right to dictate a grown woman's choices.

"She wants to keep peace. She is good woman."

Did that mean she'd be a bad woman if she didn't please her father? This thinking was so foreign to me but, as a guest in another world, I sealed my lips.

I had to admit, the anonymity of the hijab and trench coat suited my purposes. If not for my pale complexion, I could have blended in with the Istanbul street population. Many women wore the hijab here. Those who didn't, brandished their individuality, relaxed and open, while others found artful ways to wear their hijab and still be fashionable. Despite my unease at wearing Muslim clothing, I preferred not to advertise myself as an obvious outsider, either.

When we reached the arcade, I paid him up to that point and explained again that I needed him to wait. By then, I knew him as Mr. Burek.

"But no stopping here," he pointed out. "No place to wait."

"Could you drive around the corner? I will be back, I promise. No, better still, I'll call you." He nodded his agreement and I took his phone number, entering it into my speed dial as he drove away.

I slipped into the shoppers strolling the arcade. With my head down, my backpack over my shoulders, I headed towards the Chanel shop. Nobody gave me a second glance.

I approached the shop, standing just outside the plate glass window, studying my cell phone while covertly glancing inside. I couldn't see a thing from that vantage, but I couldn't risk entering, either. My solution was to slip across the promenade and stand against a wall, watching, the cell phone as my ruse.

Humans fixed on a tiny screen was the new norm worldwide. I watched and waited, pretending to be texting. So many minutes passed that I was certain I had either missed Maggie or she was very late. Either way, I couldn't stand there all day. Eventually, even a forever-texting woman would look conspicuous.

Then a man in dark blue trousers, a white shirt, and tie, wearing a peaked hat, stepped from the shop and lit a cigarette. He leisurely paced outside the store, his gaze slipping across me without interest. A security guard taking a break?

I stood, flicking through my iPhone photos and re-reading email for what seemed ages while covertly watching. When his phone jangled, he ground out his cigarette under his shoe, and slipped back into the store, exiting moments later burdened with black boxes and Chanel shopping bags. Head down, he rapidly dashed off down the street.

Seconds later, out swept a shapely woman, coiffed with shiny black hair seemingly shellacked to her scalp. Her lips slicked brilliant red above a priestly white-collared black jacket belted over a pencil skirt. It was a startling juxtaposition of wanton severity and so Maggie, the fashion slave, paying homage to couture.

I watched her five-inch heels peck the ground like foraging fowl as she proceeded down the arcade in the direction of the man.

The sight erupted a fire storm in me so strong, I wanted to shove her to the ground, wipe that gash of lipstick from her mouth, and shake her until her eyes bulged. Instead, I fell in among the pedestrians behind her, clenching my teeth. She would not escape me this time.

We emerged onto another road, heavy with traffic, all one-way, but I couldn't see a street name anywhere. I pressed the speed dial and waited for the cab driver to answer while Maggie darted across the street to a limousine.

My call got snagged in a telecommunications loop. An automated voice fired away in Turkish. I hadn't done something necessary to connect with an international call. Blah blah. Several clicks followed in quick succession until a London operator asked how she could help.

Maggie's black car slipped away from the curb while I barked frenzied orders to the operator, who coolly informed me that I needed to add the Turkish country code to my number and, if I'd provide the number, she'd connect my call. Only, I didn't have the number, seeing as my phone was currently pressed against my ear and Maggie was getting away.

Then, incredibly, blessedly, I saw Mr. Burek on a sidewalk ahead, smoking outside his car while chatting to a minivan driver. I sprinted up to him and gesticulated towards the speck of black car stuck in traffic. "Follow that car!"

Startled, he stared where my finger pointed. "Like the movies?"

"Yes, hurry, please!"

He tossed away his cigarette and leaped into the driver's seat while I dispensed with formality and climbed in beside him. "I must catch that woman! She's my aunt but I haven't been able to call." I waved my phone. "No connection, you know?"

Mr. Burek, nodded, intent on keeping the black car in his sights as we merged into a four-lane road. We proceeded along a broad avenue graced by large white buildings, apartment complexes, and a lovely mosque. "Suleyman Seba Caddesi," he said.

I had no idea what he referred to, so fixed was I on keeping Maggie in view. We wove in and out of traffic, losing the limousine only to have it reappear moments later as a bus passed or a corner straightened into another boulevard. We entered a curving road that wove through a park.

"Yildiz Park," Mr. Burek told me.

"Okay."

Now we were on a divided highway running parallel to the Bosporus. Yachts and large pleasure craft bobbed on the blue water while parkland and grand houses occupied the opposite side. The limo took a left-hand turn, diving under an overpass and across the highway to the parkland.

We hit a traffic light and ground to a halt. Mr. Burek seemed unconcerned. "Slow traffic among houses," he remarked. "Your aunt must be very rich."

"Very." Pulling out my iPhone, I opened my Google map app and dropped a pin on our current location so I could follow our route on the map.

When finally we caught a glimpse of the limo slowing down on a tree-lined hill in front of us, I cautioned the driver to stay back and pull to the side.

"I can drive right up," he offered.

"No, it's okay. I want this to be a surprise." And it would be a big one. I saved the location on the map and pocketed the phone.

I hastily paid Mr. Burek, thanking him profusely and adding a generous tip. He pulled away, leaving me standing on a deeply shaded hill, the trees framing the Bosporus behind me and secluding grand houses all around.

I began to climb, keeping beside the tall manicured hedge. The limo had turned into a driveway ahead, and when I reached the spot, it was no shock to find an ornate gate locked against intruders. Peering through the iron bars, I saw a tiny guard house positioned beside a curving driveway that disappeared amid the foliage. Though the gatehouse appeared unoccupied, the camera beside the intercom didn't encourage lingering.

I left the gate and slipped along the hedge until I found a break wide enough for me to squeeze through. All that got me was a scraped cheek, and a view through the fence at broad rolling lawn.

There had to be an alarm system rigged with all kinds of fancy burglar detection devices here, not to mention employees. I burrowed deeper into the hedge until I could better peek through the rails. A white three-story mansion with wraparound balconies, tall arched windows, and green lawns abloom with flowers indicated that Maggie, possibly the whole trio, had nabbed an impressive hideaway. But how was I supposed to get in?

I backed outside the hedge, surveying the quiet street, considering my options. I almost missed the sound of an approaching car before diving back undercover just as a white van pulled up to the gate. An exchange of Turkish followed over the intercom.

I could hear the gates creaking open and counted ten seconds before leaping out behind the van and scuttling through, the gates closing behind me. I ducked behind a berry bush, adrenalin racing.

After several minutes hearing no alarms, I crawled from bush to bush until I was deep inside the garden. There I found the perfect hidey-hole: a copse of ornamental palms surrounded by banks of glossy-leaved jasmine bordering a tinkling fountain. By scooting deep into the fragrant underbrush, I could rest my back against the fence in what turned out to be a leafy little tent.

I took a few minutes to allow my heart to return to normal before leaving my bag and crawling on my hands and knees to the edge of the shrubbery. There, I found a great view of the back patio. Large French doors opened to the garden. A maid was setting a table under a kind of arabesque-style loggia with a fireplace and big comfy chairs. A manservant dashed about in a fez and short jacket, adjusting a coffee urn and setting a bouquet of flowers in the center of a white tablecloth.

I waited and watched until, at last, Maggie slipped into view. Gone was chic Chanel along with the glossy wig. In its place she had donned a long pale blue silk robe patterned with stylized tulips, her blond hair loose over her shoulders. The manservant pulled out her chair as she lowered herself down, crossed her legs, and waited while he adjusted a napkin over her lap.

In minutes, the maid appeared carrying a coffee urn and a tray of snacks that seemed to be a variety of artfully constructed vegetables. Though not close enough to see the particulars, I guessed she had ordered some near calorie-free mid-afternoon repast that could be inhaled without chewing. I nearly gagged. Maggie playing to the manor born on her stolen loot while Max drowned his broken heart.

Waiting and watching, I keened for a glimpse of Toby or Noel, but Maggie seemed alone but for her staff. She kept checking her phone for messages, looking tense because maybe someone somewhere didn't contact her when she expected.

Finally, she snapped an order to her man who leaped over to light a cigarette. Back to smoking? Bad nerves, maybe? Several minutes passed before I grew weary of watching Maggie flip from bored to frustrated while picking away at some carrot escargot or eggplant tartar. I couldn't make a move in daylight with so many people around, so my only option was to stay hidden until nightfall.

Scuttling backward, I returned to my jasmine bower, made myself comfy against the fence, and settled in to wait until nightfall. Knitting, my constant companion, kept boredom at bay.

Before resuming the ornamental stranded border which would frame my design, I positioned the project on the ground, added a sprig of jasmine, and took a photo with my iPhone—one more addition to my Knitting Exotica digital photo album. To date, I had knit in the Tower of London, on the London Eye, and in a beautiful little cove in Bermuda. Today, I would add Knitting in a Jasmine Hedge in Istanbul.

Content, I knit while working out some semblance of a plan. Something almost plausible began taking shape. With a little luck, it might actually work. Time slid by until all light drained from my bower. I checked the time at 7:45—still too early to penetrate the lair, yet too dark to continue knitting. I tucked my project back into my carpet bag, plumped the satchel behind my head, and allowed myself to drift into a doze.

When I awoke, it was cold and surprisingly dark. Sleep had left me chill and disorientated. Stiff from lying propped up with knees pressing against branches, I tried to shake myself awake by wiggling my limbs.

My iPhone registered the time as 8:45. I'd slept that long? On the other hand, the air wafted sweet jasmine and I could see lights twinkling through the foliage.

Though my stomach complained and my throat felt dry and scratchy, I had stores stashed deep in my bag. Finishing off the last of my water bottle, I dug around until I retrieved a cube of halva and an apple stashed from breakfast. By the time I'd finished eating, I was nearly alert.

I set my iPhone to the record app before shoving it into the inside breast pocket with the mute ready to deactivate. Next, I shifted the burner phone to the coat pocket and left Foxy's buried deep in my carpet bag next to the fence.

That done, I crawled on my hands and knees back to the edge of the lawn. Though the patio doors were still open with the fire burning low in the grate, the house sat blanketed in dark except for a few lights burning here and there. One by one I watched them click off as if someone were going about tucking the house in for the night. My suspicions were confirmed when I saw a maid shut an open casement on the bottom floor.

Springing from the foliage, I dashed across the lawn, diving for cover at the edge of the patio. I heard someone call out to another in Turkish, the tone along the Did you lock the front door? variety. I leapt from the bushes and kept low to the ground as I skirted the perimeter of the loggia and slipped inside the French doors.

It was a dining room with a long central table dressed in brocade and lined with a sentry of chairs. A single lamp burned on a sideboard against the wall.

Footsteps were tapping down the hall towards me. I scrambled between the forest of chair legs and overhanging tablecloth to press deep under the table. There I lowered my head to my hands and forced my breathing to still.

Footsteps clattered into the room, marching with efficiency towards the doors. I heard them click shut, the latch fastened, and the curtains slide across. The footsteps turned and started back the way they'd come but suddenly stopped. I couldn't bear to look, keeping my eyes squeezed shut and my breath shallow. Seconds ground by. I heard the maid fiddle with something, muttering under her breath. Seconds later, the light doused and I was alone.

My heart pounded in darkness so dense, I couldn't see my hands in front of me, but at least I was safe. All I had to do was wait until the staff retired for the night before proceeding with part three, or was it part four? For the most part, the house felt surprisingly empty and I sensed that Maggie occupied the residence alone but for servants.

Hopefully the motion sensors weren't engaged. Maybe Maggie was awake in her upstairs salon and wouldn't activate the security system until going to bed? Too many maybes drove me crazy.

Approximately twenty minutes later, I shuffled out from under the table and stood. I could hear nothing, see nothing. Fishing for my iPhone, I flicked it on and used the ambient screen to illuminate my way to a door which opened soundlessly onto a long hallway. Night lights positioned over wall sockets allowed me to proceed with ease.

Pocketing my phone, I carried on down the hall into a cavernous kitchen humming with electronics where various pilot lights glowed in red and amber—an espresso maker, a stove, and, a refrigerator.

The kitchen opened into another hallway, which led to a smaller dining room adjoining a lounge and a library, all grand spaces lit by tiny night lights at baseboard level. I had circumnavigated the house without finding a single stairway. On a hunch, I retraced my steps to the kitchen, where I tried yet another door, this one opening onto narrow steps heading upward, steps which I took two at a time until reaching the top.

My guess that this was a service route to the bedrooms proved right. A spacious landing overlooking a central curving staircase spanned ahead, the other side of which a bar of light glowed beneath a door.

A total of five rooms encircled the landing, all dark with the doors either ajar or closed except for one. That had to be hers. Targeting the room next door, I sprang, ducking across the hall and into the darkness, easing the door shut behind me.

Mounds of boxes and trunks loomed in the half-light gleaming from the windows. I flicked on my iPhone and beamed it across the piles. Luggage, I realized, lifting a lid and peering inside. Maggie had either just arrived or was planning a speedy getaway, probably both.

I tiptoed through the piles, my light brushing over clothes, shoes, a small carton of new cosmetics—a year's supply?-and finally halted by a map spread open over a Louis Vuitton steamer trunk. Bending in, I held the phone over its surface, following the geographical contours until I read the letters spelling ANATOLIA stretched across the terrain. I nearly dropped the damn phone.

Pocketing the phone, I crept to the adjoining door and pressed an ear against the wood. No sound. The door turned easily in my hand. A huge bedroom spread before me, all red silken pillows, quilted divans, and mirrored walls.

No Maggie in sight, but ahead two doors flanked the enormous silk tented bed; one door lay half opened revealing clothes and a vanity desk, and the other closed with a light beneath the door—the bathroom. Maggie would be immersed in her nightly bubble stew.

I padded across the wooden floor to the dressing room. Nothing but hanging clothes, stacked shoe boxes, and unopened Chanel packages, yet one dress appeared to have been freshly unsheathed and now hung on its padded hanger in a prominent position.

I unhooked the black silk from the mirrored wall and draped it over one arm before my gaze landed on exactly what I sought: Maggie's bag plunked gaping on the vanity table. I plunged my hand deep inside, fumbling until I gripped the little pistol I knew she carried everywhere the way most women carried lipstick. Pulling it out, I studied the pearl-handled Colt before hiding it under the dress.

Scanning the top of the vanity next, I spied the gold-plated antique scissors she used for snipping off tags. Pocketing those, I raced back out to the bedroom and dove for a corner chair.

There I sat, heart hammering, the dress draped over my lap, hiding gun, scissors, and phone, the latter with the recorder activated. I waited, counting the seconds to 32 before spying another bag, this one a fur-covered tote squeezed in between a lamp and a clock on her nightstand. Another bag meant another gun. No sooner had I lifted my butt to check it out, when the bathroom door flew open.

19

Maggie swept into the room in a long pink robe, hair wrapped in a towel. With her cheeks flushed and makeup-free, she seemed both older and more vulnerable than I had ever seen her before. She plucked her phone from the bed, jabbed her thumb at the screen as if checking for messages, and then tossed it back on the silken spread.

I squeezed the gun handle beneath the couture. "Isn't it aggravating when people don't do what you expect?"

"Holy shit!" She backed up against the bureau, knocking a jar to the floor. Her eyes widened. "You!"

"Me," I agreed.

"How did you get here?"

"It wasn't all that difficult."

She crossed her arms. "How did you find me?"

"Also not difficult. You leave a Chanel trail wherever you go."

"So, what do you want?"

"What do you want? You sent that goon after me, remember. If you wanted to talk so badly, I'm sure we could have arranged something. Anyway, here I am."

She looked me over as if inspecting a cockroach infestation. I pulled the pistol out from under the dress and wiggled it, thinking that might increase the intimidation factor.

Her eyes flicked from the gun to my face and smiled. "Put that down before you hurt yourself."

My grip tightened. "I appreciate your concern but I'll just hang on to it for now."

She shrugged. "You'd never pull the trigger even if you knew how."

"Are you sure about that? Noel taught me the basics of gun usage in Bermuda. I particularly recall the release-the-catch- and-pull-the-trigger part. Oh, wait—I forgot. You didn't stick around long enough to see me fire those shots. You'd already scuttled off."

"Yeah, but I heard all about it. You nailed lover boy in the shoulder while aiming for Hector. That showed real expertise."

I remembered that moment too clearly. "He wasn't my lover." I stopped myself from launching into another diatribe. "Thing is, I'm bound to hit something at point-blank range and chances are it will be you."

"You'd likely just hit a wall and ding my security deposit."

"Want to risk it? Sit down and let's talk. I repeat, why did you send that goon after me?" It felt damn good to be in control for once, even though I sensed I was only fooling myself.

"I knew you were in town and just wanted to talk."

"So we'll talk now. I'd like answers and, since I've got the gun, you can give them to me."

"Think so? What kind of answers?"

"Like where are Toby and Noel?"

She pushed a damp tendril from her forehead. "Boggles me how you can be so smart yet do so many dumb-assed things. Must run in the family."

Walking across the room, wafting the scent of some exotic bath oil, she sat down in the chair opposite mine, crossed her legs, and proceeded to study me. "That napkin on your head suits you. Keeps that Raggedy Anne hair of yours in place. Couldn't have found a better style solution myself."

"It's called a hijab." I tried to appear cool and relaxed, desperately hoping she couldn't see my gun hand shaking. I tried propping my elbow on the chair arm.

"Why do you have my dress in your lap—trying for a bit of chic? Forget it, hon. I'm a size four and you're what, a twelve or fourteen?"

I smiled at that. "I don't want to wear your dress, Mags—not my style. No, I thought I'd rip it to shreds before your eyes just to see your face crumple."

"Bitch."

I laughed. "Don't worry, I'd rather shoot you than damage silk any day. Where are they?"

"I hear Max gave you half of Baker & Associates, like he ever did anything like that for me."

"It's Baker & Mermaid now and, yeah, I'm going to resuscitate the business after you bled it and Max dry. Max gave you everything he had and then some. How could you do that to him after so many years?" That just slipped out.

"You mean, how could I last so long without doing it sooner? He totally took me for granted."

"You could have left him instead of kicking him in the nuts."

"Oh, poor baby. Is he all heartbroken?"

"Why wouldn't he be? His girlfriend of twenty years left him hanging and ran off with his money in the heist of the century."

Her face brightened. "Are they calling it the heist of the century?"

"Yes, but the century's still young. Like I said, you stole millions of dollars' worth of priceless artifacts from Alistair Wyndridge." I needed her to admit it, hopefully embellish it, make a confession so the iPhone recorder would catch every word. I had the thing activated in my lap.

"It wasn't Wyndridge's. Like Noel said, it belonged to museums, the world, all that shit."

"Justify it any way you want, you stole it."

"Not me. I was only the assistant. Your brother and his buddy, Noel, were the real masterminds. That pissed me off. Like, here we go all over again with the man on top shit."

My mouth went dry. "Where are they?"

Maggie gazed over at me, her expression pained. "Poor Phoebe. They fooled you, too, didn't they? They plotted to steal Wyndridge's treasure while we women sort of hung on like women do. Yeah, I helped out a little here and there but I got screwed in the end, too."

"I presume you mean figuratively?" Stupid question.

"Maybe I do and maybe I don't. Your bro is gay but Noel is as virile as they come and I'm in pretty good shape." She licked her lips. "Figure it out yourself."

My hand tightened on the gun. This wasn't going the way I'd planned. "Where are they?"

"How the hell should I know?"

"Maggie, if you're lying to me again, I'll—"

"You'll what? Slice the hem off my dress? Shoot the wall? Give me a break. You don't have the guts to do anything like that. You're the type of wuss who takes spiders outside rather than squish them. Look, I lied about not knowing where Toby was back in Bermuda but I'm not lying now. I don't know where the hell either of them are. I know one thing, though: your brother's only half the man you remembered him to be."

"What in hell does that mean?"

She smiled. "Let's just say that he'll never forget how screwing with me doesn't pay."

I raised the gun a little higher. "What are you talking about? What did you do?"

"Chill, hon. I don't know where they are, I said. They dumped me."

"Dumped you?" Why is it that in time of stress I can't utter a coherent sentence?

She sighed. "It was supposed to be a three-way partnership with all of us equal, right? Only, the moment things started heating up, they cut me out. Noel said I was too big a risk. He wanted us to stay low, not fence the loot, though there were enough buyers ready to pounce at any minute. Wait? What the hell is the point of having millions worth of stuff if you're just going to sit on it? Meanwhile, we're on the run going from dive to dive—a farmhouse here, a shack there."

"No five-star hotels?"

"Yeah. Give me a break. If I wanted the simple life, I would have stayed with Max. I was in this for the money, you know what I mean? No delayed gratification for me, thank you very much. So, I contacted some of the collectors myself and took just one piece to sell, just one piece. Big whoop. What's wrong with that? I deserved much more. The bastards got pissed and shafted me."

I breathed slowly out and in, trying to steady my heart. "Never were a team player, eh, Mags? So, they finally realized it's always been all about you."

"Listen up, hon. You're supposed to be some kind of a feminist, right? You fit the description—no boyfriend, dresses like shit? Well, I said we three were supposed to be equal partners, which means that the men don't get to call the shots without my approval. I never agreed to not fencing the loot, see?"

"What happened next?"

"They just left me in some little shack in France and took off. All I had was the money from the necklace. God, it paid good but it won't keep me living like this forever. They've got the rest of it hidden somewhere and part of it is mine. I could kick their asses, the pair of them. If they think they can cut me out of their next heist, they got another thing coming. I've got things organized in ways they haven't." She fixed me with her chill blue eyes and breathed deeply. "See, we're like two peas in a pod, you and me—both of us kicked to shit by the men in our lives."

I nodded. "Sure. We could be twins only you're much, much older."

"Shut up. You always thought you were smarter than me—everybody makes that mistake-but being smart doesn't mean shit if you don't use the brains you've got."

"We're just motivated by different things," I said carefully. "I figure Noel and Toby are here in Istanbul which is why you're here, too."

"Yeah, maybe. After all, why else are you here along with Foxy and that dingbat professor you've been hanging out with? Yeah, I know things. Did you bring that old rug?"

"Look, who's holding the gun here? I'm asking the questions. What old rug?"

She wagged her finger at me. "Oh, Phoebe, don't pretend. You're so not good at it. Toby sent a rug to you for safekeeping, like that would work. That's why you're here, why we all are. Noel claimed there's a clue about the whereabouts of this next hoard embedded in that thing. I saw it but I don't get it. Besides, if it's that important, you're the last person to send it to. You never think, you just react. You brought it with you to Istanbul, didn't you?"

I had sunk back against the chair, brain spiking, heart hurting, the fever burning all over again. Foxy was right, they were hunting down another find, here in Turkey, related to the Anatolian Goddess kilim. Toby sent it to me for safe-keeping and risked my

162

neck all over again. I suspected as much but now the pieces were falling together. Toby and Noel were hunting the Anatolian Goddess and Maggie was hunting Noel and Toby.

In those flash seconds of preoccupation, Maggie lunged across the space between us and snatched the gun out of my hand. Now she was standing over me with the gun pointing at my skull. "You're way out of your league again. You need to be ruthless for this game and you're a sheep in bad clothing. Listen up. I know Toby sent the rug to you in London thinking he could keep it away from me—silly bastard—and you brought it right back here because that's the kind of idiot thing you do. Never think it out, just knee-jerk your way into a shit-fest."

I gazed up at her, fearing she was right. I'd lost the upper hand, lost everything. "Was that Jason Young character working for the three of you?" I still hoped to get something out of this disastrous meeting.

"Hell, no. Jason worked for Noel and Toby. The guy who killed him works for me. Noel hired Jason to keep an eye out for you and Max after we parted company. He had Jason hide the kilim in the storeroom and I had my guy try to get it back, only when that didn't work out so well, I had him kill Young instead." My face must have crumpled. "Do you know what that kilim really means? Does it have some kind of map in it or something? Tell me." She pressed the gun closer to my skull.

"This is why you tried to kidnap me, so I could tell you something I don't know?"

Her eyes had narrowed. "Maybe Foxy knows or maybe Ava told you something?"

"It's Eva and nobody tells me anything. They just drag me around using me as bait for their own damn purposes." I sounded so petulant, I nearly convinced myself.

She considered that for a moment, rolling her tongue inside her month as if test-tasting a flavor. "Yeah, that's true enough. Poor little Phoebe. Why would anybody tell you anything? I sure as hell wouldn't. They're just trying to get the kilim away from you, same as me. So, where is it?"

"I don't need the actual rug. I brought a photo, instead."

"You're lying but it doesn't matter. I've got a good idea where the kilim leads." She'd backed against the bed, gun still pointed at me but no longer quite as threatening.

"Can I go now?"

"Sure, but first, I want to show you something. Don't move." She kept the gun pointed at me as she turned to the dresser, but I took that opportunity to slip my iPhone back into my breast pocket. With a little luck, I had enough evidence to nail her.

She pulled out a drawer, returning moments later holding a framed photograph in her free hand. "See?"

I studied the photograph she held. Maggie in her slick black wig, bejeweled in a stunning pectoral cross encrusted with pearls and gems, stood wearing a long red gown. "That's the piece you fenced, Queen Isabella's?"

"That's the one. May as well go for the biggies, right? So, remember I told you how I wanted to have myself photographed like Sophie Schliemann wearing the diadem from Troy? What do you think?"

"You were trying to look like a Spanish Queen? Are you kidding me? You look more like some punk Cleopatra turned loose in a theme park."

"God, you're such a spoiler. Couldn't you just be happy for me for once?" She tossed the picture on the bed. "Next, I want a picture of me dressed like an ancient goddess."

"You could pull off ancient, Mags, but I doubt you'd nail the goddess part. So," I inched myself to standing. "On that note, I'll just leave."

Maggie wagged the gun at me. "Sit back down, Phoebe. I was lying when I said I'd let you go. I can't do that. Who knows you're here?"

"Interpol. I alerted them before I came."

"Stop taking me for a fool. Sit, I said."

I remained standing. "Look, Maggie, I know we never really got along, but I tried to be the surrogate daughter you wanted, only I had parents of my own and my style and yours clashed."

"You were always jealous of me."

"Not true. I just didn't get you anymore than you got me. I didn't grasp why you craved so much stuff, why you always made Max buy you more and more expensive things."

"It doesn't matter now. It's all in the past."

"I don't care what you do. Let me go."

"You do care what I do, that's the problem. Now, stop wasting time. We're done." She picked up her cell from the bed and pressed a number. "Hi, Hali? Yeah. Come up to my room ASAP, only keep your pants on this time, okay?"

I inched my way towards the door. She tossed the phone onto the bed and fired once, the shot so close it zinged the table beside me. I froze.

"Unlike you, I do what has to be done, even if it means pulling the trigger on a girl I used to care for. Where's that stupid carpet bag you lug everywhere?"

"Back in my hotel room. Don't think I'd drag it here, do you?"

She held out her hand. "Pass me your phone."

I dug into my other pocket and handed her the burner.

"What the hell is this? Where's your iPhone?"

"I lost it, okay? I bought that one as a replacement."

"Can't you do anything right?"

"Guess not." I eyed the door, wondering if she'd shoot me in the back. Yeah, she would.

Then in walked the chauffeur, his eyes raking over Maggie's half-clad body like a panting puppy.

"Not this time, hon. We have to take care of her first." Maggie pointed to me.

Hali turned, his fine aquiline face rigid with surprise.

"Don't worry, she's not Muslim. That's her idea of a disguise." Maggie bent over and retrieved the dress and scissors from where they'd slid to the floor. "This little shit has to go."

"She got in?"

"Yeah, she got in but get her out, as in far away, you know? I don't want her getting in my way. Do something with her. I don't care what. Don't even tell me the details. Just arrange for her to get out of sight and out of mind for a long, long time. Make it permanent."

A slow smile spread across his handsome face, reminding me of Errol Flynn in those old films, only Flynn played good guys and this man clearly had another role. "Yes, I comprehend. I have connections."

"So, go connect."

"I tie her up, okay?"

"Do it."

"I go get stuff."

"Good. We'll just wait, won't we Phoebe?"

Hali left to make arrangements for my disposal, the details of which I tried not to imagine. Maggie stood watch.

"Are you going to add kidnapping and murder to your list of accomplishments?"

"Don't worry, sweetheart, he won't murder you, or at least, not right away. I want to make sure you're going someplace where you won't be getting in my way this time."

Hali reappeared in moments, nodding to Maggie. "Arrangements made," he told her. "She go someplace far. No coming back."

Maggie nodded. "Good."

"They pay me to take her," Hali grinned, "She dangerous?"

Maggie laughed. "Her? More like a nuisance, the kind you don't want buzzing around your house or landing on your food. She always lands on shit. Have your connections keep her out of my face any way they want."

Hali grinned.

I turned to Maggie, my heart galloping wildly. "You're going to let them hurt me? I thought you said you had guts? You're just a coward who gets someone else to do your dirty work."

"Don't want to break a nail." To Hali she added: "How are you going to keep her quiet? She can scream like a stuck pig."

He held up a napkin and an ominous-looking bottle, the contents of which began dabbing into the cloth, smiling all the while. "She'll sleep." Then he put down the bottle and lunged at me while I scrambled away over the bed. Maggie blocked my path on the other side, wrenching me off the mattress by my arm onto the floor and throwing herself down on my back.

I lay winded, pinned to the spot with my face squashed into the rug.

"Never come into a place and wave a gun you can't or won't use. Should have shot me when you had the chance. Hurry, Hali!"

I bucked and raked my nails over her bare thigh.

"Ouch! You little bitch!" She whacked the back of my head.

Hali shoved Maggie off me, straddled me with his heftier weight, and wrenched my neck from the floor until I thought he'd snap it off.

"Now breathe, bitch," he said. He pressed the cloth over my mouth while I struggled to breathe and not breathe at the same time. Impossible. Reflex took over. I inhaled, gagging into blackness.

20

I was lying on my side. Ahead, a red light shed a bloody glow across mountains of crates in an otherwise shadowy realm. I tried to shift but couldn't—hands tied behind my back, feet bound—and the headache whamming against my skull threatened to black me out again.

The last thing I remembered was trying not to breathe. Hali must have tied me up and thrown me in a storeroom of some kind but where? Not at Maggie's. There was nothing residential about this place. It smelled faintly of diesel and I could hear swishing sounds accompanied by a steady drone.

I struggled to sit upright when the floor suddenly shifted, pitching me off a platform onto a metal surface stomach first. I managed not to retch as I heaved myself to my knees. The floor was rocking, a slow swaying back and forth. The hold of a ship!

Supported by the sacks, I struggled to my feet, knocking against boxes and tripping into a wooden crate. I leaned, trembling, my heart hammering. They were going to throw me into the Bosporus! No, wait. Think. Surely they'd have done that by now. No, they had something else in mind. They were transporting me somewhere.

I slid down to the floor and leaned forward, trying to free my hands. The bastard had tied me with some kind of nylon, which cut into my flesh and numbed my hands. I couldn't feel my fingers behind me let alone work myself free. I spent minutes, maybe hours, trying to loosen those knots to no avail.

Then lights flashed on overhead. I squinted around as men's voices approached. Two men arrived. I didn't register features at first but knew they were thickly built and strong.

I looked up. Maybe they didn't realize I was an unwitting stowaway? "Help me," I pleaded.

One laughed and motioned to his companion who stepped closer, hands in pockets. They spoke a battery of some language I didn't recognize, like Turkish but not Turkish. Russian, maybe. Both wore dark pants over matching shirts—a uniform of some kind. The man standing closest pulled out a switchblade, a wicked-looking thing that sliced the air as he waved it before my eyes.

"Wow. Such a big knife for a little tied-up woman. Aren't you mighty?"

No understanding flickered in his face. No English, then.

He grabbed my neck. Shoving my head down, he began slicing off the hijab, the blade close enough to my skin to nick me. I cried out and bucked against this onslaught until, finally, he vised my head between his knees and finished slicing without interruption, tearing away the last of the fabric in shreds. Then he yanked at the pins securing my hair until he'd freed a mass of unruly strands, which he grabbed by the fistful to haul me to my feet.

Both men now stood on either side of me. Each grabbed an arm and tipped me on my back over the sacks and proceeded to discuss my attributes while squeezing my breasts through my clothes. I didn't need Russian to get their drift.

One lifted my coat, unfastened my fly, and pulled down my jeans and panties while the other pinned me down by gripping my shoulders. Thus pinioned, I lay helpless squirming with humiliation. I tried squeezing my legs tight but the man in charge pried them open with his knees and began digging his dirty fingers into my flesh.

I screamed and spat and bucked. I couldn't stop struggling even though I knew my efforts probably excited them further. When I screamed at the top of my lungs, one of them whacked me across the cheek.

My head fell back on the sack. I thought I was going to faint. A whistle blew somewhere and both men sprung away, one returning seconds later to pull my jeans up and hastily rearrange my coat, kicking me over onto my stomach in the process.

I lay there stunned, churning with disgust and shame, feeling dirty as if I was somehow to blame for the violation. How could this be happening? My brain scrambled for a coherent thought.

If I was on the Bosporus Strait headed for the Black Sea, I could be easily sold into the sex trade. It was rampant all through the area, in Russia in particular. I was no more than a piece of meat.

Hunger, thirst, and despair darkened all the colors in my heart. I drifted in and out of consciousness, effected by the drug I had inhaled and the abuse I suffered.

At some point, my eyes opened as someone rolled me onto my back. Three men stood over me arguing—the two from before plus one other—a big meaty man built like a heifer. This new one wore a peaked cap with an insignia on his shirt. The captain? The captain!

"Help me, please," I gasped.

The captain glanced at me with little interest before returning to his discussion. With the impact of a fist to the gut, I saw myself from the outside in: a woman, worthless in of herself. Weak. A sexual toy to be enjoyed and traded like livestock but otherwise possessing no brain, no heart, and no soul, certainly not worthy of respect. To these men, I was less than an animal. I felt cheap and useless, a born victim.

Why had I ever come here? What made me think I could tackle this brutal world alone? I couldn't do it, I just couldn't.

I swam up from the bottom of despair long enough to try understanding what the men were saying. The two underlings seemed earnestly attempting to convince the captain of something. My worth on the black market?

The bastard who had roughed me up gesticulated wildly, pointing to me then towards the door. The captain cut him off—I heard the name Sergei—as he pointed at my bruised cheek. I guessed he didn't like the boys battering the merchandise. Leave that for the buyers.

He snapped an order which sent Sergei scrambling away while his buddy stood by silently. The captain approached me, looking me up and down as if inspecting a particularly troublesome bag of potatoes until Sergei returned moments later with a bottle of water and a plate which he lowered to the floor beside me—a wedge of bread with something slimy that reeked of cabbage.

The captain nudged me with his foot barking an order I deduced might be "EAT!" I shook my head and hunched my bound arms helplessly.

Sergei muttered angrily, lurching me to sitting, and pointing to the plate before slicing off the twine binding my wrists. I moaned, bringing my raw and swollen hands in front of my face. The men were already heading for the door.

The captain must have insisted they at least feed and water the cargo so it would stay in reasonably good condition. How much would I fetch half-dead? And I couldn't very well eat with my hands bound, could I? He couldn't spare a man to spoon-feed me on this working ship, either, so he must have ordered everyone back to their post, confident that with the door locked, I wouldn't be going anywhere.

Shaking the circulation back into my hands, I stared at my wrists through my tears, still feeling that man's disgusting grope. If only I had the time to retch and wail and cry. Instead, I fumbled for my iPhone with my numb fingers. The phone remained buried deep in my coat pocket where I'd managed to hide it. Maggie took my word that I had lost it, and then nobody bothered to search.

I plucked the sleek surface out with fumbling fingers, dropping it on the floor beside me. The battery was almost dead and the reception weak, but it might eke out enough juice to get a message out.

Agent Walker was on speed-dial so I pressed his name and waited. The call rang and rang, me cursing every wasted second. I kept my ears keened for the men's return.

When Walker's answering machine clicked in, I rasped into the phone. "Walker, it's me, Phoebe, in Istanbul. I've been kidnapped. I'm on a ship in the Bosporus—don't know the name, Russian, I think. I found Maggie. Please help." Then I clicked off, switched to email and sent him a link to Maggie's Google map address, still open on my phone. Whether that posted successfully, I had no idea, since my phone blacked out seconds after I hit SEND. I noted the time before it died—12:45 a.m. local time.

A long shot is better than never pressing the trigger. I'd remember that the next time I saw Maggie.

Shoving my phone back in my pocket, I wrestled with the water bottle until the cap popped off, downing nearly the entire contents before reigning myself in. Next, I tackled the cabbage thing and the bread, which snaked down my throat like a glutinous mass followed by a block of wood. I needed energy so didn't care.

Thus fortified, I tried untying the knots binding my ankles, but my hands, though gradually regaining circulation, were nearly useless for dexterity. I fumbled, spending precious seconds picking the knot loose until finally I could shake my ankles free.

On my feet at last, I stumbled across the floor, banging into crates labeled in Turkish, making my way to the door. Metal like the floor and walls, the door stayed solidly shut. It probably locked automatically from the outside but still required a key. Not so modern a ship to go with digital locks, either. I turned away to begin exploring my world, shaking the blood back into my limbs as I went.

God, I so did not want to be a victim. Women suffered worse abuse than I just had again and again. Why had I never really grasped how half the female world survives? I'd been protected and cosseted all my life without realizing it.

Now I teetered on the edge. I would not go down without a fight. If I didn't do something, I'd end up living in the worst kind of subjugation.

My captors had switched off the overhead fluorescents before leaving but I flicked them back on. The room flooded intensely bright, revealing an industrial metal space stacked with crates and sacks. Some country brought cargo to Istanbul and filled the outgoing ship with goods for home, me being the bonus.

I scanned every shelf, up and down, until I found something useful: a utility knife sitting on a stack of papers along with a dirty coffee mug and a half-smoked cigarette. Thank you, Ivan, or whoever this careless sailor was. Maybe he'd just saved my life.

I returned to my sack, sat down, the knife concealed in my trench coat, and considered strategy. Every avenue was as risky as the next but none more so than doing nothing. I didn't yet know what I was made of, what I was capable of doing. I only knew that if I didn't take desperate action, I'd spend a life of the worst kind of subjugation. I'd rather die than be pawed and prodded by a bunch of brutes for the rest of my days. The sheep had to turn wolf fast.

The door opening roused me from a doze. I bolted upright into the still brightly lit space, every sinew tensing as footsteps approached—one set only.

Sergei slipped around the corner, eyeing me speculatively. Bastard probably sneaked from his berth thinking he'd have me to himself. Who would know if he raped me? Everyone but the bridge and night watch would be asleep and no one could hear me scream in here. Who even cared?

Play the game, I warned myself. Women had been playing the same one for thousands of years, so I figured I should be able to do the same. I forced a shy smile, trying to appear submissive. "Please don't hurt me," I said aloud. "I'll do what you want."

Some communication went beyond words. I unbuttoned the top of my trench, smiling, patting the floor with my hand.

"Come join me," I whispered. "Just don't hurt me."

Sergei's face lit with eagerness. He must have known he'd get in big trouble if he bruised me, but if I was willing to offer myself freely, he wouldn't need to slap me around.

On my knees, I smiled up at him as he unzipped his pants and let them drop. I did my best to appear eager, excited by the prospects of this wormy little man about to ravish me. Suppressing nausea, I smiled in anticipation.

He gestured for me to pleasure him by mouth. Oh, hell, no. Hurry. He ordered me in Russian.

I moved closer and, as he swiveled to check the door once more, I pulled out the utility knife, clutched it in both hands, and raked it deep and hard across his scrotum—such a vulnerable piece of the male anatomy—sending him screaming and toppling backward on the floor.

I sprung forward, blinded by fury as the slick knife fell from my hands and skittered away. Picking it up again, I came after him knife outstretched.

The pants bunched around his ankles kept him flopping helplessly on the floor like a beached tuna. I should stab him, realizing I couldn't just half do this thing, but blood slicked the knife and gummed my resolve.

Instead, I sliced the straps off the nearest crate and heaved it down on top of him. Hearing him cry out made me bellow in triumph like some warrior queen. With the crate pinning down his upper half, I could now pluck the keys from his pants pocket.

Shoving the gooey knife into my pocket, I ran for the door, trying multiple keys until the right one fit.

The corridor was empty as I eased the door shut behind me, hearing the lock catch at my back.

I just knifed a man. I was covered in blood. Who was I?

Lights bleared fluorescent inside wire cases as I slipped down the hall towards the stairs. I climbed up to the next deck and heaved open the door. Outside, the ship plied the strait under a starry sky, lights beaming from the headlands on either side. I could see other vessels to the left and behind us on this busy thoroughfare.

Since only a skeleton crew would be on duty this time of night and they'd be manning the bridge, a lone person scuttling along the lower deck could go undetected.

It was a small tanker, a bit rusty and probably old, which meant I couldn't expect new-model escape pods or maybe not even inflatable rafts. I looked for traditional lifeboats fastened to the sides on winches and found them straight ahead, two lifeboats suspended on ropes bound to the side.

They reminded me of the kind used on the fishing trawler where I'd worked my summers as a student. I'd spent my day filleting haddock for the freezer hold but had learned the basic abandon ship drills: break the glass, activate the pulley, and be prepared to leap in. Since the written instructions were in Russian, I needed to apply memory with a touch of resourcefulness.

I wouldn't have much time after activating the pulleys before the alarm sounded. I removed the fire ax strapped to the ship's side, whacked the glass, pressed the pulley, and watched as the dinghy shook once and began lowering by winch.

The alarm shrilled immediately. Men shouted overhead. The lifeboat was taking too long to lower. They were going to recapture me, me who had just knifed their crewmate and robbed the captain of his bonus!

I leapt on top of the dinghy's canvas cover as the boat leveled with the deck. The winch snagged and jammed to a stop. There I crouched, suspended on a boat swaying at least thirty feet above the water, going nowhere.

Flat on my stomach, I inched to the edge and peered over. It was a long way down but I'd jump if I had to. Yet, something else was happening out there: a spotlight raked the darkness ahead.

I squinted into the blaze unable to see anything. A loudspeaker sounded off to my right, as if from another ship. The tanker bridge responded by megaphone and I could feel the ship slowing down. As the spotlight swept to the right, I watched a small craft approach with flashing red lights and uniformed men.

"Phoebe McCabe? Stay where you are. We're coming to get you down." Agent Sam Walker's voice blared over a loudspeaker.

I sunk back down on the tarp, dizzy with relief mixed with a different breed of fear.

21

I sipped apple tea and tried again to focus on the questions instead of my bandaged wrists. The world around me had taken on a surreal haze as if I played a starring role in someone else's nightmare. I may have been on a police boat sailing towards Istanbul, but nothing about the woman I now inhabited felt familiar.

Earlier above deck I asked, "Where is Sergei? Where is the man I knifed? Is he going to live?"

"I have no idea. Too early to say. They're rushing him to hospital. You can give us the rest of your statement below," Walker said. Not unkind, just understandably brusque.

Back in the galley, I told my story to the Turkish police, with Walker and his Istanbul colleague looking on. They requested I repeat several aspects, especially the part where I stabbed Sergei. My responses appeared to satisfy the local police, if not myself. "It was in self-defense," I said repeatedly.

"Of course," Agent Walker said. "We don't believe that you boarded a Russian tanker and knifed a sailor for entertainment."

I looked at him. "Right." So why did I have that sick pang in the pit of my stomach?

Russian kidnappers and human traffickers didn't have many rights under Turkish law, apparently, so the police seemed more admiring of me than anything else.

Once the police captain had exited the galley, it was just Walker, the Turkish Interpol agent, Adalet Kapitz, and me sitting around the chrome table like we were sharing tea at the bazaar. My iPhone needed recharging so I couldn't check what the recorder had captured. I wanted to hear it first in private, anyway. "You followed me to Istanbul?"

"Your phone helped us pinpoint your exact location today. Did you really think I believed you were just coming here for a carpet sale?" Agent Walker asked.

"An Antique Carpet and Ethnographic Exhibition is hardly just a carpet sale," I countered, mustering energy. "I'm in the trade, remember?"

"And since you arrived, you've hardly been behaving like someone in the trade. You've been seen with Dr. Eva Friedrich and Sir Rupert Fox."

"Both are connected to ethnography."

"Both are on Interpol's radar."

"Dr. Friedrich is assisting me with the provenance of a carpet I purchased, and Sir Foxy is wooing me because he wants to buy the gallery." Oh, how truth can also shield a lie.

"We believe both may be interested in a secret archaeological site in Turkey."

"Really? Nobody tells me anything."

Walker leaned towards me, fixing me with his unsettling gaze. "And you tackled a holy man at the opening event."

"A Sufi," Agent Kapitz pointed out, hardly suppressing his pique.

"A case of mistaken identity," I stated.

"Who did you mistake him for, one of the Twelve Apostles?" Walker quipped. "He wore a white robe, as I understand."

"Most people attending were in some kind of costume so he could have been anybody."

"But you thought it was Noel Halloran, didn't you? You suspect he's in Istanbul."

"I don't know where he is," I said. "I only found Maggie by tracking her to a Chanel store on a hunch. Have the police arrested her yet?"

Walker turned to Kapitz who shrugged. A man of few words, I gathered.

"The police are on their way. We'll know more when we dock. Don't change the topic. You came here to find your brother and Halloran, admit it. Did they contact you?"

I sighed, looking down at my hands. I wondered if I could still knit now that I needed that consolation the most. Then my mind wandered to my carpet bag still stuffed under the jasmine hedge back at Maggie's. My attention refused to anchor.

"Answer my questions," Walker said. "Did your brother contact you or did Noel Halloran give you instructions when he visited you in London?"

"No and no," I said. "I haven't spoken to my brother in fourteen months. I told you that. I want to see him again, sure. Who wouldn't want to see their brother after all that's happened? But I swear I don't know where he is. I thought Maggie knew, but she insists they dropped her once she started fencing the jewels without their knowledge."

"How did you know Maggie was in Istanbul?"

"Someone attacked me near the Grand Bazaar, who I later discovered was working for Maggie. She has a penchant for Chanel so I went on a hunch." I added, "Anyway, she told me she'd fenced the Isabella necklace to finance her habits and insists the men had been planning to sit on the cache but she got impatient."

"Did she say to whom she fenced the necklace?"

"No, she didn't disclose that. She bragged how she stole the piece from Toby and Noel. She has access to all Max's old clientele—the wealthy private collectors that feed off the black market. It could be any of those."

I kept my gaze fixed on my hands.

Kapitz leaned forward. "Just understand, Ms. McCabe, if you are withholding anything, we will consider this aiding the fugitives, which is a serious offense in international law. You are already in big trouble."

I glanced at him. "So, I'm either with you or against you, is that it?"

"That is it exactly," the agent nodded. Kapitz's dark hair and penetrating eyes reminded me uncomfortably of Noel. The Turks were handsome men. He rose to his feet. "I will excuse myself and check the pilot house to see if there is word from the shore team."

That left me alone with Walker, who sat across from me gripping his mug while that scarred eyebrow jutted under his wool cap like the skid mark from a crash scene. I shifted in my seat.

"You're hiding something," he said flatly.

"Maybe you mistake shock for reticence. I've had a grueling night. What will happen to me?"

"I'll be escorting you on an 11:00 a.m. flight back to London in the morning. Charges will probably be laid, something which you could lessen the extent of by assisting me now."

"You have insufficient evidence to charge me with anything."

If possible, the ragged eyebrow peaked further. "I forgot you studied the law. Who are you protecting, Phoebe?"

"No one accept myself, Agent Walker. Look, I led you to Maggie's lair, didn't I? Sure, I admit to wanting to find her—all of them—but I've told you everything I know. I came for the carpet exposition and to purchase pieces for my shop. I located Maggie by luck, if you can call what just happened to me luck."

"How do you know Dr. Eva Friedrich?"

I turned the mug around in my cupped hands. "Her name was given to me by a carpet dealer at the Arasta Bazaar when I was inquiring about authenticating Anatolian kilims for the gallery. In my business, a carpet that comes with provenance is instantly made more valuable, making it necessary to bring in experts on occasion. Dr. Friedrich and I hit it off."

"Do you know she's had dealings with the police in the past?"

"I don't know much about her either way."

"Which kilim were you inquiring about?"

"I purchased several Anatolian tribal kilims of a certain type. That's my job. They are being shipped back to the gallery."

"I will need to inspect them all once they arrive in London."

"Of course." Nausea and desperation roiled over me. "Look, could you grill me some other time? I'm exhausted and I just knifed a man."

"In self-defense."

"It doesn't matter." I held up my hands. "These just committed an act of horrific violence and I can't just shrug it off, okay? I'm exhausted."

"Of course. I understand. We can continue our dialog tomorrow en route to London." He got to his feet and exited the cabin, feet clattering on the metal stairs as he dashed above deck.

That left me alone in the small galley crowded by memories of leering men, Maggie's sneers, and the impact of knifing a man in what could be a fatal blow—terrifying acts inflicted on me and by me. My bandaged hands felt all wrong, as if still sticky with the blood I'd washed away countless times.

Fifteen minutes later, I felt the boat slowing down followed by the thrust of engines navigating a pier. Walker clattered downstairs to tell me to come above deck.

"I'll deliver you to your hotel, where you'll have a few hours to rest before we head for the airport."

"Wait, the police must have reached Maggie's address. Let me go with you to the site on the way back to the hotel. I need to retrieve the bag I stashed in the shrubbery and maybe I'll get to spit in her face. Surely, I deserve that much?"

He hesitated. "I thought you had enough for one night?"

"If she gets what she deserves, I'll get the best sleep I've had for ages."

He finally he allowed me to accompany him, and we wove through the darkened streets and up into Maggie's leafy neighborhood. I could barely contain myself. With Maggie finally apprehended, I might consider the night a partial success, or at least not a total disaster.

We pulled into the open gate, the driveway now crowded with police vehicles. It only took Walker a moment to inform me that Maggie had escaped. By the time the police arrived, she had already vacated the premises.

I stood on the lawn, reunited with my bag but awash with sick disbelief as the police continued fanning out across the grounds. But for the pre-existing furniture and stores laden with food, the place was empty.

"If you had informed me the moment you caught sight of her, she might be in custody now. As it is, she obviously had enough sense not to risk hanging around," Walker said, his authoritative voice banging against my skull.

Without saying much further, he delivered me to the hotel with strict instructions to pack and be ready for pickup at eight o'clock sharp.

I stepped into the hotel room, inserted my key card into the slot, and turned just as the light automatically flooded the room.

I stared. Everything had been ransacked. I swung towards the safe, saw it gaping open and fell to my knees, clawing the empty cavity. It couldn't be gone, it couldn't!

But it was.

My spare cash lay in a wad on the floor along with my passport. This was no ordinary thief. If Maggie took the kilim, she'd destroy it. I sobbed uncontrollably.

An hour later, I sat perched on the edge of the bed staring at the curtains. They mimicked real silk brocade but were mere clever forgeries. I needed a shower. I could do with some sleep, too, but the world hung black and miserable all around me. Everything seemed false and cruel with nothing worth the effort of doing. People stole, murdered, tortured, and abused one another, and otherwise decent people became twisted. Such a warped, warped world.

What can we do but keep on moving? I plucked the Foxy phone from the bed, and dialed. The phone rang imperiously in my ear until someone picked up the call.

"Eva Friedrich here. Who has the unmitigated gall to call at this hour?"

"Me, Phoebe. Does the offer to go with you to Cappadocia still stand?"

Five seconds' hesitation. I counted the beats. "Certainly."

"Good. Can you be ready to leave within the hour?"

22

Istanbul felt surreal in the early dawn, quiet but active with the occasional car whizzing by and men pouring into the mosque across the street.

The five o'clock adhan sounded just as I turned the corner, a haunting demarcation of the breaking day. I might have prayed myself if I knew how with conviction. All my childhood attempts had sounded like pleading and today wouldn't be much different. I need to get away and find Toby and Noel. Please help me. Amen.

Pressing against the wall, I waited. Moments later, a little gray car pulled to the curb and the passenger door clicked open. Eva leaned towards me. "Phoebe, are you all right?"

I hauled my luggage to the curb and bent towards her. "Interpol wants me gone," I said.

"Did you steal something?"

"Absolutely not."

"Get in."

"But I am withholding evidence, just so you know. Technically what I'm doing is illegal. I'm probably the last person you should be connected with right now."

"I could say the same applies to me. We'll form a perfect pair."

I tossed my bags into the back seat and climbed in beside her. After taking a quick check in the rear view mirror, I fixed my gaze on the streets ahead, watching the city awaken on this early October morning. "Someone stole the kilim, Eva. It's gone."

I heard her sharp intake of breath. "Who do you think would do such a thing?"

"I have no idea but I'm thinking Maggie, possibly Noel, but that doesn't make sense because he's still tight with my brother, and it was Toby who sent it to me. Maggie admitted that much. It's incredible how strongly I feel its absence, like someone ripped the rug out from under me, literally. Maggie wants it destroyed. She seemed to know my whereabouts—who I saw, what I did. Maybe she found my hotel information and had her goons break into my room? Oh, God, what have I done?"

Eva gripped the steering wheel. "Who is this Maggie to you?"

"My nemesis, though she'd think that implied I was her equal, which she clearly doesn't believe, but she's vicious and dangerous, and why the hell didn't I realize that sooner? Though, I feel a little dangerous myself right now."

"Phoebe, try to calm down. Why do you believe it was Maggie?"

I squeezed my eyes shut against the brilliant sunrise. "Who else could it be? The kilim is a key to the missing site, isn't it? She's after it, too. She knows the site lies in Cappadocia. She's probably imagining another Troy."

Eva remained silent. I turned to check behind us again. We'd have a good lead on Foxy, at least. "How will we know if someone's following us?"

"You mean Interpol?"

"Anybody. I have quite an entourage."

"If you can't identify anyone in particular, I'd say it will be difficult to determine, but we'll be thoroughly evasive, never fear."

"Where else could I have hidden the kilim to keep it safe?"

"With me, as I asked. If a dark energy knows you are in possession of it, then keeping it in a hotel safe was a mistake."

I looked at her. "A dark energy?" Hell, were we talking voodoo and Darth Vader types here? I really wasn't in the mood.

As if she sensed my thoughts, she added: "Think with your spirit, Phoebe. I mean dark against the light, the contrasts that keep the universe in check. Balance is everything. Whoever wishes to destroy the kilim is an agent of darkness."

I sighed and rubbed my eyes. "My friend, Nancy, would get your drift in a nanosecond, but my mind's too filled with concrete traumas like knifing a Russian sailor to think about that stuff now."

"Knifing a Russian sailor? Phoebe, you truly are in shock."

"I probably am but I really did, knife someone, I mean."

"You must tell me everything that happened once we're safely away from Istanbul. The Goddess made me delay my excursion longer than I expected—I meant to leave yesterday—and now I know why."

I stared straight ahead. If Eva was unhinged, as I was beginning to fear, what was I doing in the car with her? "Is there time to pick up a coffee?"

"Definitely not."

"Interpol wants me on a plane back to London this morning but I can't leave. I'm still in the best position to find Toby and Noel, especially now. Besides, Maggie knows roughly where this place is located, too. She's after the same thing you are." I paused. "What is that, exactly?"

Eva took a corner onto one of the main arteries. "Details later. When do they expect you on that plane?"

"The flight leaves at 11:00 a.m., but Walker is picking me up at 8:00. We have to avoid planes. As soon as they know I'm gone, they'll be watching the airports. No worries about Maggie, though. She thinks I'm on the Black Sea readying for a career in the sex trade."

"Great Mother of Goddesses! The sex trade?" Eva abruptly signaled onto a side street and headed in the opposite direction. "No airport, then. Alternate routes required."

"I should have told Interpol about the kilim. Maybe if I had, it would be safe, but maybe not. What do I know? But I do know I don't want police intervention. Toby needs to see me as much as I him, only for different reasons. He wants absolution and I want retribution. How do you factor justice into all that? I never could. I mean, I can't. There's a reason why I left the law. I've got to build up stronger stuff, be able to defend myself, not let people victimize me, ever. And Noel tried to contact me last night. That must mean something. I didn't know I had it in me to knife Sergei. On, hell, I knifed a man! I knifed Sergei." And then I started crying, bawling, really.

Eva kept her eyes on the road. "Phoebe, keep it together long enough to remove my phone from my bag and engage the speaker. Hold it up while I make a few calls. I need to organize our escape."

I did as she bid, remaining silent while she made several calls, speaking rapidly in Turkish to three men and one women.

"You know a lot of people here," I commented, wiping my eyes on my sleeve. I'd ditched the trench and put my freshly showered self back into my own clothes—skinny jeans, boots, my leather jacket.

"When you marry a Turk you inherit his family, and his friends, plus a network of former colleagues, all over the country. This is my brother-in-law's car, one of them anyway."

"How long ago did Borek pass?"

"Ten years and two months ago." She kept her eyes on the road, hands fused to the steering wheel. "Time for personal histories later. Now I must concentrate on getting out of Istanbul."

Eva drove through the tributaries of city traffic, pushing on through the huge metropolis until the buildings clustered into apartments followed by a gray spread of factories and industrial spaces.

"Where are we going?"

"We'll catch the ferry across the Marmara then drive cross country to the Aegean. My nephew will convey us down the coast in his fishing boat. We'll dock some place where we'll less likely attract attention. From there, another nephew is lending us a car and we'll drive across country. Have you had any sleep in the last 24 hours?"

"Not unless being chloroformed counts."

"By the Goddess, Phoebe! Once we're on the ferry, you must sleep."

And sleep I did. After bundling myself from the car to the passenger deck of a ferry where all the windows looked out over a sea streaked with tankers, I turned my back, rested against my carpet bag, and slept until Eva roused me.

Soon, we were back in the car driving once again. I glimpsed long stretches of farmland, more industrial buildings, mosques, and tiny villages in between sleeps, only rousing when Eva shook me awake to have lunch in a little cafe. She ordered me something she referred to as "Turkish pizza" and strong, hot tea. I drank and ate as if in a daze, only dimly aware of people talking and laughing around me.

My throat felt scratchy and raw, my head ached with a relentless thud. Eva felt my forehead. "You're sick. Little wonder after what you've been through. Here, take these."

I watched her shake two red pills into my palm.

"Standard issue ibuprofen. Take two."

I swallowed the pills before climbing back into the car and falling into a deep, fast sleep. The world slipped beneath and around me in perpetual motion with hills, valleys, pavement, and briefly glimpsed farmlands flying by.

When Eva roused me again, it was dark.

"We'll stay here at my niece's for the night. You'll have Pinar's bed and I'll take the couch."

I don't recall much about the young woman who opened her house to us except she was petite, very pretty, and smiled broadly. I went straight to bed and slept so deeply, it was if I tumbled off the edge of a velvet cliff.

When I awoke, the sun was slicing sharp and bright through the curtains, and I heard people talking outside the door. Feeling restored, I dressed quickly and stepped into the small living area.

Eva, in a long cotton gown with her hands waving, was in an intense discussion with a young man, all conversation ending abruptly at the sight of me. "Phoebe, this is my nephew, Deniz. He'll be taking us down the coast today."

The young man smiled and nodded, saying something quickly to Eva in Turkish before dashing out the door.

"Are you feeling better?"

"I'm feeling much better, thanks. You look nothing like yourself. Does it bother you to don the traditional Muslim dress?"

"Why ever would it?"

"Because you're not Muslim. Do you feel like a fraud?"

"Phoebe, it's a disguise, not a mockery. Besides, I hold Islam in the highest regard. It is a beautiful and noble religion, the exact opposite of how these extremists and terrorists corrupt it for their purposes. In any event, Pinar had to go to work but sends us best wishes on our journey. We'll have some breakfast and then meet Deniz at the dock."

"Where are we?"

"Dikili but we'll head down the coast to Kusadasi which, as a tourist destination, should grant us sufficient anonymity to get lost in the crowd. Once there, another nephew—Borek had five brothers who all have children—Ege, is meeting us with another car. In any event, here's your disguise. Pinar found it for you. Try it on." She held out a patterned silk scarf accompanied by a long plain cotton dress, both predominantly an unflattering mauve pink.

"It belonged to Pinar's mother, I believe. It's probably too big for you but it will do."

I dropped the dress over my head. It fell from my shoulders like a sack, the sleeves dangling to my fingertips. At least that feature disguised my bandaged wrists, but otherwise, I felt like a kid going trick-or-treating in a grape-stained bed sheet. Eva wrapped the scarf around my head in quick, efficient motions.

"You've done this before," I commented.

"Many times."

"So you could fit in with Borek's family?"

"As a sign of respect, yes, but I was always an anomaly."

We grabbed our bags and hurried off in the borrowed car across bare, dusty hills until at last the Aegean came into view as a haze of blue against an equally flawless sky. We turned onto a small two-lane road running parallel to the water and carried on for another couple of miles until the road curved up and away from the water and into a densely wooded area.

"Keep an eye out for signs."

"What signs?" I hoped she didn't mean Goddess signs like three birds flying in formation.

"He said to take a left-hand turn into the village but, for the life of me, I don't see a village anywhere let alone a sign," Eva said.

I looked behind us. A little green car could be seen in the distance, its roof glinting like a beetle's back in the sun. "I think we just passed a sign back there."

We turned around until we found the road again—one lane jutting straight up into the forest. The green car had disappeared. "This must be it," Eva muttered, carefully nosing the car onto the lane, "Though it doesn't look much like a fishing village to me." The road wound through the dense growth for at least another mile before white buildings began appearing amid the trees.

I rolled down the window. "I can smell the sea."

And soon I could see it, too, but only in glimpses through branches as the road abruptly plunged downward. The forest fell away as the road took a sharp turn against a cliff edge and razor-backed downward towards the shore. "By the Goddess!" I heard Eva exclaim, "Why don't they believe in guard rails?"

After a dizzying decline, the car leveled out in a little village where a crowd of white three-story buildings tumbled against the shore. Dories and boats of all sizes had been pulled up on wooden slats along the water's edge while a few larger boats rocked gently in the cove.

Eva parked the car under a tree, leaving the keys on the floor, and urged me out. "Deniz can make sure this gets back to Istanbul. Come along."

"But won't someone steal it?"

"Not here."

The curious stares of countless eyes followed us as we made our way along the shore. I could only imagine how we appeared to the villagers. Eva carried only a knapsack tossed easily over one shoulder. I followed behind her, hoisting my carpet bag over one shoulder while dragging my roller bag over the pebbles with my other hand until a man suddenly came up to us, smiling and nodding. He took my roller bag from my hand and Eva's backpack, exchanging a few words to Eva before dashing on ahead.

"He's offering to help us take our bags to the boat," Eva explained with a grin.

"Oh, that's wonderful," I said, plunging my hand into my carpet bag. "How much should we pay him?"

Eva shook her head sharply. "Tipping could offend him. Phoebe, he's doing it to be helpful and because helping people is just the way things are done here."

After that, I thought maybe it was best to watch and learn. Playing the follower wasn't easy, but I didn't see an alternative just then.

Despite my aching wrists, I savored the calm sea with the little fishing boats rocking gently in the cove. Gone were the skyscrapers, the congested streets, the crazy schizophrenic beauty of Istanbul's cultural jumble and, in its stead, the peaceful glory of the Aegean Sea spreading a cool balm of blue and white. Cleopatra may have gazed out on a vista much like this.

We carried along the rocky shore until we caught sight of Deniz waving to us from the only wharf.

On instinct, I turned suddenly to look back the way we'd come just in time to spy a small green car parked beside ours under the tree. "Eva, I—" but she had already scrambled ahead, our volunteer porter loping ahead. Well, damn. I scuttled after her, catching up just as we reached the jetty, where several fishing boats were moored.

"Eva," I whispered, "I think we've been followed."

"Pardon?" She turned, staring at me with an affronted expression. "Impossible, well, at best, unlikely. You must be mistaken."

I turned back but couldn't see the tree from where we stood. "Let's get on with it."

A man shouted up to us. I could just see the top of Deniz's head three feet below on the deck of a small white fishing boat lashed to the wharf. Deniz and another man were hoisting the bags from our helper's hands into the bottom level of a three-deck pilot house.

Eva was already climbing down the ladder. I tossed my carpet bag to Deniz and followed after, negotiating my cumbersome robes as gracefully as I could, frustrated by the cocoon-like sense of being wrapped like a sack of groceries. Once on the deck, I gazed around at the mound of fishing gear secured under a blue tarpaulin and inhaled the scent of motor oil and fish offal, the perfume of my childhood.

"I don't suppose women work fishing boats much here, but I can help untie ropes, handle the anchor, anything," I said to Eva. "I practically grew up on a fishing boat."

Deniz didn't understand much English but apparently grasped enough to shake his head vigorously and point towards the lower cabin of a three-story pilot house. "Must stay inside," he said. "We drive boat."

Eva beckoned me towards the cabin. "Come, Phoebe. Today we make like the locals. We don't want to attract attention."

I looked up to wave goodbye to our kindly porter. "But I think we already have." A crowd was gathering on the wharf, as if some telepathic communication had spread through the village alerting them to the spectacle of two strange women in an unconvincing disguise about to sail away on a fishing boat.

Eva looked up and shook her head. "Oh, blast them!" She called out to Deniz while tugging me by the sleeve towards the cabin.

We bundled ourselves into the cramped lower cabin, a narrow space dominated by two long benches with a table fixed to the floor in between. Here the fishers would eat a hasty lunch, maybe swig a mug of tea, but not much else since the work took place on deck outside or one floor up in the pilot house.

Regardless of the discomfort, being aboard a fishing boat again delivered such a memory punch that I fought back tears. Dad, Toby, me, and the sea. For the first time since arriving in Turkey, I felt truly home yet totally lost. I wanted to man the wheel, let the salt air tangle my hair while steering towards the blue horizon, straight back home.

Remembering where I'd been while longing to know where I was going left me nothing to cling to but the empty horizon.

"How long a ride is it?" I called out to Eva as the engine rumbled to life.

"Approximately six hours," she shouted back while unpacking a small feast from her knapsack. Bottles of water, waxed paper wrapped pastries, and a plastic container of what looked like slices of roasted eggplant were deposited on the table, along with forks and knives. We'd only just had breakfast a few hours ago, but Eva attacked the meal with gusto, nodding to me to join in. I tucked into the eggplant and drank a bottle of water, smiling at her companionably across the table. "Pinar made these for us."

"Oh."

"We're off to find the Goddess, Phoebe," she called to me like a child excited over a day at the fair.

I nodded. "And I'm off to find my brother. Let's hope the two are connected."

"They are."

All I knew was that this path to Anatolia pitched me in the same direction as the kilim, possibly Maggie and Noel, and by association, Toby. It was the only lead I had and, since remaining in Istanbul was no longer an option, I chose to be a fugitive hurling into the unknown. Hell if I knew where I'd land.

Real conversation was impossible over the throbbing engine, so I tried to knit. Just as I feared, my aching wrists made that challenging and very slow yet I persevered.

Out the grimy window where the crowded wharf had long shrunk into the distance, long stretches of bright blue sea soothed the eye. Green cars couldn't follow us here and a boat on our tail would be noticeable. Maybe I could relax. Well, maybe not relax exactly, but at least escape for a few moments of solitude.

I studied my knitting, gently combing the butterflies of colored yarn free. Intarsia required both halves of my brain, the left to adhere to patterns and color boundaries, the right to flow deeply into my unconscious where yarn wove in and around the human heart. Nothing painful touched me here. I glanced once at Eva, finding her slumped against her knapsack snoring heartily in a similar tempo as the engine.

I just knit. I'd add Knitting in a Fishing Boat on the Aegean to my list of extraordinary places, soon editing the title to Knitting in a Fishing Boat on the Aegean While Escaping Interpol, which added a certain panache. I took photos with my now-charged iPhone.

Hours later, I looked up to find the water surrounding us populated by numerous boats, including sailboats with their sheets unfurled with both wind and light and, to the left, a band of heat-smudged land rising ahead. We were cruising into port.

I shook Eva awake. One glance out the window put her into instant alert. She sprang into action, shouting up to Deniz who called back.

I carefully tucked my project back into the carpet bag and poked my head outside. The air felt warmer here with a balmy breeze tugging at my robes. The sight of so much activity ahead startled me. I had conjured images of a rocky coastline where Eva and I would stealthily disembark in a secluded cove and scramble into the undergrowth. Instead, we were navigating a crowded waterway crammed with speedboats and pleasure craft, with two huge cruise ships rising like apartment buildings away to our right.

"How is this safe?"

But she was already on deck calling orders to Deniz, who yelled back excitedly. The boat puttered into a marina populated by little fishing boats about half a mile from the port's epicenter, which I could see on the left.

A battlement or fortress of some description rose on a spit of land linked to the fishing marina on the right. Deniz and his companion called out to another boat owner, presumably for permission to tether next to another craft since there were no free berths available. It appeared we were to boat-hop to the jetty.

Eva pulled me inside. "Take your robe off. Kusadasi is filled with western tourists. We'll fit in better dressed as Westerners."

I happily tugged off the robe and hijab, leaving them on the bench as I followed Eva outside. A fisherman was helping Deniz lash our craft to his amid many pleasantries and what I took to be an offer of tea. Deniz laughed, nodding while indicating Eva and myself.

"He just told them that he took us out on a tour of the coast for a little authentic Turkish flavor but now we have to catch a ferry," Eva told me before launching into a stream of Turkish herself.

The man nodded with a broad smile. In minutes, the fishermen were passing our bags from one craft to the other while helping us leap from boat to boat towards the shore.

We landed on the sidewalk in the midst of yet another Turkey.

23

We stood on a long congested promenade among cruisers in shorts and sunglasses poking through the market stalls like flocks of festive parrots. My roller bag made us conspicuous, since most visitors didn't lug anything heavier than shopping bags.

Eva scanned the streets. "Where is Ege? I neglected to ask what color of car he'd be driving." Hand shielding her eyes, she peered down the promenade.

"This doesn't look like the main road, Eva. Maybe we have to get through all these restaurants and shopping arcades where he's probably waiting."

"Yes, spot on. Let's go."

I fought the rise of unexplained panic. We were hundreds of miles away from Istanbul and yet I still felt as though we were being watched.

"Madam, would you like to see my beautiful handbags? Many more inside," a shopkeeper called.

"No thanks." I indicated to Eva to hurry with a jerk of my head. She caught my alarm and picked up her speed.

"I should have had Ege define a meeting spot," she admonished herself. "How will we ever find him?"

"Is he familiar with the port? This place is so rambling."

"I don't know."

"Someone is definitely following us." Foxy and Evan would have just waved. This one felt more threatening. "We've got to shake him, whoever he is." A large cement complex lined with pottery and leather shops rose ahead. "Quickly, in there!"

We scrambled into the arcade, blocking offers of hopeful shopkeepers along the way. My roller bag had become a liability. Not only did my wrist hurt from dragging it, but the extra weight slowed us down. But how could I just leave it? On the other hand, what did I really need now that the kilim was gone? Bare necessities like my knitting, that was it.

I made a flash decision and slipped into a public washroom. There, I removed the two silk tunics, the amulet against the evil eye, toiletries, plus a change of clothes from the case and tried stuffing them into my capacious carpet bag. Not everything fit. With the remorse of an amputee, I transferred some of my yarn into the roller bag, zipped it closed, removed all identification, and left it against the sink. It would probably be destroyed as a possible bomb threat.

Back in the arcade, Eva had disappeared from her watch. Frantically, I scanned the plaza, catching the eye of one man seemingly leisurely investigating a shop window two stores down. I turned and sprinted down the mall, checking over my shoulder just long enough to see him on my heels. I was almost at the outside door when Eva beckoned to me from a side utility entrance. "In here!"

"I thought you'd left!" I said as she shoved me through and slammed the metal door shut.

"I spied a bloke watching us so I opted to find an escape hatch. I'm trying to strike a deal with Amhad here."

Amhad, a bony little man standing but a few feet away, gripped a cigarette between stained teeth and pointed towards an equally senior rickshaw bearing a tattered blue canvas awning. Around us a warehouse space soared in aluminum roofing with loading bays lining one wall.

"Amhad?" I asked, looking at the man quizzically.

"Amhad doesn't speak much English. He and his son operate a little tourist trap here. They pick up the unsuspecting from the cruise ships and offer to deliver them to the shops but actually divert them in here, where they insist they buy a leather jacket before leaving. See the racks over against that wall? That's Amhad's shop. The man waving at us is his son."

I waved back while Amhad beamed tobacco-stained teeth, nodding pleasantly.

"Extortion must be a crime in Turkey, too."

"Of course it's a crime, Phoebe, but the tourists never lay charges. Are you ready? Amhad is going to drive us out to the main street, for a price, of course. Do you have cash? He says 100 euro fee but that's robbery."

"Tell him we'll give him the 100 euros," I said as I climbed into the cart. "It's either that or we buy a jacket, which hardly seems preferable. Amhad doesn't look strong enough to haul us anywhere," I pointed out.

Eva climbed in beside me, plunking her utility bag on her lap. "Looks are deceptive. Those skinny types are all sinew and muscle like a goat. Did you leave your hijab behind?"

"I did."

"Most unfortunate," she said, tying hers back over her head. "Try to stay hidden."

Amhad lifted the rickshaw's handles and spun us towards the open bays. Soon he was loping down the drive in an easy gate like a geriatric hackney horse. No one looked in our direction as our driver trotted us along the long paved drive and out into a kind of cul-de-sac populated by seafood bars and pomegranate stands. Two streets converged, one jutting uphill and the other forming a road lining the cove.

"Isn't that bay where we docked?" I asked, peering behind us through a crack in the awning. I caught a glimpse of our tail standing by the arcade entrance studying the crowd.

Eva saw him, too. "By the Goddess, what does he want?"

"Who knows? We're obviously the target of competing interests. He could be in Maggie's corner."

Eva called out to Amhad, pointing down the road. The man protested, arguing vehemently with his hands waving around like an agitated chicken. "He wants another 50 euros."

"For taking us few hundred feet further? Is he nuts?"

Then Eva shot forward. "Wait, I think I see Ege up ahead. See that white car parked midway down on the other side of the road with the young man standing beside it?" She waved her hand to Amhad to get moving.

The rickshaw jerked its way down the road, keeping close to the sidewalk. We were only 500 or so feet away from our getaway car when I turned to check for the arcade stalker, skimming my gaze over a restaurant patio in the process. By chance, I caught site of Agent Walker sipping coffee from a paper cup next to a restaurant stall. And he saw me. He jerked as if electrocuted, tossed away the cup, and lunged towards us.

I tugged Eva's arm. "Interpol! Run!"

Slinging our bags over our shoulders, we bolted from the rickshaw and sprinted towards Ege's car while Amhad launched into a string of Turkish at our back, dropped the rickshaw handles, and bolted after us. Sam Walker had cut half the distance between us, with Agent Karputz joining him from somewhere on the side. Eva was shouting at Ege, who spun around and jumped into the car. We reached the vehicle as it rolled towards us just seconds ahead of the infuriated Amhad.

"Drive!" Eva shouted at the kid as I threw our bags into the back seat and leaped in after them, each of us punching down the locks while we were at it. The car rolled forward with Amhad pounding on the window.

Sam Walker halted in the middle of the traffic, dead center of the road with a phone pressed to his ear, shouting at us and at whoever was on the phone simultaneously. Ege swerved to miss him, running up onto the sidewalk and smashing into a daily special sign. He gunned the accelerator, pulling off the curb and back on the road by forcing a car to jam on its brakes to let us in. Pieces of signage flapped from our grill. We could just see Walker leaping over the sidewalk debris towards us.

"Drive, Ege!" Eva shouted.

"Who is he?" the young man cried.

"Just get us away from here!"

But the traffic on either side was too thick to move.

"Hell, we're buggered," I muttered, resorting to a Maxism.

The phone rang from inside my bag. Pulling it out, I saw the caller ID of AGENT SAM WALKER and knew exactly how he'd traced me to Kusadasi. I powered my phone off and called to Eva to do the same. Why didn't I remember to turn it off when we left Istanbul?

Eva bellowed at Ege. "Drive, boy, drive!"

"But the traffic, Auntie!"

"Forget the traffic. Make like one of those getaway drivers you see in the American movies. Drive like James Bond with the bad guys chasing us."

"James Bond?"

Eva sighed in impatience. "James Bond, the master spy in his Porsche or whatever."

"But my Toyota is no Porsche, Auntie!"

"Don't be so literal, my boy. Use your imagination!"

Ege straightened his shoulders and made a masterful attempt at stunt driving, at least as far as swerving back over the sidewalk went. This sudden diversionary tactic, though causing pedestrians to scatter screaming, zipped us out of Walker's sight and across the grass into the driveway of a huge hotel parking lot. He drove around to the back of the building and hit the brakes behind a garage. "Now what?" he asked, wiping his forehead on his sleeve.

"We need another car and a route out of town."

"But, Auntie, this my only car."

"Do you know anyone with a spare car? Think, Ege, think."

"Soon everybody on the Aegean coast is going to know that two women are attempting to escape," I said, my anxiety rising to a pitch. "They'll figure out we've left the road soon enough."

"I'll phone my friend. He may have extra car," the boy said, thumbing a number into his phone. "Will they arrest us? Will I be thrown in jail?"

"Nonsense," Eva said. "You're not a criminal."

The sound of approaching sirens screaming away to our right was unmistakable.

"But you are?" Ege asked. "Auntie, are you in trouble again?"

"Stop worrying."

"Again?" I asked.

"Stop worrying," she repeated.

"The police are coming," I said as calmly as possible.

Ege was talking rapidly into his phone, his young face brightening with relief. "My friend has extra car and will lend it to you for small price."

"What price?" Eva asked.

"It doesn't matter. We'll pay what it takes," I interjected.

"Nonsense," Eva scolded. "Here, you must bargain for everything."

Ege turned back to his conversation, adding in a moment: "500 euros per week."

"Robbery!" Eva exclaimed. "Tell him a 250 Turkish lira flat rate and not a penny more."

Ege said the amount to his friend and listened for a second, nodding to himself.

I checked behind us. If Walker rounded that corner, we'd have to bolt on foot and how far would that take us? And the sirens were now on the main road.

"No Turkish lira, he says. Only euros. He says 350 euros flat rate," Ege said. "He says final offer."

"250 euros, then," Eva insisted.

"We'll take it at 350!" I cried. "Tell him yes. Eva, we don't have time for this. Where will we meet him, Ege? It has to be some place Walker would least expect us to go. He'll think we're heading for the main highway, which means we can't hit the highways until he's far ahead of us."

"The House of the Virgin Mary," Eva said, clapping her hands together. "Perfect! Tell your friend to bring the car there in, what, twenty minutes?"

"House of the Virgin Mary?" I asked. "We're going to a Catholic shrine in a Muslim country?"

"The Turks call it 'Meryem Ana' or 'Meryem Ana Evi' but it's more than a Catholic shrine. The Muslims honor it, too. Ege, get us there."

"How?" I asked.

"It's located on Mt. Koressos about 5 miles away."

"I don't mean in terms of directions, I mean we're blocked in."

"I know where it is," the boy said.

"Of course you do. You're a good Muslim son," Eva remarked.

"Why do I not feel like a good Muslim son with the police chasing?" Ege wailed.

"Hush. You'll be fine. Now all we have to do is escape this blasted parking lot undetected."

I took out my Foxy phone knowing damn well I was about to give Sir Rupert my precise location. I considered that an insurance policy as I tapped the icon with trembling fingers. The pin found our current location and in seconds I was studying a satellite view of the surrounding streets.

"Look," I pointed. "There's a service drive at the corner of this building leading to a parallel street."

In moments his little Toyota was weaving through the parked cars to a narrow lane bastioned by dumpsters and overhung by fig trees. Soon we were merging into traffic, cutting up one of the vertical tributaries heading for the hills. Looking down, I could just see the road running beside the water below. Police lights flashed amid the congestion surrounding a tour bus that seemed to be blocking the route in both directions. We took the first right-hand turn off the highway and onto a side street packed with hotels and restaurants.

"I know a back way," Ege stated.

"Of course you do!" Eva exclaimed with an air of triumph.

"Will I be arrested?" he asked again.

Eva turned to me. "Phoebe, you are a former lawyer. Tell him."

"I never wrote my bar exam and wouldn't know Turkish law anyway but I doubt you'll be arrested, Ege. They're not interested in you and, frankly, don't have the time to put you through the legal finagling. They'll question you, that's all."

"You must not tell them that we've taken another car," Eva added. "You'll say you dropped us off in town."

"They won't torture me?"

"This is not the CIA, my boy!"

"No, it's Interpol," I said glumly.

"Interpol? That's bad, yes?" Ege asked.

"They're not into torturing people for information, as far as I know." But what did I know? A face like Sam Walker's looked torturous enough.

"We'll soon be long gone and you certainly cannot be held accountable for my misdeeds," Eva added.

"Ege, you are still taking a risk in helping us and thank you for that, but I really don't think they'll do anything to you."

Or so I desperately hoped. Though I didn't share Eva's cavalier attitude, I really didn't see Ege as a big enough player to catch anyone's attention. On the other hand, I couldn't deny that my desperation was driving me to use people.

The car had begun to climb more steeply. We traversed the town through small back streets that cut a modern line across the port town but now were on a two-lane road heading straight up the side of a deeply forested mountain. Far below, the Aegean Sea basked in a luxurious blue with distant marble columns spiking the shoreline zenith. I took a deep breath. "Ephesus!"

"Ah, yes," Eva sighed, "one of the most beautiful cities of the ancient world, yet what we seek far transcends the Greeks and Romans, Phoebe, though they embraced our Goddess in Artemis. How I wish I could take you to see Her temple, once one of the seven wonders of the ancient world, now reduced to rubble by the narrow perspective of long ago marauders. But today we visit another goddess."

"We do?"

"The Virgin Mary is the closest to a goddess we have in the present time. The Goddess has been with us through the eons, appearing in many guises and by many names, including in this life as Mary, Mother of God. We hunger for the Divine Feminine in any manifestation. She figures prominently in the Muslim faith where she is recognized as the mother of a great prophet."

"I didn't realize that Islam intersects anywhere near Christianity or Judaism."

"Of course you didn't. Religions rarely highlight their commonalities, but prefer to pound us over the head with their differences; there is only one Universal Spirit, one God, rising far beyond gender boundaries. Man has claimed Him in his image, while we women claim Her in ours. We are both right and yet not."

"And Mary reportedly came here at some point?"

"According to legend, Mary was delivered here by Joseph, where she lived until her Assumption. Though archaeology hasn't confirmed it as truth and Catholic tradition places her Dormition in Jerusalem, I have no doubt as to its authenticity. A real archaeologist must work with her spirit as much with her investigative strategies. How else are we to understand the history and structures of human societies if we don't allow in our humanity? Only, I hold that the Virgin Mary is the modern manifestation of the Goddess, not just mother of God but a manifestation of God Herself. Everything we do here is in Her name."

"So it follows that we are breaking multiple laws, including breaking a bargain with a rickshaw driver plus a mass of other infractions, all in the name of the Virgin Mary? Somehow I doubt she approves."

"You are fixating on too small a picture, Phoebe. Consider the whole fabric."

In reality, I kept my attention fixating on the back window, keening for police cars and sirens, my mind only half on goddesses. This couldn't be me, the upholder of all things legal, climbing this hill to parts unknown on a quest to find a goddess by any name.

The higher we climbed, the thicker the forest on either side, until far up on what seemed the apex of the incline, a golden statue of the Virgin Mary glowed to the left. Tour buses parked on either side, the statue's base amassed by visitors. All I could do was look up and gasp.

I was not a religious person. I couldn't abide or condone the murderous tyranny inflicted on humanity in the name of any dogma, yet, for one brief instant, I felt the impact of faith in its purest form. It was not the statue itself but the power of light the statue invoked that touched me on some level I couldn't understand. No words existed for that moment of sudden illumination but the effect quickly dissipated.

"Are you Catholic?" I asked Eva as the car eased between buses and continued up the mountain.

"Certainly not. I embrace all religions yet follow none. More commonalities link the faiths than differences separate them, when all is said and done, so why pledge allegiance to only one? I am a child of the One. Power and politics blind us into believing that division and war are critical to protect one's secular view. Our Virgin, our Goddess, does not represent these things. She, like Jesus, Mohammed, Buddha, and most of the true prophets, speaks of peace and love. Only man corrupts that message to his own ends."

"Auntie, I'll park over there in the far corner, okay?"

We had pulled into a large parking area filled with tour busses, taxis, and other vehicles lined with more trinket booths and cafeterias than I'd seen outside of a city center. This is a holy sanctuary?

"Yes, fine. Phoebe and I will just take a brief jaunt up to the shrine while you wait for your friend. Phoebe, give him the money, if you please. I am distressingly low on funds until we find an ATM. Ege can pay for the car while we disappear for a few moments."

I dug around inside my bag.

"But, Auntie, shouldn't you be here to make the deal?"

"The deal has already been struck, my boy. Just give him the 250 euros and let him have your car to get back into town. You can wait for us here and take a cab home yourself. Phoebe will give you the fare."

I counted out the euros. "Phoebe's almost running out of euros at this point, just so Eva knows, but here's 350 euros, as agreed. Hopefully that works." I passed a rolled wad of bills to the young man. "Your aunt's right, though: it makes way more sense to keep your friend out of it to avoid another witness for the police to interrogate."

The word "interrogate" caused the young man to pale.

"It will be fine," said Eva patting her nephew's hand. "Just wait for your friend. By my estimate, we have at least ten minutes before he arrives. I do not see it as remotely likely that the police will follow us here, in any case. They'll expect us to be heading out of town."

"Unless someone caught sight of us," I said, but Eva was already marching towards a ticket booth on the other side of the parking lot. I scrambled after her, wading along with the crowd to a path leading between concession stands selling religious memorabilia, books, bottles of holy water, and refreshments.

The noise and bustle soon hushed into a leafy parkland threaded through by the upward-leading path. Sunlight filtered through the canopy, a butterfly danced in the sun motes, and I was suffused by a deep envelope of peace. People stopped speaking. I was only vaguely aware of Eva. Though she walked beside me, part of my destiny in some way not clearly understood, we remained separate.

The path led steadily upward, past the footprint of an ancient structure to the left and, though I expected my archaeologist companion to launch into a lecture, she continued past without a word. The sanctuary evoked a profound inward-seeking communion I had never experienced. Like being in a church without walls, even the air seemed holy. Words were not encouraged or necessary.

We arrived at a small tree-shaded stone church at the hill's crest. We pilgrims threaded through the building into a central chapel graced by a candle-lit altar holding a black Madonna. Some visitors cried, most prayed. I lit a small white candle to place before the altar, something I did every time I visited a place of worship, regardless of denomination. Whether it be a cathedral in Italy or a Buddhist shrine, I didn't care. Something within sought hallowed ground to honor my dead through a small light of remembrance.

Since we were gently encouraged to keep moving in a building that could only hold a few supplicants at a time, I moved into the smaller anteroom, which I later learned was an area of worship for Muslims. The sight of a handful of hijab-wearing women clustered at the shrine praying struck me as poignant.

Back outside in the sunlit glade, people either sat on the benches in silent prayer or continued down the other side of the hill following the path to the gate. I quickly caught up to Eva, who I found fixing a message onto a stone wall lining the right-hand side of the downward path, a wall bristling with feathery messages of frayed paper, tissue, photographs, and written prayers. Others were doing something similar, and still others filled bottles from the faucet of a nearby spring.

I watched in silence as supplicants approached the wishing wall. I remained still yet deeply moved. Words seemed superfluous for this communion.

"Phoebe," Eva roused me, returning from her supplication. "We had best get back to the car park."

I nodded, falling into step beside her. As we wove down the path, people around us resumed speaking. "Obviously it's been restored, but does that chapel truly date to Mary's time?" I asked.

"My former colleagues believe most of the building dates from the sixth or seventh century, but it has foundations that may date to the first century AD, which places it firmly in the apostolic period. It was a small domicile originally, which lends even more credence to the story, but perhaps the most fascinating aspect of all is that its existence came to light through nothing short of a documented miracle." Eva's face seemed rapt with wonder, though her professorial tone continued.

"A miracle?"

"Verifiably, or as much as any miracle is verifiable. In 1812 a German nun, one Sister Anne Catherine Emmerich, a bed-ridden woman who had not journeyed beyond her own front door, began manifesting stigmata and experiencing visions, including one describing the Virgin Mary and Apostle John traveling from Jerusalem to Ephesus. She described Mary's house in detail right down to the location and aspect, all of which was recorded at her bedside by a man named Brentano. Brentano scribed that Mary had lived in a house built by John for her sole use, a stone building with a fireplace and a rounded back wall. According to the report, the room currently assigned as a Muslim chapel was once Mary's bedroom and had a spring running through it—perhaps an early form of indoor plumbing—which is the same spring flowing through the wishing wall. Because it's true makes it no less extraordinary."

We pressed through the congestion around the concession stands and bypassed the hawkers on our way to the parking lot. At first, we couldn't see Ege, since the recognizable white Toyota had disappeared, but his agitated waving finally caught our attention. He stood beside what at first glance looked to be an ancient army vehicle. Painted a dead-bird green, the scarred little truck bore numerous battle scars along its battered sides.

"What in the name of the Goddess is that?" Eva demanded.

"It's a 1983 Series 3 Land Rover, Auntie," Ege said, clapping his hands together.

"It looks like it hails from World War Two."

"Mustapha says it is in very good condition for its age."

"I've heard the same thing about me and don't consider it remotely flattering."

"He says it is very reliable since he fixed it last. Four-wheel drive, nearly new tires for bumping over rocks. He say he would charge most much more to rent it but for you, he gives excellent deal. You must return it in same condition or he will charge more."

"Pha! It doesn't look worth 350 euros if we bought it outright." Eva surveyed the truck with suspicion. "It does rather look like it's bumped over quite a few rocks already. Where did he get it? Oh, never mind. Blast it, anyway. We must make haste. Pass me the keys, dear boy. Thank you for everything." She embraced her nephew heartily, patted his cheek, and bolted for the driver's seat. "Come, Phoebe."

I hugged Ege, too, and climbed up into the passenger side. Inside, a tree-shaped air fresher dangling from the rear view mirror emitted a piny scent that couldn't quite mask the reek of dirty socks. Otherwise, the truck appeared relatively clean despite the tattered upholstery.

Ege poked his head through the open window. "He says he keeps my car until this returned in same condition in one week."

Eva let out a bark of laughter. "It will take far longer than that for our business to conclude, tell him. Get your car back, Ege. That wasn't the deal. Tell him we'll get this returned when we can."

"Ege, here," I passed him my last 200 euro. "Please give whatever is left after your cab ride to the rickshaw driver working the pier where we came in. You saw him chasing us earlier? Tell him we owe him more, which I'll try to get to him as soon as I can. Will you do that for me?"

The young man nodded, pocketing the money.

"Phoebe, we must go." Eva turned the key, and the truck started with a cough and pitched forward, spewing black fumes as it went. Ege backed away with his mouth covered as we lurched our way towards the exit.

"The police should be well ahead of us by now," Eva said. "We'll cross the back routes. I know some tracks through the villages they'd never suspect we'd use. The manpower for these local police forces is minuscule, so as long as they don't call the army on us, we should be fine."

"Why would the army be involved?" I asked.

"Interpol often work with the Turkish army in the rural regions. They are usually much better manned in the outreaches, which is where we're heading. My point is that matters may get more challenging."

I threw up my hands. "What, you don't find this challenging enough?"

And then, as if determined to emphasize the moment, the truck sputtered to a halt.

24

The Rover coughed before chugging down the hill in fumy protest.

"Hopefully this heap will remain equal to the task. Pray that the Goddess will lead us to Cappadocia without issue."

"Does the Goddess do spark plugs?" I asked.

"Why do you ask?"

"Because this thing is suffering from serious oil issues. I used to tinker with my dad's boat engine. Burning oil this badly in something this vintage probably means clogged spark plugs."

"Then, to answer your question, yes, the Goddess does spark plugs. As soon as we get someplace safe, you can have a look under the hood in Her name. Meanwhile, we need a map."

"We've got to keep the phones turned off or they'll track us."

"Not your Google maps, Phoebe, real maps. A paper version is always preferable to gadgetry. Until we obtain such, I'll take the back routes. Borek and I used to journey from the coast to Cappadocia all the time. He loved this land. He was, indeed, a true Anatolian boy."

We cut up alternative roads threading through thick forests, along lanes climbing between orchards of figs and pomegranate, and into winding strings of concrete villages. We stopped in one tiny place, estimated population fifty or less, and dropped into an alcove serving as the community's general store.

Besides the map, my remaining funds bought water, juices, crackers, a hunk of thick white cheese, oranges, and two meat-filled pastries. It amazed me how much that closet-sized depot could stock.

For good measure, Eva filled the gas tank at the nearby garage while I checked the plugs. As I suspected, they were gummed to death. After wiping them clean, I replenished the oil, and bought a roll of paper towels.

"We'll just have to hope she'll get us to wherever we're going, which is where, by the way?" I hadn't asked earlier, but now that a map spread across my lap, the time had come.

"Goreme and environs."

I located the area on the map, an estimated 600 miles away. "It will take hours to get there."

"I'm estimating 12 hours without stopping except for gas, bathroom, and spark plug resuscitation. What else can we do? They'll be watching the airports and the main routes. Cutting across country is our best option."

Settling in for a long, bumpy ride, I tried to keep my eyes open for possible pursuers in a vehicle that had probably lost its suspension a decade ago. Every bone in my body rattled but I had to admit, those back routes, even if it meant taking us miles off course, probably kept pursuers off our tail. Besides, the truck definitely ran better with the pedal down, since pausing or stopping only invited vehicular petulance.

I passed Eva one of the meat pies and devoured the other along with an orange, the map serving as my place mat.

"All right, Eva, we're in no immediate danger, so tell me your story," I said, wiping my fingers on a slice of paper towel. "I want to know exactly why you were disgraced with the Turkish government and what you're after in Anatolia. It's time, no excuses. Once you tell me everything, and I mean everything, I'll tell you my story, okay?"

"I am agreeable to that, Phoebe," she said, biting into the pie, scattering crumbs onto her cargo pants. I passed her a piece of paper towel, which she ignored. After chewing for a moment, she added, "but I must ask that you not judge me. You'd think that, at my age, judgment would no longer matter but I fear it does. I do want you to trust me, no matter what."

"You ask me to trust you unconditionally?"

"I ask that you have faith."

"Faith in you?"

"Just faith, faith that things will work out as they are meant to, regardless of how it may disrupt our lives in the progress. Faith doesn't judge."

"Just talk, Eva."

"Very well. In 1979, Borek and I were noted authorities, published widely, excavating at renowned sites, and enjoying a certain international status as guest lecturers. We were oft called upon by Turkish authorities to provide provenance for important artifacts and regularly contributed expertise to museums. Indeed, it was such a heady time for us both. To be partnered in such significant endeavors with one's mate can be so inspiring. We never competed. Ours was a true partnership based on love and mutual respect."

"What happened?"

"Borek made a significant discovery. He had such a gift, that man. It was as if he had an instinct for locating tombs and hill fortifications, though he would claim that topographical maps and research combined with an astute ear for local legend led him to such finds. The fact remains that he located sites where others did not. More importantly, people would tell him things. Why would they not? He was well-known in Anatolia, one of their own made good in the world of academia, a star, if you will."

"He was already famous then?"

"Oh, among archaeologists, quite. In any case, on one occasion, he was traveling the region of Yalakinar Malalles, or so he claimed, though he never told me exactly where. I was away lecturing in London at the time. He loved to journey around this ancient land, meeting and talking with the locals, always keeping his ears open for local traditions that might indicate the existence of ancient settlements."

"And?"

"Don't be so impatient, Phoebe. Good stories take time. And one night, he was staying as a guest in a village, something he often did to further his research, when a young woman approached him after dark, claiming that her family had stumbled upon an ancient treasure hidden in an underground city they had been guarding for generations, maybe centuries."

"An entire underground city?"

"They are relatively common in central Turkey. An estimated 50 miles of tunnels and cave houses exist underground in Cappadocia alone."

"Okay, so go on. A young woman approached Borek one night..."

"Clearly she was fearful. She claimed that it was only the women who guarded this secret, afraid to reveal it to their menfolk in case they were exposed to the Turkish Antiquities authorities and the find ripped away from them or worse. More than anything, she feared the riches they secured would be leaked into the black market and the significance of the site lost forever."

"She was educated?"

"She was a university student returning home for a visit and understood the historical value of the find, yes. She spoke English fluently, but her mother and aunts saw the site as more religious than archaeological. It had a deep spiritual connection for them."

"So she showed the treasure to Borek?"

"Oh, indeed she did but not in a way that he could easily relocate or identify. She led him there in the early hours of the morning, part of the way blindfolded, not an easy maneuver considering that the route traversed rough terrain and involved caves and cliffs. You'll better understand the landscape once we reach Cappadocia. In any case, once inside an underground cave system, this young woman revealed a shrine buried deep within the cliffs, an amazing Bronze Age find that Borek dated as possibly from the time of Troy 1V."

"Homer's Troy?"

"No, this civilization would have predated Homer by over a thousand years. Borek estimated 1200 BC, making it contemporary with Mycenae, but it needed much more thorough study. The young woman refused to let him photograph anything or even to make a return trip. He had just that night to record the findings, which he did through a series of hasty sketches by lamplight. I've studied those sketches—gold daggers, goddess statuary, necklaces, and gold cuffs. The overriding images in the shrine were of a female deity counterbalanced by a bull—male and female represented in primitive yet powerful symbolic form."

"Gold," I said, thinking of certain thieves.

"But, Phoebe, there was also wall art of incredible intricacy. Preserved in the dark for thousands of years were these motifs of an early version of Cybele, the Vulture Goddess, motifs almost exactly like the ones on your kilim. Don't you see? Borek had discovered a lost Goddess shrine protected through the centuries by Her very own daughters! Is that not extraordinary?"

I swallowed hard. "Oh, yes, but how could they keep that secret against all the village men?"

"Borek believed that some men may have been entrusted with the secret but had kept it safe in honor of the Goddess or, as I suggested, more likely for fear how such a find might impact the life of the village, inviting violence, treachery, and the like, as gold is wont to do. The other fear is that it might be absconded by the government, thus secreted away from the village, eventually resulting in some foreign-financed archaeological dig to disrupt their village life. This was before cable TV bristled on every roof, which is so often the case now. They were trying to preserve their lifestyle."

"I get that but what did Borek do with these sketches and the information?"

"Nothing. The young woman had only taken him to the site to verify its age and attribute it to a specific civilization, something the mothers had no interest in, but she made him promise not to reveal the village name or vicinity. He could publish his notes but nothing more."

"And he agreed to that?"

"Certainly. Borek was a man of integrity. His word was rock; thus he would never reveal the details of the location to another soul, even to me. I knew the rough area, but with miles of cave formations and many tiny villages, that told me little enough. Yet what Borek showed me was convincing as to the significance of the find."

"But, as an archaeologist, keeping such a find secret must have been terribly hard."

"Difficult for him, excruciating for me. It proved my thesis, you see, confirming my life's work. Still, we knew that, without tangible evidence, these notes were worth nothing in the scholarly world. To publish them, or even tell of this incredible discovery, would only heap ridicule upon his head, possibly ruin him. And yet there it was, the extraordinary story of a generation of women guarding a secret of incredible cultural, social, spiritual, and archaeological value for centuries. If he published findings without proof, he'd be ruined."

The silence that followed was relieved only by the sound of the tires rumbling along the dirt road. "So you published them in your name," I said after a moment.

"He didn't want me to, tried to stop me, in fact, but I had to get the word out, let the world see those incredible images with their own eyes, see the Goddess's arms extended into the vortex of the sacred feminine, sacrosanct, perfect, timeless, in Her glory, as is Her right. I had to connect those images to the same motifs we find in Anatolian kilims today, proving our need for balance in the cosmic, female balanced with male, the bull and womb, the Polat energies in harmony, rather than this destructive dysfunction of presumed male superiority over female! I had to, Phoebe!"

"And you published those raw notes without proof?"

"I tidied them up but did not submit them to an archaeological journal but rather the London Illustrated News in my name. I wrote of how this proved that the ancients were far wiser than we in the balance of the universe, that the Goddess was still alive in the hearts of Her priestesses."

"That doesn't sound very archaeological."

"Well, no, that is not the spirit in which it was written. Nevertheless, Turkish authorities demanded to know why they had not been informed. The antiquities laws are very strict here, as they should be. If ever a citizen or visitor should stumble upon an ancient site, which happens fairly often, the authorities must be informed immediately or the finders arrested."

"But you couldn't reveal the site because you didn't know where it was."

"No, so I claimed that it was I who had made the promise to the village woman not reveal my source. The Turkish authorities demanded that I take them to the village but, of course, I couldn't. They responded by banishing me from Turkey, treating me as if I were a bad girl who wouldn't obey her superiors. The impact of that moment was excruciating. My banishment was not as a man's would have been. Mine was humiliating as I was barraged with condescending diatribes best reserved for children caught raiding cookie jars. On the other hand, that same attitude probably kept me out of prison."

"And Borek just stood by while you were humiliated?"

"No, of course not. He protested loudly, stating that he believed me absolutely-which he did, of course—and even wrote an article countering the vilification I received at the hands of my colleagues."

"But didn't he stand up and explain?"

"I did it without his consent so, no, of course not. I wanted his reputation to remain unblemished, which it did, after I took the experience as being totally my own. The Turkish authorities banished me and I returned to England without Borek."

"He wouldn't even come with you?"

"Why should we both lose our careers and reputations? He stayed in Turkey but visited me in London sometimes."

"Did he forgive you?"

"Of course he did. He loved me."

"And you forgave him for choosing his career over his life with you?"

"It could be argued that I did the same."

"But his love for you should have put you first, and your commitment to your lives together should have done the same."

"Phoebe, you are a romantic. I consider myself an idealist but not a romantic. You, I fear, are both."

"You made a promise to one another, a contract which you both broke. Promise and commitment are part of marriage vows. That's not idealism, that's an issue of morality as well as legality."

"You are right. I failed him and he failed me but we loved one another despite it all. As the person I was then, head-strong and driven, I did what I had to. What I regret most is that I was not with him when he died. Until that moment, I always believed we would be together again, even if only in our retirement. I believed we had time, which we didn't. As it was, he was here in Cappadocia trying to find the site and thus exonerate my name when he slipped from a cliff and fell to his death. We never have enough time. That's the one fact we must all grasp. Time is finite. Love is not."

"I'm so sorry, Eva. I can only imagine the heartbreak you've experienced."

"Heartbreak is part of being human. None of us escape unscathed. We all have dark amid the light."

I closed my eyes. "I like to think of a life as a complex weaving. There are patterns in the mix of light and dark—joy and sorrow, good and bad—but the balance determines the strength of the design. Do we have enough light to counterbalance the dark? What if we have so much dark amid the light that it leaves our weave warped beyond repair?"

"Dear Phoebe, no weave is warped beyond repair. It's all in how you see it and how you make it. You are still the weaver, remember. You may not have the whole picture but some of the design is in your jurisdiction. Blend your warp into the bigger pattern, move on, and on no account dwell on the flaws. Where there are holes, let in the light. That's where faith comes in."

"Are you about to bring up the Goddess?"

"Would it help if I said God?"

"I'm not religious."

"Neither am I in the true sense. It's enough to be truly awake."

We drove along in silence for a while, lost in our thoughts as the sun sank deeper, a glory of red-gold hues intensified by deep ultramarine riding overhead. I remained fixed on the luminescence pooling on the horizon as it seeped away into the twilight. There is no light without dark. The impact of that adage had never affected me so profoundly.

"Now I understand why and where we're going," I said, after a while. "You want to find that village and locate the secret cache to protect the find, maybe exonerate your name. You needed to see my kilim to confirm the location. And the Bronze Age gold?"

"Gold is not my interest. My overriding impetus is to prove the strength of Goddess worship across time and patriarchy."

"Gold is interesting to somebody, lots of somebodies. And don't the same considerations still apply? I mean, if you find the site, won't Borek's promise have been for nothing and the site will be exposed?"

"It's already been exposed. I neglected to tell you what might be the most important part. A young archaeologist friend informed me a few months back that certain ancient artifacts from the Anatolian region had begun appearing on the black market—daggers mostly, but very distinctive in design. He sent me a

213

picture, and the artifacts exactly matched one of the designs in Borek's notebook. Somebody has infiltrated the cache and is leaking the pieces into the black market."

I leaned forward. "Ah, now I understand Noel's and Toby's interest in the site."

"Don't be so quick to judge, Phoebe."

"Judge what, who? You knew my connection all along. That's why you've never pressed me for details on my side of the story. You already know it."

"Not all of it, I don't. I know about the Bermuda heist, certainly. Every archaeologist knows that story. My point is that you may have incorrectly attributed the identity of criminals chasing the Goddess hoard."

"I know Maggie and Noel are after it."

"Perhaps not for the reason you suspect. Phoebe, I knew about your kilim long before I met you in Istanbul."

I took a deep steadying breath. "So our meeting was staged?"

"Our lives are interwoven. The meeting only served to forge our alliance."

"You knew who I was all along."

"I am a researcher, Phoebe, and I have many connections."

"Why didn't you say something?" I stared straight ahead, my fingers icy in my lap.

"When have we had the chance? We have been on the run from the moment we meant, and first I needed to establish trust between us. We will find this site together and you can confront your demons just as I must battle my own. Finding this site is our mutual salvation. I said I will help you and so I shall."

"By withholding the truth, by lying?"

"I never lied, though I withheld the truth, certainly. You have trust issues, so I realized I had to tread carefully. There is more that I have to say, but perhaps I've said enough for now."

I closed my eyes and took a deep breath. "I can't wait to learn the next segment but first, I need to pee. We've been driving for hours. Let's find a station. How far away are we?"

"Maybe another three-hour drive. We are somewhere near Mustafapasa. There will be gas stations there and restaurants but that means entering a busy town. On the other hand, I doubt even the police can cover every mile of this place."

"Let's take that chance. Oh, and I'll drive the next leg." I had so much to think about and plan. Right then, I yearned to be back of control of something, even if it was just that ancient Rover.

So far, the truck had bombed along without too many incidents, other than the occasional stall, but the engine was misfiring more frequently now. We had to enter a populated area and do what had to be done. Meanwhile, I had to think. Eva had misled me to what end? On the other hand, she could help me get to a site that drew Toby and the others.

Electric lights began appearing embedded in the midst of weird organic rock shapes ahead. Mushroom chimneys? Strange flood-lit turrets and irregular twisting pinnacles rose from the earth all around.

"Did Gaudi hit this place with a wicked sense of humor or is this landscaping via deranged djinn?"

Eva laughed. "Natural earth formations, the effect of rain and wind on the soft porous rock indigenous to the area. The terrain is riddled with cave systems, some natural, some man enhanced—entire subterranean cities—all once inhabited by ancient civilizations, including the Hittites, and even the Christians escaping the Romans."

A magnificent cave hotel soared in flood-lit fairy spires along a main street where we stopped at a gas station. While Eva filled the tank, I used the bathroom and splashed water on my face as if that would shock clear thoughts into my brain. I bought an orange juice and stood outside waiting, gulping in the high cold night air along with the liquid.

We were at a much higher altitude, far from the humidity of the ocean, making the starry sky so clear it penetrated the haze of town lights. My gaze climbed upward, brushing the stars, before diving down again to the cave hotel, staring up at the glowing terrarium-like rooms.

Each room was unique, each suspended in the darkness like pools of warmth and light. My gaze dropped further, landing by chance on the lobby directly across the street. A man stood outside the glass doorway shooting furtive glances in our direction while talking urgently into his cell phone.

"Eva," I whispered. She stood by the gas attendant watching him refill the oil. I jerked my head towards the hotel. "We've got to get out of here."

She turned to the attendant. "Never mind that. Do you take credit cards?"

I jumped into the driver's seat and tried the engine. Nothing. I checked the lobby again. Two men stood there now instead of one.

I watched as the new arrival, a tall bearded man dressed in a hat and scarf over a leather jacket yanked away the other's cell phone and smashed it against the cement doorstep, bringing the heel of his boot crashing down on the little flip-top.

The first man responded with a swinging punch, which the tall man easily deflected following up with a jaw-cracking upswing of his own. The blow pitched the shorter man backward onto the tarmac, after which the victor flexed his hand, and bounded across the road towards us.

"Oh, shit!" I cried, the moment I identified that long bearded face. I rolled down the window. "Go to hell!"

He climbed into the passenger side. "Hello to you, too, Phoebe. Where's Eva? How the hell did you two get the Turkish army after you?"

25

Eva dove into the back seat. "I wasn't expecting you so soon, Noel."

"Change of plans," he commented.

"I suppose this scum-bag bastard is the young colleague you referred to?" I said.

"Phoebe, I—" Eva began.

"Talk later," Noel ordered. "That man alerted the cavalry. Could you force this rust bucket to move, Phoebe?"

"Think I'm not trying, you thieving butt-head? The engine is fried, get it?" I kept turning the key in the ignition. "Eva, did you plan this all along?"

"Certainly not," Eva said. "It's not what you think. If things worked according to plan, we would have all connected in Istanbul."

"Where you had plenty of time to explain."

"Not so. I—"

"Let me drive." Noel interrupted, placing one hand on the gear shift.

"No!" I elbowed him away. I couldn't deal with either of them right then, being too intent on getting the engine started. Maybe having Noel in the front seat was preferable to being captured by the Turkish army but not by much.

Of course, the engine refused to catch. "Damn!" I whacked the steering wheel, glancing towards the hotel in time to see the wounded man limping into the lobby.

"They'll be here in minutes," Noel said, his voice smoothed down to honey and tonic. "Ease up on the accelerator. Don't flood the thing. Stay calm. What's wrong with your wrists?"

"Don't tell me to stay calm, shit-head."

"I bring out your best adjectives, don't I?"

Headlights barreled towards us.

"Do what he says, Phoebe. The Goddess is on our side," Eva said.

"I know well enough not to flood the damn engine!" I kept trying the ignition, shocked when the Rover finally bolted forward in a string of jerky lurches. Praying to the power of momentum alone, I shifted gears, jammed on the accelerator, and rolled onto the road just as an army truck squealed to a halt beside us.

"There's a hill ahead," Noel said. "Switchback turns, no guard rails, straight down for maybe two miles. Can you handle that?"

"Of course I can handle that. It's double-crossing swine like you two I can't handle."

The truck hitched forward for another 500 feet, reached the crest of the hill, and stalled with the wheels still rolling. Uniformed men were running towards us.

I released the clutch, switched to neutral, and allowed gravity to barrel us downhill, thinking I'd worry about the bottom once we got there. Shots fired, bullets pinging against the fender and hitting the rear tires, first right then left. Rubber burst, sending the truck veering towards the cliff edge.

"They're firing at us!" I gripped the wheel and wrenched the truck back on the road as we careened around the bend grating on the back rims.

Noel whistled, his hands gripping the dashboard. "You're good!"

"I'm damn good," I said between my teeth.

"There's the sign to Goreme!" Eva called.

Letters flashed white on green in our dying headlights as I took the turn with a peal worthy of the Formula 500. For a few giddy seconds, I thought we'd crash into the rocks but instead we ground to a halt half-way up the rise before gravity kicked in and we began scraping backwards.

"Run!" I shouted.

I slammed up the handbrake, turned off the lights, and left the keys in the ignition while flood-lit rock formations rose on either side. I snatched our belongings from the rear seat, throwing Eva's knapsack and my carpet bag onto the road while stuffing the last of our food supplies into my pockets. Noel slung our bags over his shoulders and bounded towards the rocks.

"I know a shortcut through the valley!" Eva called.

A glimpse of headlights below fueled my adrenalin. I ran towards illuminated rocks thrusting into the night sky like gigantic penises, a sight made weirder by our elongated shadows shrinking towards us. I bounded deeper between twisting spires, oblivious of anything but plunging forward.

The ground changed from grass-bristled sand to rock. The moment we broke away from the floodlights, the surrounding shadows thickened like glue on tar. I stumbled, righted myself, and kept running.

Visibility shrank. Eva and Noel appeared like distorted lumps two shades lighter than the background, but they kept disappearing around corners leaving me hissing at them for directions. Finally, Noel picked his way back to me and clasped my hand firmly in his, tugging me behind him. I shook him loose and struggled on.

Men's shouts trumpeted the air at our backs. I imagined flashlights sweeping the area while we stumbled along blindly. And it seemed endless, those tortured rock towers. Large and small, they clustered in all directions, as dense as trunks of giant stalagmites frozen in some ancient dance. Sometimes the formations briefly fell away into a moon-bleached expanse which we'd sprint across until safely undercover.

We ran for what seemed like hours until Eva slumped against a rock trying to catch her breath. As I leaned nearby, I realized I could no longer hear our pursuers.

"They'll give up the search for tonight," Noel commented, as if reading my thoughts. "Probably resume in the morning with helicopters."

"Why is the army after us again?" I panted.

"Because you count Interpol among your fans, obviously." Noel took a swig of water from a bottle he pulled from a bag slung across his body. "I suspect they've engaged the army to bring you two in. Eva, how are you holding up?"

"Fine, thank you. Don't you worry, I'll make it."

"How far away from the valley are we?" he asked.

"I have no idea," she said, sinking onto her haunches. "I lost my way some time back. I am so very tired."

"Best to keep moving," Noel urged, helping her to her feet. "If they tracked you this far, they may guess the general direction we're heading."

"That they may, young man, but I know this terrain in ways they don't," she said, steadying her breath. "If I can reach the valley, I know many hiding places. It's got to be near here somewhere."

"Hold on to me. There, that's it." Noel tucked her arm into his and smiled down at her. "We'll be all right."

"I shouldn't have dragged you into this," she said to him. "You've risked so much for me."

"I'm here willingly. Let's see this thing through."

"Have you two been in contact from the beginning?"

"I'm sorry, Phoebe," Eva said. "I asked Dr. Halloran to help me locate Borek's hidden site long ago and he promised to do so. The timing has become even more critical."

I wrapped my arms around myself to keep from shivering. Stay calm, I cautioned myself. I was thousands of miles from home being pursued by the police, army, and God knows who else, in the company of a black market thief and a disgraced professor. All I could do was go with the flow until I could figure something out.

"Keep moving," Noel urged.

"Give me my carpet bag, please. I can manage perfectly well handling my own stuff." I held out my hand.

"I'm sure you can," he replied smoothly, shifting the weight of the two bags on his considerably broader shoulders, "but it's easier for me."

"It's fine to accept a little help sometimes," Eva said. "I have learned that much over the years."

"So, as a man, he gets to play predatory bastard while I, the lowly weaker sex, am helpless by virtue of my feminine nature, is that it?" I couldn't stop spewing juvenile garbage.

Noel laughed. "For the record, you drive more like a trucker than an earth mother."

"Can we just stop this?" Eva gripped Noel's arm and pointed between two boulders opening ahead. "Head that way." Together they continued picking their way over the rocks with me following.

The temperatures fell alarmingly. We had begun our day amid balmy Aegean breezes and now stumbled about in this frigid moonscape.

I soon lost all track of time. One minute blended into the next with sequence after sequence of stark shadows juxtaposed against ghostly peaks. Above, the stars spangled over moon silvered turrets, while at our feet, shadows clung so thickly I could be wading in pitch. Nothing but a slight wind in an otherwise supernatural stillness accompanied our ragged breathing. Exhausted, I began stumbling more and Eva, too, but she clung to Noel. At one point, they turned a corner and disappeared, leaving me to face multiple paths with no idea of which one to take. I plunged left and the ground dropped sharply under my feet. The stone walls fell away as I hit the ground hard before tumbling downhill. Flashes of moonlit cliffs flipped over again and again, but nothing could stop my rolling trajectory.

* 26*

A heavy weight landed on top of me, grinding me to a halt and walloping the breath from my lungs. I spent winded seconds on my back looking up into Noel's shadowed face. Only when he shifted his knees to straddle me, did I force the air back into my chest.

"Are you all right?" He shoved the hair from his eyes.

I inhaled sharply. "Get. Off. Me."

He slowly climbed to his feet and offered me his hand. I stood there, knees trembling, my hand firmly in his, recalibrating my balance.

"Are you all right, Phoebe?" Eva called down.

"Bruised not broken," Noel shouted back. "Stay where you are. We're coming up."

I yanked away my hand. "Not so fast. Where's Toby?"

"Istanbul."

"Why not here?" I began toppling sideways, he caught me, and I endured him pressing me even closer.

"I'll tell you later."

"I'm sick of later. Tell me now. He sent me the kilim so I'd find him."

"Will you listen? I said we planned to meet you in Istanbul, but matters got complicated so we had to thwart that initiative."

"I need to see him."

"You will."

"When?"

"Not now, obviously. We're standing on the edge of a bloody cliff!"

"I'm so sick of this!" And without thinking, I shoved him hard, too hard. For a terrifying moment, I watched him skidding downward towards the edge. In seconds he caught his balance and scrambled back up towards me.

"Do you want me dead, is that it?" his voice more pained than angry. "Would that make up for all I've done?"

"I didn't mean to push you so hard but, to answer your question, no, I don't want you dead. I want you in prison suffering for years and years, and just so you know, there's no way I'm going to let you get away with another theft. I don't care what I have to do."

"I'm not here to plunder, Phoebe. I'm here to help Eva."

"Do you expect me to believe that?"

Eva scrabbled down towards us in a flurry of pebbles. "What's taking you two so long?" she called. "I was up there looking out over that cliff and realized that's it, that's the valley I've been seeking right below us. All we need do is find our way down and be delivered to the perfect place for the night."

"We'd better start searching," Noel said, turning away.

It took at least another hour to find a suitable descent, which turned out to be no more than a gorge eroded into the side of the soft tufa by eons of rain and wind.

As a path, it was steep and pebbly but had enough small trees and bushes springing on either side to offer handholds along the way. Noel, taking the role of scout, proceeded first, followed by me, then Eva, each of us making cautious progress down the cliff. Only with my bandaged hand and sore shoulder, I barely inched along.

"Everybody all right up there?" Noel shouted up.

"Just wonderful," I replied.

"Coming along," Eva assured him. From her labored breath above, I knew she was in no better shape than I.

There were moments when I found myself clinging to a bush under the moonlight with my feet scrabbling beneath me, wondering why in hell I put myself into these situations when I could be miles away safely tucked into a warm bed. Only then I remembered I'd lost safety long ago and all I could do was forge ahead.

We arrived at the far end of a narrow valley where a stream threaded through a band of trees. Overhead the moon-limned cliffs soared, accenting arched openings.

"Caves," I whispered, collapsing cross-legged onto the sand, relieved to be on solid ground at last.

"Yes," Eva said, landing beside me with a grunt. "Fourth century, mostly. Anchorite communities began forming through the leadership of Saint Basil, who brought his brothers here to avoid persecution. There are cells and chapels carved throughout Cappadocia, too many to count, but none of these contain the Byzantine frescoes that made the area famous. Those you'll find in other valleys and, of course, in Goreme."

"No one deemed these important enough to properly excavate," Noel remarked.

"Borek and I excavated here one summer but the funding soon dried up."

"It still makes a perfect refuge," Noel commented.

"It's been a sanctuary of one kind or another for thousands of years." Eva stretched out on the stony ground. "I could just drift off to sleep here."

Noel offered her his hand. "But don't. We still need shelter."

I gazed up at grill-like formations. "Are those dovecotes?"

"They are," Eva said. "They once used doves as both messengers and food."

"And their excrement also served as fuel. Pigeon poop is surprisingly versatile," Noel added.

I climbed wearily to my feet. "Any place in particular you see us spending the night?"

Noel hoisted Eva to standing, tucking her arm into his. She pointed towards the nearest cliff wall. "Over there. If memory serves me, there's a range of small cells clustered near to the valley floor. I'm sure none of us feel like climbing any more tonight."

One glance at the ghostly openings far overhead and I swore I'd rather sleep impaled on rocks. As it was, my teeth chattered and all I wanted was a roof over my head and a fire. Food would help.

Eva trundled over to a ragged opening a few hundred feet further along. Inside, the soft tufa rock had been carved into a Spartan three-room domicile. Ledges and niches hewn into the rock encircled a small fire pit with a hole overhead to funnel out smoke, though exactly to where I couldn't tell.

Noel foraged for twigs while Eva and I worked to clear the sleeping niches of animal droppings and debris.

"He really is here to help me find the site and protect the remaining artifacts," she told me while using a leafy branch as a brush.

"I just can't believe anything either one of you says."

"Oh Phoebe," she sighed. "Open your mind and heart."

We continued without speaking until Noel returned with a bundle of branches and proceeded to build a fire. Once a blaze crackled away, we gathered around cross-legged or perched on makeshift seats trying to warm ourselves while downing most of our food and water.

Noel contributed two protein bars and another water bottle to the feast. We split everything three ways, with Noel carefully slicing cheese and oranges with his knife. After devouring our meals, we each portioned a little something for breakfast, in my case half an orange and a piece of protein bar.

I studied Noel furtively in the firelight. With his shaggy hair and the kaftan worn under the battered black jacket, he could pass as a cross between a Serbian rebel and a motorcycle dude. When I first met him, he was clean-shaven but the beard did nothing to diminish the fierce angles of his face or obscure the full mouth frowning down upon the orange he segmented with careful deliberation. With different clothes he could hail from Cappadocia or Pakistan or even downtown North America, as if his mixed heritage granted him a visa for half the world without offering a passport to a single country.

He sensed me watching and his eyes briefly touched mine across the fire.

"What's the plan tomorrow?" I asked, dropping my gaze.

"We'll proceed to a village through the cliffs at the end of the valley," Eva said. "I'm known there so I can find someone to shelter us until we can catch a lift to Goreme, where I own a house. It will be easier to sink into the woodwork there."

"You own a house?"

"A small one, yes. Borek and I bought it when we were excavating in the region. It's relatively central. Oh, and I loved the view so much he wanted me to have it. We can use that as our base while we work to find the exact location of the site."

225

"And how will we do that exactly?" I asked. Noel studied me as if he sensed I had no intention of going along with their plan, whatever the hell it was. He'd be watching me as closely as I him.

"We must ask questions, Phoebe. As women, we may be in the best position to elicit trust among the womenfolk. If the community is the one I suspect, it will be most difficult. Somehow we must convince them to allow us to help before the last of their heritage trickles away into the hands of the unscrupulous. Thieves are already at work, no doubt assisted by some villagers."

"And these thieves must be watching every stranger who passes by." I looked pointedly at Noel. "Do you have any idea who's infiltrated the site?"

"Probably a local," Noel said, biting into an orange. "He or she is filtering artifacts out one by one, selling them to multiple buyers through an intermediary. It's the middleman who fences them on the black market."

"Could the middleman be a middle woman?"

"If you're thinking Maggie, I doubt she would have got this far yet, and besides, she'll still have to cooperate with the local contact." He was feeding twigs into the fire.

"She had a map of Anatolia spread out in her room. She's in this somewhere."

"Her ruthlessness is boundless."

"She had Jason Young killed to--"

His head shot up. "She killed Jason Young?"

"Not personally but had him killed, yeah. She told me as much. Jason was your man, wasn't he?"

"Yes, but—"

"And you had him crawling all over my gallery while I slept upstairs."

"He would never have harmed you. He was your bodyguard, instructed by Toby and me to keep you safe. We were trying to ensure you and Max had everything you needed and, yes, I see now how this only complicated your life further and I apologize for that. I would have explained all that if you hadn't pulled the alarm."

I rubbed my eyes. "Oh, right, so it's my fault."

"I'm only trying to explain how things went wrong."

"And keep going wrong."

"And we are now charged with setting all to rights." Eva held up her hand. "The Goddess has brought us together so that we can protect Her history against the ravages of the greedy. Perhaps her gift to us will be to help heal our wounds along the way. That is all that matters."

I thumbed toward Noel. "Does he really look like Goddess material to you?"

Noel spit a mouthful of seeds into the fire. "The Goddess chooses strange bedfellows."

"We are all Goddess material, Phoebe," Eva told me sternly.

"Maybe the Goddess should choose her partners better. This one betrayed his own father while conniving with his father's girlfriend and my brother to steal a fortune of artifacts. If that's not the ravaging of the greedy, I don't know what is."

"You're the only one I wanted to ravage," said Noel mildly.

I shot him a foul look. "My point is you're a cheat, a thief, and a—"

"'Scum-bag bastard' is my favorite. There, you hit poetic stride while touching on the truth of things, since I am technically a bastard," he said. "'I am bastard begot, bastard instructed, bastard in mind, bastard in valor, in everything illegitimate'."

"Do you always need Shakespeare to express your feelings? And, just for the record, Max would have done right by your mother had he known she was pregnant."

"He told you that?"

"He did."

"And you believed him."

"Yes." I paused. "Why do you hate him so much?"

"I don't hate him; I hold him in contempt. There's a difference."

"But why? He didn't know that your mother was pregnant."

"I realize that. After all, he didn't know my mother, period. It wasn't uncommon for a white man to drive into an Aboriginal community and knock up some local girl for a spot of fun. Most of them just drove on, too. No, I hold him in contempt for how he treated me once he knew the truth, as if I should be grateful that he deigned to pluck me from my shabby little Aboriginal community and accept me as his son in the first place. Supposedly, I should spend my life groveling for affection and recognition from that day forward."

"He loves you!"

"How the hell do you know?"

"Because I'm the one watching him blubbering into his drink every night while going on and on about how he wasn't a good enough this or a good enough that. He even begged me not to turn you in. You are his son, he said, and that's all that matters."

"Too little too late."

"It's never too late!"

"Stop it, both of you," Eva interceded. "Fathers and sons can brew a complex relationship, especially with the divisiveness of misunderstanding. I don't know Max, except by reputation, but I'm sure he does love you, Noel, and must be proud of all you've achieved—"

"Like what a fabulous double-crossing crook he's become."

"Like father, like son," Noel remarked.

"Only now he's come clean while you're just getting dirtier by the minute." I hated this miserable sniping but I couldn't stop myself.

"Maybe I'm defining my own version of justice."

"Are you back to that Robin Hood of archaeology shit again?"

Eva climbed to her feet. "I said stop! It's been a long day and, in my case, heaped upon an even longer life, and I'm weary of your arguing. Don't you see how you are poisoning yourselves? Grow up, both of you. Noel, maybe your father doesn't know how to express his feelings—men don't always have the emotional vocabulary to articulate these matters. Perhaps you could give him another chance. And, Phoebe, you are so driven with bitterness, you can't see the light in the stars. Noel's as wounded as you are, only bears his scars in different places. Open your eyes, both of you. For now, we're all too tired and overwrought to think straight. We need sleep. Maybe forgiveness will come later."

I sighed, knowing the truth of her words though unable to process them in any way that mattered. True enough, I couldn't see the light in the stars. Nothing shone for me anywhere, any place.

Though I said goodnight and made to go to my sleeping niche, I ended back at the fire, still roiling with the desperate need to make something right, though I wasn't certain what.

Noel continued to feed sticks into the blaze with focused intensity.

"I meant what I said about Max," I said softly. "Whatever you did to him, he forgives you, even accepts what you did as his due. Try to forgive him, too."

His eyes met mine. "You speak of forgiveness as if you know it well."

"I have to relearn a lot of things I understood better when I was younger. Seems as though I've lost everything over the past year. I'm trying to mend the best I can. Maybe you are, too, but neither of us know how." I turned away towards one of the alcoves.

Eva had already claimed a niche and lay curled on her side under her army-green parka, her scarves wrapping her head like a colorful mummy. Of the three of us, she had come best prepared with her thick quilted jacket and multiple layers. I, on the other hand, didn't have a single useful fabric to keep me warm, unless my half-knit yarn counted, which it didn't. The irony wasn't lost on me.

I picked up my carpet bag and chose another niche, plumping up the bag into a makeshift pillow. Meanwhile, Noel stretched his long body into the bench opposite mine, the space so constricted, his legs hung over the edge sideways.

Even with the fire blazing, the cave remained tomb-chill and Eva's snoring did nothing to improve the comfort. I lay staring into space, my heart pounding, thoughts live-wire twitching. It felt as if all the lives and deaths that had passed in this ancient place had fractured the air itself. I couldn't breathe without inhaling pain. My teeth chattered miserably. I wrapped my arms around myself wondering how I'd ever survive the night.

I was in that cocoon-like state with my eyes closed when something like a bag of potato chips landed on my chest. I looked up to find Noel standing over me unpacking a silvery blanket thing from its pouch. "An emergency blanket," he said, as if discussing the weather. "One of the items I packed for just such nights as these. It will help keep you warm, though it won't feel very cozy."

I tried to sit up, nearly whacking my head on the alcove wall. "You use it. You're no better dressed for the elements than I am."

"I'm just doing the manly thing. Couldn't you just play along for once and pretend you're the weaker sex?"

I laughed. "Well, thanks. I'll accept this token of your gallantry."

"You're welcome." He hesitated, making no move to return to his niche. "We could always share body heat."

"Considering the size of these alcoves, that would be logistically impossible, though probably worth a few good laughs."

"Good point. try to get some sleep. we have a long day ahead of us tomorrow and must leave before dawn." He turned and walked back to his niche alone.

27

The predawn traipse through the valley was a mute, frigid stumble along the narrow valley with companions as numb with hunger and cold as I.

We followed the stream to the end of the valley before climbing up a narrow path leading sharply upward. Eva, though groggy and stumbling even with Noel's help, knew the way with an unerring sense of direction. She led us to the crest of a stony hill and pointed to a cluster of cement houses below, smoke curling up from their chimneys and windows beaming squares of light into the chill dawn.

"They take great risk in harboring fugitives," Eva told us, "but I have yet to meet a Turk who will turn away someone in need."

"Is this village connected to my kilim?" Though I still felt its absence, at least I had my tattoo.

"No. That one is on the other side of the plain but these people may still know something."

We skidded down the steep incline until we reached a dirt road curving into the village. The community consisted of maybe twenty humble houses clustered around a tiny domed mosque, with the occasional battered car or truck parked haphazardly in the street.

The first call to prayer blared from the mosque's single minaret as we approached, prompting Noel to urge us deeper into the shadows of an outbuilding. Men began pouring from their houses to the mosque, some still wiping their faces from morning ablutions.

"Which house is your friend's?" Noel whispered while a donkey bayed from a paddock behind us.

"The big one across the street," Eva told him, nodding towards the boxy two-story building opposite. Other than size and the occasional portico, all the houses looked the same. "It is good that the men will be attending the mosque, since that will give me a chance to speak to Cari alone. She was the one I came to know best. Here they keep to the old ways."

We watched the men enter the mosque in single file accompanied by the melodic chant that seemed to suffuse the entire town. After a few minutes, Eva beckoned us to follow as she slipped out behind the building and hobbled across the road. For seconds we were exposed mid-street with the sun rising in a shimmering red-gold overhead. While darting past the open mosque door, I glimpsed thirty or so robed men bent over in prayer. Maybe I only imagined the roar of a far-off truck accompanied by the thump-thump of a helicopter, but the urge to dive for cover overwhelmed me.

Eva reached the door and knocked loudly, beckoning to Noel to turn away, which he did, keeping his gaze fixed towards the street. Several agonizing seconds passed without a response until, finally, the door inched open onto the startled face of an older woman wearing a long skirt and a headscarf.

She stared out at Eva without recognition while Eva spoke in rapid Turkish, waving her hands about and pointing to me and then Noel. The woman's gaze fixed on Noel's back for what seemed far too long before beckoning us in.

The woman spoke to Eva who translated. "Quickly. First remove your shoes and then we must descend to the kitchen. Cari's husband and sons will return soon. Noel, Phoebe and I will be in the kitchen but you must wait apart." Noel had already removed his battered boots, he being familiar enough with the customs to know one never wears shoes in a Muslim household. "It is not fitting for a strange man to be in the company of women in this community, so Cari wants you to wait in another room until the men arrive."

He nodded and kept his head down.

I caught impressions of brilliant rugs covering every bit of floor and wall space. We descended the stairs while the scent of wood smoke mingled with spices rode the air. Once on the bottom level, Cari kept her face averted while pointing through a door where Noel was instructed to wait as Eva and I continued into the next room.

Here, two women sat around a low flat grill where something fragrant sizzled. They turned startled faces towards us and then promptly burst into excited Turkish. I was bid to sit between them on the rugs as the women smiled and asked me questions I couldn't understand.

"This is Canan and Berna, Cari's daughter and daughter-in-law, respectively. They want to know if they can offer you tea and breakfast."

"Oh, yes, please." I smiled, wishing desperately I could speak the language. "And a toilet."

Eva informed me toilets here consisted of a hole in the ground in a shed outside. We followed Berna to a tiny outbuilding, scattering foraging chickens as we went.

Inside, it was dark and cold, not to mention incredibly small for maneuvering jean removal and squatting over a hole. Thankfully, Eva had prepared me with tissue, not that I knew where to deposit it afterward. Since it was socially impossible to question people on their toilet habits, I kept my maddening questions to myself and figured things out as best I could.

Back inside, Canan led me to a wash basin set against one wall so I could clean my face and hands. Eva stood nearby waiting her turn and translating the women's excited questions.   "They are so delighted to see us. They don't meet many women from other worlds here and are asking a million queries which I can only begin to answer. They have never seen red hair like yours and want to know if you have used henna to honor the prophet. I have explained that you are not Muslim but respect their beliefs."

"True enough," I said wiping my face on the towel offered. "But I saw a satellite dish on the roof. Don't they see lots of different things on television?"

"I'm not sure which programs they watch here-maybe only the Turkish soap operas-and perhaps the television is viewed mostly by the men. I think it rude to ask since this is one of the more conservative communities. Best not to pry. It is bad enough that I am going to request that they illicitly transport us to another town sixty miles away."

I passed Berna my towel and she handed me a mug of hot, sweet tea. "Will they do it?"

"No community takes on the army's scrutiny lightly. Fortunately, they remain suspicious of the government on principal. I've told them the truth: that we aim to stop a robbery of an important archaeological site and that the government misunderstands our intent and wishes to block us. Governmental red tape will only halt our efforts, I said."

"Did you say Interpol is involved?"

"That would only complicate matters." She paused to catch her breath. "Whether they turn us over to the army will be for Erol, Cari's husband, to decide. Erol owns the truck parked outside as well as the biggest herd of sheep in these parts. The fact that many of these villages keep archaeological findings to themselves is in our favor. For now, we must wait. Besides, this gives me a chance to ask the women a few questions."

I settled into a warm spot on the floor beside the grill, watching in fascination as Berna flipped a flat pancake-like bread in front of me, dousing it in olive oil, and sprinkling cheese. The tension slipped from my neck and all I could do was continue smiling while extending my hands towards the warmth. When the offer came for breakfast, I gratefully accepted, devouring the warm pastry while the women prepared the men's.

"Usually women are to wait until the men have their meal before eating." Eva said between bites. "We are exceptions as guests."

Cari took off upstairs with a tray, leaving Eva and me alone with the other two. As soon as she'd disappeared, Eva launched a battery of questions at Berna. By the tone of her voice, I sensed she was attempting to keep her questions casual but casual wasn't Eva. Soon her voice tensed into something more clipped and demanding.

Canan brushed crumbs from the floor rug with a broom while Berna kept pressing more food on us with a smile fixed tightly in place.

"Eva, this isn't going anywhere. Lighten up a little."

"They know something and we're running out of time. Do you have a picture of the kilim?"

"On my phone but turning it on might send out a tracking blip."

"I doubt that there is much of a cell service here but we'll have to risk it. Pass it to me, please."

I pulled my carpet bag towards me, fished out the phone, and reluctantly turned it on, reminding myself I meant to pry out the SIM card but had forgotten.

"Can you hurry?"

"It needs to reboot. What's the rush?"

"I want to show them the photo before the men come down or call us up. If I guess correctly, a secret of this nature is kept safe among the women only."

The phone finally came to life and I thumbed through my photos until I found the portrait of my kilim. "I miss it," I remarked, passing the phone to Eva.

"She is always with us, Phoebe."

"I mean the kilim itself."

"I know what you meant."

She spoke in earnest tones to Canan and Berna as their two heads leaned together over the photo. A quick look passed between the women before Berna handed the phone back to me. They shook their heads in unison.

Berna rose to her feet, smoothed down her skirt, and began gathering the dishes. I offered to help, but Eva informed me that, as a guest, I was to sit.

Eva added. "They're making more tea."

"Guess we can always use more tea."

"They say they know nothing, yet I'm sure they do."

"So I gathered."

"They're hiding something."

"Of course they are, but why would they tell us?" Just before returning the phone back to my bag, I glanced at the icons. Not surprisingly, there was no cell service out here, but several messages had come in before I'd turned the phone off back in Kusadasi. Two were from Serena, one unknown with a London number, a string came from Sam's Interpol number, and one from Max.

My breakfast suddenly churned. Supposing something had happened to Max? What if the gallery was broken into or Serena harmed? Nothing I could do about it anyway. I turned off the phone and returned it to my bag. Canan stood watching me. I smiled back.

"Eva, please ask them if there's a place where we can bathe."

She did as I asked, prompting a response from Canan that included pointing over her shoulder. Berna chimed in with more detail, part of which included some kind of negotiation with her sister-in-law.

"They say there's a small haman in town which the women use between 1 and 4 p.m. every day. The rest of the time, the haman is used by the men. They've agreed to take us with them later in the afternoon, if the men agree."

"Why do the men have to agree to everything?"

"A haman is a public bath. Other village women will be there, too, and the news of strangers in town will spread." Eva rubbed her eyes and sighed. "I don't care one way or the other. I'm well used to Spartan living conditions. I'd be happy just to rest for a few hours."

"I care. For me, cleanliness is next to goddessness. I haven't had a proper bath in days."

At that moment, Cari returned and beckoned both of us to follow her upstairs.

We were ushered into a large sunlit room hung with vibrant red-based textiles with ceramic plates nestled within the occasional bare spaces. Cushioned benches lined the walls with a low carpeted table surrounded by big kilim-covered cushions centering the floor. Three men sat around the table cross-legged, one of whom was Noel, who appeared to be enjoying the male company along with his breakfast.

Cari quickly cleared the table and bid us join the men before she hurried downstairs. I arranged my limbs lotus position but Eva found this more challenging. After seconds of awkward shifting, she finally settled. "My apologies."

Noel introduced a small man with crinkled brown skin and sharp darting eyes as Erol, the family patriarch, while the handsome younger man sitting across from him was Polat, his son.

I smiled and nodded, which seemed the only kind of communication I could manage. More smiling and nodding followed until I thought my face would freeze and my neck bob off as the conversation continued in Turkish. Eva and Noel did most of the talking.

I sat in mute observation sipping tea and watching as something Eva said prompted Erol to shake his head vehemently.

Polat intervened as if attempting to counter his father's position. The two men erupted in excited debate until Noel said something in halting Turkish. They studied him in silence for a moment.

"What just happened?" I asked.

"We requested that they drive us to Goreme but Erol said it was too risky," Eva explained. "Polat is willing but father is not. Apparently the government has made some heavy-handed statements about citizens dealing with foreigners over protected archaeological sites."

"And?"

"And they're considering the prospect."

Noel extended a warning hand for Eva to stop talking as he further pitched our case. Erol spoke next in a series of brief sentences checked off on the fingers of one sun-browned hand.

"He has agreed to take us tonight after dark providing we stay hidden in the meantime," Noel said. "He doesn't want the other villagers to know we're here because at least one family has a son in the army."

"So, no bath," I remarked.

Noel raised an eyebrow in my direction. "Bath?"

"I was hoping to use the haman."

"It doesn't sound like that's going to happen."

The incomprehensible drone of voices stirring together with a big breakfast lulled me into an upright doze. Before I knew, Eva was nudging me awake. "Come along, Phoebe. We'll go to the sleeping quarters and rest for the day."

I blinked into an empty room. "Where have they gone?"

"Noel is resting in another building."

Though the cushioned benches in the main room looked tempting, we were ushered upstairs to Polat and Berna's quarters, to sleep on the floor by the fire.

I glimpsed a bed behind a curtain but the floor suited me fine. By that time, I had redefined comfort. Food in my belly and a safe, warm place to sleep rated right up there in my new luxury category.

Eva dropped to the floor, pulled a blanket over herself and fell into a deep sleep. I joined her on the rug and slept as though berthed in a 5-star hotel.

Hours later I awoke with a start. Flinging off the blanket, I sat upright, keening my senses. Eva snored away on the floor beside me, but otherwise the surrounding house seemed unnaturally still.

The unmistakable rattle of truck tires grinding the village dust outside must have kick-started me awake. I shuffled over to the tiny window and peered out onto the street. A green army truck had just pulled into the village center.

28

"Eva, wake up. Grab your things!" I shook her once, snatched my carpet bag, and scrambled downstairs calling for the others.

No one answered. The kitchen, main room, and every space between, lay empty.

Wait, it was the woman's bathing time. My heart galloping, I checked out the window again. Six uniformed men were now spreading up the street knocking on every door.

Eva arrived downstairs moments later, rumpled and dazed.

"We have to get out of here before the army arrives." I tugged her out the back door towards the outbuildings. Huddled together amid the squawking chickens, I scanned for the safest hiding place. Two squeezed together in the toilet shed? No room. Hide with the goats in the animal pen? Too predictable. The soldiers were bound to check the outbuildings. And where was Noel and why did I even care? I couldn't worry about him right now.

We slinked between the sheds, ducking under a pomegranate tree into a neighbor's yard, passed a table set with a backgammon game in progress and an ashtray filled with burning cigarettes. Men's voices called from inside the house as we sprinted into the next yard. More fruit trees strung with laundry offered a bit of cover as we crouched behind a drying blanket and strained to see the street.

"They must be starting from the far end," I whispered. "Maybe they won't get here for a few more minutes. Where's the haman?"

"Haman?"

I turned to her. "Would male soldiers storm into a bath house during women's' bath time?"

"Good thinking."

I waited until the street was free of soldiers before clutching Eva's hand and dashing across the road. Two elderly men sat on their doorsteps watching us. I put a finger to my lips as we scurried by, my destination a small elaborately tiled stone building beside the mosque.

In moments we were descending marble steps into a dark, moist sanctuary. At first I couldn't see much but heard the agitated voices of women coming from somewhere.

We stood in a little tiled vestibule. On the right a curtain, on the left steam wafting up from under a tiled door. I glimpsed two other doors down the hall but Eva was already leading me towards the right. "The dressing room must be this way."

We stepped into a large shelved room with coat hooks and alcoves where Berna plus four other women were hurriedly dressing. Their excited chatter stopped the moment we entered. Eva launched into some too-long explanation while waving her hands and pointing towards the door. One woman responded, then another, with Berna having the last word.

"They are cutting short their bath to return home but some refuse. Berna will remain with us."

"Eva."

"The short version is they have told me that 'women as women are safe.' I believe it's an idiomatic expression but—"

"But we get the gist. They'll help." I stepped further inside and accepted the towel Berna offered. Most of the women had finished dressing and stood in their head scarves and skirts studying us openly. Berna indicated for us to undress while she shed her clothes again. The other women just stood, waiting. I turned to Eva, who had already shimmied from her gear to stand naked like some ancient fertility goddess.

"Wouldn't it be better if we stayed dressed?"

"Whatever for?"

"Because we may have to make a run for it."

"We can't stay clothed while our hosts are naked." She pointed to my towel. "Get on with it, Phoebe."

"But they're watching." In fact, a couple of them had stepped forward to help me disrobe. I gently pushed them away.

"They're curious. They've never seen a redhead before, probably never a naked Westerner, for that matter. They'll soon discover our equipment is basically the same. Hurry, the sooner we're with the other women, the safer we will be."

I packed away my modesty along with my clothes, piling everything on top of my carpet bag in one of the niches. Aware of their scrutiny, I wrapped the towel around my middle bits before the inspection grew too intimate. My tattoos may as well be outlined in neon so I kept them shielded. Satisfied the show was over, the women shuffled away, chatting amongst themselves up the stairs.

Inside the steam room, various tasks of grooming and washing suspended as we entered. I sensed they were at least as surprised by my hair color as our sudden arrival. While Berna explained, I scanned the tiled room with its taps and porcelain basins, shelves and benches. Some women were in the midst of washing their hair while others rubbed oils into their skins or received a massage from maybe a friend or a relative. We had interrupted a pajama party minus the pajamas.

"Here women share their secrets," Eva whispered. "Isn't it marvelous?" She greeted Canan. "It's all about bonding and dates from long before the Romans when public bathing centered the community."

Berna pointed to a marble platform in the middle of the room.

"She says you are to lay on the marble and she will tend you while Canan tends me."

"Define 'tend'."

"Rough bliss is my best explanation." Eva climbed onto the slab and lay on her back, sighing in pleasure as Canan poured warm water over her body.

Reluctantly, I climbed on the platform beside her, the marble uncomfortably cold and slick under my skin as I lay facedown. Nothing so far aligned with my definition of bliss. Two women even came up and giggled over the mermaid tattoo on my butt.

"Eva, being naked while a bunch of heat-seeking soldiers tromp around outside and women study me like I'm a zoological specimen makes me feel as vulnerable as hell."

"Relax," she murmured. "You could never be anywhere safer than with women in a haman," she murmured. "We are enveloped within the Goddess's womb among sisters, mothers, and wives. They are only curious."

"Wish they wouldn't giggle."

"Enjoy every moment while it lasts. Ouch!" She said something to Canan who made soothing sounds as she kneaded Eva's shoulders.

I couldn't wait for it to end at first. Berna washed my hair with some herbal-scented shampoo—rosemary or maybe sage—which was pleasant enough, though a bit robust when her fingers dug into my scalp.

Otherwise, I felt splayed on a pedestal like a sacrificial lamb in the midst of some ritual I didn't understand. The impression intensified when Berna finished with the shampoo and began rubbing pumice over my skin as if intent on scraping off the first two layers of epidermis. I had to force myself not to yelp. After exfoliation so intense my skin tingled pink and tender, she poured a warm stream of lemon-scented oil over me and began to massage my aching muscles with firm strong hands.

Finally, my tension melted into fragrant pliancy. By the time I flipped on my back, thoughts of soldiers and kilims had retreated. I felt Berna pause and opened my eyes to find her studying my goddess tat. She nodded, and approached that still-tender area with considerable care while her hands soothed and comforted.

I'm not sure how long the bliss lasted, certainly not long enough. After the cocooning hot towels had begun to cool, Berna nudged us gently and spoke hurriedly to Eva.

"She reports that the soldiers are still here and a car drove into the village a short time ago with a damaged man—I'm not certain of the exact translation—accompanied by another policeman not in uniform. She says they insist upon performing their own search and are cooperating with the soldiers."

"Interpol?" I bolted upright. "The 'damaged' bit must refer to Sam Walker's facial scars. He wears them like a badge. Damn, I knew he'd catch up with me sooner or later."

"These agents are asking different questions, she says, and insist upon exploring the village themselves. The villagers are incensed by this since they show little respect for the customs the army have afforded them. The villagers are requesting the army protect them against this insult."

"What if they search here and find us?"

A short exchange followed between Berna and Eva. "None of the villagers have betrayed us, she says, at least to her knowledge, but they don't know where Noel is hiding. The soldiers have been informed that many women are choosing to remain in the haman rather than be subjected to watching strangers invade their homes. It appears the captain has accepted this even if the two Interpol agents haven't. The captain is holding firm."

"This isn't good."

"No, but we have no choice but to remain here for now."

"I think I'd rather dress and wait in the dressing room until dark. Are there other rooms?"

"I'll ask." Berna pointed towards the vestibule. "There's a cold room and a men's dressing area at the rear. They don't use the cold room often in the cooler months."

"All right, I'll wait in the dressing room. I can always knit."

"I'll remain here." Eva sank back down on the marble while I climbed cautiously to the floor.

I followed Berna towards the vestibule, both of us entering the dressing area to change. I dug around in my carpet bag for clean clothes. There wasn't much to choose from: a slightly less grubby pair of jeans and a black turtleneck. I couldn't very well wear one of the silk tunics. Everything else had gone the way of the roller bag.

Berna touched my shoulder and held out a deep maroon robe. I nodded and thanked her. In a moment, she was gone.

The single bulb dangling overhead gave such feeble light, knitting would be a challenge and after the steam room, I was cold. Even dressed, I shivered.

Leaving the robe with my bag for now, I followed the urge to move. I strolled down the hall towards the back rooms, wondering if the building had a rear entrance or at least a more comfortable knitting area.

The first door opened onto a dressing room much like the one I'd just exited, only previous occupants had left a robe hanging on a wall peg with a tumble of clothes shoved under a bench. I quickly closed that door and opened the one beside it, stepping inside a larger room alive with the sound of running water and brightened by a circle of windows high up in the domed ceiling.

For a moment, I simply focused upward, appreciating the effect of the reflecting water on the blue tiles until I sensed movement. My gaze dropped to the rear view of a magnificently naked man with a tattoo curving around his body, standing not more than a few feet away. Busy toweling himself down, he didn't see me at first until a quick glance over his shoulder froze him to the spot.

"You don't knock?"

"The haman is still for women only."

"It's past 4:00."

"The village are extending the women's hours while Interpol searches the houses again. At least now we know where you're hiding."

"Hell."

"It's not that bad. You look rather good from behind."

"Phoebe..."

"Yes?" I waited while he just stood there in a half-turn. "Oh, I get it: you're shy. You did promise once to show me your full Kangaroo Dreaming tattoo, remember?"

He slowly straightened and turned, letting the towel drop to his side so that he stood before me full frontal, watching me study him wearing nothing but a little smile and that incredible Aboriginal Kangaroo Dreaming tattoo curving around his entire body in ochers, rusts, and black dots. Not that I was focused on the art, exactly. "Is this what you want to see?"

I scrutinized him up and down, taking my time, admiring his tall, lean build. Perhaps he had grown a bit too thin over the months since Bermuda, maybe his ribs protruded too starkly against his skin, but his shoulders remained as broad as ever until they tapered down to his waist, all properly muscled and impressively male.

I especially liked the way the dark hair brushed across his chest to stream into a tiny line that thickened with furious intensity around his groin. His groin. I dragged my gaze to his face.

"Remember, it's cold in here."

"I have an excellent imagination." He looked so damn good right then I may have licked my lips. "Is there a back door?"

"Pardon?"

"A back door, a way to escape if Interpol tries to search the haman?"

He breathed out slowly. "Oh, yes. Ah, there's a door at the back of the men's dressing room. I guess they use that during the changing of the guard. Mind if I get dressed now?"

"Sure, but you don't want to bump into any of the women still in the building. Stay here while I get your things. I presume that's your stuff in the dressing room?"

He nodded.

By the time I returned carrying his bag plus the boots and robe, he had wrapped the towel demurely around his waist. I stifled my disappointment while passing him the clothes. "They don't look like yours."

"Erol lent me a few things. You've had a bath yourself, I see. Your cheeks are pink and your hair all—". His hand waved as it trying to snare the right word.

"Bushy?" I knew my hair had taken on the consistency of a deranged banshee.

"Joyfully uninhibited."

I laughed. "That sounds like wishful thinking. I'd better get back to the women's side. See you later, at least your public parts."

But I didn't see any of him until much later.

29

Eva and I escaped through the back door camouflaged in borrowed robes, our instructions to wait for Erol across the field.

Noel had already disappeared.

By then it was so dark, we could barely see one foot ahead of ourselves but, luckily for us, neither could the army. We could hear them banging through the haman from where we huddled in the dark even though the village had shrunk to no more than lights clustered in the distance.

"Where did Berna say we were to wait exactly?" I whispered as we crouched behind a rock.

"In this direction is all she said. Erol will drive out to collect us once the army leaves, which I hope will be soon. My knees can't take much more of this."

"Here, sit on my bag. Yarn makes a perfect cushion." I shoved it under her bottom and urged her into sitting. "How's that?"

"Oh, much better, thank you."

"How about a piece of bread? Cari gave me some for later."

"She gave me some, too, but right now I just need rest."

I slumped against the boulder beside her, oblivious to the pebbles biting into my skin.

"Dear Phoebe, forgive me for keeping so much from you." She reached across the dark and took my hand.

I squeezed it back. "You didn't know how I'd react. I get that."

"When I received Noel's message about the artifacts hitting the black market, I had to find my way here, no matter who it affected. In truth, I have been incredibly selfish, but I see all the casualties along the way a necessary sacrifice."

I stared at the town lights without seeing them. "A necessary sacrifice," I repeated.

"I just need to get there, Phoebe, for the sake of history, for the Goddess, for all women. Thanks to you and Noel, the Goddess's mission and my life's quest are about to reach fruition."

I steered the conversation onto less hallowed ground. "How long have you known Noel?"

"I met him while guest lecturing in Queensland when he was still a student, and over the months we grew quite close. Perhaps he needed a mother and I needed a son, so we filled those roles for one another. I always believed the Goddess brought him into my life to ease my way after Borek died."

"You know him that well?"

"Oh yes. When in London, we'd often meet for dinners, and once or twice he'd even escort me to the theater. Such a caring man. He knew how much I needed to return to Turkey and find this shrine and, even though he is risking his life and freedom, he is here for me now."

"You believe he came to Turkey for you?"

"He's an archaeologist so, of course, he wants to protect what's left of the shrine, but, yes, he came to Cappadocia at my request and for you, too. He and your brother initially thought that Istanbul would be a reasonably safe place to rendezvous with you. They had no idea what forces had already been mobilized. Once that became clear, they conspired to keep you in London but it was already too late. All has aligned according to the Goddess's will."

I had so much I wanted to counter, to argue against, but I knew there was no point. Sometimes the best that two opposing views can manage is to coexist on some common ground. "You think you can protect the shrine somehow?"

"We must. Noel believes there is little in the way of artifacts remaining but the shrine itself is the true treasure. Besides, if I can stand for one moment in that ancient site and feel the power of the Universe as our species first imagined Her thousands of years ago, I will consider my life a wondrous success, despite the sorrows. Noel believes the robbers may yet destroy the site after they've ravaged it. We need to get there before that happens."

"I wish you had told me this earlier."

"Would that have made a difference?"

"Maybe not but I still wouldn't have felt so betrayed."

"I know I used you and I'm sorry."

We didn't speak for a while. She broke the silence with: "I do wish Noel would appear."

I scanned the surrounding darkness. "Me, too."

It took over an hour more before Erol's truck rumbled across the field to meet us. A dark ride in a battered truck down more ruts than roads followed as we bounced across sheepherder tracks and over the hills towards Goreme. Nearly three hours later, he pulled to a stop at the edge of town, announcing to Eva that we must walk the rest of the way. I tried to argue against that, since I didn't think Eva had the stamina for another long trek, but she cut me short.

"Let us just go, Phoebe. Erol is afraid his truck will attract too much attention and he has risked enough."

She leaned on me as we scrambled along footpaths and over fences in the dark, the details of which blurred together in a fast-forward of images and exhaustion.

We finally reached the town and trudged through the shadows uphill towards Eva's house, a little three-story stone structure perched at the top of a road scattered with similar homes. My feet screamed with fresh blisters, but I was beyond caring about anything but sleep.

"I called ahead to request my friend Ela light the fire and fill the larder. She looks after the place and rents it out to tourists in the summer. With luck, no one else will even know we're here. You may take the top floor bedroom and I shall claim mine on the next level."

I hauled myself upstairs, tossed my carpet bag on the floor, and dropped onto the bed fully dressed. When I opened my eyes hours later, I found myself inside a dark room hazy red by sunshine pushing patterns through a kilim-covered window. Pulling back the rug curtain, I peered down at the street, empty except for a foraging dog.

Had I only dreamed the last few days? Nothing seemed quite real anymore.

The scent of coffee lured me down a narrow stairway to a landing, where I glimpsed Eva through a half-opened door. I tiptoed in and found her sleeping deeply.

I carried on down to the bottom level with its tiny kitchen living area crowded by a table, two chairs, and one counter. A cushioned bench hugged the wall nearest the stove. Otherwise, the room was empty, yet coffee warmed on a hot plate on one counter with space enough for a single basket of bread and a plate of dolmades covered in cloths. Her friend must have been and gone.

After food and jolts of caffeine prompted a swell of gratitude, I stood in the center of the room, brushed crumbs from my jacket, and finally had time to panic. We were in such trouble—Interpol was after us, thieves, the army. I wasted a few minutes spinning in adrenalin until my gaze landed on Eva's duffel bag. She had dumped it on the floor when we entered the house last night, but now it sat on one of the chairs like a rumpled gnome.

I thought I'd bring her coffee along with the bag to her room but, as I reached down to pick it up, the bag tipped, dumping the contents to the floor in an orderly pile.

Eva had organized her stuff with clothes and fabric on the bottom and smaller items neatly tucked along the sides. I was just about to upend the pile and replace it in the bag when something caught my eye. The frayed edges of the bottommost layer hit me with a bittersweet pang. I unfolded the Goddess with Vultures kilim across the chair and stared.

Eva had stolen it?

I flashed back and forth between joy at the reunion and a wrenching sadness. Of all the things I expected of Eva, this wasn't one. For a moment, I thought I'd upchuck breakfast or, at least, burst into tears. She stole my kilim? She spouted faith and trust while ripping me off?

How sad, how horribly sad. What kind of inner conflict twists a person like that, what makes them say one thing and do another? How could she truly believe such an act was justified?

My legs buckled beneath me and I slumped into a chair with the kilim spread across my lap. For a moment, I gazed down at the goddess motifs, struck anew by the energy woven there. She needed to go to that shrine at all costs. Nothing and no one else mattered. She said as much.

It would be so easy to judge, to criticize, but for some reason, I couldn't stir the necessary anger. That didn't make my next decision any easier.

Returning the kilim lovingly to the duffel bag, I carefully reconstructed the contents roughly as I found them. Scarves, two plastic zip bags—one stuffed with soap and toothpaste, the other prescription bottles—our grease-stained map, extra shirts and undies, her wallet. Her wallet? Without so much as a pang of guilt, I unfolded the leather and investigated the contents. She had a wad of euros in there plus at least as many pounds sterling. So she lied about that, too. I stuffed the wallet back and returned the bag to the chair.

When I climbed the stairs moments later, it was to tiptoe past Eva's snoring form and carry soundlessly to my top floor room. Fishing my two phones from my bag, I powered on both. I needed someplace utterly private. I couldn't risk Eva overhearing.

It was then that I noticed the pull-down ladder propped against the wall opposite the bed. It had to be a ladder to the roof. After checking the thing for stability, I climbed upward, bumped open the trap door, and climbed out into a bright chilly vista.

I stood blinking at an amazing landscape of twisted dawn-cast castle mounds, dancing conical hats, and far away plains rimmed with more of the same as the sun pushed molten peach into the horizon.

Hot air balloons rose in the sky like some aerial ballet adding to an unready majestic landscape. Below spread the town with lazy swirls of smoke threading the still air. I pulled out my iPhone, relieved to find a strong signal, and pressed redial for the last Agent Walker call.

The routing was nearly instantaneous. "Phoebe McCabe?" His voice grated over the line as if he'd been ripping apart fenders with his bare teeth. I must have woken him up. "Where are you?"

"I don't have much time so please listen, Walker. Remember how you said I should try to find out information when the opportunity presents itself? Well, I hitched a ride hoping it would bring me closer to the truth. As I see it, opportunity is now presenting itself in 3D and Surround Sound—oh, and balloons."

"Are you serious? You're a fugitive and a co-conspirator with art thieves and now you're implying you planned this all along as an undercover move?"

"I'm not saying I planned anything. I'm an impulsive creature who wasn't ready to return to London with so much unfinished business hanging over my head. I took a risk that coming to Anatolia would bring me closer to Noel and Toby and, so far, I'm half-right."

"Stay where you are, we'll pick you up, and just possibly I can get your sentence reduced for turning yourself in."

"You're not listening. I said I'm about to discover the truth, as in the location of this Bronze Age site everybody's excited about. Do you really think you can find that without my help? The locals aren't talking to the government officials, which means they won't talk to you, either, especially not you."

Silence spoke volumes. "Are you listening?" I prompted.
"I'm listening."

"Good, so I'm here with Eva Friedrich along with Noel Halloran, who is temporarily missing in action but can't be far away. Do you want me to lead the authorities to the site and help you apprehend Halloran or not, yes or no?"

A pause followed. I could almost hear him considering the limited alternatives. "If you try double-crossing me again, I swear you'll be in such deep trouble, no amount of finagling will set you free."

"First, I want both you and the army off my tail until I locate the site." More negotiations followed and I didn't agree with all his conditions nor he of mine, but we compromised.

Afterward, I pocketed my iPhone and picked up the Foxy phone, waiting for long seconds before he picked up. "Sir Rupert Fox here."

"Phoebe McCabe here. Are you ready to be friends?"
"Phoebe! Where are you?"

"The question is, where are you? I figure we might have lost you back in Kudesai. Am I right?"

"Partly, yes, but we since deduced that you are somewhere in Cappadocia, as am I, by the way. I am currently ensconced at a lovely cave hotel just outside of Goreme." "Excellent. I'll contact you again later with where to meet."

30

Eva stared down at the map of Cappadocia anchored on top of the diminutive table. "This is the village near where I believe lies Her shrine. Those hills are riddled with unexplored tunnels, most of which we believe were originally Hittite retreats, though this one is far older. Borek often mentioned the region. When I think back, perhaps too often."

I cleared the breakfast dishes and refilled our coffee mugs. "Are you sure he didn't drop other clues?"

"No, I don't believe so but I don't remember. Why hadn't I paid closer attention?" She scraped one of the wooden chairs closer and collapsed into it, her gaze fixed on the floor. "I still miss him. I wish he were still here. There's so much I'd like to say. Everywhere I look, I see his face, remember his voice, especially here."

I slipped the fruit plate back on the table and laid my hand on her shoulder. "All these memories must just crowd in around you."

"Yes, they do. I had no idea it would be like this. I've been here before since he died, but this is different. Phoebe," she laid her hand on mine. "I told you that I had no regrets but that's not true. If I had my life to do over again, I would never have published that article or left his side. I would have found another way to reveal the shrine."

"I understand," was all I could think to say. "Is Goreme where the kilim hails from?"

"Not here but close. I'm convinced it's near Begüm, which is not far away."

"Would seeing the kilim again help at all?" It was only a desperate hope that she might yet confess her theft.

"No," she said. "I have gleaned all I can there."

"Oh." Even now she wouldn't tell me. "I guess what the Goddess giveth, the Goddess taketh away."

She shot me a quick look. "The Goddess works in mysterious ways, Phoebe. It's best not to mock. In any case, Begüm is not more than 5 miles away but may as well be 20 leagues without a car."

"I'm not mocking. As I see it, nobody really owns anything. We just keep something treasured for a while before it lands in someone else's care, either by design or circumstance." I removed my hand and tapped the map. "So, how do you plan on getting to Begüm?"

"Unfortunately, Borek has no relatives still in this region and it's too risky to rent a car in either of our names. Perhaps I could borrow one from Ela's brother, providing I can do so without attracting suspicion? I could sweeten the pot with a few euros."

"I'd lend you some but my funds are gone, if you recall. I figure what 'the Goddess giveth the Goddess taketh away' applies to money most of all."

"I have a few euros in reserve, Phoebe, in the interest of expediency. And you're still mocking the Goddess."

"I am not. I'm only using humor to navigate treacherous waters. I figure the Goddess would get the joke, seeing as She makes plenty Herself, including lots at my expense."

Eva still wasn't about to tell me about her money stash, either, yet anger didn't flood me. Anger, above all emotions, seemed so irrelevant somehow. "So a car may take care of the transportation problem, but once in the village, how do you propose to locate the shrine?"

"For that I must win the trust of the local women. I will need to devise a plan for that but first, the transportation issue. Perish the thought of having to use the local bus. Interpol would find us for certain. In any case, relax here and enjoy the respite while I proceed to my friend's house to see if borrowing a car is remotely possible."

"Don't exhaust yourself. I'll find a car while you rest."

"You don't know the language, Phoebe. It's better that I go alone to attract less attention. Stay here. Noel may yet make an appearance and it would be good to have one of us meet him."

"I'm sure he could manage by himself. I still think I should go with you."

"And I still think you should stay put."

I watched her throw on the same brown robe borrowed from Berna. She paused at the door. "Phoebe, thank you."

"For what?"

"For not hating me despite everything." And out the door she went, blinking out the bright slice of sun as the door closed behind her.

Well, she was right about that. I didn't hate her.

I waited only long enough to make sure she had a good head start before I scrambled upstairs and tossed on my own borrowed robe and hijab. Up on the roof minutes later, I called Foxy and arranged for him to pick me up outside the one landmark I recalled from our flight the night before, a carpet shop anchoring the corner at the bottom of the hill where a footpath connected with the main street. Soon I had bolted out the door, keeping my head down.

Foxy arrived a little later than planned but so did I, since it took me much longer than expected to retrace the tangled steps taken the night before. By then, I'd become adept at traversing backyards and footpaths weaving behind public streets.

Sir Rupert and Evan sat idling in a white Rover outside the carpet shop. In a testament to my disguise, neither recognized me until I knocked on the window.

"My dear, do get in. I am very relieved to see you well, though admittedly you led us on a merry chase, indeed. Brown is a good color for you, may I say. Not everyone can carry it off."

I slid into the back seat, taking in Sir Rupert's exquisitely tailored cashmere long coat and yellow knitted scarf, a combo worn incongruously over a pair of knife-pressed jeans decked out with a brand new pair of hiking boots. "Good morning Rupert, Evan. Would you drive, please, preferably to the main highway heading east?"

Though today I wasn't concerned about either Interpol or the Turkish army, that didn't mean I felt totally safe, either. Maggie's men had to be in the area somewhere. I pulled out the map tucked into my carpet bag and passed it to Foxy. "We're going to the tiny village circled in pencil."

"And just why is that?" Foxy flicked his wrist to Evan who pulled away from the curb heading out of town.

"I'm researching the location of a certain site I believe interests you, too, but it would have made things so much easier if you had shared what you know earlier."

"I could say the same thing to you, Phoebe, and besides which, you are assuming I knew the details earlier, which I did not."

"But you do now?"

"Not totally, no, but the pieces are coming together rather admirably. Once I understood you were traveling with Eva Friedrich, all the dots connected—isn't that a tiresome phrase? I shall banish it from my lexicon henceforth. Anyway, as I was saying, Dr. Yilmaz is known to me. In fact, I knew her late husband, too, and the sorry tale of their parting heated up the scholarly world for a while. Now I understand what everyone is after and must say, I am thrilled with the prospects. The question is, why are you including me in the dance at this late hour?"

I smiled at him and meant it. "You extended the offer of assistance, any time, anyhow, so I'm taking you up on the offer."

"But why now and what exactly is the how?"

"The now is that I need help, specifically a ride to the village, which is the probable site of the final dot you're connecting. As for the rest of the picture that makes up the how, it's still unfolding. I mean, I'm hoping to convince someone to lead me to the shrine but, obviously, I don't want to do this alone."

"Why not with Dr. Friedrich?"

"I plan to take Eva along but not on this leg. She often alienates people rather than inspires their confidence and I have reason not to completely trust her."

"And yet you trust me?" He clapped his gloved hands together as if receiving a long-awaited gift.

"Up to a point. I figure you're devious in an honest way. I know that's a contradiction but, as underhanded as you are, you haven't told me a single lie, as far as I know. It may seem simplistic but I appreciate that, which doesn't mean I'm willing to help you steal precious artifacts. You do get that, don't you?"

"I would expect no less of you but, in turn, it may surprise you to know that I am not in the business of stealing precious artifacts, period. I haven't the stomach for it. I have personally stolen nothing."

"But you're interested in dealing with artifacts once they're stolen, kind of like an ever-circling commercial vulture?"

He laughed, slapping his thigh in delight. "That is it exactly! And I do appreciate vultures for the manner in which they tidy things up after the predators, don't you agree?"

"You mean, like a cosmic housekeeper? Vultures have risen in my estimation but I'm still not willing to kill to feed one."

His laughter filled the car. "Never fear, Phoebe, my dear. We will both meet our ends without resorting to murder."

"That's the idea. But maybe the two of us will be at cross-purposes?"

"I don't see it that way at all. It's just that we seek the same things for different reasons."

"An interesting distinction. Did you knit your scarf?"

"I did. It's brioche stitch. Quite a pleasant experience, if you don't mind two-color knitting. How I wanted to add three or four more shades into the mix but the pattern didn't call for it."

"Maybe someday we can just talk knitting."

"That would be delightful. You could visit me at my estate in Wiltshire—lovely old pile, though a monster to sustain. Now, where exactly in Begüm are we to go?"

The road stretched ahead as a curve of pavement plunging around and among those tufa towers, the landscape bleached an ashy white. Finally we turned onto a paved road clearly frequented by tour busses and jutted upward across the hills. By the time we pulled into the village, it was nearly 2:15.

I had expected to find a gathering of humble houses, but the modern structures rising from either side of the tiny street took me by surprise. Freshly minted three-story homes marched on either side of a little gold-domed mosque along a tidy street featuring a single glass-fronted-carpet-cum-coffee shop that would look at home in downtown Istanbul.

"How very interesting," Rupert mused. "I would hazard a guess that this is indeed the correct village."

"And that the community has been benefiting from some source of income." I hauled the robe over my head and removed the scarf until I had peeled down to my jeans, jacket, and turtleneck.

"Well, well." Foxy tapped his chin and peered out the window. "Touristic efforts appear to be especially lucrative or, no doubt, that is what they wish everyone to believe. Look at the sign in the carpet shop window. It seems the village sits on an underground city to which the community offers limited tours."

"An underground economy."

While Evan remained with the rental, Rupert and I entered the shop, which turned out to be a multipurpose carpet store, tour-booking depot, and coffee shop presided over by a young man busy working an espresso machine and an older one unfurling a brilliant kilim at the feet of a seated couple in an expansive gallery area. The four tables that ran beside the long marble counter were occupied by a mix of people sipping coffee or eating pastries while studying guidebooks and maps. I walked up to the counter and picked up one of the brochures stacked by the cash register.

"Hello. Be right with you," the young man said over his shoulder as he zipped around the counter carrying a tiny cup of coffee to place in front of a lone man scanning his phone. So, good English was spoken here along with German, judging by the guy's passing comment to the two women hikers.

I handed the brochure to Rupert. "This looks fascinating. I'd love to visit an underground city, wouldn't you, uncle?"

Foxy unfolded the glossy pamphlet and beamed down at the photos of tunnels. "Oh, indeed I would. Looks terribly dark and cramped, though."

"Very sorry," the young man said, returning to his post. "One tour only per day. The next one is tomorrow at 10:15 in the morning. Do you want to book?"

"My, yes, dear boy, but we really only have today. We would be willing to pay extra for a private tour. Can that be arranged?"

The young man hesitated, taking in Foxy's expensive attire. "I am not sure that is possible. My sister leads the tours and she is not available."

"Could you ask her for us? We can wait, can't we dear?" Rupert said, turning to me.

"Sure."

"I will try to contact her but no promises. Very busy in cafe right now."

"Take your time, dear boy. Shall we investigate the carpets, Phoebe?" Foxy asked me.

We strolled around the gallery while I pointed out what kilims attracted me most and why. Though none were as old and venerable as my Goddess with Vultures kilim, several bore a modernized motif in rich reds against a cream background. The workmanship was still exquisite with crisp detailing at least 20-40 knots per inch.

"If I hadn't already blown my budget, I'd buy those two," I told him. Still, I was distracted and kept scanning the shop. "Maybe I'll just go across the street to the haman while we wait."

"Splendid," Sir Rupert said as he accompanied me back to the counter. "Dear boy," he hailed the cafe attendant. "I don't suppose you serve proper tea with milk?"

"Yes, see?" The young man pointed to a row of tin teapots beside a jar of mixed bags on the shelf behind him and grinned. "Any kind, even green."

"Green? No, my, that won't do it all. I prefer English breakfast but any tea served in such a manner would be deadly tepid. Tin is not meant to brew anything more notable than canned beans in some dreadful camping scenario. Do you have real china?"

I slipped away, leaving Rupert regaling the poor guy on the specifics of English tea preparation, and stepped into the sunshine. Evan, leaning against the hood of the car reading a paperback, nodded to me as I crossed the street.

The haman I spied midway down bore the same signs of prosperity as the rest of the village, only more noticeable by its size and marble exterior. Two entrances, one for men, one for women, meant that both genders could enjoy their ablutions any time.

Inside, I paid the attendant the last of my change and descended into the women's side of the bath house. In a modern dressing room, I stripped, determined to banish modesty in the name of research, and entered the women's area with head up and chest out. It took time to adjust to the light in the steamy interior but I soon realized I was not the only Westerner there. Most of the locals shampooing and soaping down took little notice of me. The haman was busy with at least fifteen women in the main steam area alone.

I wasn't certain what I was looking for or even why I'd come, except on some hunch that the Goddess motif must hold power for the women of this community. Where better to feel it than naked?

Some bathers were clearly tourists, especially the young blond having a pedicure in an adjacent room, and no one seemed particularly interested in me, though a couple smiled in welcome.

I circled the round steam room as if looking for an ideal spot to land my naked rump when I noticed one woman staring at my chest. She paused in the midst of towel drying her hair, bent over seized in a state of apparent shock. Somewhere on either side of thirty and probably Turkish with a cloud of thick dark curls, she slowly straightened and waited until I approached. By then I knew my breasts weren't as fascinating as the goddess tattoo rising beneath. Our eyes locked. I strode over to stand directly in front of her.

"Are you a sister of the Goddess?" I don't know where that question came from, but it seemed to suit the gravitas of the moment—one naked woman regarding another in a steamy interior.

Without replying, she gathered her towels and steered me from the steam area into a nearby sauna, empty but for us. She turned on me the moment the door shut behind us. "Who are you and why are you wearing that mark so openly on your chest?"

"I'm Phoebe McCabe and I'm here on the Goddess's business." I actually said that and, more strangely, even meant it. "Who are you?"

"I am Nadira Sonar and you should not be here, a stranger wearing Her mark so openly." Her English was excellent. "What do you think you know?"

"I am here with Eva Yilmaz. Does that tell you anything?"

She lifted her hands and let them drop. "No Yilmaz is welcome here, especially not Eva."

"Why not? If you know the story, you also know Dr. Yilmaz kept his promise to the village."

"He did not." She emphasized "not" with a hammer's force, her lovely face fierce. "He returned many years later trying to locate the shrine, but already our men were suspicious, thanks to Eva Yilmaz. The women of this village had kept this secret for centuries, but as soon as she published that article, it came to light that we were hiding something. Then men watched and pestered their women trying to pry the secret free but no one talked. Then Dr. Yilmaz returned and sought out my mother again, and all our efforts were for nothing."

"Your mother was the mystery woman who first brought him to the shrine?"

"That was a mistake she lived with all her days. Dr. Yilmaz's arrival brought it all to light again. My uncle—her brother—followed her and Dr. Yilmaz to the shrine one night and discovered the truth. He killed them both on the spot."

"Your uncle killed your mother and Borek Yilmaz?"

"Ssh! Keep your voice down. Yes, that is what I'm saying. You understand now the danger?"

"But why, why would he kill his own sister?"

"You don't understand. A woman couldn't just creep away some place at night with a man who was neither her husband nor a family member. My mother was married and yet she was alone with another man."

"She didn't have intercourse with him, did she?"

"Certainly not, but in my uncle's eyes she still dishonored her family. Do you understand now?"

"Oh, God, they were killed together?" I buried my head in my hands. "But how did you find out?"

"I followed my mother that night. I saw it all."

"Oh, Nadira. How awful to carry around that burden. Your heart must be broken."

"Many hearts are broken in this village. Many necks, too. Mine is only one casualty. You must leave. My uncle controls the site now and the village. All of the treasures have long ago seeped into the town and to foreign buyers. He would stop at nothing to keep secret what he has done."

"Are you safe?"

"I am lucky he didn't kill me, too, but my uncle could not bring himself to murder a child. I am his servant now, as we all are. I run his tours to the underground city, my father and brother run the carpet shop across the street. We work, we live, we survive, like the rest of the village."

"But what about your mother?"

"She is lost to me now, and if I dare share what I know to anyone, he will have my father and brother killed. That is what he said and I believe him. Many have already died here. No, I am not safe but I am trying to impress on you that neither are you. Go now and take Eva Yilmaz with you."

"No, please." I grabbed her shoulders. "You can't remain a slave and allow your mother's murderer to get away with this. Maybe she did make a mistake, but does that mean they both should be punished with their lives? That's just barbaric. That's not what the Goddess stands for. You're Her daughter, too, aren't you?"

Nadira pushed me away. "Would you get us all killed?"

"We can end this once and for all. If the treasure's gone, turn the site over to the authorities. Let the Goddess speak. What do you have to lose?"

"My life, my father's, and brother's."

"I have a plan. Help me play it out."

31

When I emerged from the haman an hour later, Evan stood outside the car in conversation with another man with no Rupert in sight. I strode over to them, shielding my eyes against the sun.

Evan smiled as I approached, holding a hand towards the older man, the same one who had been displaying carpets to the young couple earlier. "Ms. McCabe, meet Mr. Sonar. His family runs the carpet shop cafe."

"Hi," I greeted Nadira's father, a short rotund fellow with graying hair wisping around a high forehead. When he smiled, his face crinkled into a thousand lines. "Your uncle has bought many fine things today, many nice carpets."

"Has he?" I looked around. "And just where is Uncle Rupert now, still inside drinking tea?"

"He is with my brother-in-law, Sarp."

"Buying more things," Evan added with a knowing smile. More like a smirk, actually.

"Really? Where?"

"Just up the street. We're to wait until he returns."

"You come inside," Mr. Sonar insisted. "I give you tea or perhaps you prefer coffee?"

"Tea, thanks." I followed him into the shop, almost empty now but for the lone man still reading his phone. How could anybody read a Blackberry screen for so long?

I took a seat a few tables away and waited for my apple tea while keeping one eye on the man. His jacket looked more Sears than Turkish leather, so I pegged him as possibly American or Canadian. After a few moments, he rose and stepped outside to talk into his phone.

I watched him uneasily. Where was Foxy? We had things to do, places to go. At last, in he walked, his face rosy and beaming. "Hello, Phoebe, dear. Did you enjoy the haman? I must say, I had a most excellent afternoon."

"Did you? Are you ready to head back to the hotel?"

"Are we not to take a tour of the underground city?"

I got to my feet. "Not now. Let's go."

We said our goodbyes to the Sonars and climbed into the waiting car, the phone man still talking on the street outside.

"That man is definitely a spy for somebody," I said, the moment the doors closed.

"Indeed he is but, never mind, he is quite toothless by himself," Rupert said, settling down in his seat wearing something like a beatific smile.

"I'm glad you're so relaxed about it because I'm not. He could work for some black market syndicate."

"He's a scout for Maggie's syndicate, as it turns out. She knows we're here but what of it? There's nothing left for her to steal, as you said."

"Maggie has a syndicate?"

"A network of hired guns and contacts sounds quite like a syndicate by my definition. She's been here asking questions but to no avail, as far as I can tell."

I studied him closely. "You've been vulturing, haven't you? You look like what my mother would have called 'the cat who ate the canary'."

"Phoebe, I'm either a vulture or a cat. I can't be both. In any case, I have been actively doing business, yes, and have, in fact, just spent a fascinating hour in the company of one Sarp Onur, the veritable mayor of the village in charge of all things related to the underground city."

"Including keeping the community under his control and acting as the kingpin for black market interests? I know. He murdered both Dr. Borek Yilmaz and Mr. Sonar's wife ten years ago."

"Pardon me?"

"I met Mr. Sonar's daughter in the haman. She told me everything, like how her mother was murdered by her own brother in a kind of disgusting honor killing. He's got a stranglehold on this village and it has to end."

"Oh my."

"I'm coming back here tonight at 10:00 with Eva for a personalized conducted tour."

"Oh, dear. Is that wise, given what you have just disclosed?"

"It's necessary. Eva needs to see the shrine, which she will at last, and I'm bringing in reinforcements to set up a sting or whatever it's called. Evan, as soon as we're on a hill somewhere outside of town, stop please so I can make a call to Interpol."

"Interpol?" Rupert's alarm was almost comical.

"Interpol. Look, if the business you did with Sarp today is the tiniest bit illegal, I don't want to know about it. Don't even try disclosing the details."

"I always operate within the margins of the law, Phoebe."

"Margins being the operative word. Now, would you stop the car so I can make my call?"

Rupert nodded to Evan, who pulled off on a viewing area overlooking a breathtaking valley of caves and conical hills. I scrambled from the car and climbed a rock, trying to fix the strongest signal. It didn't matter who tracked me now. Everyone knew where I was and it suited my plan to have Interpol keep tabs on me. And Maggie, too, for that matter.

Walker answered the call after four rings. He actually sounded awake, if not necessarily pleased. "Phoebe?"

"I'm here outside Begüm. We need to speak in private. Can you meet me somewhere?"

After I'd arranged to meet him at the back of Eva's house within the hour, I took the opportunity to call the gallery, only soon realized it was past closing time. I left a chirpy voice message telling Serena I was in Cappadocia on a hunt for more kilims but should be back in London soon. Duty served, I returned to the car and grinned at Sir Rupert. "Fabulous scenery," I remarked.

"Glorious, indeed. Is all well?"

"So far. Could I ask you for another drive to Begüm tonight?"

"Yes, of course. Consider me at your disposal, but I am most anxious. What you are doing is excessively dangerous."

"I won't be alone, Rupert.

"Yes, I understand that, but what help can I be among murderous cutthroats? We shall bring Evan along, of course, but nevertheless, this is all very risky."

"Evan can't come inside the shrine and neither can you. I'm sorry, Rupert. Nadira believes her Uncle Sarp will agree only to taking Eva and me to the shrine and, even so, we're not sure she can convince him of that."

Rupert slapped a hand over his heart. "Surely you're not proposing to use yourself as bait?"

"If necessary."

"No, Phoebe. I must protest!"

I patted his knee. "I'll be fine, Rupert. Let Interpol handle this. You stay on the sidelines and try to maintain your innocent facade."

No amount of badgering could shake my resolve, and by the time he dropped me off at the bottom of the path leading to Eva's house, he had reluctantly agreed to pick me up at the same spot at 9:30 that evening.

I climbed the stony path in my robe and hijab with my head down. It didn't seem worth walking all the way up to Eva's house when I'd be meeting Walker nearby in a few minutes. Instead, I found a sheltered area under a tree halfway up the path and waited.

Though a few pedestrians passed, nodding as they trudged uphill, mostly the little byway remained empty. It would be supper time soon and people were already home for their evening meal. The scent of grilling meat spiced the air from the nearby houses as the sun poured liquid tangerine over the horizon. Sun juice, I thought idly. Yum.

My mind wandered to food and Noel with equal hunger, my appetite for all things enhanced. I kept picturing one in a glass and the other naked when I noticed a man in a long white robe approaching from the main road below. I recognized the authoritative gait at once.

Stopping only a few inches away, he took in my robe and nodded. "Finally, face to face at last. Make this good, Ms. McCabe." He'd darkened his skin in disguise, but the effect only enhanced his Most Wanted look.

"All right, I'm going to fill you in on everything that happened today, plus everything I now know. Listen carefully." I

launched into a rapid description of Begüm's secret, of Sarp
Onur's role in the murder of Dr. Yilmaz and Nadira's mother, of
the noose that kept the village in a chokehold of black market
dealings. Describing Foxy's role and how Noel fit in was a bit
more challenging, but I could honestly share only what they
claimed; one was here as a dealer, the other as Eva's former
student and substitute son. By the time I'd finished, I may have
only imagined the tinge of reluctant admiration warming Walker's
expression. I preferred to believe it real.

"I propose to act as bait at the shrine tonight. I asked
Nadira to inform her uncle of how much I know and, of course,
he'll want to bump me off like he did her mother and Borek."

"That's madness. You've just turned yourself into an even
bigger target."

"If you can think of some other way to entice that man to
reveal the secret site he has been plundering for years, bring it on.
While you're at it, figure out a way to get him to provide a guided
tour for me and the wife of the man he murdered. This is the only
way I can take Eva to the site she craves to see so much while
preserving what remains of this ancient shrine. Besides, I'm
hoping to have the cavalry on my side for once."

He held up a hand. "Are you referring to the army? This is
going to be enormously challenging to organize and there's not
much time. I'll need to involve the Turkish Antiquities divisions,
not to mention my colleagues in Istanbul all, in what, four hours?"

"You'd better get busy."

"You'll be underground, I presume, with people who know
every twist and turn in what is bound to be a labyrinth of tunnels.
Where exactly do you expect your backup team to hide, and
supposing we can't find you in time?"

I hesitated. "Surely you guys can figure that part out?"

"You'll need to be fixed with a wire, presuming I can get
the equipment here in time, and possibly we can use a kind of dye.
If you sprinkle it along the way, we can then use an ultraviolet
light to follow."

"Oh, like a techno Hansel and Gretel. That sounds good." I
didn't even try keeping the relief from my voice. "Sir Rupert Fox
is picking me up at 9:30 to drive me to back to Begüm. There's a

stretch of road between the main highway and the village where we can pull over and wait for you at, let's say, 9:45ish?"

"We'll be there." He turned to leave, then hesitated. "Phoebe, stay vigilant between now and the time we meet. A lot can happen in four hours." "I know," I said as I turned and marched up the hill."

32

"Eva?" I shrugged out of my borrowed robe and scanned the room. The duffel bag dumped by the door told me she'd returned, but still no response met my call. Anxiety drove me to take the stairs two at a time up into her bedroom where I found her spread-eagled on the bed as if she'd collapsed.

"Eva?" Perching on the edge of the bed, I shook her gently until her eyes fluttered open.

"Oh, Phoebe, there you are. I was worried to find you gone. Have you seen Noel?"

"Not yet. I'm hoping he's hiding out somewhere safe and will show up soon."

"As do I. If anything should happen to him because of me, I could never forgive myself."

"How are you feeling?"

"Tired, and after all that, I still didn't manage to get a car. Nobody wants to get involved with me, and in truth, I don't blame them. My name is known in these parts but not as I'd hoped."

"Don't worry, I think I have part of the problem solved. I have so much to tell you, but the short story is that I've arranged for us to see the shrine tonight. Before you get too excited, there are lots of strings attached and maybe a couple of nooses."

Eva propped herself on her elbows. "Tell me! How the Goddess smoothes our paths! This is extraordinary news, Phoebe."

"It's also complex, convoluted even, and dangerous. I also discovered something that may cause you pain."

"Pain is a relative matter to me these days. Spare nothing."

"I'll explain as much as I can." And I did, finishing off with: "So you see, this Sarp Onur couldn't let Borek return to Istanbul to reveal the site's location and his black market operation, which is why he killed him. I'm sorry, Eva."

"Borek was murdered," she said, staring up at the ceiling. "I'd always suspected that he'd run into trouble on that last journey. Now I know. And you will bring me face to face with both his killer and the Goddess? I am almost too overwhelmed with gratitude."

"It's going to be a very dangerous trek, Eva, and exhausting. I have no idea how far we'll have to walk or even if Interpol can set up what has to be a complicated sting. The more I think about it, the more convinced I am that the whole thing is crazy."

"Nonsense. I care nothing about the danger and, if you will help, I'll walk as far as it takes. What's crazy about taking risks and forging forward with spirit? Thank you, Phoebe, for doing the Goddess's work so magnificently. No matter what happens tonight, She will ensure that all will turn out as it should. I am happy, will be happier still. That's all I can say. You have brought this to my worthy fruition."

"We haven't arrived yet, so hold the thanks. Get some rest. We still have a few hours before we have to leave." I got to my feet, about to head for the door when she clutched my hand.

"Wait, Phoebe, please. I must tell you something."

"If it's about the kilim, I know."

She gazed up at me in surprise. "You do?"

"I do. Let's not talk about that now. I still have a few things to get ready before we go out tonight. Can I fix you something to eat?"

"No, thank you, but about the kilim—"

"Later. Rest while you can."

"I took it to keep it safe, that's all, but you must take it back when this night is over. She wants you to have it."

"Get some rest."

***

Upstairs in my bedroom, I perched on the edge of the bed running the details of the plan over in my head. Of course, I wouldn't

269

have the full logistics until I met Walker later, but I knew enough to understand how unprepared we all were. None of us had enough information on the tunnels to make a decent plan. We were delving deep into uncharted territory.

How many things could go wrong? All the bravado I'd mustered leeched away.

Supposing the army refused to play or Sarp Onur didn't trust his niece, or worse still, Nadira didn't trust me and backed out at the last minute? Or maybe she had no intention of helping us from the beginning? Why should she disrupt her life because some stranger with a carpet tattoo implores her to set her people free? Just who did I think I was? After all, the community had prospered by draining antiquities into the black market over the years. Maybe Sarp was their hero. What did I know?

I was so busy biting down on reality pills that I didn't realized that a cool breeze was ruffling my hair. I brushed a tendril from my eyes and paused. Did I leave the trap door open? I must have, since a square of dusk-hued sky marked the ceiling overhead. Well, damn.

Cautiously, I climbed the ladder, reaching the top to poke my head out into the descending night. I had planned only to fasten the trap shut but the sky held me captive. All I could see were stars emerging a billion miles above. Billions and trillions of galaxies and worlds, a cosmos of mystery and possibility, all spinning with an energy so fierce, it pushed through time itself. Maybe energy was time? Stars died, collapsing into dark holes, to be born again in brilliant swirling nebulae light years away. Who could measure such magnificence or relegate it to mere science alone?

All I could do was breathe, allowing a flood of conviction that everything would work out as it should wash through me. By the law of possibilities, that conviction made no sense at all, but its impact hit me so powerfully it was if I'd been ambushed by a comet.

"Phoebe?"

I whipped around. "Noel?" He was sitting under what looked to be a mound of carpets, silhouetted against the luminescence like an island in a starry sea. "You're safe!"

"I am."

"I was afraid Interpol picked you up and forgot to mention it. How long have you been here?

"Only a few hours. The house was empty when I arrived, and this seemed the perfect place to rest after spending last night dodging the army. I didn't want to risk making myself too comfortable downstairs. This is ideal."

He stood up and stretched. "It's secluded, and once you pull up the ladder like so..." I watched as he crossed the distance between us and offered his hand to help me topside. He kept my fingers laced in his while he hauled up the ladder and closed the trap door single-handedly. "The roof is private both inside and out."

"Privacy which you need right now because?"

He kept holding my hand and I didn't mind at all.

"In case Eva comes up and we lose a chance to talk."

"Eva's downstairs sleeping so deeply, she won't be going anywhere for a few hours. She finally told me the whole story, well, most of it."

He gently pulled me closer, wrapping one arm around my shoulders. I didn't mind that, either. "I've gone along with her obsession for years. She believes, Phoebe. She's convinced that a public and academic endorsement of the Goddess shrine will somehow make the world a better place."

"Do you believe that?"

"It can't make it worse, in my view. All is twisted out of balance at the moment, and we need a strong dose of the feminine to balance out the forces destroying our planet, destroying our humanity. Yes, I believe it."

I peered up at him, trying to see his face. "You surprise me. I'm in this now and I'm taking her to the Goddess shrine tonight."

"How did you manage that?"

"It's a long story."

"We have time."

"I'll tell you that Interpol is helping."

"So you're back on friendly terms with the police?"

"More like a truce in the name of the higher good, the higher good being the capture of black market thieves, murderers, and assorted miscreants, while preserving what's left of the Goddess shrine."

I could feel the warmth of his breath on my hair. "I must be lumped in the miscreant category."

"Actually, you also qualify as a black market thief."

"Overqualified, then. Have you actually located the site?"

"Yes and no. Tonight at 10:00 I've arranged for a private tour for Eva and me. Sorry, but you're not invited." I couldn't tell him the details in case he tried to prevent us from going. Or followed us and Interpol captured him. "You have to stay away."

"I'll follow you anyway."

"Don't. Look, Noel, I've never hidden the fact that I intend to assist with your capture."

"And yet you're not calling Interpol right now to say where I am."

I shivered despite how close I stood to him. "That wasn't the agreement. Besides, you still haven't told me where to find Toby."

"I'll remedy that right now." He pulled something from his pocket, holding it palm up in his hand. I could just see a little fold of paper glowing ghostly in the starlight. "Take it. It's an address, instructions, really. You'll find specific information on how to find Toby in Istanbul. He wants to explain what happened in person, and it's only fair to you both that he gets that opportunity. Read it, memorize it, then burn it. I promise you, he's waiting."

I took the folded paper and shoved it deep into my jeans pocket. "Thanks."

"And yet you're still not calling Interpol. Does this mean I'm forgiven or that maybe you've come to recognize a few of my redeeming features?"

"I hope you're not referring to the redeeming features I glimpsed in the haman?"

He laughed. "Glad you appreciated something."

"I figure Interpol will capture you soon enough, so why rush the moment?" I gazed up, trying to see his face.

"Let's not rush a thing."

When be brought his lips to mine, I was waiting. His kiss was long and deep, both leisurely and urgent all at once. Fire breeds fire, energy explodes into possibilities. I pulled him tighter, feeling his arousal against me as he framed my face with his hands and continued kissing deep and hard.

Soon, we were lying back against the rugs, his mouth on mine plunging me into the heady realm of not caring or maybe caring too much. My hand snaked under his sweater, and until I touched smooth skin dusted by hair, the ripple of sinew and muscle, the steady throb of heart under palm. My hand wandered lower.

With one quick twist, he pulled a rug over us, a rough weave smelling faintly of goat and smoke. The sky overhead burned sharp and cold while beneath the blanket I was heating up.

"Phoebe," he murmured. "I love you."

I helped ease his jeans down over his hips, spending a few wanton minutes exploring the exposed terrain.

We wrestled out of our clothes, laughing at the entrapment of shoes and socks, jeans and underwear, until our naked bodies pressing together stifled mirth under a battery of sweet, urgent kisses. We couldn't see each other in the dark, but other senses rose to the challenge. I craved the strength of him, of everything that made man different from women: body hair, muscles, and the long hard length of him.

Did I love him? I didn't know. I only knew I loved everything at that moment—the stars, the sea, the universe, especially the universe and everything within it. I was open to the energy while stirring up my own with his.

I called out his name when he entered me, and cried harder in the release. Had I been propelled into a joyride across the galaxy, I couldn't have felt more alive.

Afterward, he held me tightly against the chill of the evening and we stayed locked together unwilling to break the spell for a long time. Too long, in fact.

"Noel, I have to go," I whispered, disentangling my limbs. "I have to wake up Eva and prepare for tonight. If I don't get to see you again after this, if Interpol brings you in, I promise to visit you wherever they imprison you." I kissed him one last time before climbing to my feet. He never saw my tears though one may have dropped on his chest.

"Phoebe, wait."

"No time left." My voice hitched. "Could you replace the ladder?"

"If you think I'm letting you do this fool thing alone, you don't know me."

I pulled on my clothes while he repositioned the ladder, the air chill against my skin. He was balancing on one leg climbing into his jeans when I lowered myself down the steps.

"Wait, I said I'm coming down with you." He hopped towards the hatch.

"And I said you can't." And I pulled down the trap door and secured the latch.

He pounded on the roof while I tidied up. His muffled shouting reverberated through the wood while I pocketed my phone and stuffed a bottle of water into my jacket pocket for later.

I could hear his anger and frustration as I opened up the little fold of paper with Toby's whereabouts. It was more a string of coordinates than an address, so I committed it to memory and swallowed the paper, forcing the pulpy wad down with a wash of water.

"Phoebe, let me out! What the hell are you doing?"

Minutes later I was down on Eva's level calling out for her to get ready. "Our ride will be here in fifteen minutes," I said, bursting into her room.

The rumpled bed was empty.

"Eva?" She must have gone downstairs to have a bite to eat. I called her name all the way down to the bottom level, stunned to find it dark. I flicked on the lights and scanned the room: chairs knocked over, her duffel where she dropped it, the door wide open. No Eva. Something moved behind me but I turned too late.

33

My captors gagged and blindfolded me before tossing me face-down into what felt like the back of a van. Everything rattled. The gritty mix of gas fumes and dirt hurt my lungs. Panic surged uncontrollably until I reined my emotions into calm.

I struggled onto my back. Better. At least I could breathe. I lay there with all my senses stretching outward. We were traveling over a rough road very fast. Where were they taking me? What would they do once they got there? Why had I locked Noel away? Veering into panic again, I fought back the surging adrenalin, trying to breathe as deeply as possible. Several minutes passed in a jiggling, bumping state of suspended terror as I locked panic down.

Something groaned to my left. I wiggled over inch by inch until I felt warmth against my thigh. Eva! My relief spiked then nosedived when I realized that she'd be bound, too, only how could she endure this brutality? I tried to communicate through the gag, managing a muted hum at best. Eva made no response. I nudged her and she groaned again. I settled for inching as close to her as I could go, hoping she'd sense the warmth of a friend nearby.

We bumped along for at least another hour, the van hitting potholes and rumbling over gravel. Suddenly, it squealed to a halt. Voices speaking Turkish, two, maybe three men. The doors slid open and someone dragged me out by the feet. Fresh air hit my face as I was slung over a shoulder and bounced along in a loping jog. I went limp. Let them think I was unconscious like Eva. Eva! Surely they'd have the decency to carry her properly?

My carrier slowed his pace. A woman's voice now, sharp and angry. Men arguing back. Yet another voice barking authoritatively, which seemed to prompt my carrier to continue. Steps going down now, many, many steps, my head lolling like a rag doll over this guy's shoulder. I felt sick but I couldn't afford to vomit. I'd suffocate.

Then without warning, I was dropped backwards against a wall. Someone ripped off my blindfold and peeled off the utility tape sealing my mouth. I blinked into an earthen room strung with electric lights. Many people stood around, some in shadows where I couldn't see their faces, but I recognized Nadira crouching, shaking Eva on the ground nearby.

I roused myself. "What are you doing to her?"

Before Nadira could answer, the man hovering over me spewed verbal vitriol launched in Turkish but quickly changed to English. "You think we are stupid?"

I looked up at him, this man in his middle-fifties wearing coveralls and a baseball cap. He held a pistol in one hand. "You think I let you trap me and come here with police? This is my home, my village. This site belongs to us, not government. It is our land. No one steals our secrets! Tonight you die. How we kill them, Nadira?" He stooped long enough to pull the young woman to her feet, holding her by the arm while she tried to shake loose. "You decide. Your mother and her friend were killed by falling, yes?"

"Maybe we should sacrifice them to the Goddess?" Maggie stepped from the shadows. "That would be a good end, don't you think?"

I groaned. "I should have known you'd be involved in this somewhere."

"You should have known lots of things, hon, but you're not real swift. I work with people, like Sarp here, see? You could have bought some useful friends for once." She shrugged, a vision in fashion perfection in total black leather. "Too late now."

"Buying friends is an oxymoron, Mags."

"You're the moron 'cause my way works. Isn't that right, Foxy?"

Rupert emerged from the shadows, his expression apologetic.

Damn. Damn. "Were you working with Maggie all along?"

"No, in fact, we only forged our collaboration this afternoon." He twisted his hands together and actually had the nerve to look guilty. No need. I was the fool here, not him.

I closed my eyes and leaned against the wall. "Please don't hurt Eva."

"As if we can let either of you go," Maggie said. "You two have to disappear—simple. Get that? I told you in Istanbul. You never listen. Besides, Mr. Onur here promised to silence you permanently."

"This must be hurried," Sarp interrupted, shoving Nadira away. "We shoot them now."

"Now, now, Mr. Onur, no need to be hasty." Foxy said, refusing to meet my eyes. "We agreed that all would be handled in a civilized fashion. No rough-housing, no unnecessary haranguing, and that taking the two ladies to the shrine would be a fitting end, dare I say poetic? Shall we proceed there now?"

"How is murder ever civilized, Foxy?" I asked.

"Too much time." Sarp cut the air with his hand. "We kill now."

"No, no," Rupert insisted, waving his hands. "No guns, didn't I say no guns? Yes, I did. This must look like an accident. They are to fall off a cliff, didn't we agree?"

"Great story: two women were strolling the Cappadocian hills at night...'

"Hush, Phoebe. You are not helping," Foxy said sternly.

"I have idea." Sarp beckoned to four men standing against a far wall. I recognized Evan and a man that could have been my pursuer in Istanbul. The others I registered as just men with guns. "No more arguments. Take them to shrine. Nadira leads the way."

One man yanked me to my feet while Evan rushed to scoop a limp Eva into his arms. All formed a single file behind Nadira, with me being pushed along directly behind her, Foxy behind me, followed by Evan with Eva, and the others in a ragged string behind them. Sarp brought up the rear.

"Where are we?" I asked.

"The underground city," Nadira said over her shoulder. "This part once served as the grain storage area. We will pass through a wine cellar next. A city of several hundred people lived here once. At least fifty miles of tunnels have never been explored."

It was a subterranean world of hewn stone with niches and vestibules, low ceilings, and multiple tunnels cutting off in all directions. I imagined hundreds of people living here long ago, forced underground by religious persecution or the expansion plan of warring empires. Now it became the warren of tourists and thieves.

We skirted three large amphorae set into the floor lit above by recess lights. "For olive oil," Nadira, ever the guide, told us. The path dipped steadily downward.

"Watch your step," she cautioned.

How ironic, I thought. We were to tread carefully only so our captors could kill us later. Nadira didn't seem happy. Had she told her uncle my plan or did Foxy? Foxy. I didn't feel betrayed as much as stupid. My character assessment needed serious recalibration.

The tunnels narrowed so low we had to duck in parts, with Evan proceeding sideways with Eva. So far underground and hemmed in by stone, claustrophobia threatened me at every step. I focused on the electric lights illuminating the ceiling, floors, and walls. I kept my eyes fixed on Nadira's slim form ahead.

"Where's the air coming from?" I asked, feeling a breeze on my face.

"There are ventilation channels leading to the surface all through the city. Careful." She raised one hand. "The first door lies ahead."

"Door?"

"The inhabitants used boulders to block various sections against their enemies. They are designed to be secured from the inside only. They are impossible to dislodge from the other direction."

"How ingenious," I heard Foxy say.

We squatted through a portal past a gigantic round stone that must have taken many hands to roll into place. Foxy poked me in the back as I scrambled through. I turned and caught him winking at me in the half-light. What?

Soon everybody pressed in after us. We crammed into a kind of hewn vestibule. That gave me an opportunity to check on

Eva. She had flung an arm over Evan's neck by now and sat half-raised looking alert. Evan must have offered her water, since she held a bottle in one hand. I touched her arm and she mouthed something at me, nodding to Evan. I didn't get it. A quick glance up at him unsettled me further when Evan shot me a friendly smile.

"Can you imagine living down here?" Maggie asked no one in particular. I fought back a smart-assed reply.

"From here, the people moved off in many directions to their homes. Many families lived in each cave carved in these walls."

"Nadira," Uncle Sarp snapped. "No guiding! We are not tourists. Go."

We re-formed our line and continued deeper and deeper into the earth. Nadira had stopped the commentary except for pausing long enough to point out a Plexiglas-sealed hole in the floor. "If enemies reach this far, hot oil would be poured on their heads."

"An old and time-honored strategy," said Eva, rousing. By now, I figured she must have assessed the situation.

Many twists and turns on uneven ground followed until the ceiling lights ended and Nadira flicked on a flashlight, as did Foxy and three others behind us. "The rest is not open to the public. Very dangerous."

Without the lights, I could barely stay upright and twice tumbled into Nadira. "Is this leading to the Goddess shrine?"

"Yes," she said. "The two sites are separated by walls of stone. An earthquake uncovered it decades ago and we discovered it by accident."

"Keep moving!" Sarp shouted.

We wove over loose rubble, some of which had been cleared into an uneven path I imagined trod by the feet of many local thieves. Sarp considered the site his because the village lay near it. Did proximity equal ownership? Not by any law I knew.

Earthquake damage stood out in fallen walls, mounds of earth.

"Why is there damage here but not back where we've come?"

"The tufa is more porous," Nadira said, "and many caves exist close together with little support between. The earth shakes, it crumbles."

Many dark and twisty paths followed; many slip-slides down scrabbled hills into narrow valleys followed that. It was dark, the air constricted around us. I began to heave oxygen into my lungs. At last Sarp yelled, "Halt".

Nadira turned around to wait. "I did not want this," she whispered in my ear.

"Then why?" I asked.

Sarp pushed his way through. "You and you stay here and watch," he said, indicating two of his minions. "You, too," he said to Maggie. "Sir Rupert and the two women only go to shrine."

"I'm going," Maggie said.

He pointed his gun at her. "You wait here, I said."

"Don't tell me what to do. I came a long way to see this place so I'm going, too."

"I said no."

"Play your macho bullshit somewhere else. I'm coming." Maggie never did temper tone to circumstance. "I've got a gun I can wag, too."

Sarp nodded to one of his dudes to restrain Maggie, which prompted her man to intervene. A brief scuffle erupted.

"Stop!" Foxy cried. "This is folly! Mr. Onur, permit her to come. What is the harm?"

Sarp muttered away in Turkish before jerking his head towards a ragged opening in the wall ahead. "Go." Maggie won again.

Nadira picked her way through, beckoning us to follow. We were inside another dark tunnel, wider than the others, which at first seemed to be more of the same, only soon even I could tell that the walls were hewn differently.

The blocks were more squarely cut, with few round pieces. The mark of another, far older civilization rose around us. Occasionally, the flashlight beams licked across bands of relief so startling they seemed to leap out from the wall—a procession of bulls, a bird. I heard Eva gasp, but we were shoved along relentlessly.

Finally, Nadira came to a halt. "We enter the Goddess shrine now. Do not touch anything."

Sarp squeezed his way to the front. "No matter if they touch. All gold is gone. Move."

We stepped inside a large square stone room decorated by relief chiseled deep into the rock. Multiple flashlights flicked over a carved life-sized goddess featuring pronounced breasts and enthroned with leopards. Her outstretched arms held carrion birds in each hand. Though chiseled bull heads also decorated the shrine, the Goddess reigned supreme, like birth triumphing over death, the bearer of life signaling hope in the internal cycle.

"Phoebe, look!" Eva whispered. "Evan, set me down at once." He lowered her gently to her feet. "Phoebe, quickly! Take pictures."

My gaze flew to the wall opposite, where brilliant color danced in Nadira's light, a wall of Goddess with Vultures motifs similar to my kilim only larger, more detailed, and almost as electric with energy. I pulled out my phone, hit the camera icon, and began filming. Here the Goddess manifested symbolically in still-vibrant pigments—blue, red, white, ocher—dancing across time itself.

"Do not touch," Nadira warned, her voice choking emotion. "Already the colors fade. All our lamps and the fires they've burned here are destroying the paintings. She will disappear soon."

The closer I came, the more I focused on where flakes of color had slipped to the floor.

"My maternal ancestors guarded Her for years. We kept her secret safe. Now look."

"She was this Neolithic civilization's idea of universal deity, balanced with the male, a spirit merged in the great giver of life," Eva marveled.

"Ancient beyond ancient, older than even the Egyptians," I whispered.

"Far, far older. We worship Her still in the Virgin Mary but she is... God's compassionate side, the Divine Feminine in partnership with the male and, as God, She has many faces, of both genders."

"Oh, my, how remarkable," Foxy effused. "What an honor to be here."

"Blasphemy!" Sarp interrupted. "Nadira, all of you. Move away. This place is an abomination to Mohammed. No woman is to be above man. It is written in the Koran and your Bible."

"Both are freely interpreted by man and steeped in the cultural and social morass of the ages," Eva pointed out. "This is how it began, how it is supposed to be."

"Silence! I will not hear such blasphemy! This place is an affront to Allah and must be destroyed."

"Uncle, no!"

"This shrine is to Allah, only by another name," said Eva.

"Wait, wait," Maggie stepped forward, running her own light around the shrine's parameter. "These paintings are all very nice but where did you find the gold? I mean, let's get practical here."

Sarp jerked his head towards the empty niches centered above each bull's head. "All around this room, gold vessels and other things, all gone now."

"There were ritual daggers embedded in cabochons, necklaces and bracelets on the Goddess's arms and feet, a magnificent headdress fashioned with tiny gold leaves," Nadira explained.

"There was a friggin' headdress? Sarp, you didn't say anything about a headdress. Did you hear that, Foxy?"

Rupert, standing beside me, seemed distracted. He kept nudging me in the arm. "Pardon me?" he asked while I pocketed the phone.

"Sold long ago," Sarp said before he could answer. "The first piece sold gave us the haman."

"Well, damn. I mean the bracelets and dagger I bought are real stunners and all, but a headdress, wow. I would love to be photographed wearing that. I'll have to settle for a phone selfie. Foxy, will you take my picture sitting on the throne?"

Before he could respond, one of the minions left behind leaped over the threshold, shouting Turkish to Sarp.

"What's happening?" Maggie asked, swinging around with her phone in one hand, flashlight in the other.

"Interpol," Eva lowered herself down to sitting. "He says there are men coming through the underground city, our rescuers, presumably. Sarp wants to proceed to the next plan."

"Evan!" Foxy called to his man while turning to me. "I was afraid they'd never get here," he whispered, shoving something into my hands. "Flashlight and map. There's another exit through the tunnels leading to the other side of the village. Nadira highlighted the route. Use it to find your way out should we get separated. Matters are about to get rather messy."

Maggie swung towards him. "What? You chubby little bastard! You're double-crossing me?"

But Sarp was shouting, Nadira screaming, Evan wrestling one of the minions. Flashlights fell, rolling to the ground. A gun went off, then another, bullets ricocheting off the ancient bull's heads, lodging into the walls. I grabbed Eva and pulled her into a far corner, whispering "We have to get out of here! Rupert, where are you?" I called.

"I must stay." Eva told me.

"Here, Phoebe! Run!" Foxy's voice.

The shrine plunged into darkness, but for one fallen flashlight beaming light against the far wall. More shouting, with Sarp's voice rising above the rest.

"Go!" Eva pushed my arm.

I fumbled with the flashlight Foxy gave me. "I'm not leaving you."

But the Goddess had had enough. First came an earth-ripping explosion and then the ceiling began to fall.

34

I shielded Eva with my body as the mountain tumbled around us. Shrapnel plummeted my back. Chunks of stone flew from the walls amid a horrendous rumbling that sounded like the earth being ripped apart. Something huge crashed nearby. I huddled, waiting for the final blow, fully expecting to die.

Then the earth stopped thrashing. I risked lifting my head, finding the air thick with dust and blacker than black.

Eva shifted beneath me. "Phoebe, my leg," she gasped.

I pushed to my knees, coughing in the saturated air. My hands found the pillar that had landed on her calves crosswise and hefted it to one side.

"Can you stand?"

"No. My left leg is broken...I believe."

"Hello. Is anybody there?" My muffled call barely projected so I tried again. Nobody answered. I felt around nearby searching for the flashlight Foxy had offered but my fingers dug into nothing but rocks and dirt. "We have to get out of here," I told Eva, fumbling for her hand. "Here, lean on me."

"You go. I will only slow you down."

"Stop saying that. Get up. Here, hang on."

She grunted. Struggling to stand, she slung her arm over my shoulder. "Do you have the pictures?" she asked.

"Yes, and videos, too, but let's worry about that later."

"They...are more important than ever."

"Of course."

I stumbled, banging against what felt like walls of dirt, while Eva hobbled, gasping at my side. Totally disoriented, probably stunned, I had no idea which way to turn. Mounds of rock blocked every direction.

"There." Eva nudged me to look down to where a bleary glow penetrated the settling dust.

A flashlight. I dug the thing out and shook it off. Now, the full destruction of the ancient site jumped into view as the light revealed mounds of stone and tumbled walls.

I moaned at the severed head of the fallen goddess staring stone eyes up to a ceiling that no longer existed. Eva began to cry but I was too fixed on escape to mourn.

A gaping space overhead swallowed the beam I shone upward, hinting that one, maybe two, tunnel levels had collapsed during the explosion. Where I thought may have been the direction of the entrance was now chocked with rubble. The light flashed on a ragged opening that had appeared in the far wall.

Clutching Eva's waist, I helped her over the mounds towards the opening. The light caught the edge of a hand so dusty I thought it was carved stone. Brushing away the dirt revealed a wrist below a frayed sleeve. Not Foxy, not Evan, but probably one of Sarp's men. I felt for a pulse. "Dead," I pronounced. "Rupert! Nadira!" I called out.

"They are gone, Phoebe. Sarp planned to blow the shrine. I heard them talking...while we traveled through the underground. Fools didn't comprehend how...I know Turkish." She fought to catch her breath. Recovering, she continued. "He wanted to shoot us but your friend, Rupert Fox—I knew him in London—said no. Some agreement...previously struck."

"Sir Foxy was playing a double game. He's a player and he played them for our side. Are you in pain? Why am I asking? Of course you are. Come on. We have to get you to a hospital. Interpol is coming to our rescue. All we have to do is get to them." I pulled her with me towards the opening.

"Phoebe, Sarp set explosives...intending to bury us...while he escaped through an alternate route. We must assume the route we came is...destroyed...and possibly our rescuers with it."

"No! We can't assume anything. Sam Walker would have alerted the army. There are lots of people coming to rescue us. Why are you hesitating? We have to get out of here. Nothing is stable." The earth rumbled as we stood.

"All the more reason..." she began coughing, "for you to go without me. I will only slow you down. I will stay here with the Goddess. You must go and tell the world what you've seen. Publish the pictures. Tell my story."

"I said stop saying that!" I pulled her by the arm towards the opening, flashing the light into the dark beyond. At first, I couldn't grasp was I was seeing. The relief-walled corridor leading up to the shrine had collapsed, not into mounds of rubble like inside the shrine but simply gone, fallen away into the abyss.

I held the light out over the edge waiting for the beam to brush against something—a floor, a wall, anything, but it didn't. All light was swallowed by the subterranean maw.

Eva, standing behind me, touched my shoulder. "Phoebe, the floor is gone. Probably...many levels, many centuries of underground networks...fallen."

A cold fear trickled down my spine. I swept the beam closer to the opening, illuminating a sliding mountain of rock to the left and the abyss bordered by a narrow ledge no more than six inches wide disappearing into the darkness to the right. Maybe I could cling to that lip of stone and shuffle along to whatever lay beyond, but not Eva.

Leaning out, she saw it, too. "Go, Phoebe. Leave me, please. Let me die...where and how I want. Thanks to you...I have found the Goddess and she will hold me safe...for my next journey. In all the ways that matter...nothing will destroy Her or me."

I pulled back. "I'm not leaving you. We came to Anatolia together, linked in our fates, like you've been saying all along. If we're meant to die here together, then that's the way it has to be. We'll just wait until we're rescued."

"Phoebe, listen. Focus on my words...these tunnels were carved thousands of years...ago. Think, thousands of years. Their tenuous relationship with the earth has been... shattered. Publish the pictures. Tell the Goddess story. Go now, please. I am happy...and filled with joy. I cannot explain it. Just trust what I say."

"No." I fumbled in my pocket. "I brought water. You take a deep drink and you'll feel better. They know where we are. They'll find us soon. We'll just wait. Everything will be fine. I have pain killers, too, in my pocket." I pulled out the water bottle and a fold of paper fluttered to the ground. I picked it up. "Oh, the map Foxy gave us."

Eva eased herself down to perch on the edge of broken wall, her back to the bottomless darkness. Taking the map and flashlight from my hands, she tipped light down over the diagram.

"That way," she pointed over her shoulder towards the ledge, "is a tunnel leading to the surface. Original entrance to Her shrine, probably a...processional avenue. This is Sarp's... escape route and...yours." She passed the map back. I stuffed the page into my pocket and handed her the bottle, which she didn't take.

"Give me back the flashlight and take the water. Drink, Eva."

"Phoebe, you have so much to live for. Your brother...Noel told me...and Noel himself is such a good man. He loves you. I know you two danced on the roof like Borek and I once did... before I left him. I have lived my life. It has been full and...though not perfect, the most wondrous weave. I am so very grateful and...I see you as a daughter-friend, a gift...and I thank you and Her for sending you to me. But I am tired and in pain...you must go now and let me fly."

She dropped the flashlight to the floor and while I bent down to pick it up, she pushed herself over the edge, and flew away into the darkness.

35

She made no sound. I never heard her body hit the bottom, wherever the bottom was but, I swear, gazing down into the blackness at that moment, I saw a light. Maybe I only imagined it, or maybe the glow was within me but it burned brightly nonetheless. Somehow in some way, the glow became a warmth wrapped in her voice pleading to me to let her fly and to keep on going all at the same time.

I thought my heart would crack in two and crumble like the earth around me, but I paused midway to despair and turned my heart towards the stars. I might not be able to see their shine but I knew they existed.

I took a swig of water and pocketed the bottle. Mustering every scrap of resolve, I turned off the flashlight and shoved it into my other pocket. Darkness pushed in around me like congealing nightmares. Then I swung my legs over the broken wall and stepped out onto the ledge.

Utterly blind, I needed both hands to feel for handholds while shuffling sideways along the narrow lip. I balanced on the balls of my feet, focused on nothing but remaining upright above the void. Closing my eyes or leaving them open made no difference. Either way, this was the darkest night. I needed every bright thing in my life to lead me forward.

I fixed on the unseen starlight, on beloved faces living and dead, thinking love survives everything. Love is metaphysical, the strongest energy of all. Should I die that night, the energy of everyone I loved and who loved me would keep swirling across the universe carrying me along.

But I wasn't ready to die. Eva wanted me to live, so I had to for her.

Nose to the rock, I scuttled two inches to the left.

Love was forever, maybe the only forever there is. It takes courage to love, more courage to lose the ones you love, but why else are we here? I couldn't think of a single thing more worth living for.

My feet moved three inches further. Once I coughed hard enough to almost lose my footing, forcing me to cling to the wall, drenched in sweat. Everything ached with strain but I recovered to continue, inch by inch.

Who said that every great effort must be done step by step? I shrunk everything down by inches and centimeters and fixed on that truth.

Finally, my foot slid across a smooth flat surface. Shifting my weight to standing, I beamed the light up a broad corridor where relief-carved walls marched a procession of bulls and goddesses. I scrambled beside the ancient supplicants until I detected a glow mingling with angry voices ahead. A bolt of caution shot my delirious relief to a standstill. I switched off my light and tiptoed towards a waft of fresh cool air.

The corridor rose at a sixty-degree angle before leveling off and plunging sharply downward. Just before the decline, the tunnel narrowed up to an opening where a huge boulder was wedged partway across.

I crouched, shielded by the rock, gazing down on dust-smeared figures huddled around an electric lamp in a small cave-like space. At least two men lay on the floor face down as if they'd been struck from behind or shot—Evan, maybe, and a minion? I couldn't tell—while two others sat backs to the wall, Foxy on one side, eyes closed, Nadira on the other, eyes glittering in the lamplight.

The two arguers were Maggie and Sarp, who stood over the others, jerking their guns at one another. Behind them, I could just make out a sliver of night sky.

One of the men on the ground slowly turned his head towards Maggie. His hair was shaggy and dark, his limbs long and lean. I recognized the boots. I slapped my hand over my mouth to keep from crying out.

"I said I'm not going to wait in this frigging hell-hole for the next twenty-four hours. Finish them off and let's ditch this place before the sun rises." Maggie punctuated her sentences by poking the air with her sleek little pistol.

"No, you listen. Police out there. If they find us, no good," and then he broke into furious Turkish.

"He says Interpol knows about the underground city," Nadira said in a weary tone, translating from her position next to the outer opening. "The army will be all over the area. They don't know this entrance, but we still have to wait until they leave or you'll all be captured, he says."

"That's nutzoid! There's a friggin' army after us! They're not going to just leave because the underground city is blocked. They'll bring in mining dudes and maybe all kinds of heavy equipment types. This place will be crawling with journalists and cops. We have to leave now, while we have the chance. We're wasting time. I have people waiting for us back on the main road. All we have to do is get there."

While Nadira translated, I scuttled far back into the tunnel to pull out my phone. Though probably impossible to fix a signal deep underground, I'd left it alive just in case. Maybe I could hit the sweet spot now but the glowing screen registered no bars. And then I had an idea, a crazy idea. It meant risking the photos I'd just taken but I couldn't afford to let that hold me back.

I turned the phone back on, and brought up the selfie recording me strolling around the gallery that first day. Before I hit PLAY, I called into the air: "Interpol? Phoebe McCabe here. I'm in trouble! Yeah, we're at the other entrance. Fix my coordinates!" Then, I turned the volume up, hit Play, placed the phone on the floor, and scrambled back to press my back against the boulder door.

Footsteps pounded up the incline. Sarp squeezed into the tunnel first followed by Maggie, both leading with their guns. Bracing myself against the rock, I pushed hard into Maggie's back, sending the gun flying and her into Sarp, jettisoning both into a headlong tumble downward. A gun fired. I could hear Maggie cursing as I squeezed through the opening.

Noel pulled me through by the arm, tugging me aside before he and Nadira applied their shoulders to the boulder door. There was room for only two at the narrow portal.

"Do it this way!" Nadira called, showing him the ideal positioning. Noel bent his shoulder to the stone with his eyes fixed on me. "I so damn happy to see you, Phoebe McCabe!"

I watched, stunned, as the boulder rocked but remained in place. "I'm glad to see you, too," I said, shocked by the impact of the understatement.

Evan heaved himself off the floor and lunged half-dazed towards the rock, blood dribbling from his forehead. "Let me help."

Nadira stepped back. Foxy arrived at my shoulder to touch my arm. "Phoebe, you are alive! I cannot fully express my deep-felt relief! Evan, do be careful. You received quite a blow to the head."

A gun fired through the opening, the bullet pinging against the far wall. I shoved Foxy and Nadira out of range. The men continued grunting against the rock. Blood stained the tunic under Noel's jacket.

"Is he hurt?" I asked.

"Maggie shot at him but I believe he feigned the extent of his wounds. Just a graze. He managed to wrest Maggie's bloke to submission before she fired," Foxy told me.

"Look, it's moving! Push more to the middle and it will pivot shut!" Nadira's jubilance was cut short when Maggie wedged her arm through the crack and waved the gun around, firing blindly shot after shot.

"I'll kill you, you bastard!" she shouted, "You and that useless girlfriend of yours!"

Noel knocked the pistol from her hand and kicked her arm until she pulled it back.

I sprang after the fallen gun, picking it up, and sticking the muzzle through the crack.

"Phoebe, don't!" Noel said.

"Why not?" And I pulled the trigger. Only the gun was empty. Just when I needed a stupid gun, it was useless! I threw it down in disgust. Foxy pulled me back as the boulder door finally grated closed.

We stood in silence for a few seconds listening to Maggie wail and curse behind the stone.

"We made it!" Nadira cried joyously. "We made it, we made it!"

Noel turned and gathered me into his arms. I buried myself in his chest and started to cry. "Eva's gone," I told him. "She jumped, Noel. She just jumped so I could carry on."

He stroked my dust-caked hair. "Consider that her gift."

I gazed up at his lovely, bearded, dust-streaked face. "How did you get here?"

"You mean after you locked me on the roof? Rupert came to my rescue." He grinned down at me.

"Yes, I did, Phoebe," Foxy said. "Sorry to see your faith in me waver even for so brief a time, but after you insisted I couldn't accompany you, I returned to the village where Sarp was already plotting your demise. I hastened to insist I could aid him to silence you forever."

"I didn't betray you, either," Nadira added. "Mr. Fox only pretended to and I joined the game."

"And most admirably, too, my dear. Oh, my, how your uncle knuckled on to the plan. Why wouldn't he trust me after I had just purchased so many of his lovely artifacts? I do so love being the double agent. Maggie was already with him, you know. She would insist upon fouling up the best-laid plans."

"It was her idea to kidnap you, Phoebe. After Mr. Fox left, she convinced Uncle that you would contact Interpol. He arranged to have you kidnapped, all very quickly," Nadira said.

"And I arrived at Eva's house intent on sharing the details of what I believed to be the plan when I found you gone and Noel pounding on the roof."

Noel hugged me closer. "I thought I'd lost you," he murmured into my hair.

"Me, too," I told him hugging him back.

"Well, of course, I alerted Interpol immediately," Rupert continued. "Thus I became the plant—is that the term? Very James Bond like, I must say. Noel insisted on joining in, of course, but we couldn't let Interpol know of his presence."

"He was to wait at this entrance," Nadira explained. "Uncle said he planned to bring you here and throw you off a cliff but he lied. He must have planned to blow up the shrine all along but wouldn't tell me." She choked back a sob, staring wide-eyed as if only just realizing what had just happened. "He is a murderous man."

Foxy patted her shoulder. "Yes, yes, such a nasty person, your uncle. Never mind, dear. There's a black sheep in every family. Mine is my cousin, Reginald. Quite the blackguard, I must say. Now," he turned to where Noel and I stood locked together as if we'd never let each other go. "As much as I hate to tear asunder this romantic reunion, Interpol will no doubt arrive shortly. I signaled them as they instructed. They know where we are. You must leave, Noel, before you are apprehended."

"Do you want me to go or stay?" he asked me. "If I'm arrested, I might get parole for good behavior in four years. On the other hand, if I go we could connect in more interesting locales than a prison facility on visiting days."

"Are you asking me to carry on an illicit relationship with a known criminal?"

He grinned. "Definitely, with an emphasis on the illicit part."

"Noel, dear chap, I hear a truck below. You really must leave."

I pulled away. "You'd better go."

"I'll be in touch. You'll know the message is from me when you see it."

"Go." He kissed me one last time, released me, and scrambled over the rocks.

36

"Assure me that you are leaving Istanbul as planned."
Agent Walker's tone was surprisingly gentle.

I stared down at the deep Prussian blue of the Bosporus
with my Foxy phone pressed against my ear. "Of course I'm
assuring you. Why would I want to stick around here any longer
than necessary? Sir Rupert and I are booked on British Airways
tomorrow at 11:00 a.m. Besides, Max will be released from detox
soon and my assistant is going nuts with the hired help. I have to
get back home."

"Good," he said.

"What about you?"

"I have a few matters to attend to regarding returning the
remaining artifacts to the Turkish Antiquities division and will also
assist with the preparing of the report before I can return."

"Busy man."

"Very, but when I return to London in a few weeks, you
will still have a lot to answer for, Phoebe McCabe. Don't think
you're off the hook."

"Really? You have Maggie in custody plus the local black
market connection tied up plus you couldn't have broken this ring
without Sir Rupert and me. Surely I'm no longer on your Person of
Interest list?"

"We still haven't apprehended Noel Halloran or your
brother, remember."

"I can't do everything for you."

He actually laughed. "My point is, we're not planning to
take our eyes off you just yet, so expect a visit when I return."

"Just remember to bring my iPhone with you; that is, if
Maggie didn't destroy it."

"It's safe and I replayed the recording of her admission of
guilt, though I'm not sure how much weight it will hold in court."

"Glad I could be of assistance. Now, if you'll excuse me, I'm going to finish my shopping."

I clicked END and turned to Foxy, who stood beside his black rental car while Evan, sporting a rakish bandage over his left temple, leaned against the hood. Both appeared to be enjoying the view.

"Noel managed to escape Interpol," I said.

Rupert brushed the sleeve of his new leather coat. "Of course he did. All is as it should be, don't you agree? What is even more extraordinary is that you and I are heroes of sorts."

"I wouldn't take it that far."

"I would. In fact, I rather like that version. There is a certain panache to being an antiques dealer who is also known for being at the crux of a covert operation recovering priceless artifacts at an ancient site. Very Indiana Jones meets James Bond, don't you think?"

"Considering that even the shrine has been destroyed, we didn't exactly recover anything."

Foxy smiled. "Maybe not officially, but I assure you I will not be returning to London empty-handed."

"Foxy, surely you're not implying that you plan to smuggle artifacts out of Turkey? They'll throw you in jail for half-past forever."

"Calm down, Phoebe, and I do prefer Rupert to Foxy, as I have said before. I assure you, the pieces are on their way to London as we speak and no one will ever be the wiser. There are ways and means, my dear."

I made a show of covering my ears. "I know nothing and I'd rather keep it that way."

He rubbed his hands together. "Of course you do. I shall never sully your ears with the details, and let me assure you that Onur had plenty of amazing pieces left in his safe. What Interpol recovered from Maggie alone will grace some museum admirably. Even Noel should be satisfied with this outcome."

"All those artifacts should remain in Turkey for the same reason I donated the Goddess kilim to Tayla today. It hurt to let it go, it really did, but she's going to request that it enter the Islamic Museum of Art with Eva's name as the donor. She's the real hero, Rupert." Thoughts of Eva twisted a double-edged knife of both joy and sorrow. "I definitely have a story to tell but the best part will always be hers."

"The story is of utmost importance. I am rather surprised that you parted with the kilim, however. It would have fetched a smashing price with this story surrounding it. Nevertheless, I have sent your gallery all those carpets you pointed out to me in Bergun—my thanks to you for taking me on this most excellent adventure."

"I didn't take you, you followed me, but I can't accept your gift either way."

"Of course you can. Consider them a finder's fee. Besides, as soon as I return, I shall contact all my decorating friends and implore them to purchase their antique carpets from you alone. I shall quite turn your business around, Phoebe, dear, now that we are friends."

As tempting as it was to argue the whole friendship concept, now wasn't the time. "We'll carry this conversation along some other time. Right now, I'm on to unfinished business."

"Your elusive brother, of course."

"I could turn these coordinates over to the police and apprehend Toby in minutes."

"But you won't any more than you aided in Noel's capture. He knew you wouldn't."

"Maybe I'll surprise him yet."

"Nonsense, Phoebe. You'll make the right choice once again." He stepped closer to me and peered over my shoulder at the phone screen. "Where is he?"

"When I key the coordinates, the pin drops directly into the Bosporus somewhere over there." I pointed across the congested strait just as a ferry coasted past.

"He is on the Asia Minor side?" Foxy marveled.

"I think so."

"We must proceed there directly."

"We? Rupert this is something I have to do alone."

He studied me from under his caterpillar brows. "Very well, but permit us to drive you to the other side, at least."

Moments later, we were back in the limo cruising over the bridge spanning the two continents, my fingers twisting the handles of my carpet bag.

We were following the car's GPS this time rather than my phone version, Evan taking every turn the automated voice demanded. Soon the car was sliding downhill towards the water, pulling to a halt beside a large marina of floating berths crisscrossed through a quivering forest of masts and radar antennae.

My heart was racing. "He's on a boat."

"So it seems."

We got out of the car and stared across at the watery parking lot. Similar marinas to this could be found in any port city around the world, only the craft here ranged from humble fisher craft to every imaginable form of sailboat and pleasure yacht.

I keyed the coordinates into my phone again, watching as the dropping pin formed a circle somewhere dead ahead. "Thanks for the drive, Rupert. I'll take it from here."

"Phoebe, let me stay with you just in case."

"No, but thanks. I'll see you tomorrow."

I strode through the chain link gates, nodding at two men who were lugging equipment to some waiting boat. The smell of brine mixed with motor oil pinged my memory receptors, taking me home in a bittersweet instant. Once I reached the steps leading down to the berths, I paused.

Toby loved boats better than any other vessel. He'd bought a sailboat with his first big software check and often spoke of buying another, bigger version, but somehow I couldn't picture my brother living on the run with a sailboat. The fact that he was on the run and would stay that way until the day of his capture, struck me hard.

The steps clattered under my heels as I descended. I had no choice but to stroll the walkways between every berth, hoping that a name might jump out at me or even Toby himself would flag me down.

As the gulls wheeled overhead, I walked the boards, recalling the games we'd play as kids, me the spunky little tomboy shadowing my bigger brother's heels. How I adored him. We'd dive together, gunkholing around our bay's tiny islands, swimming the beaches near our cottage, the two of us inseparable until time and tide peeled us away.

On the day of our father's eighty-third birthday party when Dad's biggest surprise didn't show up as planned, my life plunged into a spinning vortex, leaving a hole I still struggled to mend. Grief, loss, and betrayal warps the weave but, as Eva claimed, nothing is irreparable.

All the boats looked the same at first glance, just a fuse of white streaked with color. My tears blurred the specifics. I was so sick of hunting, worn to the bone with waiting, that these last few steps had become unbearable.

And then I realized someone stood at the end of one of the floating walkways. He looked familiar yet I didn't recognize him at first—short hair, close-trimmed beard, sunglasses. With a start, I realized I'd seen him in London multiple times in different guises. He stepped forward.

"Phoebe?"

"Yes."

"My name's Kevin. I work for Toby. Follow me, please. He's over this way."

"You were tailing me in London."

"Yes, sorry. I was one of your bodyguards of sorts." He turned and shook my hand. "Hope I didn't frighten you."

"Not really. You had too much competition in that department."

I said nothing more as I trailed behind him two berths over. At the end of the berth, a magnificent yacht bobbed in its mooring, one of those sleek millionaire-types the wealthy sometimes moor in Halifax during the summer, all luxury and seclusion.

I seized to a standstill, staring at the glorious painted bow. A mermaid curled her tail along the white sides in a kaleidoscope of rich turquoise and trailing seaweed greens, long tendrils of red hair tangling in the gilded currents. I gasped.

"Stunning, right? The male version is on the opposite side. Are you ready? He's waiting."

I ran up the gangplank, across the wooden deck, and through a door that whispered open automatically. He was just inside an expansive cabin, sitting in a pilot chair of some kind. I hardly noticed as I dove into his arms, remaining bent over since he hadn't time to get to his feet.

"You bastard!" I mumbled into his shoulder, feeling his big arms squeezing me tight. My brother. Finally. "Why did you do this to us?"

"Phoebe." He was sobbing, "I'm sorry beyond words."

I pulled back, wiping my eyes on my sleeve. "Sorry doesn't cut it. You'd better do better and fast."

He had grown stockier from when I'd seen him last and now sported a full auburn beard like some Viking prince in a green hoodie. Only my brother had tears in his eyes, too, and my prince seemed different in so many ways. Older. Sadder. Reduced. "Why aren't you standing? Stand up."

"I can't."

Then I realized the pilot seat was a kind of souped-up wheelchair. "Maggie?"

"Yeah, she shot me in a pique when Noel and I ditched her in France—long story—but it's not your sympathy I'm after."

"Good, because you're not getting it."

"Noel told me you helped put Maggie away. Thanks for that."

"Don't bother thanking me since you might be next. Why, Toby?" I lowered myself onto a stool across from him, never taking my eyes from his face. "Why did you betray Alastair, desert Dad and me, become a criminal, why?"

"I didn't plan it that way. It all happened so quickly but, first, Alastair is not the noble victim he's played himself to be. I thought I loved him at first until I discovered he was using me for a bait-and-switch scheme. He asked me to make the forgeries to keep as mementos, claimed he would donate the real treasures to the respective museums—all very up-front and legitimate. Only that wasn't his plan at all. He intended to sell the forgeries to private buyers as genuine artifacts, make a few million dollars on the side, while keeping the real treasure all along. He was using me. I was totally hoodwinked by a consummate actor."

"So, you decided to retaliate?"

"Not exactly. Noel and I devised a scheme to expose Alastair, but it ran aground when Maggie found out and threatened to tell Alastair and Max. Max was a wild card. We couldn't trust him not to mess up, so we hatched a plan to escape with the treasure and offer it to Interpol as a sign of our good intentions."

"But it wasn't that easy."

"No, it wasn't. Because I had created a complete set of forgeries, I looked as guilty as sin. It was my word against Alastair's, the famous author/historian and Bermuda's shining glory. And then there was Maggie ready to play witness to my supposed duplicity. It all went to hell really quickly. We escaped with our lives that night. There was a point when we realized the world was crashing down around our heads and we had to make a decision to jump or be beaten to a pulp by the law. We jumped and here we are."

"International criminals on the run."

Toby spread his hands. "More like on the roll, in my case." Then his green eyes held mine. "Forgive me, Phoebe. I made a hell of a mistake, messed up my life and Noel's, plus yours and Max's, maybe Dad's, too."

"It was you who came to the nursing home that day, wasn't it?"

"Yeah, it was me, the wayward son crying in my poor father's arms with him bawling, too. He understood something that day, Phoebe, I swear he did."

Tears streamed my cheeks. "Maybe pain breathes life into fading memories."

"And maybe love does, too."

"So now what? You could give yourself up, face the consequences. I know you have the rest of the treasure stashed somewhere. You could turn it over to Interpol."

"And spend ten or more years in jail? We're guilty one way or another, regardless, and there's no guarantee that Alastair won't make a strong enough case to make my sentence longer still."

"Noel thought four years, max."

"He's an optimist. He never expected any of this to go this far. He loves you."

"Are those two points remotely related?"

He smiled, a brief flash of his old merriment escaping lockdown. "Yeah, sure. The optimist is almost happy with his lot right now. He intends to continue his artifact do-gooding knowing that the woman he loves loves him back."

"I never told him I loved him."

"But you do. You can't fool me, or him. In the few hurried calls I've had from him, he seems convinced."

I stood up, beginning to cry really hard, sobbing, really. "Toby, I need to process all this and I just can't right now. So much has happened." I wiped my eyes again, heading for the door. "I have to go."

"Wait! Phoebe, I don't know when I'll see you again."

I stopped and turned to face him, my beautiful, wounded brother looking like Neptune defrocked. "You're going to keep on running, aren't you? You'll continue living like this, both of you?"

"Yeah, I'll help Noel on his mission and try to build a life for myself along the way. I'd only die in prison, Phoebe, especially like this. You know I would."

I did know. "You made some horrible, horrible mistakes."

"I did."

"And I'm having a hard time processing it all."

"But you know I love you despite what an ass I've been."

"Ass is too mild a word."

"You never let me swear in front of you."

"Damn right. The F word is a lazy man's substitute for verbal effort."

"And I'm not a lazy man, whatever else I am. I've just run aground right now. Phoebe, you know I'll still be there for you wherever I am. I have the financial means to help you."

"I don't want your money, Toby. Please stop laundering your funds through my bank account."

"That's all money I've legally earned through my software sales, which I still keep going through multiple holding companies. It's not laundered money. I earned it the hard way and it's a gift from me to you. I have far more than I need. This was never about money, you must know that."

"I still don't want it. I need to make it on my own." I took another step towards the door, pausing as it whooshed open.

"Tell me I'm forgiven." He said behind me.

I turned towards him again.

"Say it, please."

"I can't just yet but I will say I love you and maybe that's the same thing. Maybe when you love, the forgiveness follows. I love you, Toby." I stepped out into the late afternoon sun.

Brushing past Kevin who waited on the dock, I strode up the walkway.

The sun would set soon. It would dip a golden orb into the ocean, gilding the horizon a brilliant orange-red. The stars would sail up into the velvet darkness, spangling the depths with bright pulsing illumination. Even in the fog and rain, the world never is truly dark. Somewhere the sun shines, the moon spreads her silver sails, and a human heart pours light into the shadows.

All I needed was to pull back and imagine the full design to be content that nothing and no one is perfect and yet everything is.

THE END

My thanks to Fran Mues for her astute editorial eye and enthusiastic support and to Heidi Hugli for always being in my corner.

ABOUT THE AUTHOR

Jane Thornley has led many lives, including school administrator, teacher, librarian, travel host, knitwear designer, and artist but writer will always be her default position. Please check out Jane's other novels, including *Rogue Wave*, the first book in the *Crime by Design* series, and *Frozen Angel,* both on Amazon and other book sellers.

Visit janethornleyfiction.com for more about Jane and follow her on
Facebook

Made in the USA
San Bernardino, CA
19 April 2016